The Secret of St. Andrews

All rights reserved.
Printed and bound in the United States of America. Except as permitted under the U.S. Copyright Act of 1976: Without limiting the rights under copyright reserved above, no part of this publication may be reproduced, stored in or introduced into a retrieval system, or transmitted, in any form, or by and means (electronic, mechanical, photocopying, recording, or otherwise), without the prior written permission of both the copyright owner and the below publisher of this book.

PUBLISHER'S NOTE
This is a work of fiction. Names, characters, places, and incidents either are the product of the author's imagination or are used fictitiously, and any resemblance to actual persons, living or dead, business establishments, events, or locales is entirely coincidental.

The publisher does not have any control over and does not assume any responsibility for author or third-party Web sites or their content.

The scanning, uploading, and distribution of this book via the Internet or via any other means without the permission of the author or publisher is illegal and punishable by law. Please purchase only authorized electronic editions, and do not participate in or encourage electronic piracy of copyrighted materials. Your support of the author's rights is appreciated.

Copyright © 2008
First Edition – First Printing November 2008
Library of Congress Number pending

ISBN # 978-1-934615-20-1
         1-934615-20-X

Published by Main Street Publishing, Inc., Jackson, TN.
Copy Editing by Shari B Hill
Cover Design by Shari B Hill & John Scofield
Editing by Pat Little & Shari B Hill
Printed and bound by NetPub, Poughkeepsie, NY.

For more information write Main Street Publishing, Inc.,
206 East Main St., Suite 207, P.O. Box 696, Jackson, TN 38302
Phone 1-731-427-7379 or toll free 1-866-457-7379.
E-mail: editor@mainstreetpublishing.com for managing editor and
           mspsupport@charterinternet.com for customer service.
Visit us at www.mainstreetpublishing.com and www.mspbooks.com.

WITHDRAWN

*The Secret of
St. Andrews*

The Secret of
St. Andrews

A Novel By
John Scofield

This book is dedicated to

Sandra

Special thanks to the following for making this novel possible:

Zach Reilly, Tim Forrest, and Harvey Boyd.

For the Gaelic Translation, a very special thanks goes out to:

Dr. Catriona Mackie, Lecturer in Manx Studies, University of Liverpool, Centre for Manx Studies

The Secret Of St. Andrews

John Scofield

1979
Bristol, England

FRANCIS TAILBY FELT WORSE THAN HE HAD IN ANY OF HIS TWENTY-ONE YEARS. He was to have picked up the Triumph Herald at nine o'clock sharp, had overslept by half an hour and now, as he staggered off the bus at the Temple Meads Railway Station, his only thought was the chewing out he would surely catch for being late.

Thank God he worked for his uncle...

Tailby, in spite of his grogginess, recognized the vehicle at once. He couldn't remember the geezer's name that owned it but knew that by the fourteenth of November he'd be back. He'd left the city of Bristol with complete faith that Wood Mechanics, Limited would have his Triumph right as rain.

Not a bad set of wheels, Tailby had to admit. If Kate Vickery could see him in this, she might possibly be more receptive. The thoughts of the young woman vanished as a sense of revulsion quaked through his stomach once again. Tailby ran a clammy hand across his face, reached for the hidden key, where his uncle assured him it would be, and closed the car door. Great upholstery. Comfortable. Real leather. A stereo system that was first class. This beauty had it all.

Tailby drove the key into the ignition, started her up, noticing at once the knocking coming from the motor. As Tailby was about to ease the car into reverse, he could control his urge to vomit no longer. He jerked the emergency brake on, threw open the car door, and realized he was about to be sick for the second time that morning.

Tailby took three steps toward the men's room and got no further. The force from the explosion hurled Francis

Tailby against a nearby automobile, causing him to black out at once. There was little left of the Triumph Herald, save a smoldering, blackened shell.

The young lad was fortunate. He suffered a broken rib, a badly twisted ankle, and torn groin muscle but was, thanks to his overindulgence in alcohol with his mates the night before, miraculously alive.

***

Northern Scotland

IT WASN'T JUST THE DARKNESS. The rain and the wind made matters much worse. The rain was pouring down with incredible voraciousness while the wind pounded the automobile about like a kite in a March sky.

He was already late. He'd planned on reaching his destination no later than eight, and it was already half past seven. Being late was the worst thing possible, but in spite of the fact that winter was approaching, the bad weather was something he hadn't counted on.

The storm had blown in suddenly.

Like her.

The Scottish mountain highway on a clear day was nothing less than breathtaking. Known as the Great Road North, the A-9 is famous for its storybook castles, rising majestically atop sheer cliffs overlooking the North Sea.

The road had a reputation for being one of the most scenic highways in the world. Ross Burnham was no tourist, however. On a dangerous November night for driving along the formidable stretch of mountainous highway, he began a sharp descent while veering sharply to the right. Braking lightly, he began to have his doubts.

Being late would mean the unthinkable. Challenging this road was inviting disaster. His hands gripped the leather-covered steering wheel, eyes riveted to the blanket of rain that clung to his windshield like steam in a cramped shower.

For an instant, and only an instant, his eyes dropped to the illuminated speedometer. Sixty. To the clock once again, which rested in the oval space next to the speedometer. Back to the road where his tires suddenly steered across, a churning noise emerging from the bullet-riddled left front wheel.

Burnham reacted at once, gripping the steering wheel even tighter as he tried to ease the car into the direction of the skid.

He was too late. The automobile slid towards the rocky embankment. At the same time, he figured it was now or never. The Jaguar's passenger door flew open and Burnham, who never wore a seat belt in the best of times, was thrown from the vehicle.

A second later, the car went into a flip, coming to rest on its four wheels.

A new Jaguar moments before was now a crumpled heap of metal.

She had found Ross Burnham.

**

BRISTOL, ENGLAND

THE HIGH SPEED BRITISH RAIL EXPRESS TRAIN PULLED INTO ITS FINAL DESTINATION AT BRISTOL'S TEMPLE MEADS STATION, MAKING THE TRIP FROM LONDON TO BRISTOL IN A REMARKABLE EIGHTY-FIVE MINUTES.

A man wearing sunglasses and a smart navy blue Austin Reed suit underneath his Burberry emerged from the train with the throng of passengers. With briefcase in hand, his grey eyes roamed the parking lot in search of his Triumph. Following a scan of the railway car park, he realized his vehicle was simply not there.

He covered the lot thoroughly once again, swearing to himself when he finally conceded his car was missing. He gave a curious glance at the work crew, repairing a section of the parking lot that had been roped off. He thought nothing more of it as he strode briskly into the terminal, found the nearest pay telephone, and dialed the number of Wood Mechanics, Limited. When he heard the voice on the other end speak, he shoved the coin home.

"Neal Edwards, here, I'm calling about my Triumph. This is the fourteenth and my car should have been here, should it not?"

Edwards was hardly an impatient man, but the voice on the telephone seemed hesitant, and that irritated him.

"Are you there?"

"Indeed I am, Mr. Edwards. I don't quite know how to break this to you, sir. Your automobile was blown up in an explosion the same morning you left for London. Nearly killed my nephew, Francis. My advice to you, Mr. Edwards," said the voice, "would be to contact the police. As soon as possible, mate. For your sake as well as ours. Cheerio."

The line went dead.

What raced through the mind of the young man at that moment was the unthinkable.

It could not be.

Not now.

"Mr. Edwards?"

Edwards spun round to find two plain-clothes policemen standing there.

"We'd like a word with you, sir, if you don't mind."

The significance of the construction in the parking area suddenly struck the young estate agent.

The repair work was taking place at the very spot where he'd left his Triumph.

She had found Neal Edwards.

Edinburgh, Scotland

HE WAS CLOSING IN FAST. Her slippery trail had brought him here to Edinburgh. Each time he had closed the gap a little tighter, but to no avail. To Daniel Harper, finding his prey had grown more intensified over the past seventeen months and certainly more complicated than he could have ever imagined in the beginning.

He'd known absolutely nothing about her, prior to his trip to the Netherlands. Had he not come down with his most severe encounter of influenza to date, ending up in an infirmary in The Hague, he would have never known.

Harper, a burly mid-level supervisor at a West Virginia coal mining operation, spent five years working to save for his trip across the Atlantic. He managed to scrape up a few thousand dollars, bought a low-cost round trip ticket on a British no-frills airline, and found himself in London on the fringe of the summer holiday season.

He caroused about in the west end for a week, met up with a group of Texans one evening, and was advised, over several pints of bitter, to see the Continent before the hordes of tourists began arriving. Having planned on leaving London the next day anyway, Harper assured the Texans he would heed their advice.

Harper, at one point, chose a train ride to Dover to be followed by a ferry to Calais. At the last moment, he changed his plans, went to Harwich instead, and boarded a ship bound for Hoek van Holland. The Hook of Holland.

That hasty decision would change his life forever.

The Hotel Cok is one of the many youth hostels in Amsterdam, which provides modest accommodations at affordable costs. The Hotel Cok was the place where Daniel Harper came in contact with the flu.

He'd been in Amsterdam for three days, planned on visiting Den Haag before moving on south to France, and virtually ignored the raspy sensation in the back of his throat, as he boarded the fast and comfortable train that would carry him across the beautiful Dutch countryside.

By that evening his throat had worsened. He spent a restless night in his hotel room. The following morning, Harper inquired at the hotel's front desk as to the whereabouts of the nearest medical facility.

At 25, Harper could not remember a sicker day in his entire life.

Once at the hospital, the Dutch physician was most helpful, assuring the young American that the strain had been common throughout the Continent all spring; and in a couple of days, he would be fine.

The doctor's strict orders, however, included Harper remaining in the hospital—at least overnight.

They checked him into a room with two other male patients: one an elderly man recovering from a minor automobile accident, the other an Englishman, gravely ill, who seemed to receive constant attention from the hospital staff. Harper, meanwhile, was given medication that left him quite sedated throughout the day and allowed him a reasonably restful night's sleep.

When Harper awoke the next morning, he noticed the older man preparing to check out of the hospital, leaving Harper and the Englishman the sole occupants of the room. Harper sat up in bed and, in English, wished the gentleman the best of luck.

Not that he expected to be understood.

To Harper's surprise, the man not only understood but spoke English.

"Thank you," he said, motioning across the room. "Too bad about this one, I am afraid he has a long road back."

Being able to swallow in comfort for the first time in twenty-four hours, Harper managed to ask the Dutchman what was wrong with the other patient. Before he could get an answer, the man's wife walked in. This was obviously a happy day for her. She smiled at Harper as she took her husband's arm. At one time, Harper thought, the Dutchman could have been a policeman.

"Severe blood loss."

"Blood loss? Was he in an accident or something?"

"The poor fellow's an Englishman. Been supporting himself by donating his blood for money. Looks like he gave too much, doesn't it?" he said, shaking his head. "Doesn't look good."

At that point, the couple left the hospital room, leaving Daniel Harper alone with the young man.

***

Paris, France

STUART CASHMORE ADJUSTED HIS TIE, KISSED HIS YOUNG FRENCH FIANCEE GOODBYE, AND WALKED THE SHORT DISTANCE FROM HER FRONT STEPS INTO THE WAITING AUTOMOBILE. It was hardly a bitterly cold morning in Paris, but Cashmore, for some unknown reason, shivered as he settled into the back seat of the limousine.

Less than ten seconds later, before Claudine could close her front door, she heard the gunshots. She bit down on her lower lip, where moments before Stuart had so lovingly kissed her, and tried in vain to suppress the tears. Something inside her said the gunfire had been directed towards her lover.

The chauffeur would later describe the two gunmen as being young, no older than 25. They were well-dressed Europeans, both knowing how to use an automatic pistol with skill.

The administrative assistant to the American Ambassador to France heard the shots before he or the chauffeur saw their faces. The first bullet caught Cashmore's left shoulder, knocking him sideways against the right rear door. Not losing consciousness for a moment, Cashmore was certain he was a dead man. In less than six seconds, the young man took slugs in his lower right arm and left thigh, in addition to the shoulder wound. A bullet also grazed his left cheek.

By the time the chauffeur could increase his speed, they were gone. In all, the gunmen emptied twelve rounds of ammunition into the car at close range, absolutely certain they had killed the American.

They had not. Hardly able to speak, Cashmore ordered his driver to take him at once to Neuilly. To the American Hospital.

She had found Stuart Cashmore.

***

Edinburgh, Scotland

HER FEELINGS TOWARD HIM WERE BEGINNING TO FLOURISH. No question about it. She was still uncertain about her future. So many things were coming together these days. Since her husband had passed on, she'd become one of society's most courted and eligible widows. There had been a brief romance during a summer holiday following her husband's death, but it was just that— brief. She was presently involved with someone who had completely made her feel whole as a person.

No one suspected.

Alas, it wasn't exactly a fortune he'd left behind, but she would manage to maintain her copious lifestyle.

She emerged from the bubble bath, reached for her towel, and began to dry herself off. The image in the full-length mirror was not at all unpleasant. At 41, her body was as firm as it was beautiful.

Age indeed had been merciful to her, with the faint hint of crow's feet only beginning to make themselves visible.

Once dry, she slipped into her blue silk robe. It clung to her body. She spent her usual twenty minutes brushing the full mane of brown hair that had become her trademark since her youth. It fell an impeccable three inches past her shoulders, the length she'd sported for the past ten years.

She felt the carpet engulf her bare feet as she headed down the spiral staircase into her sitting room. She sat down to the elegant Wurlitzer baby grand, stretched her fingers and began, slowly at first, the 1st Movement of Beethoven's Sonata for Piano Number 14 in E sharp minor. She caught a glimpse of the rising moon as her fingers worked the keys in a slow, rhythmic movement.

It was far and away her favorite piece of music.

She was extremely fastidious when it came to her music. The fact that the phone began to ring, as she was truly beginning to enjoy the Sonata, annoyed her.

Two minutes later, she hung up the telephone with a growing sense of disbelief that eventually turned to rage.

***

Urbana, Illinois

THERE IT WAS. Faded, torn in one corner and lying amongst the batch of papers he hadn't been through in years.

The list.

Most of the names he had virtually forgotten since last seeing their faces, which was ten years ago.

During the summer between his junior and senior high school years, Alan Albright spent six unforgettable weeks in St. Andrews, Kingdom of Fife, Scotland. Over the years, the list of students had been put away, reshuffled, and ultimately misplaced in the attic of his parent's house, only to turn up as he was searching for his boyhood baseball card collection.

Albright was sixteen and a half then, gregarious, B-student, and devoted to rock and roll. He was nearly twenty-seven now. Reading over the names, he suddenly realized he had no way of knowing what had become of the people he'd met in St. Andrews—people like Stevie Galloway. Rich Palmer, Sam Kipp, and Karen Henderson.

So many memories.

No name stirred up the summer of 1969, however, quite like the one halfway down the second page of the tattered list. Ten long years had passed; many loves had come and gone. In spite of the excellent holiday feast at his parents' house and the time spent that Thanksgiving weekend with the Albright family, he was making little progress in recovering from the wedding plans, which had been called off at the last minute on St. Valentine's Day, no less earlier that same year by his bride-to-be.

Like from an unwanted illness, Albright was slowly recovering.

Now this.

Now her. Jennifer Tavistock.

One discussion determined their future. One discussion over an issue they simply could not agree to. One discussion. She lived in Massachusetts; he was in Illinois. In June of 1970, following graduation from Urbana High School, Albright's decision to join the Marines for three years ended their future.

Until the list turned up.

Albright spent the remainder of the Thanksgiving weekend enjoying the comforts of his parents' home, dined well, and returned to Chicago that Sunday night with a Beacon Hill address. Granted, it was the address of her family, but at least he hoped she would remember him.

Albright had few illusions of ever re-kindling a decade old relationship with someone as rich and beautiful as

Jennifer Tavistock. Particularly in light of how they had parted. He simply wanted to send her season's greetings. The next day, he picked out a simple Hallmark Christmas card, signed it, and dropped it in the post. After all, in a month it would be Christmas.

He needed closure.

***

THE NETHERLANDS

WHILE THE GUARDED CONDITION OF HARPER'S HOSPITAL ROOMMATE REMAINED UNCHANGED, THE AMERICAN, AS PROMISED, CONTINUED TO IMPROVE. By that evening, he was able to sip a few mouthfuls of hot soup.

His fever was still high and his body so weakened; it was a major effort just to walk to the lavatory. Once back in bed, he was about to doze off when the patient in the next bed began to stir.

He opened his eyes, focused them on Harper, and motioned with a feeble hand for the American. Daniel asked him if he wanted a nurse, and the Englishman shook his head. Harper managed to slide off the bed once again, and step by painfully weakened step; he pulled up a chair next to the bed.

"Are you sure you don't want a nurse?"

The Englishman shook his head.

"No," he whispered. "Promise me you'll believe what I am about to tell you. I know I haven't much time."

Harper, for the first time since entering the hospital, took a good look at the young man's face. What was once rugged and proud was now sallow. The blue eyes were tired, and they peered through half-open, cadaverous sockets. He had not been shaved for some time.

"I promise."

Harper felt helpless but was unable to say no. He only hoped the man would not die in his presence. He could not handle that.

The Englishman spoke softly in a low resolute voice for some twenty minutes. What Harper learned in that brief time period made his blood boil. Here was a helpless man determined not to leave this world without sharing the staggering truth with someone else.

The monumental secret.

The secret of St. Andrews.

***

Chicago, Illinois

THE FOLLOWING THURSDAY EVENING, ONCE AT HOME, ALBRIGHT'S NIGHTLY WORKOUT LASTED LONGER THAN USUAL. He spent two hours on the bench lifting weights, knocked out two hundred calisthenics, and finally topped the evening off by taking a long shower. He was about to towel himself dry when the phone rang.

"Mr. Albright?" Whoever it was sounded far away—as in long distance.

"That's right."

"Martyn Tavistock. Tell me what you know about my daughter."

"I beg your pardon?"

"You sent Jennifer, my daughter, a Christmas card, which arrived in the mail this morning." At least the Postal Service works, he almost quipped. So she's married and happy, he thought. No need for her father to be this overprotective. But then again, Albright concluded, that's what happens when you act on impulse.

"Are you there?" Tavistock asked.

"Yes, sir. I was simply letting her know that I'd not

completely forgotten her. I..."

"I'll ask you again. What do you know about my daughter?"

Albright stood in the middle of his bedroom, dripping wet, with a growing realization that something was undoubtedly out of whack.

"I know that the last time I saw Jennifer was at JFK when we said our goodbyes. That was in July of 1969 when we flew home from St. Andrews. We were close that summer. We planned to enroll in the same university. Until a discussion by telephone the day before I left for Vietnam a year later when I told her goodbye, I haven't spoken to her since. Is there something about Jennifer that I should know?"

"Yes." The voice was less hostile. "My daughter disappeared nearly two years ago and hasn't been seen since."

***

ALBRIGHT LEFT WORK THE NEXT DAY, A FRIDAY, AT FIVE O'CLOCK SHARP AS USUAL. Instead of taking the train to work that morning, he elected to drive—something he never did. Rather than heading home to his apartment on the near-north side, he drove south, heading out of the Windy City, arriving in his hometown of Urbana by 7:30.

No, he wasn't broke. Or hungry. No, it wasn't his former fiancée, Tolly Chamberlain. He never felt compelled to explain his sudden appearances to his parents, but even they thought it strange he'd be back home a mere week after Thanksgiving.

They were concerned it was indeed Tolly.

Albright's conversation with Dr. Martyn Tavistock the previous night lasted only a few moments.

He did not remember Alan, although they met for a split

second at the airport when Tavistock and his wife were on hand to welcome Jennifer home from St. Andrews. Albright decided not to tell his parents the real reason he was in town.

He returned to the attic later that evening and spent half the night going through memorabilia of his days in Scotland. The summer of 1969. The summer of St. Andrews.

Albright began with the photographs. He probably had a couple of dozen shots he'd taken of Jennifer that summer. On the beach overlooking the Old Course. In Aviemore. On the tennis court, something that made him smile. The picture that really caught his eye was one sent to him by a friend in Arizona, who captured Albright and Jennifer studying together in University Hall. She was into her books, he looking over his shoulder into the camera.

Her hair was long then. Dark brown. The nose curved slightly upward; and even though he could see only a profile, the dimple in her chin was visible.

It was all coming back.

Most of the relics meant little to him before. The luggage tag from the American Institute for Foreign Study. The map of the Parisian subway system. The letters from Jennifer.

Still there, thank goodness.

Albright sat on the foot of the bed with his shoes off. He glanced at the clock on the table to his left and noticed it read half-past two. He sorted through the stationery of a girl he'd chosen to forget for reasons he believed in then and certainly believed in now.

Serving his country.

The early letters were full of memories of St. Andrews. Of plans for college. How terribly boring it had become in Boston with Albright so far away. Above all, the consistent theme in all of Jennifer's correspondence was her longing to return to St. Andrews some day.

With Albright, of course.

He read all of the letters.

That morning, with sunlight filtering through the bedroom window, Dr. Martyn Tavistock's offer continued to gnaw away at him.

He picked up a letter and read it once more.

'If there is one place in this world I could call perfect, it would have to be St. Andrews. Being there with you this summer showed me what happiness really is."

She closed the letter with a plea.

"Please write."

***

AS FAR AS GRAPHIC ARTISTS WERE CONCERNED, ALBRIGHT WAS CONSIDERED ONE OF THE BEST IN THE CITY OF CHICAGO. His drawing abilities were average, but what set him above the rest was his flair for the unusual and dramatic. His firm was by no means Chicago's largest, but there were more than enough projects on the table to keep the staff of 20 working at full capacity.

Third Wind had been in their new location less than a year. The company was housed in a converted warehouse on Carpenter Street, just west of the Loop. Brown smoked glass highlighted the antique brick structure, and the new team concept of working without a leader was working quite well. The dress code was simple; there wasn't any.

At 27, Albright was only two years younger than the owner/founder, Gerry Windham. Windham hired Albright just out of college two years earlier. Since then, the firm had flourished in Chicago, thanks largely in part to aggressive marketing and the fact that Third Wind had a reputation for breaking new ground in artistic concepts.

Going to work was somewhat easier these days for Albright. He was, finally, realizing there was something that resembled a life after Tolly Chamberlain and understood that the breakup was something he could ultimately cope with. Ironically, his work had sparkled since the split. Albright totally engrossed himself in his projects, took risks, and unleashed a dormant corner of his creative soul.

His work was splashed across billboards throughout Chicago. An ambitious R&B radio station was spending an exorbitant amount of cash on a campaign, whose sole purpose was to become the number one station in town. Just about everywhere one looked in the Windy City, there sat the billboard.

Following that successful and highly visible billboard campaign, Third Wind became deluged with projects. As was his habit, Windham rewarded his employees with two weeks off at Christmas and Hanukkah, in addition to their regular vacation time. Which meant all work had to be finished by the end of November, with the agenda for the coming year sketched out in the first two weeks of December.

That morning, as Albright whistled into work, Gerry took note of the distinct change in his employee. No one should feel that good on a Monday.

"Morning, Alan. Everything okay?" Windham asked.

"Sort of. What about you?"

"Did you get lucky last night or something?"

As soon as he'd opened his big mouth, Windham regretted what he'd said. He and Albright were friends, hung out occasionally, and realized only too well the torment Albright had gone through over the last few months. Rather than apologize, Windham remained quiet.

"Nah," answered Albright, absentmindedly fingering his Exacto knife. If there was any indication he'd taken offense to Windham's statement, he didn't show it. His mood was bright that morning because of the photograph he placed on the bulletin board at his workstation.

It was a simple snapshot, taken a decade ago with a Kodak Instamatic. The face in the picture was smiling. She wore jeans and a sweater and stood next to a body of water.

The place was Loch Ness.

The smile belonged to Jennifer Tavistock.

Windham looked his friend over. Six feet one, 190 pounds. Square jaw, average face. When Albright smiled (and it wasn't very often these days), he displayed an effulgent set of teeth with slightly extended canines, which added to the luster of his smile. He wore his light brown hair, shorter than most, in a military fashion and was clean-shaven. His physical presence was a testament to his commitment to fitness. Women simply adored him, some in silent admiration, others not-so-silent. His fashionable clothes fit him well, and he looked good in them. What concerned Windham and his co-workers at Thirdwind was the rapid deterioration that occurred in Albright's deportment, when his fiancée walked out on him some months earlier. That encounter left Albright, normally high-spirited and friendly, retiring and habitually detached from those around him.

He did not, however, take his anger and hurt out on his co-workers; and because of that, they respected him all the more.

"Made any plans for Christmas yet?" Windham asked, trying to diplomatically change the subject.

"Funny you should mention that, Gerry. Do you know what Boston's like this year?"

"Cold and wet. By no means one of my favorite cities. Cape Cod is quite nice in the fall, but I find the city of Boston a bit stuffy for my tastes. Why don't you head south like everybody else? Barnes, for one, plans on doing the Caribbean."

"What would you think about me taking a couple of days off this week? All of my projects for January have been detailed. All right here," Albright said, pointing to the big tan portfolio on his desk, "including the Balfour project."

Windham glanced over Albright's shoulder at the girl in the photograph. She seemed awfully young.

"Sure. When do you need to take off?"

"This afternoon, if possible. I'll probably be back by Wednesday or Thursday. Friday, at the absolute latest."

"Alan, I want to tell you something," said Otto Henry, as he approached Albright's workstation."You are one fortunate bastard. You found out before you got married. Unlike the rest of us. Whatever happens to you now will be for the best."

Everyone within earshot froze. Subtlety and Otto Henry were seldom associated with one another. There was a story floating around the company that Otto crashed a pool party on the Gold Coast that previous summer sans his swimming trunks.

He simply did not care.

"Thank you for sharing that with me, Otto. My day will certainly be for the better."

Windham was stunned by the remark. There was an understanding that Albright's breakup was strictly a hands-off subject. Everyone, even Otto, had been supportive when they'd learned the news. Windham noted how little effect the remark had on Albright, which made him take an even closer look at the girl in the photograph.

"If only I had been so lucky," Otto continued. "Have you guys noticed how many women feel sorry for our friend here?"

Otto was right. Since the breakup, women felt compelled to open their hearts, for starters, toward Albright. One priority for the women of Third Wind was to take care of their own. Efforts were constantly undertaken for Alan to meet a sister, a best friend, even a cousin.

To no avail.

Albright belonged to Third Wind during working hours and fitness, exercise, and rock and roll at night. As an adult, his hobbies were few, save for what he saw as a growing trend in baseball cards.

A WGN-TV report on the value of baseball card collecting had captivated him so much that he'd searched out his own boyhood collection at his parents' house.

What he unearthed, instead, made the search for the cards immaterial. The discovery of a list with the name of an old friend was putting new resilience into his somewhat opaque lifestyle.

"Merry Christmas, Albright," Windham said. "We'll see you after the first. Enjoy whatever it is you'll be up to."

By ten he was at his apartment, packing for Boston. He caught a cab to O'Hare, boarded an American Airlines flight shortly after noon; and by four o'clock, Albright had touched down at Logan Airport.

Tomorrow morning he would call on Dr. Martyn Tavistock.

A decision had to be made.

Jennifer Tavistock—this time—would not be ignored.

He spent a tedious half-hour awaiting his luggage on the lower level of Logan Airport. Once his grip circled around within his reach, he stepped into the icy Boston afternoon and hailed a taxi to the hotel where Dr. Tavistock had made arrangements for him to stay during his sojourn.

The Parker House.

Rush hour was in full swing. In spite of the traffic, Albright's taxi made it to the hotel in a remarkably short amount of time. The drive from O'Hare Airport to downtown Chicago can be time-consuming because of the sheer distance between the two points. Albright was amazed at the close proximity between Boston's airport and downtown.

Albright found the hotel seasoned and stately. From the outside at least. The cab driver turned into the narrow School Street, unloaded Albright's luggage, and thanked his passenger upon payment. Dr. Tavistock had made the reservations the same night following his conversation with Albright.

Albright wasted little time. Within ten minutes of checking into his room, he was dialing the number Martyn Tavistock had given him.

"I take it everything is to your satisfaction, Mr. Albright."

The doctor's voice was smooth, with the crisp Boston brogue.

"Absolutely, Dr. Tavistock," Albright said. "Quite the place, this Parker House."

"The majority of my out-of-town patients who come to Boston stay at the Parker House. Their families as well. Makes it easier to deal with a singular establishment."

"Makes sense, I suppose. My apologies for contacting you so late in the day. For some reason, I was unable to get anything earlier to Boston. Even from the busiest airport in the world. It's crazy. Christmas is still four weeks away, and people are traveling like there's no tomorrow."

"That's hardly surprising," Tavistock replied. "This is simply a busy time of the year. Do you have any objections if you wait until tomorrow morning to meet with me?"

"None whatsoever."

"Good. How about ten o'clock?"

"No problem. Where shall we meet, Dr. Tavistock?"

"My home. It's not far from your hotel. Do you have a pencil?"

"Is it the same address where I mailed the Christmas card?"

"Of course," remembered Tavistock.

"I'll see you at ten, sir."

"Very good." Tavistock hung up the phone.

***

ALBRIGHT'S ALARM WENT OFF AT EXACTLY HALF

PAST SIX. To him, it was an hour earlier, with Illinois being on Central Standard Time. He eased himself out of bed, parted the curtains, and looked out onto Copley Square through his hotel window.

It was a sparkling morning in Boston.

Albright showered, shaved, and dressed in a three-piece suit. Navy blue. He found the remote control, selected a local television station, and pondered what to eat for breakfast. Like the previous morning, the main story focused on the ordeal of the American hostages in Iran. The anchor, a middle-aged gentleman with a perfectly groomed head of graying hair, was interviewing the mother of one of the hostages, who lived in Rhode Island.

He decided against room service by trying the breakfast buffet instead in the restaurant, once he made it downstairs. In the meantime Albright continued to watch the morning news program. The anchor now focused on the car bombing incident in the west of England the British police were still investigating. The prime suspects were denying any involvement whatsoever, but the troubles in Northern Ireland remained the focus of Scotland Yard's inquiries.

It was a world away, thought Albright, with no bearing on his agenda of the day.

His appointment with Dr. Tavistock was at ten o'clock. He felt a growing sense of anticipation regarding the upcoming meeting with Jennifer's father. He checked his shoes for any scuff marks, gave himself the once-over on the full-length mirror, hanging on the outside of the bathroom door, grabbed his overcoat, and closed the door of his hotel room behind him. At nine o'clock, following an exceptional breakfast, Albright spent a leisurely twenty minutes buying a few Christmas gifts in the hotel gift shop. Rather than bothering to carry them back to Chicago on the plane, Albright made arrangements to have them shipped back to his apartment. It took him less than thirty seconds to choose the first taxi lined in front of the hotel, and by 9:35 he was on his way to keep an appointment with the cardiologist, the renowned Dr. Martyn Tavistock, the man who convinced Albright to take an abrupt trip to the east coast on a moment's notice. Albright was determined, once and for all, to reconcile with a person he hadn't seen in ten years.

Or so he hoped.

Little did he know what lay before him.

***

THE CAB ARRIVED AT THE ADDRESS WITH MINUTES TO SPARE. He paid the driver, who's English was quite remarkable, leaving a generous tip to the man. On the way to Beacon Hill, he'd conversed with the taxi driver about Iran, President Carter, and whether or not the hostages would be home by Christmas time. Once he realized how close the doctor's residence in Beacon Hill was to his hotel, Albright could have easily walked, had he only known.

He wondered to himself as he rang the doorbell whether Jennifer Tavistock would be coming home for the holidays.

"Yes, sir?" the maid asked.

"Good morning. My name is Alan Albright and I'm here to see Dr. Tavistock."

***

WHILE THE WEATHER WAS SUNNY THAT DAY IN BOSTON, EDINBURGH WAS EXPERIENCING RAIN, HIGH WINDS BLOWING IN FROM THE NORTH, AND UNSEASONABLY COLD TEMPERATURES. Inside the spacious vehicle, the weather was not a factor. She'd been shopping along Princes Street for much of the afternoon. New shoes. Music. Finally, her hair.

Tonight, as part of the International Celebrity Series,

she would be performing with the Royal Scottish Orchestra. The photograph in the program booklet, she had to admit, was a good one. An evening of Christmas music was on tap at the Usher Hall, one of her favorite venues, with selections ranging from a number of the very best composers.

Her biography was all there. Her accomplishments.

Nowhere did the program mention St. Andrews.

To the world she was a brave widow. A talented pianist. An enchantress, who was the darling of Edinburgh society. Tonight, she would perform.

Tomorrow she would act.

***

"I HAVE EVERY REASON TO BELIEVE THAT MY DAUGHTER IS ALIVE."

Albright was sitting in a comfortable armchair in Martyn Tavistock's study. Deep leather. Burgundy. The doctor was seated opposite Albright behind his desk. He was in his early fifties. Tall. Fit. The dark hair, covering his temples, was beginning to gray ever so slightly. His long forehead was highlighted by the permanent worry frown above his bushy eyebrows.

His face was clean-shaven and his cheeks were ruddy, Albright suddenly remembered, just like his daughter's. The doctor wore a red tie and white shirtsleeves. Very expensive shirtsleeves. Albright had an eye for good clothing.

Albright took in the doctor's manner. Calm. Disciplined. Determined. Being a cardiologist, it was the nature of his profession to look someone in the eye and tell them they had six months to live with the ease of a repairman discussing the fact that a refrigerator motor had become obsolete.

He simply did not waste time with small conversation—something Albright discerned from the moment he first spoke to the doctor, days earlier by telephone.

"The events surrounding the day my daughter vanished have been analyzed by some of the best private detectives this country has to offer. They have concluded, to my satisfaction I might add, that she was not abducted or kidnapped. The police investigation determined nothing violent occurred that day. She wasn't forced out of this house. She simply vanished and we do not know where she is."

Tavistock sat with his long fingers clasped together, thumbs resting under his chin. He spoke in a clear and steady voice. Deep. His eyes were blue and impenetrable. It was difficult to read anything from them. Perhaps, the years of imparting grave news to his patients and their families had steeled them from any sort of emotion.

The first thing Albright noticed when entering the doctor's study was not the impressive arrangement of antiques. Nor the deep-carved dark paneling. He took in at once the photographs of the Tavistock family in general and the pictures of Jennifer in particular. She was all grown up, so unlike the picture he'd brought into work at Thirdwind. The sight of her maturity was stunning. The hair was shorter, cut in a contemporary, professional style of the day. The smile had not changed. With Jennifer's face in plain sight, it became difficult for Albright to concentrate on what Tavistock was saying, something not lost on the doctor.

"As you probably know, you're not the first person I've taken on to find my daughter. The so-called professionals have come and gone. Some of them turned up bits and pieces, but none of them turned up Jennifer."

Tavistock stood up, placing his hands in the pockets of his pleated trousers. He took a deep breath and picked up his daughter's photograph.

"This is all I ask from anyone, Mr. Albright. I have tried for two years since my daughter disappeared to find her, and I will try for two and twenty more years, if I live, to get her back. She is alive. If you can help me find her, I'm giving you the opportunity to do so with my blessings and my checkbook. One half million dollars to you for her safe return."

Tavistock studied Albright for two hours before making his decision. He drilled the young man with questions about himself, about St. Andrews and, most importantly, about his relationship with Jennifer.

Like Dr. Tavistock, Albright had a military background. The doctor had served in the Air Force as a physician. Albright had enlisted in the Marine Corps straight out of high school. This astonished a number of people in Champaign-Urbana, with the war in Vietnam going at full speed and all and ultimately led to the breakup between him and Jennifer.

Tavistock learned that Albright spent a total of four years in the Corps—three of them in Southeast Asia. He'd seen active combat and was decorated for bravery. Upon his return to civilian life, Albright returned to his home town and earned his degree in graphic arts from the University of Illinois. No one in the twin cities ever spit on him and no one dared call him baby-killer.

"Could I ask a small favor of you, Doctor Tavistock?"

"Sure."

"Do you have a photograph of Jennifer that was taken within the past couple of years that you could spare?"

"Certainly." Tavistock rose from his desk, crossed the capacious library, and reached inside a glass bookcase. He removed a brown folder and returned to his desk. Once seated, he opened the folder.

Inside were family photographs of the Tavistocks.

"These were taken in July of '77," Tavistock said, selecting an 8 by 10 color portrait of his daughter.

"Will this be adequate?"

Albright leaned across the desk, getting a closer look at

the family portraits. He noticed they seemed happy together. Glancing at a picture of Dr. Tavistock, he observed how the doctor had aged in two years. Albright, until walking into the doctor's study that morning, had never seen pictures of Jennifer's family. Her brother in the photograph was sporting a beard, and his hair was practically as long as that of his sister.

Tavistock's wife was striking. She possessed that rare quality in a human being that seemed to come with having lots and lots of money. Her hair was reddish-brown, like that of her son. Her skin was like a fine porcelain, almost doll-like. Her face was slender. Small mouth. Blue, innocent eyes. Intricate nose tilted slightly upward, displaying a sense of elusive superiority.

With the exception of the dimpled chin and her father's cheekbones, Jennifer was the spitting image of her mother.

Albright took the photograph from the doctor. He studied the face. At that moment the sounds, smells, and the people—everything he had virtually forgotten about the summer of 1969—re-emerged like the incoming tide of the North Sea at sunset.

"Absolutely. I believe this will do just fine."

"My son, Roger," Tavistock said, pointing a long finger at the young man in the photograph, "is currently on tour in Britain. A rock musician."

The words came off Tavistock's tongue like venom. His eyes narrowed, and for a moment Albright sensed the anger and disappointment the doctor displayed towards his son.

"He plays in a local band."

"What's the band's name?"

Tavistock told him.

"No kidding! Those guys are bad.... But, of course!" Albright exclaimed, suddenly making the connection. "That's Roger Tav... short for Roger Tavistock... In fact, I remember them playing a couple of months ago back in Chicago. I never associated a Tavistock with..."

"Rock and roll." Tavistock finished the sentence for Albright. There was genuine disappointment in the doctor's voice. He leaned back in his chair, pounding a fist into the palm of his hand. He looked past Albright, shaking his head to himself.

"Three years ago, he was finishing up his MBA from Sloan School of Business at MIT. Had his entire future laid out before him. But what does he do? Picks up a pair of drumsticks and starts playing in clubs all night when he should be studying. Drops out of school, no less. Now look at him."

Albright was finding this conversation almost difficult to comprehend. "Your son is playing with one of the most successful bands in this country, sir. By now, he has to be a millionaire several times over."

"He is still an indubitable failure as far as this family is concerned. The Tavistock name is not measured in dollars, Mr. Albright. It's more than that. It's about dignity. On the other hand," said the doctor, smiling broadly, "I'm sure you've made your father proud."

The unexpected words of approval from the doctor took Albright by surprise.

"You'll have to ask my father that, sir."

"What does your father do, Alan?"

"He teaches military science at the University of Illinois. Not the most popular man on that campus sometimes. Like myself, he served in the Marines."

"Tell me something, Alan. Was your decision to join the Marines made by you or your father?"

"Mine. Dad and I had talked about me going to college straight out of high school. I felt otherwise. I never thought about evading the draft. Some of my best friends felt very strongly against that war and questioned what I was doing. I questioned what they were doing by dodging the draft.

Fact is, the war's over. I believe in letting bygones be bygones." Albright decided against telling Dr. Tavistock the war was the reason he and Jennifer broke things off. It was neither the time nor the place.

At that moment, the telephone rang. Tavistock listened, thanked the caller, and stood up.

"There's a slight emergency. One of my patients has gone into arrest and requires my immediate attention. Mrs. Woodbury will see that you get a cab back to your hotel. I'd like you to meet Claire tonight. How about dinner at the Parker House?"

"Dinner sounds fine, Dr. Tavistock."

"Good. We'll meet you up at your hotel at say, 7:30?"

"Perfect." They shook hands. Tavistock rushed out of his study, followed by Albright who remembered to grab the photo of Jennifer as he left the room. The doctor dashed down the stairs to the first floor, where he was met, almost by magic, by Mrs. Woodbury, who was waiting at the front door with his overcoat and hat. He was gone in an instant.

This was not, thought Albright, the first time this has happened.

When Albright was met at the front door by Mrs. Woodbury earlier that morning, he was smothered with cordiality and warmth. Now, as he stood before her, he noticed a distinct change in attitude.

Her gaze held nothing but contempt and disdain.

"Your cab will be here shortly, sir." The voice, once sweet and melodic, was now callous and indifferent, the dark eyes alive with fury.

Albright wondered what in this good world he had done. The five-minute wait for the taxi was far and away the most uncomfortable part of his visit to the city of Boston. Once the cab arrived, he bade her good morning, feeling a sense of unwelcomeness he could not understand.

He spent the entire ride back to the Parker House, wondering to himself what he had done wrong.

***

DURING ALBRIGHT'S FREE TIME THAT AFTERNOON, HE DID THREE THINGS. First, he phoned an acquaintance he knew in Chicago, who specialized in British vehicles. His Jaguar MK9, nearly twenty years old and affectionately known as the Big Jag, was running as good as ever, save a small oil leak that the Jaguar dealerships throughout Chicago simply were unable to fix. Even on this business in Massachusetts, he did not stop worrying about the Big Jag.

Secondly, he took time out to browse through the hotel where he was a guest. Within the lobby were mementos of the Parker House, its historic beginnings, as well as a list of some of the distinguished guests, who'd slept there over the years.

Lastly, after inquiring at the front desk, he spent the remainder of the afternoon in a nearby bookstore, making nearly eighty dollars in purchases. A number of books he bought were Christmas presents. For himself he purchased a couple of best sellers. He returned to the hotel by six, took a long shower, and by seven was waiting outside the Kennedy Room for Dr. and Mrs. Tavistock to arrive.

Albright himself cut a prominent figure. He wore a fashionable suit, recently purchased on the Gold Coast in Chicago. A navy pinstripe Brooks Brothers. White shirt. Burgundy and gold striped tie. He sat untroubled on a bench beside a Revolutionary war maritime battle painting. He studied the canvas as he sat down, admiring the handiwork, while thinking to himself what it must have been like during the early days of the American Revolution.

Christmas parties were getting underway that evening, and participants were bustling to and fro across the second floor of the Parker House. Tuxedoed gentlemen and bejeweled ladies strolled arm in arm. A number of women, single and otherwise, caught the eye of Alan Albright as he patiently awaited the parents of Jennifer Tavistock.

At exactly half past the hour he saw them. Tavistock was wearing his long black overcoat and white scarf. To his right, herself in a black overcoat, stood Claire Tavistock. They had taken the stairs as opposed to the elevator. Albright rose to greet them. He and Tavistock shook hands.

"Alan Albright," said the doctor, "meet my wife, Claire Tavistock. Darling, this is Alan Albright."

"How do you do, Mrs. Tavistock. It's very nice to make your acquaintance."

"Pleased to meet you." Claire smiled, revealing perfect white teeth.

Albright had expected her to look older. Unlike her husband, she looked better in person than in her photographs, and her photographs didn't look too bad. Where Tavistock had clearly aged since their family portrait was taken, his wife looked considerably younger. She had to be at least fifty and looked ten years younger. She was a slim woman. Tall. Confident. She was poised and assured. Certain that whatever Claire Tavistock wanted she would get.

Once again, Albright saw Jennifer all over Claire Tavistock.

Dr. Tavistock led the way through the Kennedy Room, where they had reservations. It was clear that the couple were not strangers to the premises. The maitre d' addressed the doctor and his wife by name and, no surprise to Albright, led the three of them to the best table in the room.

Albright took in the looks that Claire Tavistock was getting. The doctor seemed oblivious. She wore her reddish-brown hair in a very elegant coiffure, highlighted with what appeared to be a diamond-studded hair comb. Around her slender throat lay a single strand of white pearls.

She wore a black dress, cut just within the limits of respectability in the front.

The doctor ordered wine, sampled a glass, agreeing on

the vintage. Albright seldom drank but tonight allowed for the occasion. His mind kept returning to the icy treatment he'd received earlier that day from the Tavistock's housekeeper.

Over dinner that evening, Albright found the Tavistocks to be great hosts. They were charming, witty, and full of joviality. They epitomized Boston society. They were assured of themselves. They were clearly intent upon learning everything about Alan Albright—the man. He told them all about his career in graphic arts, which both the doctor and his wife seemed to be impressed with.

Claire Tavistock, particularly. They wanted to know everything and were hardly subtle about getting

Albright to do the majority of the talking that evening. His hobbies. His favorite foods. Authors. Presidential candidate.

It took Albright less than ten minutes into the dinner to realize he was, once again, being grilled.

By 8:20 p.m. the dinner plates were removed. All three declined dessert.

"Has Boston been good to you, Alan?" Claire inquired.

"So far, I should say it has, Mrs. Tavistock," Albright answered. "The key word in this city seems to be style. Lots of it, from what I can see."

Claire reached across the table and touched Albright briefly on the arm. "We want to apologize for not being able to spend more of the evening with you. As we told you earlier, we've been committed to this date for some time now. There simply isn't enough time to do everything at Christmas, is there?" Mrs. Tavistock spoke softly, very genteel in her delivery, every syllable that came off her tongue clear and precise, surprisingly void of the sharp accent so common to her city.

Albright was in complete understanding. "Believe me, it's no problem. I'm grateful for the opportunity to meet with the both of you."

"Tomorrow night," Tavistock said, "our calendar is free. We would love for you to come and have dinner with us at our home."

"I'd love to, Dr. Tavistock. It would be my pleasure."

"Alan," Claire said, "these have not been the best of times for the Tavistock family. Our daughter means everything to us. Particularly at this time of year. Martyn and I certainly hope you consider our offer. Talking to you tonight has given the both of us a renewed faith. Tomorrow night, we'll tell you everything we know about this dreadful business."

"In the meantime, if you need theater tickets or transportation or even information about some of the festivals going on, let us know. Tonight, in fact, they're having candlelight and carol services at the Trinity Church."

"Thanks for the offer. I believe I'm just going to hang around the hotel tonight. I realize you two have to run so I won't keep you any longer."

Thirty minutes later, Albright was back in his elegant hotel room. He spent the majority of the evening reading Robert Ludlum's latest bestseller he'd purchased earlier that day. In spite of everything that had transpired, he kept returning to his encounter with Mrs. Woodbury.

Her face would simply not go away.

For the first time since being in Boston, he began to have his misgivings. He understood that people acted in hostile ways for a reason. For the life of him, he could not understand why that woman did not like him.

He was not looking forward to returning to the Tavistocks' home.

Restless, Albright found his way back down to the lobby, eventually having a couple of beers while watching the Celtics game on television in the bar. By 11:30 p.m. he was fast asleep in his room.

***

ALBRIGHT RECIEVED A PHONE MESSAGE FROM DR. TAVISTOCK'S SECRETARY THAT MORNING. The Tavistocks would be serving dinner that evening at eight, and a taxi would be there to pick him up at 7:30.

He decided to spend the day walking the Freedom Trail. He took a taxi to Charlestown and spent roughly an hour exploring the U.S.S. Constitution and Museum. It was a beautiful day in spite of the cold temperatures. From there, he visited the Bunker Hill Monument and climbed the tower, which left him exhausted. Albright was in excellent physical shape, but even he was sore, following the ascent to the top of the historic site. The view, he had to admit, was worth it.

By 4:30, as dusk settled in, he was at the end of the Trail, successfully walking off a late lunch at a restaurant in Quincy Market. He returned to his hotel by 5:00 and recovered from the walk with a long hot shower. His legs ached. He turned on the television to catch up with what was happening in the world.

All day his thoughts kept returning to the way the Tavistocks' housekeeper had treated him the previous morning. In a few hours, he would return to their home to face Mrs. Woodbury once again.

Perhaps she had simply had a bad day. In any case, as he dressed for the evening, Mrs. Woodbury would have to tolerate him, at least for one more night, and he would have to tolerate Mrs. Woodbury.

When he rang the doorbell at 7:45, Albright was greeted at the door, to his relief, by Martyn Tavistock. Mrs. Woodbury was nowhere to be seen. He was shown inside by the doctor, who took his overcoat. During Albright's first visit, he'd seen very little of the home, save the doctor's study.

This night was different. The Tavistocks gave Alan a tour of their home, which turned out to be considerably larger that it appeared from the outside.

Inside the living room was one of the largest Christmas trees Albright had ever seen inside of a home. The Scottish pine was at least eight feet in length and adorned completely with white lights and hand carved wooden ornaments. Everywhere Albright looked throughout the house was garland. Surrounding the banisters leading upstairs. Around the enormous stone fireplace. In spite of their daughter not being on hand, the Tavistocks certainly seemed to be in the Christmas spirit.

Dinner was served at precisely eight o'clock. Mrs. Woodbury appeared from the kitchen to serve an excellent beef rib roast, Yorkshire pudding, roasted potatoes and shallots, and fresh green beans.

Claire and Martyn drank red wine; Albright, black coffee. Dessert consisted of mulled-cider sorbet and homemade Christmas cookies.

Albright came away from the table thoroughly satisfied. The Tavistocks seemed to be in good spirits that evening while Mrs. Woodbury, to Albright's disbelief, was all smiles. Her eyes were void of the burning malice she showed towards Albright the previous morning. She still made him feel uncomfortable at first, but he was determined to get on with the evening.

Following dinner, as promised, the Tavistocks led Albright into the living room. On hand were photo albums from Jennifer's trip to St. Andrews in 1969. Albright was astonished by sights and people he'd long forgotten—Aviemore, Tomintul, Edinburgh, London, Paris. Even photos from the plane ride back to New York were there.

With the matchless dinner, the charm of the Back Bay wealth, and all the memories from the trip to St. Andrews, Albright felt very much at home in spite of the unveiled hostility Mrs. Woodbury had shown him.

Once settled in the living room, the Tavistocks got down to business and began to untangle the situation involving the disappearance of their daughter.

To Albright's surprise, it seemed to be a family affair.

"She was transfixed by this *Roots* business. The Alex

Haley search for his ancestors. She watched the series and then read the book."

Albright had been taking notes on everything Dr. and Mrs. Tavistock could remember about the weeks leading up to Jennifer's disappearance.

"It had to be around October of '77 when something odd happened," said Claire Tavistock. "Only we did not realize it at the time. She was beginning a potentially successful law practice with a firm in Brookline when, all of a sudden, her studies forced her to become withdrawn. Quiet. Absolutely out of character for Jennifer."

Albright noticed that the conversation was beginning to take a toll on Mrs. Tavistock. She seemed sad and faraway at times but, like her husband, seemed determined to assist the old friend of Jennifer in any way she could.

"Like we told you earlier, Martyn's side of the family is active in genealogy. In fact, one of his aunts has done an extensive amount of research into the family tree."

"So Jennifer was curious about her ancestry. I can understand that. After all, who isn't these days?

Is there something about the Tavistocks that could have caused her to suddenly leave?"

Albright could not help but notice the effect his statement had on Dr. and Mrs. Tavistock. Brief, yet discernable, nevertheless.

"It wasn't the Tavistocks. We're just a simple line of commoners from Suffolk, England."

"Whose family just happened to sail in on the Queen Anne in 1627," Claire added.

Dr. Tavistock smiled as he eased his arm over his wife's shoulder. "It was Claire's side of the family that Jennifer seemed most interested in."

"Yours?" Albright asked, directing his question to Mrs. Tavistock.

"That's right," she answered, with a trace of what Albright

could best describe as vexation. "My maiden name was Fraser."

"Fraser. That's English too, isn't it?"

"Actually," Mrs. Tavistock replied, "Fraser is a Scottish name."

Albright sat back in his chair. "Scottish? Now, that certainly makes all the sense in the world. No wonder she was so in love with St. Andrews."

"Possibly," Dr. Tavistock replied. "In any case, once she set out on this genealogical quest of hers there seemed little time for anything else. Research, phone calls, letters, general backgrounds on the Fraser name. Claire's family Bibles. Birth and death certificates, you name it. It all seemed to us like a normal reaction to this *Roots* phenomenon."

Albright thought for a moment. "Do you recall at what point Jennifer was with all of this when she left? I mean, could there have been something in particular she had discovered that would compel her to vanish? Or could it be that this family business has nothing whatsoever to do with her disappearing?"

Mrs. Tavisock nodded, as if anticipating the question. "To answer your first question, we know that Jennifer was committed to finding out every possible thing she could about the Fraser side of the family, which was not difficult. Most of our history was fairly accessible. Our ancestors sailed over from Scotland in the middle eighteenth century. Things went well. Quite well."

"At the outbreak of the Revolutionary War, however, things began to fall apart for the Frasers. In fact, our family separated. The loyalists to King George moved up to Nova Scotia while our patriotic unit remained here in Massachusetts. Some moved to Virginia."

"Jennifer focused particularly on Malcolm Fraser and his family."

"Malcolm Fraser?" asked Albright, writing down as best he could everything Mrs. Tavistock was saying.

"Correct. Malcolm sailed to America as a youth and did quite well for himself during the 1750's and '60's in the shipping business. Once the War of Independence broke out, he prospered. He had a number of ships by then that moved cargo during the war. Turns out he was a very good friend of John Hancock. Malcolm was not only a successful businessman but a patriot. And a soldier. He sired five sons and lived to the ripe old age of eighty. Come with me, Alan," Claire said.

Albright followed Mrs. Tavistock and the doctor across their living room. She stopped in front of an oval portrait, framed in gold, of a man in his later years. The little hair he had was white, and he wore a pensive expression on his face. His dark eyes were friendly. It was signed John Singleton Copley. Albright did not recognize the painter's name.

"Say hello to Malcolm Fraser," Mrs. Tavistock said.

Once they returned to the living room, Albright was more interested than ever.

"Because of the non-importation agreement," Claire continued, "Malcolm became something of a smuggler, for lack of a better term, which pretty much set the wheels in motion for the family business."

Albright sat back; impressed at the quick lesson in American history he'd received from Mrs. Tavistock. He had a fairly good idea that Jennifer's family was fairly wealthy, but only then did he discover the real story behind the fortune.

He took note of that, as well.

Over his second cup of coffee of the evening, following a number of possible scenarios about Jennifer's whereabouts, Albright found himself unable to delay the one question he had been avoiding all evening. "There's something we haven't discussed tonight that I feel we need to bring up.

Who was she involved with, prior to her disappearance?"

***

THE NEWLY RENNOVATED OFFICE WAS PERFECT. The interior designer had done a tasteful job, a strong, masculine feel with just the right touch of subtlety and flair. His list of clients was growing, thanks in part to his father's retirement. As attorneys went, he considered himself one of the greatest. At thirty, he was comfortably rich, well-heeled, and ambitious.

He'd attended all the right schools. Active Episcopalian churchgoer. More than a few blue chip stocks on the New York Board.

His name was Michael Oliver Shoesmith. Curly brown hair covered his forehead. His face was bronze from a recent fling to Bermuda. It angered him that people constantly mistook him for an Italian. For the past two years, he had worn contact lenses over his azure blue eyes. He had an upturned chin, which appropriately gave him a look of an estimable patrician. In spite of his vigorous exercising, he was on the heavy side, weighing in at 205, which made his 5 feet 10 inch frame seem heavier than he actually was.

His love for good food added to his dilemma.

He had yet to do his Christmas shopping for the year and was slightly annoyed when the call came through from his secretary that he had an unannounced visitor.

"Tell whoever it is to get lost. If they want to see me, they can make an appointment."

"Mr. Shoesmith," the secretary replied, "the gentleman says he is a friend of Dr. Tavistock. He says it's about Jennifer."

Shoesmith debated momentarily."Send him in. And get his name for me, please?"

Albright was shown into the attorney's office. He ignored the spectacular view of downtown Boston through the large bay window behind the hand carved mahogany desk and focused his attention on the man in front of him. Albright disliked him at first sight.

Whether from jealousy or instinct, there were some very bad vibes in the room.

Shoesmith meanwhile made his introduction, shook hands, and came straight to the point." Just who are you? Another detective? Or a private investigator, perhaps? Let me tell you something, Mr. Fulbright," Shoesmith said, as he raised his voice, "I am a busy man. Everything that I have to say about Jennifer Tavistock has already been said. So why don't you take your business somewhere else so I can get back to work."

Alan Albright, like most human beings, had his imperfections. The one element he had trouble controlling was his explosive and often intractable temper. Three years in the Marines did little to curb that volatile emotion. Little did Shoesmith realize how close he was to being thrown through the glass behind him onto the passersby on State Street. To the cocky young attorney, Albright was just some fancy-dressed errand boy on Martyn Tavistock's payroll.

"I have chosen to bring my business to you, punk. And you are going to answer my questions. All of them. If it takes ten minutes, fine. If it takes all day, so be it. The first thing you will do is sit down in that fancy chair and tell me all about you and Jennifer. Because if I have to come over there and sit you down, you probably won't like it. And the name is Albright. Something else you will remember by the time we're finished."

Shoesmith stared into the eyes of Albright. He remained standing, not about to be intimidated by anyone in his own office and then made his move. He'd excelled on the boxing team at Harvard; and in spite of his wealthy upbringing, Michael Oliver Shoesmith had never walked away from a good fight in his life. He came towards Albright in a flash, grabbing a heavy glass paperweight from the top of his desk. Before he could bring the object down on its target,

Shoesmith felt like his ribs had exploded.

The kick sent him crashing into his desk. Albright was on top of him in an instant, his powerful arms grabbing Shoesmith's throat.

The door flew open, and it took three of Shoesmith's law partners to pull Albright away.

"Everything's fine," Shoesmith gasped, trying to catch his breath, not for an instant losing his composure. "Just a little misunderstanding between Mr. Albright and myself. That will be all, gentlemen."

***

TWO HOURS LATER ALBRIGHT AND SHOESMITH HAD LEFT THE LAW OFFICES AND WERE DINING ON AN EXCELLENT SEAFOOD LUNCH IN AN EXCLUSIVE RESTAURANT NEAR THE CUSTOM TOWER HOUSE.

The tension between them was subsiding, and a mutual respect, formed through blood and bravery, was emerging.

Albright had learned, after they'd tidied up Shoesmith's office, and the attorney had selected a fresh shirt and suit from his extensive newly installed office wardrobe closet, that Jennifer had been nothing less than obsessed with Scotland. She'd conducted an extensive amount of research into the history of her maternal ancestry and, in doing so, became something of an expert in Scottish history.

Once Shoesmith learned about Albright's past relationship with Jennifer in St. Andrews, his attitude changed at once. He realized his visit was personal, not just for the money like the others.

"We were friends. Good friends. Like you, I fell for her. I mean, who wouldn't? We met in court soon after she'd begun her practice. We traveled in the same social circle and kept bumping into each other. It didn't just happen overnight. Suddenly, she didn't have time for anything but that family research of hers. Thing is, she never discussed it with me, and I never probed because it didn't seem important to anyone but her, if you follow me. I soon realized I was on the way out, so I did what I felt was best, which was to leave her alone. By the way, my friend, she's still a virgin. Saving herself for the wedding night."

"And when she disappeared?" Albright asked, somewhat surprised at the revelation.

"I could not believe it. Leaving behind a practice. Great career. From day one, I've been interrogated by the police, private investigators, the works. Alan Albright," Shoesmith smiled, not about to mispronounce his name, "you are the one person I've met outside of Jennifer's family, who seems truly committed to finding her. You know about the letter, don't you?"

Albright nodded. "Yes. The Heder family received it June of last year. Saying she was in good health and she still loved her family. Delivered by a personal courier. No return address or anything. All very mysterious, isn't it?"

"I still think the key is the Dove." Shoesmith finished off his clam chowder, and briefly put a napkin to his face. A spot of blood, which he wiped at gingerly, had emerged on his cheek from the fight.

"The Dove?"

"The Dove." Shoesmith acknowledged. "Franconia Edge. Jennifer's best friend. Lives over in Newport. Old, old money, even by my standards. They grew up together. They're like sisters."

"Newport, Rhode Island?" Albright asked.

"That's right. The Rhode Island Redhead. The Tavistocks spend their summers there. Franconia is an only child. Her mother passed away when she was a kid, I believe. Her father hired a governess to raise her. If I'm not mistaken, she might have a fortune with her name on it."

"Franconia is a redhead, is she?"

Shoesmith nodded.

"She must know something. I'm quite sure someone has spoken to her about all of this."

Shoesmith said, "Probably as many times as they've spoken to me. If she knows anything, which you can bet she does, she's not budging. And I can sort of respect that. After all, best friends don't rat each other out, do they?"

"No, they don't. Come to think of it, I remember Jennifer vaguely referring to her best friend now that you mention it. Ten years is a long time, Michael. Tell me something. Why have the Tavistocks been so low key with Jennifer?"

Shoesmith nodded his head, as if expecting the question. "Remember the kidnapping of the newspaper heiress on the West Coast a few years back?"

"Of course," Albright answered. "Who doesn't?"

"The Tavistocks don't want a similar debacle. The media turned that situation, which was tragic enough, into a circus. Dr. Tavistock did not want reporters parked in front of his house through all of this. That's why everything is being handled quietly. The Tavistocks, particularly Mrs. Tavistock, are every bit as wealthy as the newspaper family. Were you aware of that?"

"I learned from Mrs. Tavistock that the family had an interest in shipping. As far as getting a dollar amount…no."

"Good thing you're sitting down, Alan. What we're talking here is serious money. Serious. To the tune of two to three hundred million."

Shoesmith noticed the look of trepidation on the face of the man across the table.

"The majority of this money belongs to Mrs. Tavistock?"

"Yeah. But there's more. What do you know about the doctor?"

"Basically, that he's a cardiologist."

"Ah, not just a cardiologist, Alan. Dr. Martyn Tavistock is *the* cardiologist. Outside of Debakey and a couple of others in Europe, no one comes close. His patient list includes kings, prime ministers, ex-presidents, captains of industry, baseball team owners, maestros, current and former secretaries of state—you name it. He could care less about his wife's fortune. His thing is authority. The rich and powerful treat him like royalty. They grovel at his feet. After all, when you're keeping as many influential people alive as Martyn Tavistock, it can be a rather hardy feeling, can't it?"

Albright was beginning to like Michael Oliver Shoesmith, in spite of his arrogance. The disdainful conduct shown towards Albright in his law office, he concluded, was all part of it. Above all, Albright admired his valor. Indeed, he was an Ivy League dandy. But Shoesmith was giving insight into this situation that Albright found engaging.

Interesting, even.

The discussion turned to politics, which sent Shoesmith into a flurry of criticism over President Jimmy Carter in general and the crisis in Iran in particular. "The man is useless. Totally. Who we need leading this country right now is a man like Ronald Reagan. He was just up here last month. My father's not only one of his biggest supporters but a major contributor to his campaign."

"Did you get a chance to see him in person?"

Shoesmith laughed. "For an hour or so. He stopped by my office. With an appointment, I might add," he said wryly.

Albright realized Shoesmith was referring to the incident earlier that morning and chuckled at the irony.

"The man is no nonsense. I particularly like his stance on foreign policy."

"That's odd," Albright said. "I guess it's a mistake to assume most people up here would be supporters of Ted Kennedy."

"Not on your life. The man's okay as a senator, but there's no way he will be president. JFK, yeah.

He was a good man. A great man, in fact. A friend of Dr. Tavistock Did he tell you that?"

Albright shook his head.

"The Tavistocks attended the Kennedy wedding in Newport. Story goes Jennifer was barely a year old and cried through the entire ceremony. Yeah," Shoesmith said, the smile leaving his face as he reflected on the 35th President of the United States," JFK was a good man, but Teddy's place is not in the White House, I can assure you. He's nuts for even running, although anybody's better than Jimmy Carter."

"What about the polls? I read just last week that a straw poll says people prefer him over Carter."

"Forget the polls."

"So what's Mrs. Woodbury like?" Albright changed the subject in an effort to get some insight from Shoesmith.

"A kindly sort of person, if you ask me. Devoted to the Tavistocks. Been with them for probably twenty years or so. Don't know very much about her, actually. She was always nice when I was around. Great sense of humor."

Well, that's that, Albright said to himself, keeping his own thoughts of the housekeeper to himself.

It was clear that she did not treat others with the same malice as she did him.

"One more question, Michael. What's with Roger?"

"Roger Tav," he chuckled. "One of the most brilliant minds I've ever known. Brilliant! Everything he touches turns to riches, you might say. We hung out occasionally when Jennifer and I were dating. You'd never guess he was a pop star."

"How did he take Jennifer's vanishing act?"

Shoesmith looked at Albright, shaking his head. "Not very well at all. It turned him into something of a recluse. The two of them are very close. In fact, he's been critical of his father for not doing more to find Jennifer. He and the doctor don't get on too well these days."

"So I understand."

"He was reluctant at first to go along with the cover story of Jennifer being 'away' in Europe. He's certainly another person worth talking to. In spite of that, Roger loves his sister very much, and I'm sure he'll give you any assistance you might need in finding her. I just want to add that I'm available anytime you have a question or are working on a lead." He handed over his business card.

"Thanks."

As the plates were being removed, the waiter, a thin gentleman with white hair and a white moustache, observed Shoesmith's cut on his face with unguarded distaste. Ruffians did not frequent this establishment. His behavior was not lost on Shoesmith, who seemed amused as he addressed the man before him.

"Sir, my friend here is from the state of Illinois. He's new in town. I'm not. Michael Oliver Shoesmith is my name. I haven't been here in some time, granted, but my buddy and I would expect the same service as any other paying customers. By the way, sir, I didn't catch your name."

The waiter, by the time Shoesmith had finished speaking, had gone pale. His apologies went on and on and were most sincere. He finally managed to excuse himself, actually trembling as he walked away.

Albright observed all of this over his cup of cappuccino, trying to figure out why the waiter had panicked the way he did. Shoesmith read his thoughts. He laughed openly.

"My family owns this place."

***

EDINBURGH

SHE WAS AWAKENED BY THE PLEASANT AROMA OF FRESH COFFEE. It was 6:30, the time she arose each day. The chambermaid, a young lass from Cupar, had her usual breakfast prepared.

Toast and Dundee Marmalade. Poached egg. French Roast coffee.

She opened the morning newspaper and saw little to be cheerful over. American hostages in Iran essentially covered the news all over the world. The American wounded on the streets of Paris was making a slow recovery. Speculation on Iranian involvement was being dismissed due to eyewitness reports on the gunmen being European. She took a drink of hot coffee and leisurely thumbed through the pages, reading bits and pieces of events occurring throughout Britain and the world that caught her eye.

The Conservatives were introducing an industrial relations bill in Parliament, which would drastically change the way trade unions in that country operated. She thought of her late husband, himself a former M.P. She read in its entirety the article about Ireland's new Prime Minister, Mr. Charles Haughley. Great Christmas reading.

There was a story that was datelined "Bristol" that did disturb her. A civilian had nearly been killed in the bungled affair in that city that had investigators focusing on the Irish.

The concert the previous night would be in the evening papers. She had been in top form, taking part in the Berg Chamber Concerto for piano, violin, and wind instruments. Today, there would be two performances as part of the Christmas presentation. Tickets had been sold out months ago, and even she was having difficulties getting them for her friends.

At the end of the evening's performance, the maestro had presented her with roses, which now sat in a vase by the living room window. These were such troubled times, she mused. But yet her world was perfect. Like the rose, she was beautiful. Like the thorn, she was dangerous.

"Will there be anything else, ma'am?" The girl spoke in a soft brogue. She was rosy cheeked and extremely polite.

"That will be all, my dear. Tell me, have you finished your Christmas shopping?"

"No ma'am, I haven't," she answered.

She arose from the dining table and made her way across the room to her wall safe. She removed a bundle of ten pound notes. "Here you are, Rosie. Three hundred pounds. That should be a start, at least."

The young girl was clearly taken aback. Momentarily. "I can't take that, ma'am," she said. "I've only been working for you a week. It wouldn't be proper, would it?"

"You deserve this and more for a job well done. Mind you, don't spend all of it in one place. And by the way, Rosie, you may have the rest of the day off to do with as you please. This is Friday, and the shops will be opening in a couple of hours. Why don't you enjoy yourself?"

She was thanked profusely by young Rosie, and following the removal of the breakfast dishes, Rosie was off and running, three hundred pounds richer to do with as she pleased.

With the chambermaid gone, she showered, dressed, and went over once again her music. One concert in a day was challenging enough; two would be grueling. But no matter, she thought, it would take her mind off what was becoming more and more unsettling.

There were still no developments about Alexandria.

Those who knew had been warned. They would not be back.

But what if there were someone else...

***

BOSTON

ALBRIGHT RETURNED TO THE PARKER HOUSE SHORTLY AFTER FIVE O'CLOCK. A long day was behind him. The fight with Michael Shoesmith was unexpected but, Albright thought to himself, necessary.

This entire Boston visit was beginning to take his thoughts off of Tolly Chamberlain. He still loved Tolly. Deeply. For two years they had been inseparable; now she was gone, living her own life, leaving him to live his.

He opened the leather briefcase that lay atop the bed. He'd known nothing of the Parker House prior to coming to Boston, but the service in this hotel, Albright had to admit, was second to none.

Even though the doctor was picking up the bill for the entire trip, Albright felt slightly guilty about his surroundings.

He reached for the manila envelope to remove the 8 by 10 photograph of Jennifer Tavistock. To his surprise, he discovered the doctor had included a family portrait as well. Both were in color, clearly done by a professional.

He studied the face of his old friend. Judging from what he saw, the teenager he'd known in St. Andrews had lost none of her outward enthusiasm. At least on the outside. She wore a teal-colored dress, highlighted with a tan paisley scarf, held in place with a white cameo. The same smile and open face. The brown hair had streaks of gold throughout, indicating the picture had been taken during the summer months.

Albright had learned that week that even though Jennifer's world was elitist, he remembered her as being a down-to-earth person to all people at all times, with the exception of her occasional bouts of sarcasm, and even that was forgivable.

He brought the photographs over to the Early American desk. He kicked off his shoes, sat down, placing the two photographs in front of him. The resemblance between Roger and Jennifer Tavistock and their parents was noticeable. Roger had his father's long forehead and bushy eyebrows. The upturned chin he inherited from Mrs. Tavistock.

Albright gazed in clear admiration at the face of Jennifer Tavistock. Her most distinguishing feature was what Albright remembered the most and admired more than anything else about her extraordinary face. The dimple. Perfectly round, in the center of her chin. The Kirk Douglas dimple, someone in St. Andrews once called it. Her eyes were light brown and her hair was dark. She was looking into the camera at the time of the photograph, and she was smiling. There was absolutely nothing to indicate why, less than six months after the picture was taken, she would disappear into thin air.

Albright opened the desk drawer, removed a pad of stationary provided by the hotel, and began to write down everything he'd learned that day while it was still fresh in his memory. An instant later, he noticed the yellow light at the base of the telephone was blinking.

Albright punched in the number of the front desk. "This is Alan Albright in 416. Did I receive any messages today?"

"Good evening, Mr. Albright," the voice said. First class service. That impressed him. "You received a phone call from an Ed Napier at 3:15 this afternoon. Here's the number."

Albright wrote down the digits on the stationary pad, his mind racing as to who Ed Napier might be. He had met less than a half dozen people formally over the past two days, and Ed Napier wasn't one of them. "Thank you very much," he said, hanging up the phone. The number itself was without an area code. He dialed it at once.

"Detectives. Investigator Napier, speaking."

The Boston Police Department, Albright surmised. Ed Napier was a cop!

"Alan Albright returning your call, Investigator."

"Good evening." The voice on the other end of the phone was deep. Pleasant.

"Thank you for returning my call. I was in touch with Martyn Tavistock earlier today. He told me briefly about you and why you're here."

"And why is that?" Albright asked.

"To help find Jennifer."

"Investigator," Albright said, "that is something I've yet to decide on. I did come here, as you know, to meet with the Tavistocks about Jennifer's disappearance. I've spoken with the family. I'm considering the doctor's offer, but I still haven't given him an answer."

"How long are you planning on staying in Boston, Mr. Albright?" Napier asked.

"Probably another twenty-four hours or so."

"I'd like to sit down and meet with you before you leave town. How about tomorrow morning?

I would try and see you tonight, but I'm working on something at the moment that's high priority. Is eight o'clock tomorrow morning too early?"

"Sure," Albright answered. "Eight o' clock's fine. You name the place and I'll try and find it."

"What about the restaurant in your hotel? Over breakfast?"

"No problem. Tell me something, Mr. Napier. Were you the investigating officer when Jennifer turned up missing?"

"Indeed. The case is still open and I was, and still am, in charge. We'll talk about that in detail tomorrow, Mr. Albright."

"Investigator, just one question. How will I know you?"

"Don't worry about that. I'll know you. See you at eight."

***

EDINBURGH

THE TWO CONCERTS WENT OFF WITHOUT A HITCH. The Christmas spirit was alive and well In Edinburgh, the crowds had been enthusiastic, and she'd pulled off what was arguably her finest performance that evening. The matinee has been packed, well received, and without any major flaws; but the night belonged to the beautiful pianist, whose skill and mastery had generated not one but two standing ovations.

She had gone out for a bit of revelry at the home of the conductor, had returned home by one, and had fallen off into a comfortable rest when the phone rang. Her bedside clock read three.

"Sorry to be disturbing you at this hour, I realize how late it is in Scotland. What I have to tell you can't wait, I'm afraid."

The voice on the other end of the phone was clear, in spite of the miles between them. She sat up on the side of the bed, brushed a lock of hair from her face and said, "I'm listening."

"Someone's making inquiries about Jennifer Tavistock."

"You call me at three in the morning to tell me that? I do believe you're beginning to worry too much."

"You don't understand," the voice said. "This one is different. He seems to be an ex-boyfriend of hers."

"It's late. Thank you for being so loyal to me. I do feel that you may be overreacting somewhat. We have nothing to worry about, believe me."

"He's not just any ex-boyfriend. His name is Alan Albright. They were together at St. Andrews."

It was as if a bolt of electricity had traveled through the phone line. She was wide awake now. She stood up out of bed, her supple body silhouetted against the moonlight shining through her bedroom windows.

"What do you know about him?" she asked.

"Very little. Ex-Marine. Successful graphic designer. Doesn't talk much. Lives in Chicago."

There was silence on the other end. She was thinking. It

could be nothing. Then again...

"I'll get back with you. I must get my sleep." She hung up the telephone.

***

BOSTON

ALBRIGHT REACHED A DECISION, REGARDING MARTYN TAVISTOCK'S OFFER, WHILE WAITING FOR ED NAPIER TO ARRIVE. It was shortly before eight; and after a night's sleep and careful examination of where his career path was headed, he had made up his mind.

He'd left word with the hostess that Napier would be joining him. Albright had arrived a few minutes early and planned on checking out of the Parker House and flying back to the Windy City later that morning. He looked up as a man came walking towards him.

"Mr. Albright?"

"Investigator Napier." Albright stood up. "How do you do?" They shook hands.

Napier sat down across the table from Albright. He was wearing a charcoal gray woolen suit. Well cut. Silk tie. Albright noticed the letters EGN on his right sleeve. It was the first time he'd ever seen a policeman wearing a monogrammed shirt.

The man across from him looked fit. He seemed to be in his early thirties. He was sporting a wedding band and a gold Rolex on his left hand. He seemed to be waiting for a reaction from Albright. There was none.

"You've hardly changed in ten years," Napier said.

"Did we meet in another life or something?" Albright asked.

"The photographs from Jennifer's trip to St. Andrews is how I know you, Mr. Albright."

Of course, Albright thought. This policeman had

seemingly done his homework.

"Call me Alan, would you?"

"Sure. Call me Ed. Tell me something. You an ex-Marine?"

"That's right. I was in from '70 through '74...Camp Pendleton. 'Nam. Company E. Marine Security Guard Battalion in Saigon for a year. Finally, Lejuene. What about you?"

"'65 through '68. Third Battalion, Fourth Marine."

"The Thundering Third!" Albright was awestruck. He abruptly stood up and saluted the policeman, which made Napier awkwardly nod his head in acknowledgement.

"Yeah. Took a bullet in the back at Con Thien. August 16, 1967. Sent me home a hero and all. Joined the Boston Police Department in '70 and have been here since. For better or worse."

"How could you tell I had been in?" Albright asked.

"You can always tell, Alan. I'm a policeman, remember? Some of the worst days of my life were spent in the Marine Corps, but it still was the best thing that could have happened to me. It was my ticket out of the streets of Roxbury. It's still home; my life is just a little more focused these days.

Wouldn't live anywhere else."

"I'm not familiar with Roxbury."

"It's what's known as the ghetto. No different than Southie or Dorchester, other than those places are full of the Irish, and Roxbury is full of Blacks."

Napier over the phone had sounded like everyone else in Boston. They called a park a "pahk" and a garden a "gahden." It was only when he walked in that Albright realized he was Black.

"What about you? Where's home?"

"Chicago. By way of Champaign-Urbana. I'm a graphic

designer by trade."

At that moment, the waiter arrived, took their order, and poured them both black coffees.

"Chicago's a good town. Been there a couple of times. So is Boston. In spite of all the bad things you hear about this town, I wouldn't live anywhere else in the world, even though it's the most expensive city in America."

Apart from the neatly trimmed moustache, Napier was clean shaven. He wore his hair short with a thin part on the left side. His hands were the size of catcher's mitts. His eyes were dark and steady. Obtrusive, even. They routinely observed everyone and everything in the restaurant that morning. His face was lean and hard, and it was evident that the years on the streets of Roxbury and his stint in 'Nam had left him fully qualified to be a policeman.

"Have you decided how long you plan on staying in town?"

"My plane leaves in a couple of hours."

"Then we need to get straight down to business," Napier said. "Let me begin by telling you where this investigation stands at the present. Believe it or not, Jennifer Tavistock, as far as the Boston Police Department is concerned, is not a missing person. Officially. She left this city of her own free will, it seems. She has been in touch with her family in the form of a letter."

"Have you read the letter?" Albright asked.

Napier nodded. "We took the document downtown for examination. Had our experts run a psychological profile on the wording. Everything these days is going scientific, Alan. By all our conclusions, Jennifer wrote the letter out of her own free will. No duress or anything."

"I understand it was hand delivered. Any theories on how it was pulled off?"

"It's my guess that Jennifer has a confederate. A close and trusted friend, maybe. If I were a betting man, that would be my explanation."

"You've been on this case from day one, correct?"

"That's right."

"Have the Tavistocks been helpful?"

At that moment, breakfast arrived. Albright had ordered a full blown meal: eggs, link sausages, hash browns, and toast. Napier, on the other hand, settled for fresh fruit and toast. Napier waited for the waiter to finish serving before answering Albright's inquiry.

"Yes and no. Dr. Tavistock has been the pillar of cooperation from day one. Extremely helpful and supportive. Claire Tavistock is another story."

"Not very helpful, I take it."

"That, Alan, is the understatement of the morning. She holds me personally responsible for not being able to track her daughter down. From the beginning, there has been an antagonistic relationship between me and Claire Tavistock. She's gone to my supervisors, even the mayor, trying to get me off this case."

"Now that is strange. I've only spoken to her at length one time, which was the other night. She seems so frail. Listless, even. I really felt sorry for the poor woman."

Napier chewed thoughtfully on a bite of toast, listening to what Albright was saying. He reached for his coffee cup, took a sip, chuckled, shook his head, and said, "Alan, I like you. You appear to be an intelligent man. But you will discover, my friend, that 'still waters run deep,' as Aretha Franklin says.

Claire Tavistock is far more complex than a first encounter might indicate. In fact, depending on how far you plan on taking this quest of yours, you'll discover that this case itself is considerably more entangled that it may seem on the surface."

Albright tried to remember when he'd had a better breakfast. He realized it was loaded with a few of the things he probably did not need. Nevertheless, he tried to put away a good meal first thing in the morning as often as he could.

With his workout schedule being the way it was, he seldom ate a heavy meal at night, relying instead on breakfast and lunch for his nourishment. He felt less sluggish that way, relying on juices and maybe a bowl of popcorn at most.

"Do you have any contact with Mrs. Tavistock at all?"

"None. But that hasn't slowed me down. Dr. Tavistock and I have developed a good line of communication these last two years. Not meaning to belittle anyone, but Claire Tavistock seems to have my number."

"Has she treated you this way from the outset?"

Napier nodded. "Basically. That is hardly unusual in police work, Alan. This occupation requires constant tolerance. Patience. Claire Tavistock comes from the Back Bay. Her family practically built this town."

"So I've heard," Albright said. "Jennifer never told me much about her family when we were in St. Andrews."

"Is that why you're here? Because of St. Andrews? Okay... When this investigation first began, we went through everything she left behind looking for clues. That was before her letter to her family, mind you. Dr. Tavistock was good enough to let me examine some of her personal things. As you may know, Jennifer is an avid photographer. Half of her pictures of Scotland had you in them."

Albright smiled. "That's ironic."

"What's that?" Napier asked.

"Her father didn't even realize who I was. All this began ten days ago or so when, for whatever reason, I felt compelled to send Jennifer a Christmas card. It had been a while since we'd last been in contact with each other. Two days later, I pick up the phone; and it's Dr. Tavistock, flying off the handle at me about Jennifer."

"Now, that's interesting," Napier said. "But understandable. Jennifer's life had been moving so fast, and I mean that in a good sense. She had begun what seemed to be a lucrative law career. She'd worked over at the DA's office before going into private practice. As you know, she'd dated this attorney prior to her disappearance. Gentleman by the name of Shoesmith."

"Ran into him yesterday," Albright said, smiling to himself.

"Cocky son of a bitch. That's another one who has been less than cooperative. He's a punk.

Jennifer dropped him a couple weeks before she vanished. In fact, our case focused on Shoesmith as a possible suspect at first. Truth is, he knows nothing."

Napier looked across at Albright's plate. It was empty, save a knife and fork, which lay neatly folded atop one another. He chuckled. "Don't believe I've seen anyone eat like that this early in a long time."

"What they will serve on the plane back to Chicago will probably be minimal. I've got a few things to take care of once I get back in town so I probably won't get a chance to eat again before tonight."

Albright caught the eye of a blonde seated at a table across the room. She smiled; he did likewise.

"So Ed, is Oliver Shoesmith not your choice for man of the year?"

"You know the type. Family connections kept him out of the draft. Old money. And there's another thing." Napier looked directly at Albright. "Shoesmith is a bit of a ladies' man.

Likes to play the women. For some reason or another, women seem to go crazy over the guy. Money can be a heck of a door opener."

"I wonder if that had anything to do with why he and Jennifer split up?"

"Doubtful. She was focused on something so important that Oliver Shoesmith was probably the least of her priorities. That's why you interest me, Alan. My investigation has led me to believe that what Jennifer Tavistock was involved in had something to do with Scotland."

This was not the first time since being in Boston that Albright's not-so-wild theory had been brought up. "No kidding."

Napier took in the sudden interest from the young man seated across the table. Noticed Albright's fists lightly tapping the starched white linen tablecloth. Napier shook his head and replied, "Afraid not. If you do decide to take up Martyn Tavistock's offer and if I were you, that would be the very first place and probably only place, I'd look."

The waiter poured Napier another cup of coffee; Albright declined. He glanced at the blonde across the room. She was gorgeous. Albright admired the face, the conservative suit she wore, her poise, and well-designed manner as she sat across from him. For an instant, he saw the face of Tolly Chamberlain. The pain returned.

"Why Scotland?" Albright made himself return to the business at hand.

"Couple of reasons. First of all, she was hung up on finding her ancestors."

"That's what Mrs. Tavistock was saying. What's the other reason?" Albright asked.

"The second reason is that she took her passport with her."

"Has Tavistock sent people to Scotland to try to find her?"

Napier shook his head.

"Why not?"

"Because," he said, gazing at Albright in an austere, powerful way," Claire Tavistock insisted he not do so."

"Meaning?"

"Martyn Tavistock's wife simply doesn't think her daughter is in Scotland."

"Then where does she think Jennifer is?"

"That's a good question. Which goes back to my original statement about how complicated this matter really is."

The blonde, at that instant, smiled briefly at Albright and looked the other way.

Napier looked behind him. "You've got a plane to catch, remember? Distractions like that could be costly."

"I might be willing to pay the price. She keeps looking over here."

"Naturally," said Napier. She's a pro."

It took Albright a few seconds to catch on to Napier's reference. "A prostitute?" he whispered.

"Surely not. Just look at her! Working at eight in the morning?"

Napier rumbled a deep chuckle and shook his head. "What better time than early morning, huh?

Libidos work around the clock and so do hustlers."

The blonde suddenly arose and threw her arms around the man who had approached her table. He looked to be twice her age. The way they kissed ruled out the possibility of him being her father.

"Back to the issue of Scotland, Ed. The Tavistocks basically reinforced what you just said. About the research on her family tree."

"You know then about her obsession. I know that's a harsh word, but that's basically what it was.

She evidently hit pay dirt somewhere to leave behind everything the way she did."

"What other possible motives are there?" Albright asked.

"Basically, there are few things to go on in this case. She withdraws several thousand dollars from her bank account, packs her clothes, and leaves. Inexplicably. There are so many people in this country who simply pack it in and disappear all the time. The police simply cannot spend a great deal of time searching for someone, especially an adult, who leaves on her own free will. Even when her last name is Tavistock."

"That's understandable, I suppose."

"What do you remember most about Jennifer Tavistock?" asked Napier.

"I've never known anyone more headstrong. She never gave an inch. At the same time, there was a sense of loyalty about her from the beginning of our friendship. She had my absolute trust. On top of that, she was the most intelligent person I've ever known. Period."

"That says a lot. An awful lot. I'm going to law school at night, and I can tell you there's not a whole lot of trust anywhere these days. To trust someone absolutely, certainly says a lot about that young woman."

Albright looked at the man across from him in admiration.

"You're in law school?"

"That's right. Depending on how these next several months go, I hope to take my bar exams in June of next year. If I pass, goodbye Boston Police Department."

"Good luck to you, sir," Albright said.

"Thank you. This Tavistock business will probably eventually cost me my job anyway. Don't look surprised, man. That's the way things work in this town. Everything's political. Particularly when you're dealing with someone as powerful as the Tavistocks. Claire was a Fraser before she married and, friend, that name carries an enormous amount of weight around here. Far more than the Napier name."

Albright nodded, thinking back to what Shoesmith had told him about the Fraser wealth.

"Once I get my law degree, Alan, I'm on my own, off the force and everybody's happy."

"What if you solved the case before then?"

"I still don't think you understand, Alan. It's not just about finding Jennifer. It's much, much deeper."

"Could it be that Mrs. Tavistock is...?"

"Bigoted?" He shook his head. "Nah. The issue of race can sometimes be overstated. In the case of Claire Tavistock, I must admit that my being a Black man has little to do with her resentment."

Albright looked hard at the man across the table from him. He realized Napier could have told him a lot more that morning. For whatever reason he would not, and Albright could easily understand why Napier was making such a career move in life. The Marines brought him out of the ghetto, and law school was bringing him out of the bureaucratic trap he seemed to be caught in.

"Look," Napier said, "here's my card. You've got to get back to Chicago, and I have criminals to catch. My home number is on there as well as my office. If you do decide to follow up with this business, and I've got a pretty good feeling you probably will, let me know. My official jurisdiction, as you know, is limited to this city. You, on the other hand, can conceivably go as far as it takes to do what is necessary. You're a Marine. I don't need to tell you what that means. If you make the commitment to find this Tavistock girl, you'll understand completely what I've told you this morning. All the time I spent on this matter, I've only discovered a fraction of what this case is all about. A fraction."

Albright took a deep breath. In a couple of weeks, it would be Christmas. He looked around. The

Parker House was adorned throughout with holiday décor; and in spite of the hostage crisis in Iran, people in Boston seemed determined to be filled with the spirit of the season regardless of the adversity their fellow countrymen were enduring. Napier, meanwhile, had reached into his wallet and removed a credit card.

"What about this business in Iran?" Napier asked.

"I'm ready to go back in and finish it."

"That's precisely how I feel about it," the policeman replied. "Good luck to you, Alan Albright. I've enjoyed this conversation. It's always good to meet a fellow Marine."

"Likewise. And I insist on picking up this check. This one's on me."

"Sorry. Official business. As part of the ongoing investigation into the disappearance of Jennifer Tavistock, I called you here; therefore, I'm paying. One last thing, soldier. Be careful. Real careful.

Don't take anything or anyone for granted in this town. Remember that. If you get desperate and backed in a corner, let me know. Semper Fi, my brother."

"Semper Fi," Albright replied.

They stood up, shook hands and parted company. Albright ignored the blonde as he walked towards the exit of the restaurant.

***

EDINBURGH

ONE OF THE MORE APPEALING ASPECTS OF THE CITY OF EDINBURGH IS ITS REMARKABLE TOPOGRAPHY. The hills are dramatic, and without question the most dramatic of all the hills is Castle Rock, on which Edinburgh Castle so majestically sits. Built by Malcolm the Third in the eleventh century, the castle to this day is one of the premier sights in Britain.

She ignored the enviable view of Edinburgh Castle as she stood by her window. The phone call had not come. This was her final night to perform, and her mind was nowhere on her music. To the young girl's delight, she had given the maid the day off once again. She had needed to think, and another presence that morning would have been distracting. Ever since last night's phone call, she had been uneasy. This old friend. Could he have known? And why on earth was he back after all these years?

She realized at that moment she had to speak to her

lover. She picked up the telephone, dialed the Number, and waited. There was no answer.

***

BOSTON

BY NINE O'CLOCK, ALAN ALBRIGHT HAD PACKED HIS LUGGAGE AND WAS READY TO CHECK OUT. His flight to O'Hare was scheduled to depart Logan Airport at 10:15. He gave the room a thorough examination, making certain he was leaving nothing behind. He grabbed his luggage and opened the door.

At that moment, the phone rang.

"Alan Albright."

"Give it up. It's not worth it. Before you get in too deep, get out!"

The line went dead. The voice could have been either male or female. Whoever it was had used a voice-altering device of some sort that gave him or her a metallic tone.

The warning had come. From whom? And why?

Once again, Albright grabbed his luggage and headed for the door. He had a plane to catch. Up until that moment, he was against taking Dr. Tavistock up on his offer. Now someone was trying to discourage him—to scare him off. Ed Napier's words were coming to pass. There was, indeed, more to this business of Jennifer Tavistock's disappearance than he realized.

Albright checked out of the Parker House, caught a ride to Logan Airport on the hotel shuttle, and found his way to the American Airlines terminal. As he waited on his flight, he began to deduce exactly who in that city had known of his intentions. Martyn and Claire Tavistock. Michael Shoesmith.

Ed Napier. Mrs. Woodbury.

Five people.

The housekeeper, the ex-boyfriend, the parents, and the policeman.

His sense of trust in Bostonians was rapidly diminishing. Maybe it could have been a wrong number. Or a practical joke. As much as he tried to reason why someone would warn him off, the more convinced he became that he, indeed, had been the target.

Yes, he would take up Dr. Tavistock's offer. It wasn't the half-million dollar reward. Being one of the premier graphic artists in the Midwest, he could care less about the money. His recent accomplishments at Third Wind all but assured him that he would make his first million by the time he reached thirty.

He had been threatened and that angered him.

Albright purchased a *Boston Globe* and a black coffee and settled in the uncomfortable chair outside the boarding gate. The article about the attack on the American diplomat in Paris caught his eye. He read the first paragraph and the name of the victim, in guarded condition, began to gnaw away at him.

Cashmore. Stuart Cashmore. Where had he heard that name before? He'd seen it somewhere recently. Where was it?

Suddenly, it came to him. Stuart Cashmore's name had been on the very same list he'd discovered in his parents' attic ten days ago.

Stuart Cashmore had been at St. Andrews!

Albright could not put a face with the name. He read the remainder of the article. Police had few leads they were disclosing. The State Department was denying reports that the Iranians were responsible for the shooting. At first, Albright considered the possibility of another person with the same name. Until they listed his age. Twenty-eight. It had to be the same man.

Albright shook his head in disgust at the crime, making

the incorrect assumption that Cashmore's troubles had nothing to do with his own.

He finished reading the newspaper; and when the announcement came for his flight departure, he boarded the 727 and looked forward to returning to Chicago.

Once back in the Windy City, his first priority would be to telephone Martyn Tavistock and give him an answer.

Jennifer Tavistock would be found.

Threats or no threats.

She would be found.

***

CHICAGO

SNOWFALL IN CHICAGO DURING DECEMBER IS NOTHING UNUSUAL. Albright took it as a good omen.

He enjoyed the cold weather. If one lived in the Midwest, particularly in Chicago, there was little choice but to enjoy it.

Albright took a taxi from O'Hare to his northside residence, tipping the driver generously. He brought his gear into his apartment, brewed a fresh pot of black coffee, and searched his refrigerator for food. Just as he predicted to Ed Napier earlier that morning at the Parker House, the flight attendants on American had served precious little. He found himself settling for a sandwich.

Outside his window, the sky was a slate grey. Snow had fallen earlier in the day and, as he listened to his favorite radio station, he learned an additional six inches was possible.

Albright checked his mail and, to his surprise, discovered a note from the Postal Service informing him that the gifts he'd purchased in Boston had arrived. There was the usual assortment of bills and junk mail. Nothing important.

He slipped out of his shoes, hit the couch, and stretched out. It was only three o'clock, but it seemed to be getting dark already. Albright glanced around his apartment. Simple furnishings.

Roomy. Comfortable. In one corner of the living room sat his T-square and drawing board. On the walls were prints by M.C. Escher, Salvador Dali, and his favorite, Pablo Picasso. None of the prints were signed.

As he lay on the couch, Albright reflected on the past week. Boston itself, he concluded, was a great city. Under different circumstances, his trip would have been an enjoyable one, a welcome relief from the day-to-day routine of work. But there was something out of the ordinary about Boston.

Jennifer Tavistock's hometown.

***

NORTHERN SCOTLAND

WHILE THE WIDOW MULLED OVER HER NEXT MOVE IN HER EDINBURGH FLAT, THE EVENING WAS QUIET AND STILL IN THE NORTH OF SCOTLAND. Stars twinkled in the crisp night sky while a gentle light from a crescent moon radiated through scattered clouds. Apart from the occasional barking of a distant dog and the soothing sounds of the waves of the sea, it was a cold but quiescent December night.

Craig Castle, built in 1658, lay nestled on the edge of a precipitous cliff overlooking the North Sea.

Restored in the late nineteenth century, the castle drew unbelievable gasps of wonder from motorists along the A-9, who beheld the refined sight. Located halfway between Golspie and Brora on the Great Road North, the structure itself was an architectural wonder. There were a number of castles, historic homes, and royal residences in the north of Scotland that gladly opened their doors to the public.

Alas, Craig Castle was not one of them. Tourists who made attempts to get beyond the gates were kindly turned away. Residents of Brora and Golspie, in fact, when questioned about the dwelling, were often vague and quick to change the subject, insisting that tourists visit nearby Dunrobin Castle instead.

The occupants of the castle were private. Exceedingly so. The caretakers kept the outside grounds as immaculate as any in Britain, and the few who did manage to get beyond the gates to work on plumbing or electricity came and went about their business; they were paid generously for their services and promptly shown to the gates.

Those who did indeed step foot inside Castle Craig could tell little about its occupants.

Visitors invariably remarked about the wonders of the great hall, particularly its mammoth stone fireplace. They marveled without exception at the awe-inspiring collection of medieval weaponry, which hung along the oak-paneled walls of the main corridor. They were moved at the sight of the paintings, rich tapestries, tartans, battle flags, and meticulous woodwork which suitably depicted another time.

One painting, however, stood out above all others.

The portrait was of a man from the 18th century, quite possibly a lord or a clan chief. He stood proudly, his right hand resting upon his sword, which hung at his side. He sported a bright plumed bonnet, which covered his mane of flowing black hair.

His dark eyes were not friendly. His face was strong and clean shaven. Far and away, the most distinguishing feature about the man's face was the deep circular dimple, which lay squarely in the center of his chin.

Few men or women who ever laid eyes on the painting left Castle Craig without a noticeable feeling of unease. There were more than a few examples of the luxury and affluence associated with a castle of its size, but there was something in the eyes of the chieftain, something just beyond the surface, that contradicted the comfort and extravagance normally associated with a castle.

Something menacing. Threatening.

***

CHICAGO

AT EXACTLY SIX O'CLOCK CHICAGO TIME, ALBRIGHT PLACED A PHONE CALL TO BOSTON. Martyn Tavistock's private line. In all, the doctor had three telephones in his home: the number listed in the directory, the children's telephone that had been installed when Jennifer and Roger were still at home, and his own personal line. It was seven in the evening on the East Coast, and the doctor picked up the phone on the third ring.

"Martyn Tavistock."

"Good evening, Dr. Tavistock; this is Alan Albright."

"Alan! Did you have a good flight back to Chicago?"

"Yes I did. Thanks. Dr. Tavistock, I'm calling you to accept your offer."

"I am certainly glad to hear that, Alan," Tavistock said, genuinely pleased. "Are you unequivocally sure about your decision?"

"Yes." Albright contemplated about telling the doctor about the phone call that prompted him into saying yes but decided to keep it to himself, at least for the moment. "I'm sure. There are a few things

I have to get straightened out here in Chicago. If it's okay with you, I'd planned on getting started right after Christmas."

"That's fine. First of all, we need to sign a contract. Just to ensure that you understand that I plan on keeping my word, my attorney will draw up an agreement stating that upon the safe return of Jennifer that you will receive the half million."

"I don't think that will be necessary, sir."

"On the contrary," Tavistock replied. "I should think this agreement is in the best interest for both parties. Mind you, if for some reason you fail to find my daughter you are under absolutely no further obligation whatsoever. But something tells me that will not be the case, Alan. I have, for the first time since this unfortunate affair began, acquired a speck of hope. By the way, my wife and I owe you something of an apology."

"For what?" Albright wondered aloud.

"You might have gotten the impression when I didn't realize who you were at first that we were out of touch with Jennifer's life. Nothing could be further from the truth. Ten years ago, when the two of you were in St. Andrews, something of a communications gap, for lack of a better term, developed between Jennifer and her parents. It dissipated over time as she grew older, and we became more sensitive of our children.

"As you know, my son and I have yet to put things to rest, but the fact remains that Claire and I both love our children. Dearly."

"I understand completely," Albright said. "That is why I plan on doing everything humanly possible to return your daughter to you as soon as I can. What we need to do, sir, is to set up an itinerary, something to work toward."

"I couldn't agree with you more. We'll begin by issuing a credit card in your name. American Express. By the way, expenses are strictly on me. Feel free to use it at your own discretion. Travel, phone calls, bribes, you name it... Whatever it takes."

Albright had not considered the generosity he was being presented.

He had not considered a lot of things.

"Thank you, Doctor. I'll be in touch with you in a day or

so."

"So be it. Goodbye, Alan." The line went dead; and as Albright hung up the telephone, a song from one of his favorite groups of his youth began playing on his living room stereo.

The Beatles.

Someday when we're dreaming, deep in love and not a lot to say,

Then we will remember things we've said today.

Jennifer Tavistock would be found.

***

EDINBURGH

HE ARRIVED AT RAMSAY GARDENS SHORTLY AFTER NINE O'CLOCK. The shops along the Royal Mile, bustling with Christmas shoppers earlier that evening, were now closed up and quiet. He let himself in with his own key, as he always did. Removing his tattered overcoat, he made his way into the capacious fifth-floor apartment, taking care as always not to disturb anything. He was bushed.

A long trip was behind him.

His journey had begun in the desert sun of Morocco, where he'd been serving as a security specialist for a West German manufacturing firm who, considering what had transpired over the past month, were concerned for the safety of their executives.

He loved the desert. Returning to Britain, particularly in December, wasn't anything he fancied.

The flight to London had left him with a case of jet lag, and the jolt of the Scottish December wind once he hit the streets of Edinburgh reminded him what real winters were all about.

A hot bath was a high priority.

He walked into her bedroom. Everything in place. He removed his shoes, placing them at the foot of the bed. They were the kind worn by a common laborer. He pulled off his coarse, long-sleeved shirt, revealing a muscular upper torso, browned from the hot desert sun. A nasty looking scar ran from his right shoulder halfway across his hairy chest, a souvenir from an Omagh brawl he'd sustained at nineteen.

His coat and trousers were filthy. The looks he and his client got from passengers on their journey home from Morocco were anything but pleasant. The first impression most people had was of a pair of vagabonds. That was precisely the effect he and his client wanted to give. Nothing was left to chance while traveling. Both men had gone unshaven for several days. The manufacturing executive and his bodyguard seemed unsuitable for the civilized world and, as a result, few people paid them more than a passing glance. Once landing at Heathrow, they were thoroughly searched by Customs for opium and hashish. The German boarded a plane bound for Hamburg while his employee took a flight into Scotland.

As it turned out, the man was one of the first skinheads in Dundee a decade earlier. In his younger years, during the mid-sixties, he'd aligned himself with the Mods.

By the age of eighteen, thoroughly disgusted with his life in the slums of Dundee in the Whitfield Housing Estate and no future, save the occasional fights at the local boxing club, he'd joined up with the British Army. Nine months later, while deployed in Omagh, Northern Ireland, with The King's Own Scottish Borderers, he'd run into a drunken Second Lieutenant in a Protestant pub, who'd had one pint too many.

Both soldiers had eyes that night for the same girl. The Second Lieutenant, with fool's courage brought on by rank and alcohol; decided the young woman in question had no business with a plebian Scotsman.

The officer's first mistake was slapping the girl when she refused to have a drink with him. When the enlisted man intervened, the Second Lieutenant responded with a knife across the chest of the Lance Corporal. From that point on, pandemonium broke loose. Ignoring the cut, the enlisted man grabbed the Second Lieutenant around the neck with one hand and his right wrist with the other. With a swift jerk, he brought the knife-wielding hand behind the man's back. There was an excruciating cry of pain from the Second Lieutenant that drowned out the agonizing snap of the breaking arm.

That was only the beginning.

The last thing the soldier remembered before waking up in the hospital was his face repeatedly being slammed into the edge of the bar in a manner that the human anatomy is quite ill-accustomed to.

The young enlisted man's chivalrous behavior cost him six months behind bars and an end to his career in The King's Own Scottish Borderers. From that point on, his bad reputation and his growing disdain for the English began to grow. Upon his release from jail, he spent the next couple of years down in London serving as a heavy for a group of East End hoods, eventually drifting to the United States of America, where he met up with an old West Indian mate from his regiment who had set up a nifty operation specializing in forged U.S. currency.

The fake one-hundred dollar bills were being manufactured by an Argentine gang in Buenos Aires, who used London as their center for distribution. The success lay in the financial district, known as the City of London. There, in the heart of Britain's money center, a stream was set up to cities like Lagos and Monrovia in the west of Africa. From those points, unscrupulous businessmen from the European capitals, such as Brussels and Amsterdam and Rome, purchased the counterfeit bills at a significantly reduced rate of exchange and converted them at full value into their respective currencies.

The scam seemed on the verge of being cracked at one point by Scotland Yard until, unfortunately for the Yardies, all of the key suspects virtually disappeared off the face of the earth, never to be seen or heard from again.

With two exceptions. The West Indian who, after warning his Scottish friend of the impending crackdown, vanished into the slums of Kingston, and the Scotsman himself, David James Waters.

From that point on, from the London underworld of the East End to the Ivory Coast of Africa to the docks of Marseilles, he was given a nickname.

No one is sure who first tagged the moniker. But over the years it stayed with him; and to the criminal element the world over, he was known by the appellation, even he was growing accustomed to.

They called him Dangerous Waters.

He ran a bath in the tub, climbed in, humming a Christmas carol to himself as he lay back and closed his eyes. Waters been straight for four years now. The Tel Aviv security firm, made up of former Mossad agents, recruited him in the fall of 1975. Even though Scotland Yard knew about his past activities, they had nothing on him; and since he was working in a respectable profession, they kept their eye on him but subsequently left him alone.

As he lay in the tub, he looked back on his humble beginnings from the brutal streets of Dundee on to a life of petty crime, only to end up protecting wealthy industrialists from the threat of terrorists the world over. With the taking of the American hostages a month earlier, his firm was suddenly and understandably inundated with requests for protection.

The man he had been assigned to cover, a real gentleman with whom Waters was developing a true friendship, had returned his wife and children to Hamburg following the seizure of the American hostages. They would remain in Germany indefinitely, while the industrialist would be returning to Rabat after the first of the year.

That gave Waters the opportunity to fly to Scotland. Tomorrow, he planned on hiring a vehicle and driving over to Dundee to see his mum and dad. He'd purchased them their own home two years back; and his father, now getting up in the years, no longer had to worry about how to take care of his wife and six children—two of them still at home.

Waters toweled off and threw himself on top of the bed, not bothering to dress. In ten minutes, he was asleep.

***

SHE RETURNED TO HER FLAT SHORTLY AFTER ELEVEN. Opening the door, to her astonishment, she noticed his scent of masculinity at once. All the lights were off. She quickly found her way into the bedroom. Once there, she turned on a lamp by the bed. He was resting heavily. She stood over him, admiring his frame as he slept.

It had been months. So many times she had called. He never said yes or no. He simply would come or he would not. In all honesty, she had not expected to see the center of her universe. She wasted little time undressing. This magnificent creature was hers tonight, to adorn, to caress, to love. He would conquer her, as he always did. The one man on the planet she succumbed to was lying in her bed—fast asleep.

She turned out the light, sliding on top of him, thinking of the best way to awaken the Dangerous Waters.

***

CHICAGO

ALBRIGHT SAT DOWN AT HIS DESK INSIDE HIS NORTHSIDE APARTMENT THAT SAME NIGHT AND ASSEMBLED ALL OF THE HAND-WRITTEN NOTES HE'D TAKEN DURING HIS EXCURSION TO BOSTON. Not having the best handwriting on a good day, some of the notes he'd taken while conversing with the Tavistocks and Michael Shoesmith were difficult to translate. On the plane ride to Chicago, he wrote down much of what he and Ed Napier had discussed earlier that morning. By nine, he had organized a summary of his trip. He took a break, worked out for two hours, and then took a shower. He'd arisen that morning at six Boston time, and the bustle of the flight and the telephone call from the mystery person were beginning to take their toll on him.

He called it an evening and by midnight was fast asleep.

***

EDINBURGH

THE DECEMBER DAWN WAS SLOW IN COMING IN EDINBURGH. The skies were rough with a menacing look of snow about them. They had made love for the better part of the night. As Dangerous Waters lay sleeping, she had arisen from the bed and, as was her habit, caught a glimpse of a city awakening from her fifth-floor flat.

Waters was anything but a heavy sleeper, particularly with his background, and she took great pains not to disturb his slumber. But even he, the man she cherished, had not made her troubles go away. Even now, her thoughts drifted to the phone call she'd received from America.

Who was this Alan Albright? Was his wish to find Jennifer Tavistock strong enough to be a threat?

Perhaps the American was simply being sentimental; clinging to the past like a hapless sailor clings to a life raft in the open sea. So engrossed in her thoughts was she that Dangerous Waters slipped his arms around her without making a sound.

"Beautiful, isn't it?" He nibbled at an earlobe, exploring her with his hands.

"Why, thank you, darling," she said.

"I meant the view. To call you beautiful would be an understatement."

"Then what am I?"

"I'm learning to speak three different languages, and none of them have invented the best way to describe you, my dear. You're magnificent."

She turned to face him. His hair, jet black in color, was uncombed. His eyes were grey, and there was nothing about them that gave away what this man had done in the past or, for that matter, was capable of doing period. He could pass for an ordinary businessman, which was exactly what made people consider him dangerous.

His nose had the look of a potentate. Many women considered him handsome. What affected her the most from the moment she had laid eyes on him for the first time was his smile.

Hollywood screen idols would be envious. God had given to Dangerous Waters a gift that drove women crazy and put trust into people who, sadly, should not have been so trusting.

She knew bits and pieces about his past. Some of the things he had done. She wondered if he ever wore that smile when he killed.

"Magnificent. That's English."

"It's still early," he said. "My mind still searches for the perfect phrase. In the meantime, do you fancy a shower? Last time I checked, there was room enough for two."

***

CHICAGO

BY NINE O'CLOCK THAT MORNING, ALL OF THIRDWIND'S EMPLOYEES HAD DRIFTED INTO WORK.

The annual Christmas party was being held that evening at a nearby restaurant. Albright had purchased a sweatshirt, emblazoned with the Harvard Rowing Team for the name he'd drawn. As he entered his workstation, he noticed Gerry Windham in his office.

"Can I talk to you a second?"

"Hello, Alan!" Windham seemed shocked to see Albright. "Come in. I'm surprised to see you back so soon. Didn't think we would see you until after the New Year."

Albright spoke to Windham for ten minutes, explaining his intentions. Windham, meanwhile, listened without saying a word. Once Albright finished, Windham responded.

"Impossible. Totally out of the question." Windham sat back in his executive chair. His face was flushed and, uncharacteristically as it seemed, he couldn't look Albright in the eyes.

"Might I ask why?" a stunned Albright asked.

"Our projects for 1980 are piling up at an exceptional rate. That includes the Balfour Project, which, as you know, could spell a quarter of a million dollars for this company."

Albright was not moved. "Gerry. You and I are friends. What you and everyone did for me over the past several months can never be repaid. When Tolly Chamberlain walked out on me, you guys were there for me in my hour of need. I might not have been able to pull through had it not been for Thirdwind. As I told you before I left for Boston, the Balfour project is complete. At least, my end of it." Albright stood up. "Do you mind if I close the door?"

Windham shook his head.

"I would not be walking away from this company for just any reason. The person I've told you about was a friend from long ago. I cannot begin to explain how important this is to me right now."

"I don't want to hear your explanations. You either work for me or you don't. Period."

One thing Alan Albright did not suffer from was indecisiveness. Windham was not budging; neither was he.

"Fine!" he shouted. "You have my resignation, then. But you are making a capital mistake, buddy.

When this is all over, my main agenda will be to put you and Thirdwind out of business!" He walked out of Windham's office, slamming the door behind him.

An hour later, Albright had cleaned out his workstation—to the disbelief of his co-workers. The buzz around the office was that he had been fired for insubordination, something quite unheard of at Thirdwind. What Albright and his fellow workers did not know was that Gerry Windham was a chronic gambler. He bet on horses, football, baseball—anything.

He was into his bookie for roughly seventy-five thousand dollars. Twenty-four hours earlier that had been no problem, for his debts often mounted into the hundreds of thousands until he'd hit a lucky streak and come up with the payoff. Suddenly, from out of nowhere, he was notified that it was time to pay up, juice action and all.

There was no possible way for him to come up with that amount of cash on a moment's notice.

He was left with but one option: Force Alan Albright, who would almost certainly be approaching Windham for a favor, to leave Thirdwind. That simple. Windham thought this strange. These gentlemen, however, offered few explanations as to the reasoning behind their demands.

He had little choice but to abide. He knew the rules only too well.

She had found Gerry Windham.

***

ALBRIGHT RETURNED TO HIS APARTMENT AFTER LEAVING THIRDWIND. He was completely baffled.

Why in the world, he thought, would Gerry Windham go nuts like that? He opened up his Chinese dinner. Sweet and sour shrimp in one box, pork fried rice in the other. He poured himself a Coca-cola, sat down, and dug in.

He loved Chinese food.

Albright and Windham, for the very first time, had exchanged harsh words. His promise to put Thirdwind out of business was something he planned on keeping. In fact, the first item he'd reached for when cleaning out his workstation was his Rolodex. It contained a list of all his clients—existing and prospective.

When this matter with Jennifer was settled up, he would return to Chicago and keep his promise.

Part of Albright was furious while another part of him remained confused. He kept asking himself why Windham behaved in such a manner. His former boss, prior to this morning at least, was considered by Albright to be one of the most laid-back people he'd ever known. He and the crew at Thirdwind had been there for him when Tolly had not.

Only a few days ago, Windham had given Albright his blessings to go to Boston, with the remainder of December thrown in to boot, in order to speak with Martyn Tavistock.

Albright was halfway through his dinner when there was a knock at the door. He rose from the kitchen table, glancing at his watch as he did so. 5:20 p.m. He walked through his living room and glanced through the peephole. To his surprise, it was Otto Henry and Beth Spencer. He opened the door.

"May we come in?" Otto asked.

"Sure," Albright said. "Why aren't you guys at the party?"

"Been canceled," Beth said. "Lack of interest, you might say."

Beth Spencer was twenty-one and a recent graduate of the California College of Arts and Crafts in Oakland. She was the newest Thirdwind employee. Otto was smitten with her. She had returned home to Chicago that spring looking for work; and Windham, impressed with her portfolio, hired her on the spot. Her additional specialty, interestingly enough, was accounting. While Otto adored Beth, she simply regarded him as a good friend, a buddy, someone to escort her into bars when she preferred not to be alone. Everyone realized she treated Otto like dirt; but if he didn't seem to mind, there was little to be said by anyone else.

Her excuse to Otto was that he was divorced.

With the exception of Gerry Windham, the very foundation of Thirdwind sat inside Albright's living room at that moment. Albright was the creative director, catapulting the growing company into a major competitive force not only in Chicago but into larger markets like New York and Los Angeles with his inventive and enterprising vision.

Beth's accounting background had taken much of the burden off Windham, as she was taking over day to day operations and handling Thirdwind's financial matters. Otto's duties were not limited to artistry. He had, oddly enough, the duties of account services—something he was extremely skilled at when he wasn't being silly. His ability to deal one-on-one with clients was remarkable, and Otto made sure his agency provided for any and all client needs. Windham had turned Thirdwind into a major agency in a short period of time, and his growth potential for the 1980's was seemingly unlimited.

Until this.

"Lack of interest?" Albright asked.

"After what happened this morning," Otto said, "no one at Thirdwind really wanted to have a Christmas party. That's why we're here, Alan. There is something you need to know about Gerry."

"I don't need to know a thing about Gerry, Otto!" Albright shouted, his temper flaring up once again.

Beth spoke up. "You need to calm down, Alan. Something has happened to Gerry that might explain why he's been behaving the way he has."

She was looking directly at Albright while Otto, as usual, was looking at Beth. Albright, still steaming, sat down in his favorite leather armchair while he motioned with a quick-opened, palmed gesture for his guests to be seated on the matching couch to Albright's left.

Beth Spencer had the look of an artist more so than an accountant. Her long blonde hair was pulled back in a ponytail. She wore a black turtleneck sweater, khaki trousers, and a matching khaki photographer's vest.

"I'm listening," said Albright.

"As you know, Alan," Otto said, "Gerry and I go back several years. Not only is he my best friend but he is the brother I never had."

This must be something, Albright thought as he looked into Otto Henry's face. Otto seemed troubled for a man who never took anything seriously. He had a reputation for being trivial.

Frivolous. Light-hearted. He was, however, without question, the best air-brush artist in Chicago.

"We discovered something," Beth said, "purely by accident, mind you, that may shed some light on Gerry's behavior. Wednesday evening, two men came to Thirdwind. Very nasty-looking gentlemen. Gangster types. It was late and everyone had gone home with the exception of Gerry and me.

Actually, I had left but came back because I'd forgotten a roll of film that I needed to develop that night."

"Anyway, I came in without them realizing it. On my way out, I heard one of them mention that 'he' had to go."

"He?" Albright asked.

"That's right," Beth said. "It was unclear just what they were talking about, but they were saying something about making sure it was done and done right. That's all I heard. Then I heard one of the men tell Gerry that things would be taken care of."

"Gerry is a compulsive gambler," Otto said. "He has been for some time now. He's always been able to cover his action with these guys in the past. There's no telling just how deep he's gotten himself in this time, however."

Albright had difficulty comprehending what he was hearing. "Windham's a gambler? I never would have figured him for that type," Albright said. "But that still doesn't have anything to do with me. Are you absolutely certain about what you heard?"

"Afraid so," Beth said. "It's only a hunch, but the 'he' those gentlemen referred to could possibly be you. Which could explain Gerry's behavior toward you this morning. Think about it. You know how our company is, Alan. Granted, I haven't been there as long as you and Otto, but people don't just get fired just like that."

"I agree with Beth," said Otto. "Those two guys told Gerry that someone had to go. Then bingo! You're fired for asking for a little time off. You know and I know that what you requested is hardly grounds for termination."

Albright eased out of his chair, coiled like a cheetah about to strike its prey. "I need to talk to him," he said, pacing the living room floor. "Now. Otto, where was Gerry when you last saw him?"

"At the office. He seemed a little despondent. I asked him what he was going to do tonight and he just shook his head."

"Does Carole know about the gambling?" Albright asked.

Otto nodded. "The wife always knows, Alan. That's why I don't have one anymore." He glanced at Beth. "She's known for some time now. She and I have both tried to get help for Gerry. They have these organizations nowadays for chronic gamblers. It's just not that easy to get someone to admit to the fact that they have a problem."

Albright reached for the telephone that was on the floor at his feet. He dialed Thirdwind's number.

"Thirdwind. Windham, speaking."

"Alan Albright. We need to talk."

***

EDINBURGH

HE KNEW SOMETHING WAS WRONG. That morning, before they could get their bath together, they had made love yet again. Over breakfast in bed, he presented her with what he called an early Christmas present. She had unwrapped her gift only to find a string of the finest Tetouan pearls. He had slipped them around her throat, admiring them as they lay resting on her ample breasts. They had talked about her music and his work. While reading the morning newspaper, he'd commented on the continuing investigation of the American diplomat who'd been nearly killed in Paris. It took a great deal of restraint, but she managed to say how terrible the world had become.

Dangerous Waters had not survived in his domain without picking up on the seemingly insignificant reactions of those around him.

Fortunately, he happened to be reading the paper in bed, and her head was nestled against his shoulder as he read.

Still, he perceived something wasn't cricket.

They had been seeing one another for nearly a year. He was only the second man she'd been with since the passing of her husband three years ago. He perceived his love for her as a talented musician, a fashionable woman who stood for everything he was not. She was from the best stock; he a workingman's son.

There were undoubtedly parts of his life that Dangerous did not share with her; of that she was certain. Nevertheless, in spite of his persevering hunger for her, she remained uncomfortable. This ex-boyfriend of Jennifer Tavistock continued to torment every corner of her brain.

Alan Albright.

Whoever this person was, his timing couldn't have been worse.

By all rights, Neal Edwards, Stuart Cashmore, and the beast should all have been dead and buried.

No clues, no trace, no worry. The IRA was being blamed for the bombing in Bristol, the French authorities were searching for an Iranian connection in Paris, and the police in the north of Scotland had no idea where to begin their search.

No law enforcement agency on earth would ever tie the respective crimes together. Each job had been done by different people, who had no idea who they were working for or why the task was being carried out. The Bristol job was being paid off with Krugerrands, twenty thousand pounds worth to be exact, located in a locker in London's Victoria Station.

The Scotland job had been paid in U.S. dollars, cleverly concealed in a mailbox outside a remote Yorkshire farmhouse that had been uninhabited for some years. She paid for the French job with diamonds to be picked up in a small pouch left under a designated seat in a cinema near the Place de Republique in Paris.

None of the would-be assassins knew who their employer was. The money was gone forever, which, quite honestly, she cared less about.

She would devise another plan. This time, she would accomplish her objectives. She must. It was her duty. Her obligation.

Her single mission in life.

To protect the secret.

The secret of St. Andrews.

She would stop at nothing.

***

Dangerous Waters had left for Dundee to see his family. He hired a vehicle and had left shortly before noon. He'd kissed her goodbye, before leaving her flat, with a promise to return to Edinburgh Sunday night.

That left her 48 hours to devise, not just another strategy, but learn once and for all about Alexandria.

Another name might possibly be added to her special invitation list.

The young man from Chicago.

Alan Albright.

***

With Dangerous Waters, now in Dundee, the holiday performances with the Edinburgh Symphony behind her, she suddenly realized that Christmastime would be upon her, and she had done absolutely nothing in preparation.

"Rosie?"

"Yes, ma'am," Rosie replied.

"We are going to get this place in the Christmas spirit. Locate for me, if you will, all of the Christmas decorations. They would be in a box somewhere, perhaps in the hall closet. Do you fancy going out and finding a nice a tree today?"

"That would be very nice, ma'am."

Rosie Carstairs liked her employer. The daughter of a Cupar farmer, she had moved to Edinburgh that summer, had signed up to find work through a temporary services firm, and found moderate success doing odd jobs. She shared a flat with three other girls and preferred dancing in the clubs in the evenings. She had received word to report to the Ramsey Gardens address for what was supposed to have been an impermanent position.

Her employer was so impressed with Rosie that she offered her a full-time position the next day.

If that wasn't good enough, she bestowed three hundred pounds upon her to do with as she pleased.

Her two brothers would be surprised this Christmas, as would her dad and mum. In all, she spent nearly two hundred pounds on her family, something she'd never done. With the remaining money, she bought herself clothing, mostly outfits to wear when she went out dancing.

She planned eventually to go on to college, get her highers, and become a petroleum engineer. Her eldest brother Rob was in Aberdeen, working on an oil rig, making an inconceivable amount of money. He had urged her to take up University as soon as possible.

After all, at seventeen she wasn't getting any younger.

"I suggest that we have lunch somewhere and find ourselves the best tree this city has to offer."

Her employer had to be the kindest woman on the face of the earth. Rosie could not believe her luck.

***

BOSTON

IN BOSTON, CLAIRE TAVISTOCK'S DAY WAS JUST BEGINNING. She arose from the late eighteenth century queen-sized canopy bed, put on her robe, and headed into the master bath. Normally, she would shower, but this morning she felt like indulging herself. She drew a hot bath, slid out of her gown, and climbed into the tub.

Her hair was tied loosely on top of her head. The water was hot and found its way into her every pore. She was in no mood today for anything but Claire. For twenty-eight years, she had devoted herself to her children, her husband, countless charities and benefits, and her parents. She closed her eyes and thought of her youth. Being in her forties was difficult enough, but as of today she was fifty. Of course, she took care of what Martyn called her "exquisite body." For the last two years, she had colored her hair.

No way, she decided, would a plastic surgeon ever put a blade to her face.

She heard a noise at the bathroom door that startled her. Her eyes flew open the same moment as the door. Martyn Tavistock stood there—tall and handsome as the first time she'd seen him, with a dozen yellow roses in hand.

"Happy birthday, my darling."

She was astounded, in a most pleasant way. "But what about your patients?"

"The doctor is at your service, madam. Just where does it hurt?"

***

THEY LAY UNDER THE BLUEBELL STRIPE BEDSPREAD AND MATCHING CANOPY HANGINGS.

TAVISTOCK HAD PURCHASED THE BED AT AN AUCTION IN NEW HAMPSHIRE TEN YEARS AGO. They had painstakingly and meticulously matched the entire master bedroom around the mahogany and maple Hepplewhite structure.

Tavistock had given Mrs. Woodbury the day off, risen at five-thirty, and did something he seldom had the time to do: prepare breakfast. The breakfast, sadly, went untouched.

The same could hardly be said about his wife.

The clock on the matching bedside table read 9:35. While the city of Boston was bustling about on the outside, Claire Tavistock was fast asleep on her husband's shoulder. Tavistock could not remember a happier day he'd spent that year. No patients, no administrators, just he and Claire. Later that day, as they always did on Claire's birthday, they would be leaving for their summer cottage in Newport for the weekend.

Just the two of them.

They had met in the spring of 1950. Tavistock was a dashing young Air Force officer in medical school; she a Vassar undergraduate. He knew she came from a wealthy Boston shipbuilding family.

The first time he saw Claire, she was on the arm of another. The next time they ran into to one another, they were both unescorted.

Tavistock proposed to her the night before he was being shipped out to England.

She said yes.

Their first child had been born in Scotland on the twenty-fifth of March, 1952. A girl. They named her Jennifer Kay. Tavistock had been away in Korea quite a bit in those days and was not present when Jennifer was born. She was two months old when he first held her.

Three years later, on the fifteenth of August, along came Roger.

Following Tavistock's time in the Air Force, the family returned to Boston. Tavistock's cardiology practice flourished. Claire became involved with the arts once again, particularly the theater, and her painting. With her family position quite entrenched in the city of Boston, her scions quickly followed suit. Young Roger and Jennifer both prepped at Boston's finest private schools.

Neither Claire nor Martyn would have any part of their children going away to boarding school.

Not even Andover.

Roger was now a rock and roll artist. Where his father did little to hide his disgust, Claire was quite proud of their son. Lifestyle notwithstanding, he was indeed a Tavistock, as well as a financial ace, who was investing his millions wisely. The one cloud over their lives was Jennifer.

Martyn felt his wife stirring under him. He felt terribly fortunate to have her. He realized this turmoil involving the disappearance of his daughter would have to end before it tore his family apart.

Alan Albright, he thought, it's up to you. Find our daughter before we all go off the deep end.

It was the seventh of December.

The wheels Tavistock had set into motion by taking on Albright were slowly turning. Soon they would be revolving at top speed.

The Secret of St. Andrews was in danger.

***

CHICAGO TRAFFIC WAS HEAVY GOING INTO DOWNTOWN CHICAGO. Southbound traffic into the Loop was normally moderate, compared to the stream of northbound cars headed to the suburbs. Albright, Beth, and Otto rode in the Big Jag with Albright driving at a steady clip.

Beth and Albright were seated in the front while Otto made himself comfortable in the spacious rear seat of the Jaguar. Surrounded by the irrepressible leather upholstery, riding in the Big Jag for the first time, as Beth experienced, made the vehicles of the day, be they Japanese, German, or American, seem tame by comparison.

Albright acquired the Big Jag two years ago from a neighbor and dear friend of the family, who retired from the University and moved to a villa in Spain. Mrs. Silverman was widowed, worldly, and like a grandmother to Albright.

As a youth, he had earned extra money by caring for Mrs. Silverman's lawn and rose garden. She lived alone at the end of the block in a handsome white house.

Her husband passed on some twenty years before, and her children grew up and eventually left Champaign-Urbana, leaving Mrs. Silverman quite alone. The Albrights and others along their street took it upon themselves to look out for her. At least twice a month, she would be a guest in the Albright's home for dinner, and she would certainly be invited over for special occasions, particularly on those holidays when her children could not make it home.

When Mrs. Silverman decided to retire, she offered Albright something he had treasured since high school—her automobile. Beige in color and a condition that could best be described as "pristine," the Jaguar was habitually kept in a garage and seldom driven by Mrs. Silverman, who spent the majority of her driving time in her second car, an Oldsmobile. Being seventeen years old, the car was virtually perfect. Albright actually drove the motorcar once while in high school.

The announcement came on the Fourth of July in 1977 over a backyard cookout at the Albrights.

Mrs. Silverman surprised everyone when she announced her plans to retire and move to Spain. She planned on keeping her house, of course, but was unsure just what to do with her automobiles. In all honesty, she knew exactly what she wanted to do with at least one of them, and it wasn't the Oldsmobile.

Albright was humbled. He felt unworthy. This was a dream come true for the young man, and he felt almost guilty asking Mrs. Silverman what she would take for the automobile. His hopes were dashed at once when she informed him the car wasn't for sale. Then, with a smile, she presented Albright the keys to the Jaguar and told him the car was his.

As a gift.

Albright's father immediately intervened, telling Mrs. Silverman her proposal was out of the question. She was unmoved. The car was Alan's, since she had the title turned over to him a week earlier. All he needed to do was to go down to the Champaign County Courthouse, give them his signature, and the vehicle would be his. End of discussion.

In the two-and-one half years since the vehicle came into Albright's possession, there was no automobile in all of the Land of Lincoln better maintained than the Big Jag. When he landed his job at Thirdwind and began his search for an apartment, the one priority in selecting his accommodations was that his car would be safe—both from thieves as well as the brutal winters Chicago produced.

When he discovered the north side apartment on Sacramento, just off Addison, his search ended.

The brick duplex was spacious, affordable, and included two clean garages.

Albright never drove to work, preferring the alternative of the Chicago Transit Authority. During the winter months when driving became necessary, Albright made certain the Jaguar went through a professional car cleaning service on a weekly basis. It was costly, but well worth it.

As they neared Carpenter Street, Albright detected the faint rattle once again. The following morning, a Saturday, Albright planned on taking the Big Jag to a repair shop. Since it was operated by a group of mechanics, who specialized in British cars, he was hopeful this firm, recommended to him by a friend, who herself drove a Jaguar, could remedy the problem.

The Christmas lights and decorations brightened up an already colorful Loop that evening.

Albright swung the vehicle into Carpenter Street, hoping to find an adequate place to park the Big Jag.

"What's all the commotion?" asked Beth. Police cars and an ambulance had the north side of the street blocked off.

"Who knows?" Otto replied. "Probably a mugging."

Albright said nothing as he observed the scene. Just then, a car pulled onto the street, enabling him to ease the beautiful automobile into the vacated parking space. Even the policemen paused to admire its magnificence. The trio got out of the car, locked the doors, and approached Thirdwind. The front doors of Thirdwind suddenly swung open as a team of paramedics rushed out.

"My God!" Beth exclaimed.

Gerry Windham lay strapped on a gurney, face covered in an oxygen mask. He was whisked into the back of the ambulance. Seconds later, the driver sped off, sirens thundering, red and white lights flashing.

The whole thing happened in an instant.

The trio of Thirdwind employees was too stunned to move. It was Beth, who took the first cautious steps towards the entrance of the office, only to be met face to face with a police officer.

"Just where do you think you're going?" He was in plain clothes, clearly in charge of the crime scene. He sported a Burberry trench coat.

"We work here," said Albright. "What's going on?"

The policeman looked closely at each of them, not moving his head, only his eyes. "All three of you are employed at this establishment?"

"That's right." At six feet one, Albright stood nearly six inches shorter than the policeman.

With a motion of his hand, the policeman said, "Would you come inside, please?"

Uniformed Chicago police officers, with their signature checkerboard hats, cordoned off the front doors of Thirdwind with their crime zone strips. As they entered Thirdwind, Otto hesitated, afraid of what he would discover inside. Even Albright took a deep breath. They noticed at once the blood on the floor outside Windham's office. The policeman in charge kept them well away from the stain. Beth looked horrified. Otto remained speechless.

"My name is Detective Irving Brighton. There's been an assault, as you can see. Witnesses saw two males leaving the premises. Officers are getting statements from those who saw anything."

Brighton slipped his hands into his trouser pockets. "Your names, please?"

Brighton wrote down their names.

"Is Gerry going to make it?" Beth asked.

"Is that the name of the victim?"

"Yes," she answered. "Gerry Windham. Is he going to make it?"

"He's in bad shape. Whoever it was came in here, beat your friend to a pulp, and then broke both of his legs. The beating makes sense, almost. Especially, if robbery was a motive. The breaking of the legs is a sign of something else."

"Meaning?" Albright asked.

"Breaking a man's legs is a common form of punishment to someone who's heavily into gambling and hasn't paid up."

No one said a word.

"When did you last see Mr. Windham?"

"About 3 o'clock this afternoon," Otto said. "We did speak to him on the phone about a half-hour ago. We were on our way back here to see him."

"Let's find a place to sit down," Brighton said.

Otto led the way to his workstation. The policeman grabbed a stool, which inclined the Thirdwind employees to follow suit. As Otto reached to turn on the light over his drawing board, he suddenly remembered the stash he kept in his drawer.

"You say two males were seen leaving?" Albright asked.

Brighton nodded. "Caucasians. One had a pronounced limp." The detective looked tired. He shook his head. "Happens during the holidays, you know. This sort of thing. Guys get in deep over football, hockey, you name it. Plus it's Christmas. When that happens, people just seem to go nuts around here."

"You're not kidding," said Beth.

The policeman looked at Beth with an admiring gaze that sent a ripple of jealousy through Otto's blood. "Is there anything," Brighton asked, "that you might be able to tell me about Mr. Windham?"

"Nothing unusual." Beth lied. She wore a frank expression of guiltlessness. She seemed on the verge of tears. She bowed her head, brought her hands to her face, and looked up at Detective Brighton. "He never hurt anyone. Why would someone want to do this?"

"I can assure you the Chicago Police Department will do everything possible to find these people, Miss Spencer."

Brighton extended an arm in Beth's direction. She acknowledged him by taking his large hand in both of hers. It was a silent way of saying thank you. She took the wise initiative by remaining silent about the conversation she'd overheard the night before between Windham and the two spiritless gentlemen.

"Can we find out which hospital they've taken him to?" asked Albright.

The detective brought out a two-way radio from his overcoat pocket, keyed in the mike, spoke a few words and answered with a hearty 10-4.

"The dispatch is contacting the ambulance to find out where he's being taken. In the meantime,

I'm afraid you'll have to leave this office for tonight. We have a great deal of evidence to round up around this place."

Otto cringed.

"They'll be cordoning off the entranceway for the next few hours. If one of you could leave me a number, as soon as we find out more about your friend, we'll let you know."

Icy winds whipped through the intersection of Carpenter and Roosevelt. A light snow was falling.

Still, more Chicago policemen arrived at the scene of the crime. Detective Brighton disappeared inside Thirdwind with a fingerprint team. Albright, Beth, and Otto stood in front of the Big Jag, oblivious to the noise, the smells of exhausts from the buses and cars, the bitter cold.

"Now what?" Otto asked, speaking to himself as much as to Albright and Beth.

"We get in touch with Carole," Beth said. "She's going to need our help. I think I know a way to find out where they've taken Gerry. There's a phone booth across the street over there. Let's go."

They crossed Roosevelt Street. Unbelievably, the phone booth was not only empty but in working order. Beth placed a phone call, asked a number of questions, and hung up.

"Bingo! I know where they've taken him. Cook County General."

"That's over on West Harrison," Otto said. "How'd you find out?"

"Got the name and number of the ambulance. Called their dispatch and told them I needed to know the destination of 211. I sort of exaggerated the truth slightly. Told them I was a family member."

"Which isn't altogether untrue," replied Albright.

They climbed into the Big Jag; Albright roared the engine to life and took off.

***

Emergency rooms, no matter what city or township the hospital happens to be in, are basically all alike. Once finding a place to park the Jaguar, the trio walked through the emergency room entrance.

A receptionist sat behind a glass-enclosed case, surrounded by clipboards and paperwork. They ignored the anguish surrounding them.

Albright spoke inside the small circle within the glass

booth. "A patient was brought to this hospital a short time ago. An assault victim with a couple of broken legs. His name is Gerry Windham."

The receptionist seemed to be around sixty. She was plump, and looked Albright over as he spoke.

She was wearing a uniform, but it was difficult for Albright to determine if she was a nurse. Her blue eyes seemed fatigued. If there was any job which would show the darker side of human life, it was hers.

"Just a moment." She punched a number into her telephone. She was wearing a headset that had a tiny microphone. She spoke a few words, listened, and said thank you.

"Dr. Kenmore will see you shortly. Please have a seat, sir." She spoke with the strong nasal accent that is particular to Chicago.

Moments later, a physician came through a set of double doors and spoke to the receptionist. She, in turn, pointed out Albright to the doctor. He entered the waiting room area and introduced himself to Albright.

"Charles Kenmore."

"Alan Albright. How do you do, Doctor." They shook hands.

"You were inquiring about Mr. Windham. Right now, all we can say is he's sustained some rather nasty blows to the head. He's still conscious, in fact. He's lost a considerable amount of blood. Both kneecaps seem to be smashed up pretty badly. His vital signs, I can say, are stable."

Carole Windham rushed in at that instant. She was with a woman Albright did not know; but judging from the resemblance, it could have been her sister. Otto, who had been standing alongside Beth listening to the doctor's report, embraced her briefly.

"Dr. Kenmore," Otto said, "this is Gerry's wife, Carole. Seems he's going to be okay."

Two hours later, Albright returned to his apartment. He realized he would be unable to speak to Windham tonight, but was relieved that he was alive.

***

ALBRIGHT WASTED LITTLE TIME IN DECIDING HIS NEXT MOVE. He packed up a few clothes for the weekend, assembled his notes, photographs and other memorabilia, concerning Jennifer Tavistock and placed them in his briefcase.

Beth Spencer and Otto returned with Albright to his north side apartment. They vowed to discuss absolutely nothing with the police about the conversation Beth had overheard while at Thirdwind. Windham needed their help, and the less the Chicago police knew about Gerry's gambling problem, and whatever connection that might have to do with the assault, the better.

Following his time spent in Vietnam and his experience in active combat, Albright feared few living men. Whatever problems came his way, he met them head on—without any trepidation, whatsoever. His father, Colonel Tom Albright, trained his son at a young age to look the adversary straight in the eye and make that adversary blink.

His aggressive behavior sometimes got him into trouble, and more than a few times he'd been sent home for getting into fights while in school. His brother Dennis, two years older than Alan, beat up his brother endlessly while they were young. Once Albright turned twelve, he began to grow at a faster rate than his brother, and the tables began to turn. By junior high school, they were evenly matched. When Albright reached his sophomore year, his older brother, himself a senior, left him alone.

They hadn't fought each other in years, but Dennis still knew how to bring his kid brother to the edge of a fight with little effort.

Living in a city with the criminal eminence of the Windy City enlightened Albright in a hurry. He trusted few people in that town. His circle of friends was small, limited primarily to his co-workers at Thirdwind. He'd seen the level human beings in Chicago would descend to in pursuit of riches. He had little tolerance for the social climbers and jet setters— regarding them all as bogus prima-donnas who would stop at nothing to get ahead.

He'd seen his share of victims in Chicago. Those who'd been robbed, had their homes invaded, their cars stolen. To Albright the criminals, be they street hoodlums or high-ranking gangsters, deserved little commiseration. Those who were behind the attack on Gerry Windham could have very well pressured Windham to force Albright from Thirdwind, or so Albright was starting to believe, and would ultimately be dealt with.

He closed his apartment door behind him, felt the unmerciful sting of the winter winds upon his face, and unlocked his garage. He threw his gear into the back seat, backed the Big Jag out of the garage, and locked the garage behind him.

He needed to return to Champaign-Urbana.

He needed to think and he needed to act. Unbeknownst to Albright, he was being brought into history. The simple urge to write a Christmas card to an old friend was about to alter the lives of a great number of people.

Some of those people were innocent. Others, like a young widow unknown to Albright in the city of Edinburgh, were not so innocent.

In the night skies of Chicago, stars were shining. In the heart of a young man driving his classic Jaguar towards downstate Illinois, a storm was brewing.

The widow had met her match.

***

John Scofield

THE ONE MAN ALAN ALBRIGHT ADMIRED MORE THAN ANY OTHER ON THE FACE OF THE EARTH WAS HIS FATHER. Tom Albright, USMC retired. Most referred to the elder Albright as the Colonel, his rank at the time of retirement. The Colonel was something of a maverick at the University of Illinois.

A lone hawk amongst a flock of academic doves.

Colonel Albright, rigid as he was raising his sons, still allowed his children to make decisions for themselves, right or wrong. Dennis was happily married and settled in a family environment. Alan was recovering from a relationship gone bad, single, and still finding his way to full maturity. When he opened the back door and walked in to his parents' house for the second Friday night in a row, his father knew something was wrong.

"It's Tolly, isn't it?"

"Not this time."

The Colonel was seated at the dining room table reading the *News Gazette*. At fifty-two, his full head of hair was completely white. He bore a ruddy complexion from years of being in the out-of- doors. The son of a Ford County farmer, young Tom Albright spent his formative years under arduous conditions on a farm in central Illinois. At eighteen, he enlisted in the Marines just in time to see the end of the Second World War.

As a Marine, Tom Albright earned his college degree in history. In 1964, he went to work at the University of Illinois, just in time for the outbreak of the Vietnam War. During that period of unrest during the late sixties and early seventies, he became alienated from certain faculty segments of the U of I.

His sons, thank goodness, followed the Albright tradition and served in the armed forces. The only disappointment was Dennis's decision to join the Air Force rather than the Marines in hopes of becoming a pilot. His nearsightedness prevented him from obtaining his destiny, however. As a result, he went on to become a successful electrical engineer.

As for Alan, the Colonel felt a little molding was still needed.

"What is it, then?" asked the Colonel.

"Nothing, Dad. What are you reading about?"

"Seems like Carter's forming a Marine unit to join some Rapid Deployment Force. Fifty thousand men. The guy who's heading this all up is a legend. Major General Paul X. Kelly is saying here that three brigades of Marines will be on hand to land wherever necessary. Should be full strength by 1983."

"I might just re-up," Albright replied. "Dad, I believe I may have bitten off more that I realized."

Albright sat down at the dining room table across from his father. "A lot of things have happened over the past couple of days. I mean a lot of things. First, I paid a visit to Boston at the request of Jennifer Tavistock's dad. He wants me to help find his missing daughter."

"What's wrong with the police?"

Albright shrugged his shoulders. "They've tried. At least the Boston police have. Seems she's left the city to parts unknown."

His father was not moved. "Then how does this guy expect you to find her? You're not a detective."

"That's only part of it, Dad. When I was on my way out of my hotel room in Boston, I got the strangest phone call. Warning me off, you might say. Disguised their voice and everything with some kind of electronic device."

At that point, the Colonel put down the newspaper. His son had the floor.

"What kind of mess have you gotten yourself into?"

"That's not all," Albright said. "There's more."

Albright proceeded to tell his father about the events of the previous day in which Windham gave him an ultimatum before firing him. He told him of the beating. Finally, he discussed with the Colonel the coincidence involving the attempt on Stuart Cashmore's life in Paris.

"The Iranians are responsible for that," said the Colonel," no question about it. At least, you're not mixed up in that business. Son, I must say you've had yourself quite a week. The more you tell me, the more confused I become. This Beth Spencer, for example, how reliable is she?"

"I don't know. Doesn't sound like anything she would want to make up."

"None of this business makes any sense, Alan. A doctor who hasn't heard from his daughter in two years solicits you to find her because the two of you were together in Scotland. You get a call saying leave it alone. Your boss gets the snot beat out of him the day after talking with gangsters in an overheard conversation. Now you're out of a job. What do you plan on doing for a living?"

Albright told his father how much Dr. Tavistock was offering.

"Half a million dollars? Did you get it in writing?"

"All of it."

"Where do these people get that kind of money? Look at me. I've worked all of my life just to get by, and you have the chance of a lifetime. I don't blame you, kid. I suppose I would have told my boss to take a hike as well."

"I did nothing of the kind," Albright said. "At first, anyway. But, Dad, it's not about the money. And don't look at me that way, I'm serious. It's about Jennifer. She planned to enroll at the U of I when I made the decision to enlist. She had some strong feelings against the war. When I told her I was joining up, that ended it."

"I hate to put it to you like this, kid, but your luck with women lately hasn't been anything worth writing home about."

Had anyone but the Colonel made that remark, Albright would have reacted in a violent manner.

His statement wasn't aimed at Jennifer Tavistock. Tom Albright had never approved of Tolly Chamberlain and made few bones about it.

"Well, look who's here! You're not going to believe what I uncovered in the attic." Blakelyn Albright strode into the dining room, ignoring the tension between father and son. The one thing that she insisted on around the Albright household was harmony.

Mrs. Albright was on the verge of being plump. Her hair was cut short, and she carried herself in an earthy, no-nonsense manner. Like her husband, she was a teacher—only her pupils were elementary age. She'd broken up an endless number of fights between her sons over the years and could control her husband's disposition at will. Both Dennis and Alan took after their mother in looks. Same distinct noses, same cobalt blue eyes, same light brown hair.

Where Dennis had a fairly laid-back temperament, Alan was much like his father. When Blakelyn saw the two of them about to square off, she quickly intervened, in this case changing the subject to baseball.

"Mickey Mantle. 1959 Topps. Looks as good as it did when you bought it. Or did Dennis get this one?"

"My cards!" Albright exclaimed. "Where..."

"In the attic, just like I told you. I happened to be looking for more Christmas ornaments and, lo and behold, a shoebox full of baseball cards turned up."

"I think you better sit down, dear," said the Colonel.

She ignored her husband and remained standing. "What is it now?"

***

EDINBURGH

THE WIDOW AND ROSIE, AS PROMISED, FOUND WHAT THEY FELT WAS THE FINEST CHRISTMAS TREE IN EDINBURGH.

The widow was very assiduous in her decision just where

to place the towering pine and decided on a site in the corner of the living room.

Rosie was long gone, and the widow lay awake in spite of the wee hour. Sleep would not come.

The news had come in about the botched affair in the United States. Had she been a woman who depended on drink, alcohol would have been used to console her misgivings. There was a place and time for spirits, but this was not it. This was a time for contemplation, for reflection.

She threw back the covers and arose from the bed. Down the stairs into the living room. She opened the wall safe, removing the treasured relic.

A golden cross, as beautiful as it was ancient. Missing since 1745, the treasure once belonged to James the Fifth, King of Scotland, father of Mary, Queen of Scots. Prior to being in the King's possession, the cross had something of a turbulent history.

Given to Alexander the Third in 1259 by the bishop of St. Andrews, the relic was cold to the touch and beautiful in the pool of light illuminating from the nearby lamp. As she stood next to the Christmas tree she could almost feel the force emerging from the jewel-encrusted artifact.

With this in her possession, nothing could stop her.

She held the cross in both hands and admired its handiwork. It was an item of considerable weight.

Few historians of the day even knew of this forgotten treasure's existence. The cross had been handed down through the ages, passed on from generation to generation as a symbol of what the kingdom of Scotland once stood for.

Mere men like Alan Albright, Neal Edwards, and Stuart Cashmore were powerless against her might.

The Christmas holidays were a time for celebration, she decided. Festivities would take precedent for the moment over her purpose. There were seventeen days until Christmas. She would make the most of them.

She hoped Alan Albright would do the same. If the young man from the United States got in her way, the Christmas of 1979 would, alas, be his last Christmas.

***

THE MORNING OF DECEMBER NINTH WAS A BUSY ONE FOR ALAN ALBRIGHT. The first thing he did after showering was call Dr. Tavistock. To his chagrin, Mrs. Woodbury answered the phone. The doctor was out of town, Albright was informed, and would not return before the middle of the week. He spent little time getting off the phone, not bothering to leave a message.

He made a note to discuss lines of communication with the Tavistocks.

Albright had the house to himself. At the University, finals would be gearing up before long, and thankfully the mass of students would leave the twin cities, returning Champaign-Urbana to a place that was halfway sensible. Most of the time Albright spent at his parents' home was during the summer and holidays.

The center of activity around the Albright household focused around the dining room table. It was there that poor grades were explained, reprimands for un-mowed yards handed out, and problems solved.

The dining room table was the site for more than just meals.

It was the first place where the family drifted to each day, where homework was done in years past, bills paid, vacations planned. As Albright finished a glass of grapefruit juice, he gathered his notes together from his trip to Boston. He began with the initial information he'd received from Dr.

Tavistock. That was followed by the history lesson, given to him by Mrs. Tavistock. From there, he sifted through the information presented to him by Michael Oliver Shoesmith.

He thought about the fight. Was it because he lost his temper, or was it because this person had once dated Jennifer? Albright was many things, but he was not a jealous man. When he and Tolly Chamberlain were apart, he never once questioned her whereabouts. When together, he realized that men would trade places with him at the drop of a hat.

With Shoesmith, however, something within him snapped.

The Dove. Albright had completely forgotten about the mention of Jennifer's best friend. He recalled Shoesmith's remark about best friends not ratting each other out. It made sense. Franconia Edge had to know something. How could she not know?

Albright read on. Ed Napier's perspective about the case was fascinating.

He assembled his rather unorganized collection of handwritten scribbles together, brought his father's electric typewriter down from his study, and placed it on the dining room table. He turned on the kitchen radio. It was tuned to WILL. He switched over to FM and found WPGU so he could listen to rock and roll while he worked.

Moments before, he had spoken to Otto, who advised Albright that Gerry Windham was improving somewhat; but physicians were insisting he not see anyone but immediate family. He'd spoken to Carole by phone and told her if there was anything that Albright could do, just name it.

There was little else on the news concerning what had happened to Stuart Cashmore.

Albright loaded a sheet of typing paper into the machine and briefly made a list of key names, dates, and places. As he typed, he began to realize how much had transpired on one short week.

Precisely seven days ago, he had received the blessing of Gerry Windham to take off for Boston for a few days. Now Windham lay hospitalized, recuperating from a beating that seemed to have something to do with Alan Albright.

Two typewritten sheets later, Albright had the beginning of the file on Jennifer Tavistock. He placed the sheets into a file folder, labeled it, and placed it in his briefcase. He removed the photograph of Jennifer and placed it inside of a frame he'd purchased over the weekend from a camera shop. All of the St. Andrews' relics from the summer of 1969, he brought downstairs from his room and placed them aimlessly across the dining room table. Letters, pictures he'd taken with his small Instamatic, old passport... He thought for the first time about travel.

Could this job conceivably take him overseas again? Surely not, he thought. Still, he would, in spite of his doubts, round up his new one.

Once again, he picked up the list. Out of the one hundred twenty-five or so students who were in St. Andrews that summer, approximately thirty were from Urbana High. Many of those, unbelievably, he had not seen since then. He was an incoming senior at the time, and there were students who had graduated that summer as well as a number of underclassmen, like himself, who made the journey.

Three black and white photos he could not find. One was of all the students collectively in a group shot, taken at the University of St. Andrews. Two others were of him taken in a small group with other American students. The group shot he especially wanted to see because he wanted to see if he could identify Stuart Cashmore.

Albright's inquiries regarding the wounded diplomat would have to begin somewhere. He found the list, searched through the names once again, settling on Cashmore's. His home was in Wadsworth, Ohio. The AIFS student directory contained the names of the students and their home addresses, but no telephone numbers.

Albright found a phone book, looked up the area code for Wadsworth; and when an operator answered, he gave the operator the street address and Cashmore's last name. Moments later, he had the number.

To his avail, there was no answer. At least, he had a beginning. The Cashmores, Albright concluded, could be in France at the moment with the wounded Stuart. He had no sooner placed the receiver down when the phone rang. It was Mrs. Albright. The Christmas lights needed to be put up on the shrubbery in front of their house. They could be found in the basement.

The last thing he wanted to be involved with was hanging lights on shrubbery, but he realized it was pointless to argue. Perhaps the cold air could make him think. He made a note to make three phone calls when he finished.

***

BY FIVE-THIRTY ALBRIGHT'S PARENTS HAD BOTH RETURNED HOME AND, TO THEIR SURPRISE, THE OUTSIDE OF THEIR HOUSE WAS ILLUMINATING WITH BRILLIANT CHRISTMAS LIGHTS. The Colonel was pleased. Mrs. Albright felt likewise. They found their son in the den, resting comfortably with his feet on the couch, watching the CBS Evening News.

"You realize that when Walter Cronkite eventually retires, things will hardly be the same," said the Colonel.

"Right," Albright agreed. "The guy's irreplaceable. Why is it that change is never for the better anymore? The seventies weren't that great, and there certainly doesn't seem to be anything promising about the eighties."

"I disagree with you, kid. Once I felt the same way as you. Pessimistic. Nothing to feel good about. Then I met your mom. I suppose that's when it all changed. By the way, I've been thinking about your situation all day."

"What about it?"

"This business with the Tavistock girl. There is no way all of what you told me could be coincidence. Whoever phoned you in Boston, warning you off, was doing you a favor. If you want my opinion, and you seldom do, leave this business alone. Let the good Dr. Tavistock find his daughter himself."

Albright continued watching the news. His father had never been one to discourage his youngest son away from something unless he truly believed in it. They both knew that the last time the Colonel had given Alan advice; it had been about a woman.

Tolly Chamberlain, to be exact.

The Colonel had advised Alan not to rush into a relationship with the young blonde. Wait, he had said. Albright had steadfastly refused to do so and was told, two days before the wedding was to be held, that he was no longer Tolly's choice in life.

Now, with Jennifer Tavistock's whereabouts unknown, the Colonel once again was consulting his son about what to do. That's why Albright wasn't objecting.

He knew his father, for once, was right.

At that moment, Walter Cronkite caught the attention of the Albrights. Two suspects had been arrested in connection with the shooting of an American diplomat in Paris. They were both European, described as being career criminals by the Parisian police, who apprehended the men in a bar in the seventh arrondissement earlier in the day.

The condition of the diplomat, one Stuart Cashmore, Cronkite reported, was improving.

"Well, how do you like that?" Colonel Albright exclaimed.

"I don't," Albright said. "Not one bit. I tried phoning Cashmore's parents earlier today in Ohio.

There was no answer. Dad, about your theory on coincidence. You said last night that what happened to Stuart has nothing to do with all the things that have transpired concerning Jennifer. What if there is a connection?"

"That's my point, kid. It's been bothering me all day. You knew this man from St. Andrews. You knew Jennifer

Tavistock from St. Andrews. Those men, who shot your boss in Chicago. Something about the timing of all of this. Doesn't fit. Things just don't happen at random. There's a pattern to everything. How is...what's his name?"

"Gerry Windham. To my knowledge, he's about the same. I spoke to Carole earlier this afternoon, and she says he's extremely depressed. In fact, I'll probably head to the city first thing tomorrow morning. I need to talk to Beth Spenser and Otto as well."

***

DANGEROUS WATERS RETURNED FROM DUNDEE LATE FRIDAY AFTERNOON, A DAY EARLY, HE EXPLAINED. When he arrived, he found the widow preparing for the evening. She was in her bedroom, seated at her vanity. She was dressed in her blue silk robe, brushing her hair. There was a hint of Chanel in the air. Waters stood there for a moment, hands in his overcoat pocket. She glanced at him through the mirror.

"How was Dundee?"

"Tolerable." Waters walked over to where she was seated and began massaging her shoulders.

She seemed tense. "Is something the matter?"

"Another silly party, I'm afraid. Dreading it, really. All I need is an excuse to say no."

Waters ran his fingers through her dark, lustrous hair. She smelled good. While in Rabat, there was little time to think about women. Quite often, as he spent his evenings guarding his employer on a moonlit Moroccan night, as the breeze swept in from the Atlantic, he would think of her.

"How's this?" Waters gently turned her chair around to face him. He leaned down and kissed her.

He opened her robe and began to roam with his hands. She responded by tracing her hand up his trouser leg. She found him. Irresistible, as always. She sometimes wondered if other women were equally as helpless towards Dangerous Waters as she.

With him there was no indecision, only impudence. Her state of elated bliss belied the rational.

This feeling was nothing less than surrealistic.

The dinner party was definitely out of the question. So was the radio, which incidentally included a look at the world's headlines. One of the stories centered on the arrest of two men in connection with the shooting of a young American diplomat in Paris.

They eventually fell asleep.

***

ALBRIGHT FELT LIKE GETTING OUT AND ABOUT. He needed to get away from his parents' house. He needed to ponder and meditate. He hopped into the Jag, gunned her to life, and drove down his block until he reached Race Street. He turned left on Race and headed north, past Urbana High School. The structure looked dark and menacing, just as he'd remembered. Once reaching California, he turned right and drove up to Broadway. There he turned right, drove a half block, and eased his Jaguar into a parking space in front of a two-story house. An old Plymouth sat in the driveway. The walk had been swept clean of snow. With a handful of presents in hand, he climbed the steps two at a time, wiped his boots on a straw welcome mat, and knocked on the door.

The door was opened by a child of no more than three. He had blonde hair past his shoulders, an indication of never having a haircut since birth.

"It's Alan!" Albright was attacked by a flurry of fists, some fairly hard for a three-year-old. One blow missed his groin by inches.

"Tyler! What have I told you about hitting people! How are you, Alan?"

Madelyn White looked flustered. Toys were everywhere. A tricycle was sitting in the middle of the living room floor. She was married to Alan's best friend, Eulus. Like Albright, Madelyn and Eulus were "townies." Albright maneuvered through the toys, set down the boxes, and managed to give her a hug. He noticed something quite unusual.

"You're having another baby! Congratulations!"

"June first," she said. "Yew," she yelled. "Alan's here."

Madelyn Dixon was one of the most popular girls all through school. In eighth grade, she was class president. In her sophomore and junior years in high school, she was in all the right clubs, honor student—the works.

Sometime during her senior year, she began to notice a guy in chemistry class. He wasn't a jock.

He wasn't popular. He had long hair. His grades were terrible in every subject—save one, science, in which he excelled.

His name was Eulus White. He was a nobody.

At first, it was curiosity. He wasn't cute. He didn't have his own car, and he looked disheveled all the time. He even wore braces.

By second semester, she had "volunteered" to be his lab partner. When springtime rolled around, she had turned down a half-dozen invitations to the senior prom. It was only after Yew's buddy, Alan

Albright convinced him to even consider going to the prom did he contemplate a date. He wasn't dating anyone. He honestly knew of no one he could even think of asking, until fate intervened.

Chemistry class, which Eulus had during second hour, had been disrupted by a small fire caused by a careless student. Their instructor advised the students that the remainder of the period would be held outside. Being a magnificent Midwestern spring day, little was discussed that morning in the way of molecular systems or atoms.

All talk was on who was taking whom to the prom.

Later that afternoon, Pat Myers happened to run into Eulus and Albright as school was being dismissed. She was brief. Madelyn, she said, would like it very much if Eulus would ask her to the prom. Then she was gone. It took Albright little time to figure it all out.

He spent two days in all talking his best friend into asking the most popular girl at Urbana High School to the senior prom. Eulus had his doubts. He worried little about her saying no. That bothered him not. The fact was he had never been to any extracurricular function since being at Urbana High, so why should he start now? Albright persisted. Do it, he said, as a personal favor.

The next morning, during second hour chemistry class, Eulus White asked Madelyn Dixon to the senior prom. She agreed.

Nine years, seven months, and four days later, Albright knew of no two happier people on the face of the earth. Even without makeup, a three-year-old terror of a son, and a second child on the way,

Madelyn was attractive. A habitual health nut, she ate no meat, fed her family bottled water and, when not expecting, stayed in excellent physical shape. She was also very political when it came to women's rights.

"Yew! Did you hear me? Alan's here."

There was movement at the top of the steps. Eulus came downstairs, slow as always, wearing a pair of scruffy jeans and a Led Zeppelin t-shirt. His hair was shoulder-length, long and straight, just like his and that of his son.

"Hey there." He and Albright shook hands. They were like brothers. Alan and Dennis were close, but he and Eulus were closer.

Those who didn't know Eulus took him for something of a worthless street person, still living in the 1960's. He dressed with little flair. In fact, Eulus White was a highly successful, well-paid computer programmer. For the past six years, his employers included not only the University of Illinois, but the United States Army as well. His clearance was priority, and much of what he worked on was unknown even to his wife.

Despite his appearance, he had managed to finish college, secure a steady job, and change his personal lifestyles dramatically. People were always walking up to him asking for dope. He hadn't smoked a joint since going to work for the Army. He was aware that the Army had scrutinized his past and wanted him in spite of his youthful indiscretions.

White majored in computer science at the U of I, struggled through his first two semesters, finally hitting his stride during his sophomore year.

He spent his time for the Army in a small office on Goodwin Street, spare and cold, with not so much as even a number on the glass office door. His specialty was known to few people, and his best friend Alan Albright wasn't one of them.

Eulus and Madelyn had books everywhere one looked, with candles and the scent of oil of patchouli throughout. Their furniture was old and comfortable, with the exception of a new custom-made bookcase that took up an entire living room wall.

Since Alan had broken up with Tolly, he'd seen little of Eulus. Very little. Albright had taken the time to buy the Whites' Christmas presents while in Boston, which he produced at once.

Eulus was to have been Albright's best man at the wedding. Albright and Tolly spent a considerable amount of time hanging out with Yew and Madelyn in better days. Hit the bars.

Concerts. Volleyball in the summertime. Both women realized that the lifelong friendship between Albright and Eulus ran deep.

Eulus, like everyone else, said nothing whatsoever about Tolly Chamberlain.

Nothing.

"So what have you been up to these days?" Eulus tactfully inquired.

Albright sat down, made himself at home like he always did, and started at the beginning.

Madelyn managed to get Tyler involved with a coloring book and whatever crayons she could find.

Her chores were put on hold as she, like her husband, listened in amazement and with disbelief at what Albright was saying. He covered all the main points.

"Wow," was all Madelyn could say. Her voice tended to be loud at times, something people often found somewhat unnerving. She was assertive, pushy, and used to getting her way.

Behavior like hers for men would be considered ambitious and self-confident. Since she was a woman, some men, and a number of women as well, considered Madelyn White to be overbearing and intimidating. She had little time for nonsense.

Yew meanwhile sat back, stroked his beard in his usual manner and said, "Al, be careful." Tyler had brought his handiwork over for his father to inspect, which he did, approvingly. "The world around us is crazier now than any time I can ever remember. Life means nothing anymore."

"Am I being paranoid," Madelyn said," or does everything that Alan just said smell like the south end of a sewer rat? Nobody calls someone's hotel room with a warning like that for no reason.

Someone overhears a conversation with your boss, who later gets himself attacked."

"The beating's probably a coincidence," Yew said in his matter-of-fact manner. "Crimes like what happened to your boss, a known gambler, especially in Chicago, particularly at Christmas time, happen all the time."

Albright nodded in agreement. "Yea. That's what the policeman basically said. Even my old man is worried, Eulus. And you know how he is. Face the enemy head on and all that. We've been going over this thing all day; and, frankly, I think he's really worried about me. Like I can't take care of myself."

Eulus grimaced when Albright brought up the Colonel's name. Being the lifelong friends that they were, he was punished as a young boy by the Colonel almost as often as his best friend. "Who knew you were staying in Boston?" Eulus asked.

"Good question, Yew. Dr. and Mrs. Tavistock. People at work. Gerry, for a fact, knew. Probably everyone at Thirdwind for that matter."

"That it?" Eulus began to take an interest in Tyler's drawing, turning it in several directions.

"There is someone else who knew. The...I'm not sure what you might call her. The Tavistock's maid, or whatever. Not the friendliest woman on earth. Her name's Mrs. Woodbury. Put the evil eye on me the moment we met. Great cook, terrible personality."

"Watch out," Madelyn snapped.

"That was not intended to be a sexist statement," Albright replied. This was not the first time he had been censured by Madelyn and, being as close as they all were, probably not his last. "Mrs. Woodbury acted as if I had committed some terrible crime. Cold. Vicious. Just plain mean."

"You actually let her serve you a meal?" Eulus asked. "For all you know, she could have poisoned you."

"She knew I was in Boston, but I can't imagine how she would know at which hotel I was staying."

At that point, Albright elaborated on his visits to the Tavistock household but honestly could not remember if he ever discussed where he was staying while in her presence.

"Wait a minute!" Albright said. "Of course! Dr. Tavistock made the hotel arrangements for me.

That's where all of his patients and their families stay while in Boston. I'd totally forgotten. How could Mrs. Woodbury not know?"

"Anyone else?" Eulus asked.

"You're beginning to sound like a detective," Madelyn remarked, poking her husband on his arm.

"No. That's it. Not even my parents knew I was headed to Boston."

"You're sure?"

"Well, there was this policeman. Ed Napier. A real detective, Eulus. He knew and there's someone else."

Albright told them about meeting Jennifer's ex-boyfriend and the ensuing fight.

"So what's he like?" Madelyn wondered.

"I'm not sure. I sort of lost my temper when we met. Then the strangest thing happened. We put aside our differences and ended up having lunch afterwards, if you can believe it. He knew."

Madelyn looked Albright over. She noticed something unusual that night in the well-dressed man before her. Neither she nor Eulus, Albright's very best friend, could begin to conceive what he had gone through. Almost ten months had passed since that fateful, abrupt day when Tolly broke up with her fiancé the day before their wedding. There was no way to calculate the pain and disappointment the man sitting before her had endured.

Nowhere on the face of the earth was a man more devoted to a woman than was Alan Albright to Tolly Chamberlain.

"This Cashmore fellow. The guy that's been on the news lately. How well did you know him at St. Andrews?"

"Not very well. I sort of remember him, probably drank a beer with him once or twice, but we didn't hang around together. The timing of all of this blew me away, Yew."

Yew stared out into space with the usual faraway look in his eyes. Whatever he was thinking, he kept to himself. Madelyn, meanwhile, continued to pick up on something entirely different about Albright. Something distinctly and refreshingly dissimilar. It might have been the faint gleam in his eye or that familiar edge in his voice, but the old enthusiasm was clearly returning.

Especially when Jennifer Tavistock's name was mentioned.

Something, indeed, was bringing their friend back. She decided, against her better judgment, to make sure.

"Just how important is it, Alan?"

"How important is what?"

"Finding Jennifer Tavistock."

Albright stood up, walked over to the Christmas tree in the corner of the living room, and examined an ornament. Carved in wood in the shape of a snowman. Painted white. He slid his hands into his pockets, turned around, and looked Madelyn squarely in the eyes.

"Ten days ago, Madelyn, I would have been strongly against it. That was before Gerry got himself attacked. Over something that could very well be my fault, even. At that junction, I would have told you it was a remote possibility. But tonight, even after talking with Dad, finding Jennifer Tavistock is as important as anything in my life right now. Does that answer your question?"

Tolly Chamberlain, thought a relieved Madelyn White, is on her way out of the picture whether she realizes it or not.

Eulus, meanwhile, who had said little for the past few moments, asked, "Are you absolutely sure there was no one else who knew you were going to Boston?"

"That's it."

"Whoever it was," Eulus remarked, "was telling you something to scare you or telling you something for your own good. That simple."

Albright remained at the White residence until well past midnight. Once Tyler was sent off to bed, they listened to light jazz. Albright and Eulus drank a few beers while Madelyn sipped her Perrier.

As he was leaving, Madelyn hugged Alan goodnight while Eulus slipped on his tan suede jacket and stood out on the front porch, joking with Albright as he slipped along the icy sidewalk towards his beloved Jag.

There was no better way for Albright, especially in his current dateless condition, to get in the Christmas spirit than spending time with close friends. Albright turned into his driveway at twenty till one. He let himself in the back door, locked up, turned out the lights, and went to sleep.

***

EDINBURGH

DANGEROUS WATERS HIT THE BUSTLING STREETS OF EDINBURGH THAT SATURDAY MORNING WITH THE WIDOW AT HIS SIDE. She insisted on them forgoing breakfast, and everything else, to take advantage of the beautiful weather Scotland was experiencing. People were everywhere. Children were tugging their parents into the toy shops, young couples gazed into jewelry storefronts examining wedding bands, and frustrated drivers searched in vain for parking near Princes Street, since parking along that thoroughfare was forbidden.

She was glad to have him along. She helped him choose gifts for his family. By one o'clock, they were both famished. They had a superb lunch in a small pub near Hollyrood House, washing it down with a few pints of MacEwans for Waters and a glass of sherry for the widow. They could not help but notice a young couple who strolled in moments after they'd been seated. Their clothing was so outdated. They seemed to be confused with the British currency.

The young man acknowledged them with a nod and struck up a conversation. They turned out to be Americans. Indeed. They were visiting Scotland all the way from the sunny state of Florida. A mannerly conversation ensued. The couple was fulfilling their dream by visiting Scotland, they said.

The man's surname was Campbell, and he and his wife both worked in a small library in Vero Beach.

They were in search of rare books, simply not available in America. He wore black horn-rimmed glasses, a dark suit, and a simple bow tie.

His companion was dressed in a similarly insipid fashion. They were all smiles and spoke entirely too softly. Almost like they were still in a library.

Waters chuckled to himself. There are pubs in this country, mate, he thought to himself, where that name would get you in serious trouble. Even in the late 1970's, animosity existed between the McDonald's and the Campbell's, resulting from a small and bloody disagreement in a Highland Community, known as Glencoe some two hundred years earlier.

The widow was polite but considerably cooler towards the Americans than Waters. Seeing the couple from the United States brought to mind someone she would just as well not think about.

Alan Albright.

She cursed his name, softly.

"Did you say something?" Waters asked.

"You simply must visit Scotland more often. It's a wonderful place. We simply adore having tourists in our city. Especially Americans."

Waters nearly choked on his pint.

***

ALBRIGHT HIT THE BASEMENT SHORTLY AFTER SIX THAT MORNING. The weights he and Dennis had used during high school were still set up. Nothing fancy, but good for a two-hour workout.

He felt good. He took a hot shower, dressed, and headed into the den. He opened the leather briefcase, found the phone number of Stuart Cashmore's parents, and dialed.

***

DANGEROUS WATERS AND THE WIDOW LEFT THE PUB AT TEN MINUTES BEFORE CLOSING, BURDENED WITH BAGS FULL OF GIFTS FROM THE MORNING ACTIVITY. They paid little attention as they walked out the pub to the American tourists, who themselves were making preparations to leave.

The American couple quietly put on their overcoats as they prepared to exit the pub. They thanked the kind lady behind the bar for her hospitality, tipped her generously, and asked directions for a good bookstore in the general area. They wished her a Merry Christmas and insisted she have a nice day.

Once in the street, their cheerful demeanor vanished.

"So," said the young woman," I wonder who her friend is?"

"It doesn't matter," Daniel Harper answered, walking briskly down the street. "We've found her."

"Maybe he's her hairdresser or something. He seems rather timid, doesn't he? He would probably flinch at the sight of a mouse. I certainly don't foresee that wimp giving you any problems."

Harper said nothing.

"What next?"

Harper took the young woman by the arm as they strolled down the street. Her name was Charlotte

Healy and for the past five years had been Harper's constant companion. Like Harper, she was anything but an ordinary American sightseer.

"We'll get out of this awful clothing, doll. Then we'll do as we agreed. We're going home. We'll spend Christmas with our families, and once the holidays are over, I'll be returning."

"Wrong. We'll be returning."

Harper smiled. "Yes, dear. We'll be returning. By the way, do you know the significance of that pub back there?"

"No," Charlotte said.

"They used to hang people across the street from that place. Condemned men, and women, I suppose, would be brought into that pub for one final drink before they died. Hence the name, The Last Drop."

How utterly prophetic. It may very well be her last. Listen, darling, let's go back to the hotel and pack.

After all, we've found who we were looking for, didn't we?"

***

THERE WAS STILL NO ANSWER AT THE CASHMORE RESIDENCE. On a hunch, Albright decided to call directory assistance. Once he had the operator on the line, he asked if there were any Cashmores listed in the city other than Stuart's father. There were two. He took down the numbers, called the first one, and got no answer. His hopes were begging to fade. He dialed the second number and, to his disbelief, got an answer. He identified himself at once. He asked if the caller on the other end was related in any way to Stuart. It turned out to be his uncle.

He managed to get the phone number in Paris, where the Cashmores were staying while their son was hospitalized. He thanked Clyde Cashmore profusely, hung up, and dialed the French number at once.

"Hello."

Albright could not believe his luck. "Hi. My name is Alan Albright, and I'm calling from Urbana, Illinois. Is this Mrs. Cashmore?"

"Yes, it is."

"Mrs. Cashmore, let me say that my prayers are with your son."

"Thank you, sir."

"I knew him briefly back in 1969, I believe."

"You believe?" she asked.

"Yes, ma'am. Stuart, if I'm not mistaken, was at St. Andrews during the summer of '69, wasn't he?"

"That's right."

Albright thought carefully about what he would say next. "I've been keeping a close watch on the developments surrounding your son, Mrs. Cashmore. How's he feeling?"

"He's resting."

"I think what happened to him is dreadful. I read that his condition is improving. All I can say is that I'm sorry, and I thank you for taking the time to talk to me."

"You're very kind, Mr. Albright," she said. "There has been an outpouring of support for Stuart from everywhere."

Now's the time, Albright thought. "Mrs. Cashmore, is it possible to talk to Stuart at this time? I realize that he's just beginning to recover, but I'd like to say hello to him if possible."

There was momentary silence on the other end. Albright would gladly reimburse his parents for the long-distance charges to Paris when the bill came in.

"I would have to speak to Stuart's doctor. And to Stuart, of course. If my son is up to it and the doctor has no objections, I think it would be fine."

Albright threw his fist into the air in jubilation.

"Mrs. Cashmore, thank you very much for all you've done. Again, let me express how glad I am that your son is on the road to recovery. Perhaps I can call you at say, this time tomorrow?"

"That would be fine."

"Thank you, Mrs. Cashmore. Happy Holidays."

"Same to you. Goodbye."

Albright opened his briefcase and wrote the phone number of the Cashmores' hotel into a notebook.

He'd been in such a hurry with Stuart's uncle on the line that he'd jotted everything down on a scrap of paper towel. Thinking about Stuart lying in a hospital bed brought his mind closer to home. He looked up Beth Spencer's number and dialed.

"Hello." She sounded barely awake.

"Hi. It's Alan."

"Hello there. This is a surprise."

"Did I wake you?"

"Yes."

"I need to find out how Gerry is." If Albright felt any remorse about waking up Beth he didn't show it.

"This is so weird," Beth said.

"It is?"

"I dreamed about you last night. We were in that car of yours, being chased by gangsters."

"Did they catch us?"

"No. We stopped the car, turned around, and started chasing them. And now you call. Maybe I'm still dreaming."

"Afraid not. Beth, I'm driving up this morning to see Gerry. Would you care to join me?"

"Sure. What time are you coming?"

"I'll probably get there around one. Can you meet me at Cook County General then?"

"I just realized that it's not even eight-thirty, Alan. How dare you call me at this hour?"

If she was cross, Beth didn't show it. Her voice sounded deep and sleepy.

"I only did it to make Otto jealous."

"Cute. Real cute. I've got better things to do on Saturday morning than to trade witticisms with you. One of them is my sleep. I'll see you at one. By the way, how are you?"

"I'm fine. Thanks for asking. How are you?"

"Still a little freaked out."

"Yea. Same here. Listen. I didn't tell you this before, Beth. I was impressed at how well you handled yourself with that policeman. I believe we did the right thing by not discussing Gerry's problems. Or the fact that my name was mentioned. You know, I just got an idea. Let's have lunch before we go to the hospital. Sound good?"

"I suppose I could handle that."

"How about if I pick you up at your place at 11:30?"

"Fine."

"There's just one small thing, Beth."

"What's that?"

"I don't know where 'your place' is."

"I live in Bridgeport." She gave him his address.

"11:30," Albright said.

"11:30."

Albright listened to the weather forecast as he prepared for the quick trip to Chicago. He dressed in a yellow Oxford shirt, maroon crew-necked sweater, and a new pair of trousers he'd purchased earlier in the week while in Boston. Albright's mind was racing with the possibility of speaking to Stuart Cashmore. He wanted to get that doubt out of his mind once and for all; making certain the events that took place in Paris had no connection whatsoever to what was going on Stateside.

"Where are you off to now?"

"Back to the City. Just for the day. I'll probably be home by eight or nine tonight."

The Colonel was dressed in his usual Saturday morning outfit. Loose sweatshirt, work pants. He was as fit as any man his age. "That's too bad. I need someone to help me on a small project."

"Yea, right," Albright said. With the Colonel, there were no small projects. Once a job was started, it was generally all day and half the night. "What's the project?"

"Gutters. They're leaking over on the south side of the house. Shouldn't take too long to fix."

"I'm quite sure Dennis can come over and give you a hand."

"Yea, maybe. Kid, I want to tell you something. Your mom and I are concerned about this business you've gotten yourself into. It's just not right. I thought about everything you told me. Doesn't make a bit of sense that a Boston doctor would hire a graphic artist, who knows absolutely nothing about detective work, to find his daughter. There are people who do that sort of thing for a living every day.

Professionals. For crying out loud, with what he's offering you, he could hire the best in the country."

"He's done that already, Dad. It just didn't work."

The Colonel was not convinced. The Albright stubbornness. "So what's his angle, kid?"

"He realizes that Jennifer and I were close friends. Yea, it's been ten years; and when we broke up, it wasn't on the best of terms. Still, Tavistock realizes that I care so much about Jennifer that I'm the man to find her."

"That's crap and you know it. If you or Dennis were missing for two years and I had the kind of money you say this man has, there would be a picture of you on every light pole, bus, milk carton, and magazine cover on this planet!"

"That's not what Tavistock wants. This whole business

has been kept very, very quiet for whatever reason."

"Yea, well, that makes things even more difficult to explain. And what about your ex-boss, who got his legs broken? Use your head, son."

Albright stood eye to eye with his father. He threw his overcoat across the couch and sat down next to it. The Colonel remained standing, arms folded across his barrel chest, looking down at his son. On the one hand, he was glad Alan was finding something to help take his mind off that Chamberlain girl.

He and Blakelyn did what they could, following the breakup. They knew how much Alan loved that woman. Adored her. Cherished her. Idolized her.

But she still left him.

"What happened to Gerry, as we've said, has nothing to do with my finding Jennifer Tavistock.

How could it? He was into gambling, Dad. You know how it works. That's why I'm going to the City.

I'm having lunch with Beth Spencer, in fact. I plan on drilling her again on what she heard the other night. By the way, I put a couple of long distance calls on your phone this morning. One to

Pennsylvania and one to France."

"France, as in Paris?"

"You guessed it. Spoke to Stuart's mom. She agreed to let me call Stuart tomorrow, if you can believe that. Once that's taken care of, I'll feel a whole lot better getting that loose end cleared up."

"Oh, yea? What if..."

"I know what you're thinking. You explained it all last night. It's impossible. No way. But, Dad, I need to get going. Seriously. I'm not trying to weasel out of this project of yours, either."

"Yea. Okay... You go to Chicago. I'll call Dennis and find out what his plans are."

"What about tomorrow after church?"

The Colonel smiled for the first time that morning. "You and I both know that's out of the question.

This is December, after all. Getting too close to playoff time to miss football."

"Dad, since I'm unemployed for the moment, I'm sure there'll be time to help you out with anything you might need. I mean that. I really need to get going, though. Tell mom I'll see her when I get home."

"Half a million dollars on the line and an unlimited expense account is hardly what I would consider unemployed."

***

WHILE IN THE FASHIONABLE DRESS SHOP, SURROUNDED BY THE RICH AND THE ULTRA-RICH, SOMEWHERE EVEN WATERS FELT UNCOMFORTABLE, THERE WAS PLENTY OF TIME TO KILL WHILE WAITING ON THE WIDOW. Waters sat in an overstuffed armchair sorting through the magazines that were virtually of no interest to him whatsoever. He caught the eye of the shopkeeper, herself a sight to behold, casting an admiring glance in his direction.

Waters was glad to be back home. He allowed himself another chuckle, thinking back on the Americans. The woman, he had to admit, was cute. The bloke was just too much of a twit.

Even for an American.

Somewhere in the back of his mind, a spore of uncertainty slowly entered his consciousness. It had to be pure coincidence for the Americans to sit near them in the un-crowded public house. The way the bloke had positioned himself so that he was facing Waters and the widow was surely just another coincidence. His Israeli employers had trained Waters incessantly to be on perpetual guard for anything that just didn't fit. He'd spent quite a bit of time in the States. Knew the American habits.

Found himself almost at home in that country, especially along the eastern seaboard.

Granted, some of them didn't know how to dress or hold their knives and forks properly and had a strange sense of humor.

But this man and woman seemed too American. This Campbell chap seemed the happy-go-lucky type, true. But what was it? Even as they were leaving, Waters noticed Campbell's expression as he glanced back at them. Granted, it was only for a moment, but something about the look simply was not right. Perhaps in addition to being a librarian, Campbell was a music lover and had recognized her face. Waters dismissed that theory at once.

He'd seen that look before. On the faces of men in uniform. On the faces of men in Omagh, staring at him during his short stint as a soldier. On the faces of men at football matches during his younger days as a skinhead, moments before a melee erupted.

It was a look of malice.

In late 1979, Waters thought to himself, absolutely nothing in this world could be taken for granted.

He planned on finding out just who this Yank really was and what he was doing in Edinburgh.

***

"EVERYONE'S VULNERABLE. Everyone. Just find their weak spot and strike. Like a viper. You don't think about it; you just strike."

"I'm not sure I understand."

"Let me explain it to you the best way I know how, Charlotte. This woman has a weakness somewhere. We have to locate it, single it out, and bam! It's done."

Charlotte Healy decided to accompany Daniel halfway across the world not only because she loved him deeply, but this was the first time in her twenty-four years that she'd ever done anything remotely exciting. There was something altogether appealing about dressing up in disguises and pretending to be someone she was not. This business could turn out to be rather dangerous when all was said and done, but she did not care. As a young girl, she'd read every Nancy Drew story ever written. She admired the tenacity of Amelia Earhart, revered the courage of Harriet Tubman, and felt that one of the most noble women ever to walk the face of the earth was Joan of Arc.

This was her chance to be a part of history.

This was also the first weekend in her life she'd spent outside of West Virginia.

The afternoon was waning. They were relaxing in the lobby of the Rothesay Hotel, seated side by side on a couch, watching the few people in the lobby come and go. They spoke almost in whispers as they held hands, Harper's free elbow resting on the side of the couch. So much was happening in their world. Their fellow countrymen were being held hostage in Iran, the Soviet Union had invaded Afghanistan, young Black children were turning up dead in Atlanta, and the people in Edinburgh went about their lives like nothing was amiss whatsoever.

Their plane would be leaving for America the following morning. They planned on doing little with the remaining time they had in Scotland other than having a few drinks, a good dinner and a long evening with each other.

Little did they know they were being hunted.

***

ALBRIGHT PULLED HIS OVERCOAT ON, SLIPPED HIS LEATHER GLOVES OVER HIS ENORMOUS HANDS, AND

WALKED OUT THE BACK DOOR. He unlocked the Big Jag, got in, and started up the motor. It was a cold morning and, as was his habit, he gave the Jag a few moments to warm up. He was looking forward to having lunch with Beth. He reached under his seat and found the ice scraper, got out, and proceeded to go to work on his rear windshield.

"You have a phone call," Blakelyn Albright said, looking up at the sky as she leaned out the back door. "It's Dr. Tavistock."

Now there was a startling way to get the morning going, Albright thought. If Tavistock were calling him on a Saturday morning, particularly at his parents' house, it must be important. He walked back inside and picked up the phone.

"Good morning, Dr. Tavistock."

"You aren't going to believe this." Tavistock's voice was trembling with excitement. "We had to cut short our weekend in Newport. Mrs. Woodbury phoned us last evening with the most incredible news I've had all year. After she returned from the market and checked the mailbox, she discovered something most extraordinary. Lying in the mailbox, with no stamp, return address, or anything was a birthday card to Claire. From our daughter."

***

HAD IT NOT BEEN FOR THE SERIOUSNESS OF HER BUSINESS, THE NEWS FROM PARIS WOULD HAVE BEEN AMUSING.

Whoever the French police had in custody, no matter what dastardly acts had been committed by them in the past, they were not the men who had failed her. The press continued to stress the fact that Iran was not involved in this affair. The men in custody were failed robbers—nothing else.

She wore a formal evening gown, surrounded by her admirers and well-wishers.

The crème de la crème of society was present that evening. Even the theater set, whom the Widow seldom cared to mix with, was in attendance. The maestro made his grand entrance, as always, with fervor and flair. The season was in full swing. She acknowledged the young man and his bride, who had walked over to greet her. He was an English nobleman, his wife the daughter of a Scottish Earl.

They were a handsome couple, she had to admit. She was even more surprised, following an introduction, that the young Englishman was an admirer of her work. He'd been in the audience the week before and expressed his admiration of her outstanding musical performance.

She begged Waters to accompany her that evening, but he declined, he said, for her own good. This was, after all, Scotland, not America. He was a working class bloke and, in spite of his feelings for her, had no yearnings whatsoever to mix and mingle with what he described as "that lot." Once Waters said no, that was it. Besides, he had said, your image is everything. Many of her late husband's friends and colleagues were there tonight, and most of them would have trouble accepting her with someone else, even three years after his death.

She hugged the Provost of Edinburgh, an old friend, who wished her holiday greetings. Her thoughts once again turned to Dangerous Waters. She knew he would be returning to Asilah, following the holidays, to protect those German people. She wondered what he was doing at that moment.

***

DANGEROUS WATERS, AT THAT VERY MOMENT, FELT LIKE GETTING A BIT OF FRESH AIR. He slipped out of her apartment into the evening chill. One of his old haunts was a club less than a mile from Ramsay Gardens, whose regulars included a significant number of Edinburgh's underworld.

Since it was a Saturday night, he should be in luck. As he approached the club, he noticed a dark blue Ford Escort parked along the curb, headlights off, with two men inside. The Drug Squad. They eyed him suspiciously. He ignored them. Waters walked in to the deceptively tranquil-looking establishment, filled with people who appeared, at first glance, quite ordinary. He ordered a pint of Lorimer's, something he would miss dearly once back in Morocco, and took a seat at an empty table.

The younger crowd was hanging out in this place more and more, he noticed. Hence, the presence of the Drug Squad. He searched the room with his eyes until he saw a familiar face. His man was seated at a table surrounded by a group of men, all smooth. They were eyeing up the women throughout the pub; some had whiskeys, while others drank pints. They wore expensive suits, and a few even sported diamond rings. The one common denominator was that all of the men at the table were hard. Each in his own unique way had the look of a career Scottish criminal.

They should have. Most were members of the Old Rock gang, without question the premier criminal organization in eastern Scotland. The gang was so low key that outside of the police and those involved in crime in one capacity or another, most people in Edinburgh, including the news organizations, didn't even know they existed.

Waters stood up and brought his pint over to the table across the room. The man nearest to Waters, who was bragging about his bedside prowess, stopped in mid-sentence when he noticed the stranger standing beside him. Suddenly, the entire table centered on Dangerous Waters. The boaster, slight of stature though he was, tensed like a rattlesnake. Waters did not speak, merely nodded a hello to his friend, who quietly sipped an Irish coffee.

The little man was dressed in a single-breasted suit, elegantly cut, and smoked a Players Number 6 that lay between his first two fingers.

In all, four members of the Old Rock gang sat at the

table—Waters' friend and three others. The little man was the sole exception. Waters looked all five men over as they continued to stare back at him. What the small man saw in front of him was misleading. Dangerous Waters was dressed in his favorite black blazer, brown corduroy trousers, and a simple white turtleneck sweater.

One hand held his pint, while the other rested casually in his trouser pocket. His eyes were as cheerful as always, and his cherubic face bore that faint smile around the corners of his mouth.

"There's plenty of room in this place, mate."

The voice was coarse but not loud. Although Glasgow is accurately known for being one of the roughest cities in all of Europe, the city of Edinburgh over the years had produced its own share of tough and violent men, with some of the toughest and most violent seated around that very table that evening.

By now, everyone in the club focused on what was unfolding.

"Perhaps," Waters replied, looking around the club, "but this spot seems perfect."

"Does it now?" The little man eased out of his chair, never taking his eyes off Waters. "It may not be for long, mate. You'll bloody well think twice about going somewhere else next time."

The man stood no more than five feet eight. A few of the Old Rock members looked at one another, impressed with the little man's courage. With nerve like that, a man of his size, particularly in the company in which he traveled, had to be taken seriously. While he may have been good at fighting, they thought, he was certainly lacking when it came to common sense.

The four men seated at the table silently watched the small man, waiting for him to make his move.

Waters calmly took a drink of Lorimer's.

The man who was friends with both of the antagonists

perceived the complexity of the situation.

"Maybe we should ask him to join us," he said.

"Not very likely," replied the small man. He smiled as he returned his gaze to Waters.

"Perhaps we should introduce ourselves then," Waters' acquaintance said.

A number of the patrons, seated nearby, one by one recognized the man in the black blazer, who had been out of the Edinburgh scene for a couple of years and, one by one, began to clear the area. Even the barkeep, a burly gentleman who had seen his share of brawls in his establishment, seemed a bit uneasy.

"I don't think so," said the small man.

"Ronald," said Waters' friend as he stood up from the table, "say hello to... "

"Dangerous Waters," interrupted the small man, who suddenly extended an arm to shake hands with Waters, much to the astonishment of the onlookers, particularly Waters' old friend.

"Last time I heard, you'd gone legitimate," Mackey said.

"Last time I heard, you'd gone off to jail," Waters replied.

***

THE ACCOMMODATIONS WERE, QUITE LITERALLY, FIT FOR A SOVEREIGN. All the comforts one could ask for. She'd gone for her evening stroll around the grounds, well guarded as always. There was little chance of escape, save hurling herself over the cliff into the North Sea.

The meal sat in front of her, untouched. Smoked venison, brown bread, potatoes, and French green beans. Over the past two years, she'd lost several pounds, but her overall health was sound.

Two months earlier, she came down with a severe virus

and was treated with antibiotics. She thought back on the last Christmas spent with her family. 1976. So much fun with her family at Christmas time.

The birthday card for her mother and the earlier letter were the result of an imperceptible change in the behavior of one of her bodyguards. She preferred the term *captors*. In any case, something was certainly happening on the outside that was making them very nervous.

She managed to slip a message inside the raincoat pocket of the real estate agent, who dropped in unexpectedly six weeks earlier. Nothing whatsoever had happened. It was quite possible that the gentleman had not even bothered to check his pockets or could be oblivious to the scrap of paper that detailed her captivity.

When would it end? Would she live? Would she ever see her family again?

Castle Craig, the wondrous habitat overlooking the sea, in spite of its elegance and lavishness, was her prison. She'd been at Castle Craig now for eleven long months. All the comforts available were at her beck and call. Books to read. Shortwave radio. The view from her rooms was awe-inspiring. She had everything she could possibly want.

Except her freedom.

She wandered into the great hall of the castle and stood before the portrait. From the moment she'd first set eyes on the painting, she had little doubt that this man was her ancestor. She had found what she had been looking for, and the cost had been great.

Her freedom, possibly even her life.

Her name was Jennifer Tavistock.

For months, she had planned her escape. There was no way to make a telephone call. She only hoped that the brief cryptogram left within her mother's birthday card would not go unnoticed.

She was alone tonight except for the two watchers. Normally, there were four. One was a brute, who one day would pay dearly. His name was Ambrose Dyson. Late fifties, possibly early sixties. He had not touched her physically, but his mental torment and ridicule were something in which he took pride.

It actually gave him pleasure watching her suffer.

The other man was older as well. Sixty-five or seventy. Seth Duncanson was his name. His health was not too good these days. The two other watchers had gone to an undisclosed location. One was Dyson's wife, Corra. The fourth watcher was Abigail Overby, the youngest at forty-seven.

Jennifer wore a long skirt, blouse, and cardigan sweater. The clothes were quite outdated. She had not had a haircut in two years, and she wore no makeup. She knew they were watching her. They always watched.

Particularly Dyson.

She would often walk through the castle late at night. The library was impressive. She'd read a number of the classics, and she realized there were more than a few books that were worth a fortune sitting inside Castle Craig. What she discovered over the past year was more than she had ever imagined.

It began with the cold trail of Malcolm Fraser's parentage. There was nothing. She'd contacted a number of historical societies in the United States, Canada, and Great Britain while still in Boston.

Nothing.

It was not until she returned to Scotland that she learned the truth. Her impulsiveness and poor judgment could very well cost her her life. She should have told someone where she was going and why. She chose not to. That was a mistake she was paying for and had been paying for since her captivity.

The events of the outside world were brought home via the BBC. When the Americans were taken hostage a month earlier, it depressed her even more. The whole world, at least the western portion of it, was enraged at the crime.

Her own plight was unknown. No one cared.

She'd grown accustomed to listening to Radio One on a daily basis. The rock and roll consoled her. Paul Burnett and Tony Blackburn and John Peel kept Jennifer sane. When she heard the news that her brother's band was actually touring Britain, her determination to see her family once again grew stronger than ever.

Seth Duncanson's decision to mail the two letters was not an easy one for the old man. She practically had the man turned and knew she had to act now before he had the opportunity to change his mind. She contemplated long and hard on just what she would do if she ever managed to get beyond the gates of Castle Craig. Jennifer realized that Dyson would not hesitate to kill her if she managed to get away. The two women were just as dangerous. In fact, even Seth Duncanson would probably do her bodily harm just to keep her from talking if something went wrong.

Jennifer Tavistock made the decision that she would not think about escaping without considering the possibility of dying in the process. If the decision were made to kill her inside the castle, there would be little she could do, save defending herself in a surely futile effort.

Anything was better than going down without a fight. A few days earlier, as she listened via shortwave to the fact that it was Thanksgiving Day in her native land, she had suddenly experienced, inexplicably, a sense of something lost upon her for a long time.

Hope.

Could it be the memories of her family seated around their table in Beacon Hill? Perhaps it was the optimism of the first Thanksgiving. She'd learned at a very young age on a visit with her parents and baby brother to nearby Plymouth of that special event in 1621, which would ultimately become an American institution.

That same newscast mentioned the observance that not

only was it Thanksgiving, but it happened to be the day John F. Kennedy was shot in Dallas back in 1963. Those two milestones, falling on the same day, cemented her commitment.

Even with the promise of freedom, Jennifer had steadfastly refused to give up any information they had wanted. She realized that the heat was about to be turned up. Very soon. If death must come, she thought, she wasn't about to take it lying down.

Growing up in the Methodist church, Jennifer was familiar with the Bible, believed in Jesus, and considered herself a good Christian. The captivity had drawn her closer to God and the Bible. She kept in her room an 18th century edition of the King James Version, bound in bright red leather that was part of the castle's library. She opened it, turned to the 143rd Psalm, the words of David, and began to read.

Quicken me, O Lord, for thy name' sake: for thy righteousness' sake bring my soul out of trouble. And of thy mercy cut off mine enemies, and destroy all them that afflict my soul: for I am thy servant.

She reached for the broad axe, hidden under the floorboards in her bedroom. This would be her way out.

***

NEAL EDWARDS WAS NOWHERE TO BE FOUND. He had vacated his home in Bristol, and no one— not the police, not his fiancée, not his parents nor his co-workers—had any idea what might have happened to him.

The car bombing remained in the news. There was a general belief that the Irish had struck in

Bristol, something most unusual for 1979.

Nothing could be further from the truth.

The blame actually lay in Edinburgh, Scotland, as

opposed to Northern Ireland. The motive was anything but political. Emotions being what they were, however, the customary conjecture about the political troubles placed the blame squarely on Northern Ireland.

Newspapers reported on the sad fact that no place in Britain was safe these days. In fact, the truth would never be known.

At least, if Neal Edwards had anything to do with it.

What Edwards had done to endanger his life was simply his job. An estate agent making inquiries regarding a handsome property in Scotland, Edwards had unfortunately stumbled upon a discovery that consequently sent him running for his life.

It began as a routine visit to a castle in the Scottish Highlands at the behest of a wealthy Oklahoma oil tycoon. The American spotted the castle while traveling with his wife on a coach tour along the Great Road North.

His wife wanted to know more about the little spread, and what his wife wanted, his wife usually got. By chance, Edwards had met the couple while dining in a London restaurant some three weeks earlier. He had been so covered up in work that this was the first opportunity he'd had to get out of Bristol.

The first thing he wanted to know was how much the Americans were willing to spend. They were insulted at first; then after Edwards had calmed them down, the figure of ten million pounds was bounced around. Not a shilling more, they insisted.

This was music to the young Englishman's ears. From that point, a thorough and exacting search was undertaken as to just who owned the castle. Nothing turned up. Finally, looking at the possible commission from a ten million pound transaction slipping through his fingers, Edwards decided to call on the castle in person to see if he would fare better.

Once in Edinburgh, he hired a Land Rover and drove northward into the Highlands. It was raining profusely the afternoon Edwards turned down the narrow, paved lane leading up to Castle Craig for the second time in two weeks. A knock on the door revealed the strange and unfriendly face of a gentleman who called himself Ambrose Dyson. No, Edwards was told again, the castle is not for sale.

Not at any price. In view of the inclement weather, Edwards was at least offered a cup of tea.

In twenty minutes, he realized he was wasting his time with the caretakers.

His first visit had been slightly more cordial. Miss Overby was thin and middle-aged and explained to Edwards the best way she could that it would be in everyone's best interest if the owners of the castle remained anonymous.

During his visit to the castle, he had removed his raincoat, which was drenched from the soaking he received when making his dash from the automobile to the entrance of the castle. It was not until he was halfway to London that he realized a slip of paper was in the raincoat's breast pocket, which was not there earlier.

He read the message over and over several times.

At first, he sensed something was amiss on the train trip home from Scotland. But considering it was October thirty-first, Halloween, he read the message once again, passed it off as a bizarre prank, and discarded it in the nearest bin as he emerged into the throng at Victoria's Station. Once reaching London, his fears diminished, and the trip from London to Bristol was most productive, the skies were cloudless, and he admired the fall foliage from his first-class compartment with a Canadian couple, interested in buying a summer house in Bristol.

Unknown to Edwards, Dyson had wasted little time contacting the widow. He told her everything.

This Edwards was persistent, so persistent that he had told Dyson upon leaving Castle Craig that he would; indeed, find out what he was after, meaning the owners of Castle Craig, with or without Dyson's cooperation.

Finding out who Edwards was, was simple. His card had much of the needed information. A phone call to London produced his automobile registration papers in Bristol. Edwards' mistake was notifying Dyson about his return visit. It took the hired specialist less than four minutes to enter the car park of Temple Meads Railway Station in the middle of the early morning traffic, identify the automobile as Edwards departed it, and plant the bomb.

An hour later, young Francis Tailby had shown up.

Once discovering that his Triumph had been blown to pieces, he'd been interrogated by an endless number of Bristol policemen and Special Branch officers. He was repeatedly questioned about Northern Ireland. He was honest when he told them he knew nothing. He was certain the background checks would be extensive, and he knew they would turn up empty.

At one point he almost broke and told the police everything. His instincts, however, prevented him from doing so. Having committed no crime he was free to do as he pleased, as long as he notified them before leaving town. Edwards wasted little time in withdrawing his savings from the Midland Bank and contacting an old acquaintance from the Bristol underworld.

Arrangements were made for Edwards to get out of town in a discreet manner by way of a freighter headed for the Suez.

Whoever these people were, they meant business. His career path was important, but not as important as his life. He loved Carron dearly but feared not only for her life but that of his parents as well.

He would write to them one day.

She would not find Neal Edwards again.

He still could not bring himself to tell anyone about his experience. No one would believe him.

***

TELEVISION COVERAGE ACROSS THE UNITED KINGDOM CONTINUED TO FOCUS ON THE NEAR DEATH OF FRANCIS TAILBY. He was actually being looked at as something of a hero. He even received a phone call from the new Prime Minister, urging a safe recovery. In fact, on December 12, 1979, British authorities would round up IRA suspects in Southampton, London, Liverpool, and Birmingham in an effort to prevent the threat of a Christmas offensive.

Since the IRA had nothing whatsoever to do with the crime, British authorities at that point did not know the true cause of the Bristol bombing.

His face still looked the same, save a few small scratches from the flying glass. Few men lived through what had happened to Francis.

By all accounts, he should have been blown to bits.

He'd told his story over and over. To the doctors. To the newspapers. To the television reporters.

To the police. No one, not his parents, not his uncle, not his mates, had been informed of what had occurred during the frightening period following the blast. A voice had spoken to him. During the time he lay on the Temple Meads Railway Station car park, his trip in the ambulance, even in the hospital emergency room, he had not been alone. The voice was warm and soothing, comforting him. It was close to him at all times.

People had come to Tailby's aid as soon as the blast had occurred that morning. Passengers on their way to board trains had rushed to where he lay. The voice he heard was not one of them, he was certain. At one point in his delirium, he thought he saw the person, but he could not be sure.

His parents were saving all of the newspaper clippings about the bombing. It was not until he read about just how powerful the bomb had actually been and the damage done to the Triumph and several surrounding vehicles did he realize just how fortunate he actually was.

John Scofield

This was one Christmas he would not soon forget.

***

ROSS BURNHAM WAS SLOWLY ON HIS WAY TO RECOVERY. His brush with fate had left him, miraculously, among the living. He never made it to Craig Castle that night. He never would. Not only was he responsible for his own life, he had to look out for the best interests of his wife and three children.

Some things were worth dying for and some things were not.

His claims adjuster had settled up for the damage of his vehicle. Police in the north were still following up on their investigation. So far, they were convinced that the whole thing had been a terrible accident. Crimes of that particular nature simply did not occur along the Great Road North.

The authorities had determined that the bullet which destroyed Burnham's tire came from a .300 caliber Weatherby deer rifle. Hunting was common during that time of year, and the police insisted and concluded that the shot was fired by a careless hunter.

At thirty-six, Burnham was a robust man in excellent health, which was, in part, why his recovery was coming along so well. His split-second decision, looking back on that evening, was madness. By all rights, he should have been dead.

When Burnham bailed out into the darkness, his automobile was moving at no less than fifty miles an hour. He'd been traveling sixty just past Helsmdale on his way to Castle Craig when the shooting took place; and the few seconds before the crash, he'd only managed to slow the car down no more than ten miles an hour.

He'd seen in the movies when the heroes would propel themselves from a moving car, go into a roll, and come up firing to shoot the bad guys down.

Burnham's situation was far different. He'd closed his eyes and prayed for the best. How he had survived that perilous jump he would never know, for he lost consciousness the instant he hit the pavement.

He came to a short time later—wet, shivering, bleeding, bruised and, above all, alive. He tried to move but could not. The fibula bone had shattered just below his right knee joint. There was feeling in both of his legs, however, and that was the main thing. His suit was in tatters and Burnham had looked up to see his beloved automobile smoldering some twenty yards up the road.

A lorry driver was the first to arrive at the scene of the accident. Fortunately, for Burnham, the driver knew a bit about first aid and had enough wits about him not to try and move Burnham from where he lay. An ambulance was summoned and he was carried to hospital. He nearly asked the lorry driver what happened to the other person who had spoken to him, but Burnham was unsure if what had happened was real or simply a dream. He knew somehow that everyone would think he was simply delirious. No one would take him seriously.

Burnham was a professor of history at the University of St. Andrews. He lectured on Scottish history, and his particular field was The Reformation. He currently was teaching a Senior Honors seminar that covered the Reformation to the Union of 1707. Born and raised in nearby Tayport, Burnham had made the Kingdom of Fife his home. His academic star was on the rise at the University, and he realized that in time he would eventually be Dean of History.

Until this.

His wife of seventeen years had never really been happy in Scotland. A native of New Zealand, her mum had been ill for some months now, and in spite of her discomfort, Constance remained steadfastly loyal to her husband. When Ross disclosed his offer to take a position at the University of Wellington, his wife could not believe her ears.

After all, he insisted, the weather in New Zealand was

much warmer, and he could easily adjust to the South Pacific.

History, up until that fateful night, had been his life. He lived and breathed the University of St. Andrews. The decision to come forward with what he had uncovered would have propelled him in to global prominence if it was true, and he was certain that it was.

It began some ten months earlier when he received a phone call one afternoon from an old friend over at the School of Divinity at the University. Seems the gentleman was interested in the history behind a castle. An American student was in St. Andrews searching for information about her ancestry.

Burnham was busy. Do it, the man asked, as a favor for an old friend. Reluctant as always to take on any additional workload, Burnham figured one more task could not hurt. He agreed.

The American's name was Tavistock and she was a Bostonian.

Despite his willingness to help, it was three weeks before Burnham met with the young American girl. He found her to be more than a little determined to uncover a missing link in her family tree. Jennifer Tavistock had a briefcase loaded with documents that basically led her nowhere when it came to finding out what she was looking for.

The parents of Malcolm Fraser.

There was simply no trace whatsoever of his mother and father.

That's how it all began. New Zealand was how it was all ending as far as Burnham was concerned.

He had gone out on a limb for this American, truly interested in helping her out.

Ten months later, after hearing nothing else from the American, Burnham did a little digging, discovered the phone number to Castle Craig, and made the mistake of phoning one, Abigail Overby.

He told them the day he planned on coming. One small favor, she asked. Since tourists are constantly trying to gain access to the castle, would the professor kindly describe the make and model of the automobile so there would be little trouble getting in.

That proved to be, unknown to Burnham, his biggest mistake.

His interrupted journey to Craig Castle had made that impossible. The message sent to him was indisputably clear. Ross Burnham's name would eventually be carved into a granite obelisk, the sign of his final resting place. When that would happen, he did not know.

There were enough things in Burnham's life that could precipitate his exit from this world. History itself was vital, had a meaningful place in this world, but history was hardly worth dying over.

His home would sell in no time. The doctors had given him the word that his knee, in spite of being enclosed in a gigantic cast, was well enough for his journey. His resignation from the University was taken reluctantly. He was well respected and would be dearly missed. His faculty secretary took the news extremely hard, and the current Dean expressed disappointment; but his decision was final.

Wellington was a long way from St. Andrews and an even longer way from Craig Castle. Burnham, considering his line of work, realized only too well that this was not the first time a single bullet had changed the course of history.

He simply could not stop thinking about the spiritual experience following the attempt on his life.

Time and time again since the shooting, he found himself reading the Book of Exodus, Chapter 3, Verse 2: "And the angel of the Lord appeared unto him in a flame of fire out of the mist of a bush: and he looked, and, behold, the bush burned with fire, and the bush was not consumed."

He had been spared from the burning flames of his Jaguar. The lorry driver had seen no one.

Burnham picked up his Bible once again and continued reading. This was, by all definitions, nothing less than a miracle.

***

BACK IN THE UNITED STATES, ALAN ALBRIGHT SAT DOWN AT THE DINING ROOM TABLE. He wasn't hungry. He was simply too excited to eat. Albright was contemplating whether to call Beth in Chicago and tell her he wouldn't be coming up. Tavistock's call was beginning to sink in. The doctor told Albright to call him first thing Monday morning. In the meantime, Albright had written down Jennifer's message inside her mother's birthday card. He read the message over and over. He was still reading it when he reached for the phone and dialed Beth's number.

"Hello."

"Hi, Beth. It's me again. Something urgent's come up. I won't be heading to the city this morning after all."

"Oh, I see," she replied.

"I promise I'll be there first thing Monday morning."

"You've been in a frenzy since you took off for Boston on Monday. It might be a good idea to just take it easy. Slow down."

"That's just it, Beth. I can't slow down. Not now."

"Could I make a suggestion?" she asked.

"Certainly."

"If you can't travel up here, perhaps, and this is merely a suggestion, I can make it downstate. It's been a long time since I've been to the University of Illinois."

Albright thought about it. Beth Spencer, thanks to what had transpired over the past 48 hours, was becoming more and more intertwined into this entire predicament. He was still impressed at how well she thought on her feet that night at Thirdwind. She did an admirable job in dealing with the Chicago policeman, figured out how to find where the ambulance had taken Windham when he and Otto could not, and somehow maintained her composure when the two heavies were threatening her boss.

"You actually want to come to Champaign-Urbana?"

"Why not?"

"There's not a heck of a lot going on down here, Beth."

"That's a matter of opinion. I've partied in Champaign-Urbana a few times. Besides, do you know how good it feels to get out of this town?" she asked. "You know what we've been through only too well with Gerry. I really could use a change of scenery this weekend."

"I suppose you have a point," Albright said. "Here's the phone number to my parents' house.

When you get into town, call me. I'll be here."

He gave her the number.

"Great. Since I'm already up, it shouldn't take me long to get it together. It's 9:30 now. I'll be leaving in about an hour. I should be in town as soon as I can."

"When you get here, we'll paint this town red."

***

WATERS HAD LITTLE CONVICTION REGARDING WEE RONALD MACKEY'S TRUSTWORTHINESS. As they walked along the river by the docks, he felt as if he were keeping company with a viper. Waters walked in stride with Mackey, hands in his pockets, eyes straight ahead.

Waters had left the pub an hour earlier with a pre-arranged rendezvous point agreed upon with Wee Ronald for a job. He had to find those Americans. Mackey was ten minutes late. What Dangerous

Waters wanted was anything but simple: find a tourist

somewhere in the city. Find him, and Wee Ronald would be 100 pounds richer. As they talked, Waters felt as if he and the man walking beside him were like positive and negative currents of electricity, complete opposites with absolutely nothing in common.

"A Yank, eh?"

"That's right."

"Not the easiest thing these days, is it? This town is alive with Yanks."

Waters described his prey to Wee Ronald.

"Would this chap have a name?"

"He introduced himself as Whit Campbell."

"Whit Campbell." Wee Ronald stopped suddenly, repeating the name in a thoughtful manner. "This Campbell. What d'you want done to him?"

"Leave that to me. The best way to contact me is at the club. I'll be there until midnight. If you're successful, let me know as soon as possible, right? If you run into a brick wall, call me just the same."

As the shorter man casually slipped his right hand into his overcoat pocket, he noticed the sound of a car approaching behind them. This was not lost on Waters either, who, during the entire walk, kept one eye on where he was going.

The docks were no place to be careless, particularly at eleven-thirty at night.

Waters prepared himself for the worst.

Both men heard the car stop abruptly. Mackey casually reached for a cigarette. They were standing in front of a darkened alley between two buildings. He pulled a lighter out of his pocket and lit up.

***

AS THE HUNT FOR THE TWO AMERICANS WAS BEING DISCUSSED, DANIEL HARPER AND CHARLOTTE HEALY WERE THEMSELVES PREPARING TO RETURN TO AMERICA. Their plane would be leaving at 7:20 the next morning. Following a brief layover at Heathrow, they would be departing for New York on TWA at 10:45.

The cover story Harper gave was convincing. He and his wife were in Edinburgh in search of rare books, in general, and 16th century Gaelic manuscripts, in particular. They were in Scotland to learn more about The Red Book of Clanranald. Whit Campbell was a compilation of the first name of his seventh grade gym teacher and the last name of his former college roommate.

Unknown to Waters, they were registered at the Rothesay Hotel under their real names.

For Charlotte Healy, this trip was virtually the first time she had been anywhere outside of West Virginia. She was born in Bluefield, did her secondary education in Bluefield, and attended college at Bluefield State. Eighteen months earlier, her widowed mother received a personal visit from two men in nice suits. They were attorneys and broke the news that her natural father, Charlotte's grandfather, had passed on. This meant nothing to Mrs. Healy, who had never known her father.

The lawyers produced a will. In it, the lawyers read, was a provision that Mrs. Healy be left the bulk of the gentleman's estate, which was enormous, since at one time he had been one of the biggest coal barons in the state. By the time the taxes were settled, the accountants were compensated, and the lawyers were paid. Charlotte Healy, an only child and her mother, herself an only child, were four million dollars richer.

Many people would have taken the riches and purchased everything under the sun. Not the Healys.

Mrs. Healy continued to live in the home she and her husband had purchased some twenty-five years earlier. Charlotte, meanwhile, lived in a two-bedroom apartment, drove a five-year-old car, and worked as a loan officer at the First National Bank, where she, incidentally, kept a handsome account of her own.

At the advice of Mrs. Healy's attorneys, financial planners were brought in to invest the inheritance, and despite high inflation and overall economic uncertainty that prevailed in the late 1970s, their money was doing quite well.

When Harper ran out of money not long after visiting Den Haag, he returned to the United States—despondent, angry, and broke. It was Charlotte, who suggested that she assist him financially. They were, after all, engaged to be married.

Harper had his own agenda and, knowing the dangers he faced, his beloved Charlotte would not be returning to Scotland the following January.

***

THE PHONE RANG AT 1:20. Albright's parents had to be called away to his paternal grandparents Ford County farm at the last moment. Nothing urgent, the Colonel had said, but he and Blakelyn would be spending the remainder of the weekend with his parents, something they did more and more these days.

As expected, it was Beth Spencer. She was calling from the new Market Place Mall. Albright pinpointed her exact location, grabbed his L. L. Bean goose down parka, and headed for the Big Jag.

Twenty minutes later, they were driving down Lincoln Avenue, heading for his parents' house. Once there, Beth parked her VW in his driveway, and together they took off in the automobile that for Beth was developing into a growing fascination.

Albright's first stop was Green Street. Campustown. They found a parking spot on Wright Street in front of the Illini Union Bookstore, simply because it was a Saturday, and decided on lunch at

Garcia's Pizza. Beth liked Champaign-Urbana. She was dressed in jeans and a sweater worn under a long, black overcoat. The unexpected visit, for Albright, was certainly a welcome one.

He decided to tell her everything over a pizza. Neither had eaten anything all day, and they were both famished.

The first thing Beth wanted to know, after being briefed, was more about Jennifer Tavistock. Albright described the person who created the calamity he suddenly found himself in.

"And how did you and Jennifer first meet in St. Andrews?"

***

1969

ST. ANDREWS

ALL OF A SUDDEN, WITHOUT WARNING, THERE WAS A NOISE BY THE MAIN GATES. They were supposed to be alone. A flashlight bemoaned the darkness near the east wall. No one bothered to speak; they merely looked at each other with a mutual understanding. Each of the seven foreigners realized this was the moment that could very well be the turning point in their excursion.

This was the Scotland no tourist guide would describe in one of those colorful brochures. It was one o'clock in the morning, well past curfew, and the St. Andrews police had seven American students cornered in the old cemetery.

"Well, what's all this, then?" There were four policemen altogether—two standing in front of the students, while two remained at the front gates in the Ford Cortina.

"We were on a ghost hunt, officer. Not meaning any harm to person or property, and that's the truth," said Sam Kipp, eyes squinting against the light beam directed into his eyes.

"No harm meant, eh?" The officer who spoke sounded almost friendly, but it was impossible for the Americans to read their expressions, since the policemen stood behind the flashlights.

St. Andrews certainly had a reputation for its ghosts and legends. Shortly after arriving in Scotland on the 21st of June, Kipp purchased a copy of *St. Andrews Ghost Stories* by W.T. Linskill, where he'd read about the Lady of the Haunted Tower. Kipp convinced a number of guys that this ghost was real, according to more than a few people, and they should get a good look for themselves.

This particular ghost hunt, unfortunately, was over practically as soon as it had begun. There was still one small discrepancy.

"So where's the lass who screamed? It won't do her much good to remain in hiding, lads. The hunt is over."

"That's just it, sir," Kipp said. "There are only seven of us. All guys." Like the young men around him, Kipp seemed nervous. The scream came from out of nowhere and scared the wits out of the Americans. The rest of the youths, including Alan Albright, remained silent.

"You're the lot from University Hall, are you not?"

"That's correct, sir."

"And you're certain that there's no one else?"

"Positive, officer. Nobody but us, that is, that we've seen. Like you, we too heard someone scream.

Who it was, we have absolutely no idea."

Sam Kipp was a big man. At least 250 pounds. In spite of his size, he'd made it over the cemetery wall with the rest of the guys.

The policeman who had remained silent was dispatched to the Cortina. Moments later, he returned with the two officers who had been waiting at the Cortina. They searched the graveyard thoroughly, checked the locked gates, and determined whoever had screamed was not inside those walls.

The Americans, meanwhile, were asked to remain put. Once the policemen returned, two of them joked to themselves, which set off a rumble of laughter from the officers.

"One of you might not be screaming like a lass, would you now?"

None of the students were amused.

"Look," said the policeman, who had done the initial interrogation, "you seem like good lads. It might be best for you to be getting along now. Shall we inform the University of your curiosity in spirits, or can we trust you to stay clear of the cathedral cemetery after dark? Come now! Let's hear something!"

"We shall keep our distance; you can rest assured, sir," Kipp said.

"There's not enough room for you in the squad car, so it's a fair assumption that you'll be heading straight back to your rooms, will you not?"

Somehow they had avoided getting arrested. All they had to worry about now was getting back to

University Hall. Like that would be easy at this time of the morning.

The distance from the priory ruins to University Hall is slightly over three quarters of a mile in length. The seven young men passed abreast the Deans Court mansion, headed left, and emerged into South Street, one of the oldest streets in all of Scotland.

It was cold, narrow, and deserted.

The worn cobblestones glistened in the semi-darkness as the foreigners proceeded west, passing St.

Leonard's, the exclusive school for girls. In a few hours, the banks and shops in South Street would be bustling; but at an hour when most honest people were fast asleep in their beds, nothing broke the silence of the night, save the echoing footsteps of seven grateful and most fortunate American students.

After apologizing to the policemen for their foolish and imprudent behavior, Sam Kipp, Steve Baker, Bailey Stricklin, Robert King, Nate Christopher, Donnie Patterson, and Alan Albright were glad in their own individual way to know that their names would not be called out in a Scottish police court on several quite embarrassing charges. It was the decision of the St. Andrews police officers not to place the young men under arrest nor to report their actions to the University.

Something, nevertheless, was suspiciously amiss about the whole situation. The policemen seemed almost relieved to discover that the strangers in the graveyard were only a group of harmless youths out chasing legends from long ago.

They walked in silence under the arches of the familiar West Port. Their pace was quick, and the ramifications of what could come to pass if they were discovered were beginning to sink in as they emerged through the curved beam of stone, known to those familiar with St. Andrews as a true landmark, which once served as the entrance to the ancient city.

Halfway home.

They paused momentarily in Argyle Street and strategized the best way to enter the old wing of University Hall without being discovered. Into Hepburn Gardens Road. With less than three blocks to go, they turned north and strolled beside the ivy-covered walled pathway of St. Leonard's Road.

Albright glanced at his wristwatch under the glow of a streetlight. 1:45.

Had they been missed from their rooms, the not-so-magnificent seven would surely be in for it.

Their absence would undoubtedly provoke, yet another

all-out search for an all-night poker game throughout the men's wing of University Hall, and that would spell trouble for everyone.

The circular driveway came into view. It was now or never.

The thick oak double doors swung open as quietly as they had closed more than two hours earlier.

There was absolutely no sign of life in the darkened south lounge as the adventurers crept across the reading room in the direction of the spacious, carpeted staircase. Out of the seven students, two lived on the second floor and the remaining five on the third. At the second floor landing, Baker and Albright whispered a goodnight to their comrades and disappeared into rooms 25 and 26, respectively. So far, so good.

The small alarm clock went off at seven o'clock sharp. Albright remained motionless on the straw-filled mattress for another five minutes in a futile effort to fight off the grogginess brought on by lack of sleep.

Impossible.

He surrendered his rest, eased out of the warm bed, and reached for his robe and slippers. He was still having difficulty adjusting to the cold St. Andrews' mornings, particularly being the last week of June. Like the rest of the rooms in University Hall, room 26 had a pay-as-you-go heating system, which required a shilling in the heat box in order to warm up the room. Fortunately, he had proper change. He went into the bathroom, drew a hot bath, and returned to his room twenty minutes later, where he found things nice and warm.

Albright dressed in a pair of grey slacks, slipped on a navy sweater purchased from a local woolen mill over a yellow shirt and black tie, brushed out his hair, and still had difficulty adjusting to the fact that ties were required at breakfast.

If he or any of the others had been discovered missing

someone, probably one of the monitors would inform him that his presence would be required in the office of Mr. Eberhardt. They had agreed the night before that if anyone were caught, they would insist they had been alone and wouldn't rat out anyone else.

Albright walked into the dining room shortly before eight and found a seat at the first empty chair he saw. He was in no particular mood for company. Pouring his first cup of tea of the morning,

Albright winced to himself as he saw his chaperone head to his table.

Busted.

"Good morning, Albright. You remember we leave for Aviemore tomorrow morning at ten. You will remember to pack accordingly."

Like most people from Urbana High School, Mrs. Storm addressed Albright by his last name. He flashed her his best smile and sat back in relief. Mrs. Storm was the sort of person who came straight to the point on serious matters.

It was evident she knew nothing of the night before.

"Good morning, Mrs. Storm. I had forgotten," he said, quite honestly, "about tomorrow's trip."

"Excursion," she corrected.

"But, of course. So, Mrs. Storm, what's Aviemore like? Just another fancy ski resort? There's no snow this time of year, you know."

"I think you'll find Aviemore quite exciting. By the way, do you mind if we join you?" she asked, as her husband walked up.

"Please."

Mrs. Storm was a history teacher at Urbana High School, and she and her husband were serving as chaperones for the group of students in St. Andrews from Urbana. She was thin, early thirties. He was studious, wore glasses, and seemed to be a man of perpetually good humor. Albright liked them both.

Mrs. Storm tended to be a bit too strict sometimes and, like most teachers, treated her students like children, even those who were practically adults.

There were a number of cultural traditions about Scotland that Albright and the rest of his American counterparts were learning about and quickly adjusting to. One of them was having to wear a tie at each meal. Another custom at University Hall was that not until the headmistress was seated and had begun her meal did students pick up their knives and forks.

Albright nodded a good morning to the heavyset young man who spoke to everyone present, as was his habit, before sitting down. His left leg still ached from scaling the cemetery wall the night before, and a limp was evident.

"What's the problem, Sam?" Mrs. Storm asked.

Sam Kipp felt terrible. He did his best to smile at everyone. His eyes were red from lack of sleep as the pain in his leg had kept him up all night. Nevertheless, his early morning demeanor was jovial. If it were not for his appetite, Kipp would have probably slept until noon.

"Just a little pain in my leg. Thanks for asking."

"You don't look too good," said Mrs. Storm.

"I'm fine, really."

Albright smiled to himself as he began to eat.

Rather than heading back to his room, Albright decided to hang around the lounge following breakfast. He managed to contact everyone who'd been on the ghost hunt and was satisfied that they'd somehow managed to get away clean.

His classes that morning consisted of Modern Britain and Shakespeare. Both were uneventful. That afternoon, following lunch, his afternoon was free. Albright returned to the lounge, where a number of

American students at St. Andrews were hanging out. Some were preparing to play a round of golf on the Old

Course. Others were heading to the beach for a bit of sun.

Albright, feeling somewhat sluggish from the night before, decided to head to his room to catch up on his sleep. As he stood up to leave, he felt something poke him in his side. He looked around. The object that had nudged him was a Wilson tennis racket. The person carrying the racket was dressed entirely in white. Shorts and a top. White shoes and socks.

"Careless of you, wasn't it?" She wasn't smiling.

"I'd say you were the one being careless," Albright shot back.

He'd seen her around. The American Institute for Foreign Study had its students broken into four groups; and, subsequently, whenever travel was involved, they toured on four buses. She happened to be in Albright's group. Nevertheless, they had no classes together; and, as a result, he did not know her name.

She had dark hair. Brown eyes. The one thing Albright would genuinely remember about noticing her for the first time would be her dimple... It lay in the center of her chin.

"You would say something stupid like that," she remarked.

At sixteen, Albright considered himself at least something of a gentleman. He'd been brought up not to curse in the presence of women, which he did not, at least most of the time. He was taught by his teachers and his parents to be courteous to the opposite sex, something he adhered to according to his mood. His mood that afternoon was complete bewilderment.

"Well, you would do something stupid like poking me with that dumb tennis racket of yours."

"This racket," she said, pointing it at Albright, "is smarter than you'll ever be."

"That is the ugliest racket I've ever seen," Albright countered. "May I?" he asked.

The girl's patience was wearing thin. She obviously had better things to do. Albright did not see anyone in sight who might have been her tennis partner, so evidently she was the one who was early for the match.

"Oh, why not?" she said, and extended the racket towards Albright.

As he reached to examine it, she suddenly jerked it away, but not before he managed to get a hand around the base. She held on to the tennis racket as did Albright. It took both hands for her to maintain a grip while he nonchalantly held on with his left hand. She tried twisting, turning, pulling, and pushing, but Albright would not let go. She jumped over the couch in the lounge, using her feet against the base of the couch as leverage. Had Albright chosen to release the racket at that moment, she would have tumbled over from her own momentum, but he chose to hold on.

The struggle for the racket lasted five minutes. Her face grew red from the tussle. Finally, Albright relented. He had enjoyed every moment of this spontaneous outburst.

She walked away in triumph without saying a word.

That evening at dinner, Albright walked past the table where his nemesis was seated. She didn't bother to acknowledge his presence. He did manage to discover her name, however.

Jennifer Tavistock.

Later that evening, he returned to his room to pack for the upcoming trip to Aviemore. He was still making the adjustment to the autumn-like weather going on in eastern Scotland. Cool mornings in the 40's. Cool days as well, sometimes not getting out of the 50's. The most extraordinary aspect of the Scottish summer was the fact that darkness did not occur until 11:00 at night, and the sun would come right back up at 3:30 in the morning. By 9:30 that night, in spite of the fact it was still daylight, Albright was fast asleep.

The next morning there was a flurry of activity at

University Hall. Another excursion. Albright, or few others for that matter, knew anything whatsoever about Aviemore. The trip was to last three days. As usual, breakfast came first. The coaches were scheduled to leave at nine, and Albright packed up a few last-minute items he'd not bothered to load the night before.

The sky was overcast over St. Andrews that morning, and a bracing westerly breeze made standing outside quite uncomfortable for those who were foolish enough to be without a jacket or sweater.

Albright stood in the middle of a group of students who would be traveling on his coach— one of them, Sam Kipp.

"I wonder who else was there the other night?" asked Kipp.

"You know, I'd almost forgotten about that person screaming," Albright said with a shudder.

"Strange, wasn't it?"

Kipp nodded. "Yea, it was strange. We were real lucky, Alan."

"Yea, I suppose we were. How's the leg, by the way?"

He shrugged his shoulders. "The leg's fine, thanks. What do you know about Aviemore?"

"Not much."

"Okay, gang, listen up!" Mrs. Storm had arrived, full of adrenalin and meaning business. Everyone basically ignored her and continued what they were doing before she walked up. "Let's get on the coach."

A loose, disorganized line boarded the sleek coach as the driver loaded the luggage. Albright was one of the last to climb on board. He'd slept quite well, making up for the loss of sleep two nights earlier when he and the others were out on the ghost hunt. Seats were filling up fast. He found an empty one, threw his red AIFS carryall underneath, and sat down next to the window. To his right, three rows in front of him, sat Jennifer Tavistock. Like Albright, she was seated next to a window. She wore a maroon jacket, and her dark hair was in a single braid, falling halfway down her back. She had her back to Albright and was sitting alone. Just then, Albright looked up to see Mr. And Mrs. Storm walking past. Since they were the last to board, there were no two empty side-by-side seats left on the coach.

"You guys looking for seats?" he asked.

"We'll be fine, thanks," Mr. Storm replied. I'll just slide next to you, Alan."

"I've got a better idea, Mr. Storm," Albright said, reaching for his grip underneath. "You and Mrs. Storm may have this seat."

"That's quite all right; we'll manage."

"No, I insist," he said, and slid past his chaperone. He looked up and down the coach for an empty spot and noticed there were several. He debated momentarily, thought against it at first, and then said to himself, why not? He moved up three seats towards the front and sat down next to Jennifer Tavistock.

"Hi."

Her response surprised him. She actually spoke. "Hello."

Overcast skies prevailed that morning as the coach's drove towards Aviemore. Being a first-class coach line, the students kept themselves entertained with Led Zeppelin music on the built-in cassette player that connected to speakers along the ceiling of the coach.

All of this time, no words were spoken between Jennifer and Albright. She busied herself with a paperback novel from the time the coach departed St. Andrews while Albright softly hummed "Good

Times, Bad Times," relishing the scenery in spite of the lack of sunshine. Once he pulled out his map, he noticed the girl's interest in the book was waning.

The one item the Colonel had given Albright before leaving for St. Andrews, besides a ton of advice, was a map of Scotland. They were about thirty minutes out of St. Andrews when Albright reached under his seat, found his carry-all, and pulled out the map for the second time since being in Britain. Two mere weeks ago, he had arrived in Scotland. A totally new experience beheld the young man as he and his fellow Americans departed the charter flight to a brisk Scottish morning, where the temperature was a mere 52 degrees. Once their charter plane had landed at Prestwick and the Americans boarded the coaches, Albright had pulled out the map and tracked the entire route, mile by mile, city by city, of the drive from the point of embarkation, being the west of Scotland, to the east— final destination being the Kingdom of Fife. Instead of driving the A77 Motorway, the coaches chose the A71 route through cities like Strathaven, West Calder, and across the Forth Road Bridge into Inverkeithing.

That morning, as they left St. Andrews, the coaches followed the northern route, passed through Dundee, and took the A923, which stretched along the Sidlaw Hills.

"I don't suppose you know where we are, do you?" Jennifer asked.

"Right here. In the middle of these mountains, just outside Coupar Angus."

"Oh." She nonchalantly closed her paperback. "And how far to our destination?"

Albright located Aviemore on the map and pointed it out to her.

"And how long will it take us to get there?"

"You'll have to ask the driver," he replied with a heavy dose of sarcasm.

Jennifer took in what the young man seated next to her was wearing. A tan pair of chukka boots. Straight-legged Levi jeans. Wide leather belt. A long-sleeved red and white striped Oxford shirt, sleeves folded halfway up the muscular forearms. Light brown hair. Jock haircut. She also took note that he was left-handed, as he wore his Timex watch on his right wrist.

"So where are you from?" Jennifer asked.

"Urbana, Illinois. Home of the University of Illinois."

"Well, fancy that," she said. "I didn't know there *was* a University of Illinois."

"Now you know. And just where do you come from?"

"A city in Massachusetts. Place called Boston. I suppose you've heard of it?"

"I suppose I have. Home of the Boston Strangler, right? Home to a baseball team who hasn't won a World Series since Warren Harding was President. Yea, I've heard of Boston."

"Wilson."

"Wilson, who?"

"Woodrow Wilson. He was in office when the Red Sox last won their last World Series in 1918. Babe Ruth was still playing for them."

"Oh, yea? And what do you know about Babe Ruth?" Albright asked.

"More than you know about Woodrow Wilson."

***

THE NEXT MORNING, THE TOUR OF THE SCOTTISH HIGHLANDS BEGAN. Albright boarded his bus following breakfast, and to his surprise, looked up to see Jennifer Tavistock, sliding in beside him.

"Good morning," she said.

"Hi there," said Albright, taking note of her attire. Jennifer was wearing a plum sweater and white jeans. Her hair glimmered as it lay about her shoulders. As always, she had her paperback book in hand.

"I saw you playing darts last night."

"I saw those Scottish guys flirting with you," Albright replied.

"Oh, they weren't flirting," Jennifer said. "They were just curious to know who we were."

"Did you give them your phone number?"

"Yea, right."

The four student-filled coaches traveled throughout the Highlands that morning. By three o'clock, they had reached Fort Augustus. The next destination was Loch Ness. Once there, the Americans departed the coaches under a partly cloudy, cool sky. Indisputably, one of the more famous landmarks in Scotland, the waters of Loch Ness that day were calm.

The legends of the Loch fascinated the Americans. Their guide was quite extensive in describing the length of the Loch, its surprising depths and, of course, tales of the Loch Ness Monster. Where a number of students often seemed tired of hearing about ancient Scotland, the guide had the attention of each and every American student that afternoon.

Albright, who had taken few pictures that day, took several shots of the Loch with his Instamatic.

Jennifer Tavistock, meanwhile, had her Honeywell Pentax focused on everything from practically the moment their plane touched down at Prestwick. She was into her third roll of the afternoon when, to her amazement, she was asked to pose for a picture in front of Loch Ness by none other than Alan Albright.

She consented.

In turn, she captured him in several shots, the majority of them unknown to him.

That evening, as they returned to Aviemore, they began to really talk to each other. No sarcasm, no put-downs—just talk. What impressed Jennifer the most about the young man from Illinois was his quick wit and sense of humor. He could make her laugh. Albright, in turn, was fascinated by her vast, seemingly unequaled intelligence.

The majority of American students that night drifted to the ice rink. A Highland chill had settled over Aviemore, which made conditions on the outside seem more like early autumn rather than early summer. Temperatures in the mid-forties and strong northerly winds. Football weather, Albright called it. That evening at dinner, Jennifer Tavistock and Alan Albright sat together; and as they walked towards the ice rink, Albright casually took Jennifer by the hand.

She did not resist.

They were both good skaters. Music poured through the rink as the evening progressed. Albright was oblivious to everything around him—except Jennifer Tavistock. She had changed out of her white jeans and plum sweater into a dark skirt and stockings and white blouse. Her dark hair flowed about her shoulders and she wore no makeup.

Curfew was generally relaxed during excursions, and that evening was no exception. Once leaving the skating rink, Albright and Jennifer sat in the great room of the lodge, talking and holding hands until three that morning.

***

FOLLOWING THEIR RETURN TO ST. ANDREWS, THEY BECAME INSEPARABLE. Only once was there any friction between them.

Albright caused what could have been a serious threat to their relationship by challenging Jennifer to a tennis match one afternoon. She promptly accepted. They took to the clay courts, where Jennifer Tavistock showed no mercy.

She defeated Albright soundly, without so much as a single game in the one-sided match going in his favor.

Her mastery of tennis was deadly, and Albright realized, after the match had begun, that revenge for his earlier hijinks with her racket was being served up with each volley.

She deployed the Wilson with lethal accuracy and Albright, who up until that moment thought his game was pretty good, was helpless as he tried to return her serves across the net.

In all, Jennifer aced Albright a total of eleven times.

Being the competitor that he was, Albright did not take his loss well. He left the court an angry man, his anger not so much directed at Jennifer as it was his inability to win even one game. She took note of his mood and beheld his fury for the first time.

As Albright stormed off the court, she stopped him. "Wait a minute. It's only a game."

"So it is. Congratulations." Albright lowered his head and walked towards University Hall.

"I said to wait a minute." Her voice was louder now.

Albright's face was flushed. He was breathing hard. Sweat covered his forehead, and his t-shirt was soaked in spite of the cool weather. He stood in front of his opponent, who was cool and unruffled, and wiped his tennis wristband across his brow. "What do you want?"

Jennifer Tavistock saw the anger in his eyes. She realized he was a sore loser. "Your return is weak. Your backhand is at best mediocre. In all honesty Alan, your serve is deplorable. No follow-through whatsoever. You need to arc a bit more, as well."

"I need to 'ack' a bit more?" he said, imitating her Boston accent. She had told him in a straight, pure, and simple way what was wrong with his game. It was their first and only conflict that entire summer. Jennifer had done something that moment few people were able to do: calm the volatile temper of Alan Albright.

Something that resembled a smile formed around the corners of his mouth.

"There'll be other games," he said as he took her by the hand.

The Secret Of St. Andrews

The remaining weeks in St. Andrews seemed to pass by at the speed of light. Albright and Jennifer would spend their free afternoons eating fish 'n chips at Joe's, browsing the shops, and spending time on the beach gathering occasional sun. They even spent time in some of the local pubs, listening to local musicians strum out the music of the land. One evening, days before they were to leave St. Andrews, Albright, Jennifer, and a number of others found their way into a quaint pub, only to hear a group sing a song that he would never forget.

Oh, the summer time is come,
And the trees are sweetly blooming,
And the wild mountain thyme
Grows around the purple heather.
Will you go, lassie, go?
And we'll all go together
To pick wild mountain thyme
All around the blooming heather,
Will you go lassie, go?

Albright wasn't much at sing-a-longs, but there was something about Jennifer's presence, the acoustical guitars, the laid-back atmosphere of the pub and the realization that this remarkable Scotland experience would soon be coming to an end. It was the last song of the gig, and the musicians had encouraged everyone to join in, which most of the locals did without hesitation. To the Americans, most who had never heard "Wild Mountain Thyme," it was a bit of a chore at first; but the group played round after round of the chorus that most of the visitors to Scotland in attendance that evening eventually picked up the lyrics. His appreciation of the culture of St. Andrews was burgeoning, and that particular evening in that particular pub with that particular song would be one of those defining moments he would associate with St. Andrews for years to come.

***

THE AMERICANS MADE SEVERAL TRIPS TO DUNDEE THAT SUMMER, THE NEAREST CITY TO ST. ANDREWS.

On their last visit to Dundee, Albright, Jennifer, and a few others were coming out of W.H.

Smith's Bookstore, when a group of youths appeared around the corner. The Americans had never seen the likes of them before. They wore black construction boots. Jeans, rolled up well past their ankles, held up with red one-inch suspenders. Plaid shirts. The most distinguishing attribute they all had in common, however, was their hair. They didn't have any.

It was the middle of the afternoon, just beginning to drizzle. The Scottish youths looked ready for a fight. Out of all the Americans Albright realized he was the only guy. It didn't faze him. This was the first and only time any of the Americans felt even remotely threatened during their visit to Scotland during the summer of 1969.

One of the things Alan Albright had learned from Urbana High School was how to be ready to scrap at a moment's notice, whether fighting one or half a dozen, which the youths standing before them presently numbered.

Jennifer, along with her counterparts, looked worried. She pulled at Albright's sleeve as the rest of the group quickly ran back into the bookshop. Albright jerked his arm away as he looked the Scottish lads over.

"I'll meet up with you in a bit," he told her. "Catch up with the rest of them."

"Come on," Jennifer insisted.

"I'm staying."

"Then so am I."

Most of the lads were Albright's age, some a couple of years older. He noticed the one he stood closest to was staring at Jennifer. While the remainder of the gang certainly looked like they came from and belonged in the streets with their scarred faces and chipped teeth, this one was different. He had a cherubic face, quite innocent, with friendly dark eyes. To Jennifer Tavistock, he looked like he should be studying at Eton. He smiled at the two Americans in front of him, revealing a brilliant set of even white teeth. To Albright, he had the overall appearance of an altar boy or a Shakespearian actor, anything but a street thug.

As the gang stood facing the Americans, the people in the street kept walking, looking away, not wanting to get involved. The oddly dressed gang noticed something in Albright they had not anticipated— a noticeable absence of fear.

"Is there a problem?" Albright asked.

"There is, yea," said the gang member with the perfect smile.

Albright said, "Well, maybe you should do something about it," he laughed. "If you have the balls, that is. You bastards couldn't beat us in 1776, and you can't beat us now."

He took a step closer to the short-haired man. He was a couple of inches taller than the Scotsman. At that moment, two things happened. Out of nowhere, Albright fired on the oddly dressed man in the side of his face, knocking him back in the middle of his friends at precisely the same moment a burly beat cop appeared from around the corner. At the sight of the policeman, five of the six gang members bolted.

The one who had been slugged was the sole exception. The punch had sent him reeling for a moment, but he managed to stay on his feet. The policeman began to run in their direction. In spite of being slugged with Albright's best, the young man looked at the American, smiled once again, glanced at the approaching cop, no more than a few feet away and said, "One day we'll finish this, mate," threw a kiss to Jennifer Tavistock, and took off running after his friends.

The policeman explained to the Americans that they should be more careful. After all, this was Dundee.

"Who were they?" Jennifer asked, awestruck at the bravery of Alan Albright.

"Skinheads," the policeman replied.

"Never heard of them," replied Jennifer.

***

SUDDENLY, THE DAY EVERYONE KNEW WAS COMING ARRIVED. It was time to leave Scotland. It was cool yet sunny on that early morning in late July when the lone kilt-draped piper stood in front of University Hall and played a sentimental farewell to the American students. The sounds of the bagpipes, coupled with the realization that the time spent in St. Andrews was nearing an end, caused tears to flow from nearly everyone. Even Albright fought them back. To most of the 126 students, the four weeks out of the summer of 1969 would be forever etched in their minds as being one of the truly memorable experiences of their entire lives.

Leaving St. Andrews by coach, the group boarded a train at Leuchars Junctions and began a journey southward.

Into England.

Final destination being London.

Once in London, the Americans took up residence at the College of St. John and St. Mark, located in the King's Road. The days in England's capital city were wonderful. Hand in hand, Albright and Jennifer strolled along the King's Road, sipped chilled lager in the Chelsea Drug Store, enjoyed the theatrical production of *The Canterbury Tales*, and shopped about in some of the trendy boutiques in the west end.

The three remarkable days in that city were capped off in Trafalgar Square, where Albright and Jennifer, along with thousands of others, saw history made that night as Neil Armstrong took the most famous steps of the twentieth century as he became the first human being to walk on the moon.

From London they traveled once again by coach to Dover, where they took a ferry to the French port of Calais, final destination Paris. In spite of what he had experienced in Britain, Albright would never forget his encounter at the Louvre as he laid eyes on the *Mona Lisa*. The Eiffel Tower was memorable, the Palace of Versailles, a sight to behold, but no singular occurrence in that summer could rival the sight of da Vinci's masterpiece.

***

THE MORNING THE AMERICAN STUDENTS AND THEIR CHAPERONES WERE TO RETURN TO AMERICA WAS IN SOME REGARDS A SOMBER ONE. The plane ride was both amusing and sorrowful. Entertaining and melancholy. Past moments were shared with friends, while others were eager to return to their boyfriends and girlfriends they'd not seen for practically the entire summer.

For Albright and Jennifer Tavistock, who mostly kept to each other during the flight into New York, the eight-hour flight back home was, for the most part, joyful. Promises were made. Jennifer even went so far as to pledge that wherever Albright decided to attend college, she would be there.

Once clearing customs and retrieving their luggage, bedlam broke loose. The Tavistocks had flown into JFK to meet their daughter. Things were so hurried that because of the different schedules each group of students were on, Albright missed the opportunity to meet Dr. and Mrs.

Tavistock, for the connecting shuttle back to Boston would be leaving in the next twenty minutes and the party from Boston had to hurry.

That left them with an unexpectedly and painfully short time to say goodbye.

Suddenly, the group from Massachusetts was gone and Jennifer Tavistock, gone with them.

***

1979

Beth Spencer was touched by what she had just been told. She looked across the table at her friend, who looked as troubled as the day he'd walked into his office with the news that his marriage to Tolly Chamberlain had been called off.

"When did you see her again?"

"I didn't. We both made plans to go to college right here. To the University of Illinois."

"What happened?"

"My decision to enlist in the Marines. My parents and I talked it over. They left the choice up to me on my career path, and I told Jennifer what I wanted to do. I knew she wasn't crazy about the war. What I wasn't ready for was her reaction. She became extremely combative. I'll never forget; it was on the Sunday night after our senior prom. I never should have done what I did." He spoke almost in a whisper.

Beth didn't say anything.

"We stayed on the phone for two hours that night. She was telling me about Cambodia and Laos and how ugly that war was and how utterly misguided I was becoming. I tried to tell her about my family. Our tradition in the service. We've served since the Civil War. I suppose if I did any extensive research, it would probably go back further.

Nevertheless, everything changed that night. Everything. Her hatred of the war and my determination to serve drove a wedge into our future. I respected her anti-war feelings, but she couldn't resolve the fact that what I was doing was a part of the Albright tradition.

"Yea, we're just a bunch of Midwestern farmers. But I did it and my brother did it and that's that. It cost me, but I could not change who we are."

"It's understandable, I suppose."

"You just don't walk away from someone like that, Beth. Could it be that what happened with Tolly Chamberlain is God's way of punishing me for what I did to Jennifer Tavistock? We might have worked it out. It's all so senseless."

Customers were steadily filing into Garcia's. The place was filling up with students— ordering pizza, drinking beers, taking a respite from exams. All of a sudden, the place was packed. The remnants of a pizza lay at their table. Beth and Albright had been at their table for a couple of hours now, but no one bothered them except to refill their Pepsi glasses.

"Enough of this. I'm feeling sorry for myself. Not good form for a host, is it? What do you say we get out of here and find something fun to do? How about we hit a few Green Street shops or something? Are you up for a game of pool later?"

"Sure."

They paid their bill at Garcia's and left the Big Jag parked. They strolled down Wright Street, which divides the twin cities, where they headed left on Green. Their first, and as it turns out only stop, was the Record Service. Once inside, he and Beth browsed through the record bins, loud music pumping out as always. Beth, being several years younger, naturally had different tastes than her friend. She purchased a LP by the Fatback Band and introduced Albright to a group from New York, called the Sugar Hill Gang, who performed a most unusual form of music, if you could call it that, known as hip-hop. While Albright preferred his Foreigner, Boston, Van Halen and such, Beth Spencer ended up buying a nearly dozen albums, which she had simply been too busy to pick up back in Chicago. From the Record Service, they walked down Green, crossed Wright Street, and headed into the Illini Union. Students were everywhere that afternoon in spite of the cold. After all, it was a Saturday. For the next two hours, they played nine ball. It was five-thirty when they headed out of the pool room in the Union and spent a half hour admiring photographs on display by a local artist. Beth took a particular interest in the black and white scenes of the Champaign County prairie.

"I don't know about you, but this has been one great afternoon, Alan," Beth said. She had not brought up Jennifer's name since Garcia's and knew better to even think about mentioning Tolly Chamberlain.

"I feel the same way. I was just thinking, Beth. I have close friends here in town, who would just love to meet you. Eulus and Madelyn White. Let's give them a call."

Albright reached into his pocket, found some change, and dialed the Whites' residence. Madelyn answered the phone. "Think you guys might like to go see a movie tonight?

"Do we get to pick the movie?" she asked.

"I don't see why not."

"*Star Trek*. Opened last night. It's playing at the Co-Ed."

"Hold on a second." Albright placed his hand over the mouthpiece of the telephone.

"They suggested *Star Trek*. Sound okay?"

Beth's face lit up at once. "Definitely!"

"*Star Trek*, it is. I'll meet you at your place, where we can find out when the next showing is. How tough will it be to find a sitter?"

"No problem at all," said Madelyn. "My sister and her husband would be happy to keep Tyler, I should think."

"I'll see you in a few."

When Albright walked into the Whites' home and introduced them to the lovely Beth Spencer, the look on Madelyn's face was one of total bewilderment. She was just summing up the change in her husband's best friend the night before and now this.

"Say hello to Beth Spencer."

"You're the one!" Madelyn exclaimed.

"I am?" Beth asked, not sure of just what was going on.

"Alan told us about what's happened to you guys over the past couple of days. Everything."

Beth Spencer's first impression of Madelyn White was like the first impression of many others.

Abrupt. Assertive. All of a sudden, Madelyn broke out with the warmest smile Albright had seen on her face in a long time.

"You were very brave that night with the policeman. Quick thinking. I like that. Both of you take a seat if you can find one while I finish getting ready. By the way, the next showing is at 7:05."

Albright and Beth sat down on the couch, and Madelyn, while Beth was admiring the numerous presents under the Christmas tree, gave Albright a big wink.

He wanted to say something to the contrary but just sat there.

Following the film, they dropped in at Murphy's Pub for beers and a late dinner. Madelyn naturally had iced tea. Eulus was his usual reserved self throughout the evening. Once he and Albright had a moment at the table while Beth and Madelyn went to the rest room, his attitude changed.

"How well do you know Beth Spencer?"

"I don't know," he shrugged. "She came to Third Wind not long ago. She's young and likes to hang out. Darn good photographer, who happens to have remarkable accounting skills."

"That it?"

"That's it," said Albright, knowing where his friend was going. "What's the matter?"

"You and I go back as far as Leal School. You're my very best friend. There are things about what I do that I don't tell you about."

Albright tensed, thinking about what he had just been told.

"You don't trust her."

"No, that's not it. Like I told you last night, be careful. I've been thinking all day about your business. It ain't good. That phone call you received from your hotel room is one of the keys to all of this. Take my advice. Anything that happens from here on in, keep to yourself. As far as your parents are concerned, that's different. Madelyn and myself, that's different. But anybody else, even the man in Boston who's paying you, be careful. Beth Spencer, be careful. People will warm up to you for the oddest reasons these days. Beth was the only one who was in your office the night your boss was leaned on, as I recall. To me, that's reason enough to be wary within itself."

"You don't trust her," Albright said once again.

Before Yew could respond, he looked up to see his wife and Beth return to the table. It was at that very moment that everything that his best friend and his father had been saying over the past twenty-four hours hit home.

His situation could very well turn dangerous.

***

ALBRIGHT AND BETH ARRIVED AT HIS PARENTS' HOUSE ON MICHIGAN AVENUE SHORTLY BEFORE ELEVEN. BETH STILL SEEMED REVVED UP, AT TWENTY-ONE, HER ENERGY LEVEL WAS PEAKING ON A SATURDAY NIGHT.

"If I'm lucky, I'll be home by one o'clock. Thanks for letting me hang around. It's been a great day."

"No problem. I enjoyed it myself. Whatever you do, Beth, drive carefully tonight. There's still a good possibility of more snow in the forecast."

"I will." Beth hugged Alan's neck, patted his shoulder, and climbed into her automobile, which had been warming up as they sat in the Big Jag, and backed out of the driveway. She waved goodbye and drove off.

Once inside, Albright focused on his job and went straight to work. He opened his briefcase, removed the notepad he'd written down Jennifer's birthday message on, and read it over once again.

He nearly told Beth about the note earlier that afternoon at Garcia's, but his depression over what had transpired between him and Jennifer following St. Andrews and the recurring pain Tolly Chamberlain caused him, prevented him from doing so.

Eulus's warning certainly kept the subject from being brought up that night.

***

THEY HAD PREPARED HIM FOR THE ABSOLUTE WORST. He had rehearsed time and time again what to do in a crisis situation, which he now found himself facing. Countless hours were spent instilling evasive action into the Scotsman.

The Israelis had trained Waters well.

All of this was unknown to Wee Ronald Mackey. The instant he stopped in his tracks and reached for his lighter, Waters was poised for action, although he did not move. His specialty was saving the life of the people he was hired to protect and, more importantly, his own life as well.

Waters carried no weapon. In Edinburgh, he felt no need

to do so. As the car came to a halt, he went to work instinctively. This was the first real predicament for him since his training, and one way or another; he wasn't going out like this.

Before Waters could make another move, Mackey whipped out a small caliber pistol, turned, and began firing at the approaching automobile. Waters watched in disbelief as the occupants slammed on their brakes, shifting into reverse, tires screeching, and disappeared into the darkness.

Waters maintained his position on the side of the wall, safely out of harm's way. Their prey, whoever they might have been, was long gone. Mackey calmly slipped his pistol back into his pocket and motioned with his head to Waters.

They did not need to be around when the police showed up.

"Don't worry; I fired over their heads."

Mackey found the supreme look of disbelief on the face of Dangerous Waters amusing.

Waters turned Mackey and shoved him playfully back first into the brick wall.

"Thank you."

"It's a little too close to Christmas for killing, isn't it?" Mackey said.

Somewhere in the darkness came the low whistle of a tugboat. Both men walked fast. The smells of the docks reminded Waters of where he had grown up in Dundee. His admiration of Wee Ronald Mackey was growing.

"I want you to find these Yanks for me. Period."

"What sort of payment are you talking about on this job?" he asked.

"Hundred quid."

Waters learned earlier that evening that Mackey's new trade was a chef. According to his acquaintance, Mackey's culinary skills were quite good. A chef's wage in Edinburgh, however, was simply was not adequate for the little man's munificent lifestyle.

"All right. One hundred quid, you say?"

Waters nodded in the twilight.

"You've got a deal. It's almost midnight. We need to go somewhere there's a phone. I've got some people to reach."

"One more thing," Waters said. "Once we find these Americans…"

"I forget all about you and me, is that it?"

"Right. Is that clear?"

Mackey looked around the deserted docks. There was no one. Any other man who had foiled an attempt on his life the way Mackey had done would be the recipient of serious gratitude by now. But this chap was different. Killing evidently meant nothing to him. Mackey knew enough about Waters' reputation to understand that only too well.

There was something about the way he spoke those last three words that sent a wave of unease through his bowels. He'd been around some of the hardest men in Britain while in the lockup. Even saw a man take another's life once. For the first time that evening, he was afraid. Waters was staring at him, awaiting an answer. In the semi-darkness, there was no way to distinguish the cherubic face and the warm smile. They were gone. What remained was a tanned, deathly masque. Hair sweeping about in the wintry air. His mouth was pursed shut, and he breathed through his nostrils, motionless.

Mackey nodded his head slowly.

"Relax," Waters said.

After lighting another cigarette and settling down, Mackey asked, "What has this Yank done?"

"He looked at my woman," Waters replied.

No wonder they call him Dangerous, Mackey thought.

***

ALBRIGHT SLEPT UNTIL EIGHT THE NEXT MORNING, A SUNDAY. As he lay in his old bedroom, he realized he had the house to himself. Years ago while in high school, he would come up with all kinds of ideas to do when his parents would leave him and Dennis alone for the weekend, only to have his square big brother back down for fear of catching it if the Colonel found out.

He smiled to himself as he arose. The heat had been turned down upstairs, and Albright shivered as he walked into the bathroom. The energy crisis, being what it was, one saved where one could, the Colonel was always saying these days. Once out of the bathroom, Albright turned the thermostat up to 74 degrees.

He walked downstairs to an empty kitchen and opened up the refrigerator. Full of food. He grabbed a pitcher of orange juice, grabbed a loaf of bread from the breadbox, and popped two slices in the toaster. He wandered into the dining room and flipped the radio on. He spread strawberry jam over his toast, drank two glasses of juice, and tried not to think about what this Christmas would be like with Tolly being out of his life.

No matter what happened to take his mind off of her, in spite of everything that was going on with Jennifer Tavistock, he could not stop thinking about her. He looked at the Christmas tree in his parents' house and looked back on Christmases past when he and his constant companion had spent at the Albrights' and the Chamberlains.' Like Albright, Tolly was from Urbana, and her parents lived near Yankee Ridge Elementary School. Tolly lived in a handsome apartment on State Street in Champaign, which she and Albright had planned on calling home until her sudden change of plans.

He thought of their honeymoon plans in Bermuda.

Eventually, his mind focused on what he had to do that morning. The first call of the morning was to Chicago. Once again, he awoke Beth Spencer. As promised, he was checking up to make sure she'd made it home okay.

She had.

Albright located his briefcase, found the number for the American Hospital in Paris, and placed the call.

"Jack Cashmore."

"Mr. Cashmore, My name is Alan Albright. How are you this morning?"

"Just fine, Mr. Albright," he said. "My wife said you would be calling."

"How is Stuart feeling today?"

"Better than ever. Want to speak to him?"

"Please."

"He's right here. Good to talk to you, young man."

"Nice talking with you, sir," Albright replied.

Seconds later, a weak voice was on the other end of the line. "Hello, Alan?"

"Stuart Cashmore! Do you remember me from St. Andrews?" he asked.

"I certainly do. We drank a couple of beers once at the Chelsea Drug Store while in London. You were the jock who kept talking about joining the Army when you got out of high school."

"Marines." Albright had totally forgotten the moment. "I am so sorry to hear what happened to you, man. How do you feel?"

"Blessed. Here by the grace of God. It's still a bit overwhelming, Alan, I..." Stuart began coughing abruptly, and it was several seconds before he could continue.

"Is this a good time?"

"Alan, every moment for the rest of my life will be a good time. I've seen the face of death, my friend, and he's not someone I care to see again anytime soon. What's going on?"

Albright realized his time with Stuart would be brief. "I've been hired to find someone who was with us, believe it or not, in St. Andrews. Her name is Jennifer Tavistock, and she's been missing for the past two years. Do you recall Jennifer? We hung around a bit together that summer."

"Oh, boy!" Cashmore exclaimed. "Oh, boy!"

Albright's greatest apprehension was materializing as he sat at his parents' dining room table.

"What is it, Stuart?"

"Oh, boy," he repeated.

"Come on, man; spit it out!"

There was a long silence on the other end of the phone. Finally, Cashmore said," Sure."

"What happened to you, Stuart? Your getting shot, that is. What does that have to do with Jennifer Tavistock?" Albright asked. He was not at all prepared for this conversation.

"In spite of what you're reading in the papers, it has nothing to do with either robbery or Iran. The reason I'm lying in this hospital right now is all about St. Andrews."

"What?"

"Yea. St. Andrews. Bit of a long story. My father has left to get something to eat, and there are no nurses in here, so I'm going to talk fast. About a year ago, something happened. We'd been here less than a week. Totally insignificant, it seemed to me at the time. I got a phone call from Jennifer Tavistock, requesting my help. She'd heard about my job somehow and called asking for a favor. No one knows this, Alan, so you must swear to me that this does not get out! No one, and I mean no one will know what's going on. It's too big."

Cashmore told Albright everything, leaving nothing out.

"I've got to find Jennifer," he said.

"That won't be easy. We don't have any idea where she is, or God help us, if she's even alive. Even if she is alive and in Scotland, that is a mighty big country. Plus, you'll stick out like a sore thumb."

"Stuart. I have one simple question. You have all the might of the United States of America at your fingertips. One phone call from you and you could have the President himself on the line. Why don't you come forward? This woman tried to kill you!"

"Yes, she did. Waited until now to do it, as well."

"Why don't you put the British authorities on her?"

"Proof, old man. Proof. She's the widow of one of the most respected members in the House of Commons. Everyone in Scotland, heck in Britain at that matter, thinks she is some sort of saint.

Besides, she's an accomplished and quite famous musician in her own right. Here's another point to take into consideration. Britain happens to be America's strongest ally. Think about that. Her new Prime Minister is a Tory. A female, at that. Perhaps if I had died, the truth may have emerged. But I'm still here, Alan. Battered up, yeah, but they keep telling me I'm going to live. Imagine what's going through the mind of our friend who tried to kill me. Which leads to the question you need to ask yourself, Alan Albright, does she know about you?"

Albright briefly explained what had happened to him at the Parker House.

"That's interesting. Could be someone threatening... or helping you."

"That's exactly what my best friend said," Albright replied.

"You've just answered my question, Alan. My guess is that it's a threat. I'm going to give you a piece of advice, Mr. Albright. From this point on, whatever you do must be done on your own. Listen to me. Don't trust her family one bit. It's clear that whoever called you is somehow connected with the Tavistocks. I don't claim to know everything there is to know about this business, but as the saying goes, I knew enough to be dangerous. Don't think for a moment they won't make a move on you."

"What about the guys who shot you?"

"Hired shooters. Amateurs at that. They don't have a clue as to who hired them or why. Even the French police, who are known for their persuasion techniques, have managed to come up with precious little. Sure, they'll get a conviction. But for obvious reasons, all the attention still is being focused on what's happening in Tehran right now. Believe me, I'll never let on otherwise." "Besides," Cashmore added," this could turn out to be the career move of a lifetime for me. If I live through this ordeal, I can practically write my own ticket. Providing the Democrats stay in power, that is."

Alan Albright laughed openly at the irony. Up until that morning, there had been uncertainty about exactly what had happened to Stuart. Now there was no doubt whatsoever.

"God bless you, Stuart Cashmore."

"God bless you, Alan Albright. You're really going to need it. In all truthfulness, I was willing to put this on the back burner for the moment. Jennifer Tavistock contacted me, and I was more than happy to lend a helping hand when she called me from St. Andrews. Seemed like the least I could do, considering all the fun we had ten years ago. We had a class together, you know. I contacted the American Embassy to get the ball rolling to help Jennifer, right? No problem, whatsoever. Merely needed to find out the owner of a piece of real estate. I insisted on having the information passed on to me personally. I never heard of the woman, nor her late husband. Then boom! Bullets everywhere. I'm still trying to cope with all of this. I suppose one day, when I'm healthy, I'll hunt her down and deal with it. Unless you get to her first. Even though they shot me full of holes, I still have a certain amount of assistance I can provide you. After all, we have the same rich uncle, don't we?"

"Do you feel safe?"

"Alan, right now I can honestly say that I'm one of the most protected men in the free world. She won't dare try anything else. Not on me, anyway. But I wish I could say the same thing for Jennifer Tavistock. Again, I hope she's still alive."

Cashmore left Albright with one more fragment of information. Nothing definite, but certainly a distinct possibility.

Albright took heed.

Everything had changed. Everything. The next thing Albright did was phone another hospital, Cook County General in Chicago.

"Hello? I'd like the room of Mr. Gerry Windham, please."

Two rings. Three rings. "Hello."

"Carol! It's Alan Albright. How's Gerry?"

"He's alive. How are you?"

"I've been better, gorgeous. It is absolutely vital that I speak with your husband. Please."

"Hello, Albright." It was the voice of Gerry Windham.

"It's all my fault, Gerry," said Albright. "What happened to you, that is."

"No, that's where you're wrong," Windham replied. "I brought this on myself. Betting on the Bears. Betting on the Browns. Betting on the Cowboys."

"These men who did this. What can you tell me?"

"Ah, what the heck. Someone bought my markers, Alan. I suppose I would have called you if you hadn't called me. And thanks for being there for Carol the other night. It's like this. Someone's awfully interested in you all of a sudden. Came by the office the night before I was jumped. Told me to get rid of you. Or else. Gave me 24 hours. I explained to them that I wouldn't be seeing you until after the first of the year. They bought into it because it was the truth. Your walking into my office two days later was the worst thing that could have happened. They came back that evening. Before I could tell them I'd done what they demanded, they accused me of playing games. That's when they tore into me."

"Get rid of me, as in firing me?" asked Albright.

"Yea."

"Did they give you a reason why I should be fired?"

"No," Gerry said. "That's the point. Like I told you, I said you wouldn't be back until after the first of the year."

Albright decided not to tell Gerry that Beth had overheard the entire conversation. He would leave that to Otto or Beth herself. He thought of the two people, both hospitalized, both fighting for their lives, both inexorably connected to Albright.

"I'll get them, Gerry. Whoever they were. I'll get them. I promise."

"You better hope they don't get you first. That's why I tried to warn you."

"You what?"

"I called you while you were in Boston."

The revelation caught Albright totally by surprise. Windham was the one!

"Impossible!"

"The Parker House Hotel. I guess it was shortly after eight o'clock Chicago time. Must have been around nine in Boston. 'Get out before it's too late!' I said, or something to that effect."

"But your voice—how did you change it?"

"In about three weeks, we'll be in the 1980's, Alan. Electronics is everything these days. I convinced our friends at your favorite R&B radio station that I was playing a joke on a friend who was about to get married. Nothing personal, of course. I called you from the station, speaking through a simple microphone with my slowed down and special effects added in their production studios.

"You were trying to warn me for my own good..."

"Yes, I was. A lot of good it did me."

"How much do you owe these people?"

Windham told him.

"Okay. Tell you what I'm going to do. I'll get you the money. Via Western Union. Call your bookie and tell him you have the cash. All of it. These men are only after you for one reason. Money. They were hired to lean on you to get to me. They can be bought off. Trust me. I'll have the cash for you first thing in the morning. Send the word out to whoever it is. And stay away from the Bears; they're not a good pick, Gerry."

Whatever's necessary, Dr. Tavistock had said. Bribes, payoffs, whatever. Dr. Tavistock, Albright said to himself, I am going to take you up on your suggestion.

By this time, Alan Albright's adrenalin was pumping at a racehorse level. Things were, inexplicably, falling into an order that were explaining not only why certain events had taken place, but who had orchestrated them. He studied the words given to him by Martyn Tavistock inside the card Jennifer sent to Claire.

To my wonderful mother.
Happy Birthday.
Love, Jennifer

That's what the message inside the card read. Tavistock repeated the words written on the back of the letter, and Albright carefully tried his analysis as to what she might have been saying.

Dear Mom and Dad,
   Try and understand why I've been so long without

contacting everyone. Times have been very busy, and you are justified at being angry. I hope to return to the United States very soon, and upon my return, I will explain everything.

Give my love to Roger. Don't forget to tell our next door neighbors that I can't wait to visit their shop when I return. Remember to give our uncle in Woods Hole my regards.

Jennifer.

Albright, up until that morning, had been so overwhelmed at the mere mention of a letter from Jennifer that he did not think of giving the note a final analysis until that moment. He looked at his watch. Tavistock may or may not be at church at this hour, he thought. With but one way to find out, Albright dialed the doctor's private line.

"Hello."

"Dr. Tavistock, it's Alan Albright. How are you this morning?"

"Wonderful," Tavistock answered. "Just reading the newspaper. Yourself?"

"I'm doing fine, thanks. I'm just calling to speak to you about Jennifer's note."

"Isn't that extraordinary?" Tavistock exclaimed.

"Yes, sir. By all means. I'm still having difficulty comprehending everything that's happened."

"What can I do for you this morning?" Tavistock asked.

"I read back what you gave me yesterday. On Mrs. Tavistock's birthday card, that is. I have two quick questions I'd like to ask, if I may."

"Sure, Alan. By the way, I like the way you've jumped right into this situation. That's good."

"Thanks. My first question, Dr. Tavistock, is about your next door neighbor's shop. Exactly what is that?"

"Oddest thing you mention that," said Tavistock. "The Bakers have a small wine establishment over in the North End. Just off Fulton Street."

"I see. Anything unusual about this place?"

"I shouldn't think so. Haven't been there in years. In fact, it's my understanding that the place hasn't been doing too well for some time now."

Albright wrote down everything Tavistock was saying. He had the handset against his left ear, held in place by his shoulder. "What's the name of the shop?"

"The name?" Dr. Tavistock paused. "Oh, of course. It's called The Castle."

"Right. One more question, sir. Jennifer's uncle in Woods Hole."

"Uncle Craig. Actually, he's my uncle, Jennifer's great-uncle. Likes to fish in the daytime and imbibe the rest of the time. Every family has one, I suppose."

"Is he a Tavistock?"

"Every bit."

Albright stayed on the phone with the doctor for several minutes before hanging up. He spent the next thirty minutes writing out each word that was on the card itself. He began by underlining every other word. Every third word. Every fifth word. None of it made any sense. Before hanging up, Tavistock had fetched his daughter's card from his wife and read it back to Albright once again, just to make sure there weren't any discrepancies.

There were not.

Albright spent the remaining hours of the morning and well into the afternoon going over theories and possibilities that might shed some light over what might have been in the note from Jennifer Tavistock. He began to have his doubts. Football was coming on the networks when Albright went to his room and brought down the batch of old papers that started the entire matter. He went through the papers until he found what he was searching for.

The map of Scotland, given to him by his father.

He searched the map over and found absolutely nothing that made any sense. Undaunted, he walked upstairs, showered and shaved, and pulled the Big Jag out of the garage. He drove towards campus town, stopping once again at the Illini Union. This time he did not go to the poolroom.

Instead, he found his way into the Illini Union Bookstore, which to his relief, was open for business.

The staff was most helpful. They pointed him in the direction of the travel section, where Albright bought everything the store had in the line of publications about Scotland.

Once leaving the Union, Albright drove to the Market Place Mall, where throngs of Christmas shoppers, many of them just getting out of church, were piling into the mall. Albright scoured every bookstore, finding information on Scotland. He returned home and continued his research.

He began with the Michelin map of Scotland he'd purchased in the Union bookstore. Twenty minutes later, he could not believe his luck.

It could be a coincidence. It was entirely possible he had an overactive imagination. There was, along the Great Road North, a small indication of a castle between the towns of Brora and Golspie.

He had not poured so thoroughly over a map since Viet Nam. Every square inch, beginning with the upper left-hand corner, was covered.

Albright's discovery made him shudder. He read Jennifer's words once again and scanned over the information Tavistock had given him that morning. The establishment the Bakers owned was called The Castle. The Tavistock uncle, who lived in Woods Hole. His first name was Craig.

The circle Albright had drawn in red ink on the Michelin map surrounded what could very well be what Jennifer was so cryptically indicating.

Castle Craig.

This was no coincidence at all. This, thought Albright, was what Jennifer Tavistock was trying to tell her family.

At that moment, the back door opened, startling Albright. He looked up to see his parents walking in, bags of groceries in hand.

"Give us a hand, will you?" barked the Colonel.

"Dad, have I got a lot to tell you," Albright said, as he walked out the door towards the open trunk of his father's Buick.

"Who's winning the Pittsburgh game?" the Colonel asked.

"Good question. How are my grandparents?"

"They're okay. So what exactly do you have to tell me this time that's so important?"

This was the perfect opportunity to test his theory out on his old man. If the Colonel bought into

Albright's scenario, which was unlikely, Albright knew he would truly be on to something.

After unloading groceries, they plopped down on the couch and began watching football. The

Colonel switched channels until he found the Steelers' game. "I'm listening," he said, and took a long swallow of iced tea.

Albright filled his father in on the past twenty-four tumultuous hours. The Colonel seemed most interested, quite understandably, in what Stuart Cashmore had to say. Not once did he pass off what Albright was saying as foolishness or paranoia. The Colonel had a habit, particularly when he was thinking, of stroking his chin. His interest in the Pittsburgh game slowly waned as his son continued.

The Colonel was seeing more and more of himself in his son of late. Over the past two weeks, especially. Albright was being very dispassionate and unruffled about this business. The Colonel liked that. He knew how agitated Alan could be at times. Albright gradually brought out everything Cashmore had told him about the widow. The Colonel just listened, not saying a word.

When Albright dropped the bombshell about Gerry Windam being the one who had phoned him at the Parker House, the Colonel was stunned. "Your boss? How did he do it?"

Albright gave him a full explanation. "That's not all, Dad. Check this out." He produced the Michelin map, which was spread out on the dining room table. He told his father once again about the birthday card Mrs. Tavistock received from Jennifer. He then brought forth his theory about where Jennifer might be, based on his conclusions about the references to the next-door neighbors and her great-uncle.

The Colonel stared at the red circle on the map. He sat quietly for several moments, absorbing it all in. When he did speak, it was in an uncharacteristically low tone of voice. "Kid, I must say you're a heck of a lot smarter than I sometimes give you credit for. I see why that doctor took you on to find his daughter. Are you aware of the danger you might be in?"

"Yea," Albright nodded. "I am now."

"So what are you going to do next?" asked the Colonel.

"You mean you believe me? My theory, that is?"

The Colonel nodded his head and said, still speaking in a low voice, "Yes, I believe you, son. How did you manage to figure it out in such short time?"

Albright walked over to the dining room table and returned to the couch. He handed over the neatly folded map his father had given him the night before he left for St. Andrews ten years earlier.

"This was my inspiration."

The Colonel opened the map up, smiled when he realized what it was, and proceeded to look it over." But there is nothing on this map."

"Exactly," said Albright. "That's what prompted me to go out and find a bigger one. I had no idea what I was looking for at first. No idea. I was clueless. When I discovered that castle, I honestly could not believe it myself. Until just now."

"How's that?"

"You believed in me, Dad; that's how. The most skeptical man on earth just bought in to my hypothesis. There's no way I can be wrong."

"Thank you for those generous words of support, my boy."

***

WEE RONALD MACKEY WASTED LITTLE TIME GETTING DOWN TO BUSINESS. He left the docks in his own automobile and returned to his flat, somewhat shaken about what had happened to them that evening. The next afternoon he left work early and returned home. He picked up the phone and went to work, calling the numerous contacts within the hotels of Edinburgh. All he had was Waters' description of the Campbells to go on. A quiet, timid, studious American husband and wife.

He began with the kitchen staff. Since it was a Sunday afternoon, he was in luck. Even though most establishments were busy at that hour, the key personnel were, indeed, working, and that was important. He left word that if anyone were to come up with a lead to give him a ring at his flat. His wife was gone to the bingo parlors until that evening, which was just as well. She had a knack for asking the wrong questions at the wrong time.

With Dangerous Waters involved in all of this, the less she was aware of the better.

By ten that evening, little solid information had turned

up. Americans were everywhere, just as Mackey had told Waters. The kitchen staff would make their subtle inquiries to the front desk. All very informal, of course. Mackey was very much a part of the culinary community in that city, and in spite of his occasional delvings into the world of crime, was well known and even liked by his peers. Besides, just about all of the better chefs understood only too well that one could easily be depending on the other in finding a job.

Mackey was enjoying a light jazz tune on the radio when his phone rang.

***

"SO WHAT HAPPENS NOW?" asked the Colonel.

"I make reservations and head to Scotland," Albright said.

"Got a plan?"

"No."

"Going in blind and cold, no strategy, no purpose, just driven by passion, is that it?"

What his old man was saying made sense.

"You need a plan of attack, son."

***

SUNDAY AFTERNOON FOR THE WIDOW WAS A TIME TO TAKE THINGS EASY. Dangerous Waters had risen by seven that morning, left the flat, and did not return until early afternoon. When he walked in, he seemed slightly agitated. He stood at a window overlooking the city, thoroughly frustrated at hearing nothing from Wee Ronald Mackey. He thought about the woman who was providing, however briefly, something long missing in his life. There was no need for him to be this over-protective in Edinburgh. Yet, the face of Whit Campbell kept him awake throughout the night.

The look the Yank gave them, as he was leaving the pub the previous afternoon, simply would not go away. The touch of the widow's hand upon his shoulder startled him. He turned around.

"This has been the best week I've had in a long time."

"Aye. That it has." He took her in his arms and suddenly came to the realization that he would not think twice about doing whatever was necessary to protect this woman. Waters was not an expert when it came to literary matters. Hardly. There were, however, plenty of people in Edinburgh who might be.

"Where do you keep your phone book, darling?"

Waters grabbed the phone book and started going down the list of bookstores. He rang three of them, asking the same question, all to no avail. The fourth bookseller nailed it. There is, the gentleman on the other end of the phone flatly stated, but one copy of *The Red Book of Clanranald*.

A manuscript.

Meaning these librarians were either misinformed as to their Scottish history or flat-out liars.

***

SHE INSISTED THEY STAY ONE MORE NIGHT. After all, Charlotte had reminded Daniel this was her very first trip to anywhere. The bags were packed, the hotel bill would be settled when they reached the lobby, and Harper managed to contain his rage towards the widow. He knew where she lived. He knew what she did. He even knew where she liked to dine. Everyone in Edinburgh knew her name.

"Sure, Charlotte. One more night."

Harper realized that it would not be as easy as he

thought. Initially, he planned on returning to

Edinburgh somehow following the Christmas holidays. He phoned the hotel desk to find out if there would be any problems with them staying one more night. There were none. He ordered room service with a request for a local newspaper. Fifteen minutes later, Harper was convinced what he needed to do. There would be no delays.

Tonight, he would keep the promise he had made that June morning to Leigh Katalinic.

***

THE FACT THAT ALAN ALBRIGHT AND TOLLY CHAMBERLAIN HAD MADE PLANS TO TRAVEL TO BERMUDA FOR THEIR HONEYMOON PROVED TO BE THE TURNING POINT. Both had obtained passports: Tolly for the first time, Albright for the second, since his first one had expired. The honeymoon never took place; but, nevertheless, he was set for international travel.

He was traveling lightly. Very lightly. It was not the easiest thing to book short notice travel so close to Christmas time, but the fact that his sister-in-law, Dennis' wife, was herself a travel agent made the task enormously easier. Bonnie Albright made reservations on TWA for Tuesday evening, a non-stop flight leaving Chicago at 7:30 and arriving in London the following morning. She also made reservations at the Quaich for a total of seven days.

The Colonel and his son stayed up well past midnight that Sunday evening planning strategies.

He insisted that Alan follow his plan to the last detail.

No heroics.

Ten years earlier, it would have been a simple process to pack a suitcase with a weapon inside.

The string of hijackings of the early seventies, however, did away with that option. Albright owned a Smith and

Wesson .38 caliber revolver which, when he traveled in the Big Jag, he kept locked in his glove compartment. Albright argued in favor of packing the revolver anyway. His father strongly disagreed. Getting arrested by the British authorities on a weapons charge was no way to get a mission off to a good start.

Be patient, the Colonel insisted. The first thing the Colonel did Monday morning was to cancel his nine and eleven o'clock classes. Personal leave, he told them. He pulled out his leather directory, a gift some years back from Blakelyn, and made close to a dozen phone calls. Since his only afternoon class met at three o'clock, he had the better part of the day. The clock read 1:48 when the Colonel took the long distance call.

While the Colonel was placing his calls, his son continued reading the literature he'd purchased the day before about Scotland. He was in his room studying the Michelin map when he looked up to see his father standing in the door.

"I did it. Took some time but I managed to contact someone I know over there. I'm not sure of what sort of weapon you'll be getting, but it will be there for you when you arrive in Edinburgh."

He gave him the instructions.

"Thanks, Dad. Thanks for everything."

"Sure, kid," he said, punching his son on the shoulder. The Colonel set his foot down on the edge of the bed. "So tell me about more about this girl you're risking your life over."

***

THE TIP GIVEN HIM BY STUART CASHMORE WAS AS VALUABLE AS ANY LEAD ALBRIGHT HAD PICKED UP THUS FAR. Albright landed at Turnhouse Airport in Edinburgh at 11:07 that Wednesday morning. He had notified Dr. Tavistock of his plans the afternoon prior to his departure. The doctor seemed excited. Albright asked Tavistock how his wife felt about the trip. Claire, he was told, had no objections.

Just find Jennifer, she insisted.

Albright also touched bases with Ed Napier. Napier seemed more excited about the news than the Tavistocks. The policeman wished him the best of luck, and Albright promised him an update as soon as he discovered anything—if he discovered anything.

None of the information Albright had picked from Stuart Cashmore or Gerry Windham was shared with anyone in Boston. Tavistock assured Albright that the directorate to use whatever funds necessary to find Jennifer applied to Scotland as well as the United States. Tavistock insisted that Albright withdraw as much cash as he needed from the American Express card once reaching Scotland, and Albright followed his advice.

To be in the United Kingdom for the first time in a decade, in spite of the importance of his mission, proved to be quite stimulating for Alan Albright. Unknown to the American, the British currency had gone through significant changes since the summer of 1969. Once Albright managed to get past that small adjustment, he used the American Express card to withdraw five thousand pounds in large notes.

The doctor had told him not to worry about keeping up with an expense report, but Albright was having none of that. From the moment his plane left O'Hare, he began an itemization report in a small black calendar notebook he kept in his breast pocket.

***

"HE'S GONE WHERE?" Claire Tavistock asked, barely containing her anger.

Martyn Tavistock calmly answered, "To Scotland."

"You told him to go—just like that?"

"I suppose I did," he said, never so much as raising his voice.

Mrs. Woodbury cleared the breakfast dishes from the dining room table, oblivious to the argument. Like most people who made their living serving others in the capacity in which she did, she had heard these arguments before.

Claire Tavistock was in a near rage. "You're wasting good money sending him on a wild goose chase!"

"Have any better ideas, Claire? All the detectives we've hired have been discouraged from going abroad. All because of your so-called theories. I've had it with your antagonism. You should be receptive to what this kid is doing. After all, they were in St. Andrews together. You heard him last week. You know what he wants to do and you know why. But that's not good enough for you, is it?"

"Jennifer is here somewhere in the United States," Claire said. "You know it and I know it."

This was not the first time they'd had this argument. When the Boston Police initially took on the investigation, Detective Ed Napier had given the Tavistocks a report. In it were the conclusions the policeman had reached, based on exhaustive investigation by him and his colleagues in BPD. What Napier had said was that Jennifer was, in all probability, gone abroad. Most likely to Scotland.

Claire Tavistock discounted the theory at once and was using her tremendous clout in the city to put pressure on Ed Napier. She had succeeded. He had been relegated to street gang duty, which ultimately made his decision to finish law school a top priority.

Tavistock was unmoved. "I don't know anything, Claire. Except that this Albright fellow is sharp. Quick. Tough. We haven't even given him a chance, have we?"

"Why did you tell him that he had my blessing?"

"Because deep down, I believe, darling, you know I'm right," he said, turning on the Tavistock charm that his wife, even in the worst of times, could not resist. He put down his copy of the *Boston Globe,* arose from the dining room table, and walked over to where Claire was sitting. She looked beautiful in her pink nightclothes. Mrs. Woodbury had taken the dishes away and they were alone. Tavistock reached down and opened up her robe.

"Stop it! Mrs. Woodbury will be in here any minute," said Claire. As he bent over and kissed her, she wanted to push her husband away but could not. She opened her mouth to say something but found herself unable to keep from kissing the one man who could somehow woo away even her deepest anger.

***

EDINBURGH AIRPORT WAS MODERATELY BUSY FOR A WEDNESDAY MORNING. Albright looked the part of a well-dressed businessman. Black woolen overcoat. Black suit. Polished shoes. Briefcase in hand, he found his way to the car rental desk. Once there, he produced his Illinois driver's license, passport, and credit card to the friendly young girl at the counter. They discussed automobiles. Not being entirely familiar with British vehicles, Albright took the advice from the clerk and settled on, naturally, a shiny black 1980 Jaguar XJ6. As Albright signed the rental car agreement, he took note of the listed appointments. Luxury Saloon. He smiled at the opportunity to drive another Jaguar.

Yes, he told the clerk, he was aware of the fact that the British drove on the opposite side of the road than the Americans. He thanked the clerk, who blushed slightly as he gave her a wink, picked up the keys, and headed towards his hired automobile. He opened up the trunk, placed his gear inside, and closed it shut. He automatically opened the door on the left side of the black Jaguar, which in this particular case turned out to be the passenger door. Undaunted, he placed his briefcase in the front seat and walked around and hopped in on the driver's side.

It was a cloudy morning in Edinburgh. If his father was correct, his contact would be waiting for him not far from the airport. Albright started up the new Jag, completely impressed with the state-of-the-art luxury features, not at all used to shifting into first with his left hand, and eased into the flow of traffic that was exiting the airport.

Albright drove north from the airport across the River Forth toward his destination. The highways were clear, and he understood that in the month of December anything could happen as far as the weather was concerned. A light snow began falling in the early afternoon when Albright drove into the city of Perth. He was overwhelmed at the fact that he was actually back in Scotland after more than a decade of being away. The Scottish countryside was beautiful, and each town and village he drove past was unique and, in some instances, even familiar.

All he had to go by was the name his father had given him. Once inside the city limits of Perth, Albright found a parking space near the city centre. He walked over to the bright red call box, stepped inside, and fumbled with the silver he'd received at the airport. The number he had memorized on the plane, but he pulled out his calendar just to make sure.

"Swithuns." The vice was that of a man, strong Scottish accent.

"My name is Alan Albright."

"Yes, Mr. Albright." No how do you do. No welcome to Scotland. Just straight business.

"I understand you have something for me."

"Where are you?" the man asked.

Perth was a beautiful city. A group of schoolchildren passed by on foot followed by their teachers. They seemed to be around nine or ten and were terribly excited about the prospect of wherever it was they were going. Perhaps it was the fact they were out of school in the middle of the day. He noticed that, underneath their coats and jackets, they all wore school uniforms. Albright gave his location as best he could as the throng of kids walked past the call box.

"Wait at the call box for me. Are you driving?" Swithuns asked.

"I'm in a black... Jaguar." Albright had to look at the side of his rented car to remember what model it was.

"Wait inside your vehicle. I'll be there shortly." The man hung up.

Albright climbed back in the Jaguar and warmed up. He turned on the car radio; and for the first time since his departure in 1969, he heard Radio One on the BBC. There was a steady stream of traffic where Albright sat; and as he opened his Michelin map, he looked like an ordinary tourist parked on the side of the road, which, in a matter of speaking, was exactly what he was.

The tap at his window startled him. He looked to see a middle-aged woman, white haired with a bonnet on her head, standing next to his vehicle. She was smiling at him. He rolled down the window.

"Hi," Albright said, "how are you?"

"Quite well, dear, and yourself?"

The timing couldn't be worse, Albright thought. If his contact were to drive up and see this kind lady with all of her benevolence and cheerfulness, it might scare him off. "Just fine, ma'am. May I help you?"

"Here's your Christmas gift that you ordered, son." The woman produced a brightly wrapped box, red paper, white bow and ribbon. She handed it over.

"I'm afraid there's some mistake, Miss..." He looked down and noticed the small paper tag on the upper corner of the box. The calligraphy was beautiful. When he read it, his heart nearly stopped. It read, simply, Swithuns. He looked up at the woman, bundled up from the cold, her joyful smiling face looking down at him and said, "Merry

Christmas."

"And a Merry Christmas to you, dear!" she exclaimed, when she realized the bundle of money Albright had slipped her consisted of twenty pound notes.

The exchange took less than one minute. Albright drove off slowly, well aware that if the box contained what his father promised him, it would could get him into very serious trouble with the British police. Gun laws in that country were stringent, and the fact that he was a foreigner would certainly make life difficult for him.

He drove on for some forty miles until he saw a clearing on the side of the road. He pulled over and turned the engine off. There was no one within sight. He grabbed the box and hurriedly tore off the ribbon and paper.

Inside the paper was a heavy cardboard box. Albright gleamed with anticipation. The Colonel had not let him down. The box was tightly sealed with packing tape, and it took him several moments to get it open, since he did not even carry a pocketknife. What would it be, he thought to himself. A Smith & Wesson? A Browning? Perhaps a Sig. The last strip of tape finally loose, Albright breathed deeply and opened the box.

What he beheld took away his breath. Brand new. Wrapped in its original plastic. At first, he was in disbelief but then thought carefully about what his old man told him about it being the best weapon for this job. He picked it up and examined it. It was certainly a weapon he had to agree, and at that moment, to his surprise, his level of confidence rose dramatically.

There was a small card, lavender in color, in the box along with the weapon. The writing was identical to the card that had been on the outside.

It read: *A man's heart deviseth his way: but the LORD directeth his steps.* Proverbs 16:9.

The weapon the Colonel had referred to all along was not what Albright had anticipated. What lay inside of the box the kind old woman had given Albright was not a Colt but a Scofield edition of the King James Version.

A Holy Bible.

It was a beautiful piece of craftsmanship. He picked up the Bible and realized there was an envelope at the bottom of the box. Albright opened it up and discovered it was a list of verses from the Scriptures.

Albright continued his drive, Bible in his passenger's seat next to his briefcase, through the wintry

Highland countryside until he reached the city of Inverness. He pulled into a British Petrol filling station, tanked up the Jaguar, and asked for a recommendation of a good hotel. The attendant referred him to one such place in the Fairfield Road.

Trafford Bank.

No, he said, a hotel, not a place to exchange money. The attendant, having lots of patience with visiting foreigners, explained to Albright that Trafford Bank was indeed what he was in search of—a guest house. He left the American with directions on how to find the Fairfield Road, which Albright did with little effort.

Trafford Bank was a handsome structure. Albright drove the Jaguar to the front of the villa, realizing at that moment just how tired he actually was. He expected the rates to be higher than they actually were; and once shown to his room, he was quite impressed at the good taste of the inn. His room had all he needed. TV. Telephone. Radio. Most importantly, his room had central heating.

Albright was surprised to find fresh fruit awaiting him in his room, as well. The first thing he did was change out of his suit, draw a hot bath, and relax. He had been going non-stop since Tuesday morning, Chicago time. He did manage to sleep a few hours on the flight to Scotland, but his hectic day, long driving, and jet lag made the bed seem even more inviting.

He had not eaten anything that day. He decided at this

point that food was as important as sleep.

After putting on fresh clothing, Albright found the food in the restaurant to be quite appealing. As an American, he was being viewed as something of a novelty. He struck up a conversation with a family at the next table, who were on holiday from the south of England. Later on, they had a nightcap together in the bar.

Whisky, naturally.

By eight o'clock Albright had retired to his room and was fast asleep.

***

WHEN HE AWOKE THE NEXT MORNING, FOLLOWING A RESTUL SLEEP, ALBRIGHT SPENT SEVERAL MOMENTS JUST ADMIRING HIS HOTEL ROOM. He had been on the road from virtually the moment he landed in Edinburgh, and it felt good being able to relax and appreciate his surroundings. To his surprise, snow had fallen overnight. What he saw as he looked out of his hotel window was nothing less than astounding. The ground was covered in white. Just under an inch had fallen overnight. Being so close to Christmas made it even more incredible.

Albright left his room shortly after ten. Prior to his departure, he placed a long distance call to his old man. That was a mistake in itself, for the Colonel took the call at 4:16 in the morning. The first thing asked about was the meeting with Swithuns. Albright explained the shock he'd experienced with the elderly woman. The elder Albright did what he did for a reason. He knew his son well enough that had he not suggested that a weapon would be waiting for him in Scotland, Alan would have gone against the Colonel's judgment and packed his own gun.

This would have certainly been discovered by customs.

Once Albright expressed the significance of the power of the Good Book, the Colonel sounded not only impressed but relieved. They talked for several minutes about courage and faith. Albright rang off by thanking his father once again for his assistance, asked his dad to give Albright's love to his mother, and assured the Colonel that he would be careful.

Since he had checked in for two days, Albright took a little time out to enjoy his surroundings.

He had actually traveled little over the past couple of years, since he and Tolly had been saving not only for their honeymoon but his marriage as well. Since there was no trip to Bermuda, Boston was the first time he'd been anywhere that year. Boston. Seemed like a lifetime ago. He thought of the Thanksgiving weekend at his parents' house that started all of this.

Jennifer Tavistock's name in the middle of the second page of the tattered list.

What a whirlwind of events, Albright thought. Voices and faces out of the past had come forward with staggering consequences. Claire Tavistock's birthday card in particular. The information compiled from that note either could very well lead Albright to where Jennifer might be.

Albright had a name given to him by Stuart Cashmore. A professor of history at the University of St. Andrews. By all likelihood, the man knows nothing, Cashmore had said. Inside the lobby of Trafford Bank was a pay phone. From that location, Albright had awakened the Colonel. From that location, Albright called directory assistance for St. Andrews.

Professor Ross Burnham.

The phone call with the professor gave Albright an unexpected triumphant boost of confidence. Castle Craig was the place! He could not believe his deductions had been correct. Albright was less assured of accomplishing his mission when he learned of Professor Burnham's brush with death.

Unlike the Scottish police, he had little doubt about the cause of the accident.

When asked about the Widow, Burnham did not mince words. "Be very careful," he warned. "Be careful approaching Castle Craig, and be even more aware of what awaits strangers."

Albright laid the Bible on the passenger seat as he started up the Jaguar that morning.

This was it. If Jennifer were indeed there (and he was convinced she was), she was coming out and she was coming out alive. A fine snow was blowing out of the north. The dawn gave way to cloudy, depressing skies overhead. He had phoned his old man the night before retiring. The Colonel had repeatedly stressed that the plan should be diligently adhered to.

No exceptions.

Albright was completely unaware that anyone in Scotland, other than Swithuns and Ross Burnham, knew of his existence. He was incognizant that the widow had been tipped off to his inquiries regarding Jennifer Tavistock. What ultimately saved his life was the fact that he had listened to his best friend as well as his father in sharing his plans for international travel with no one.

The card from Jennifer had dramatically changed his initial plan of attack. He never got around to contacting Franconia Edge in Newport. Nor Roger Tav. For reasons he could not put a finger on, there was no one in this entire business whom he felt at ease with.

Ed Napier, being the sole exception. Over breakfast at the Parker House, Napier had explained his hunch that Scotland would be the first place Napier would look if he were in Albright's shoes. How prophetic, thought Albright. It was Napier, who introduced the first doubts in Albright's mind, regarding the Tavistocks and their desire to find Jennifer. Claire Tavistock, in particular.

Albright sped along the Great Road North, making the adjustment to the British motorways quite well. This new Jaguar was not the Big Jag by any means, but it was comfortable and powerful. He estimated his arrival at Castle

Craig at two hours. As he drove, he thought about how he would get Jennifer out of Britain. If she were being held against her will, chances were her captors would not be willing to hand her passport over. That could mean complications.

Remember the plan, the Colonel had said. As he approached the village of Golspie, Albright looked for a place to pull over and rest. He saw a Shell station and pulled over to tank up. The wind, whipping off the North Sea, was formidable, and few people were stirring. He got out, tanked up, and walked inside to pay for his gas. The lady inside was young and almost pretty. Not homely, but not beautiful. She had short hair and lots of makeup, something he was noticing about Scottish women. He could barely understand what she was saying.

"An American," she said with a big smile. The way she spoke was totally different that the accents of Edinburgh and noticeably different from the people in Perth and Inverness.

"That's right. I'm looking for a room. I've been driving all day and I'm rather tired."

"Are you now?" she asked, her R's rolling softly off her tongue. "Just up the road there's an inn.

It's a wee bit small, but it serves a great Scotch broth and the rooms are comfortable. And affordable."

"Looks like I'm in luck," Albright said, unfolding a ten pound note. The total for the gas was seven pounds fifty. He gave her the remainder as a tip and walked out.

The hotel also housed a restaurant, which had been open less than an hour when Albright walked in. He sat down at a table and ordered black coffee and Shepherd's Pie, something he'd been turned on to at St. Andrews. The restaurant was quaint. Locals, mostly. Friendly people. Christmas decorations were everywhere. As he sipped at his coffee, he noticed a shabbily dressed man walk in. Unshaven. Ruddy-faced. Probably early sixties. To his surprise, after greeting the few people in the restaurant, who paid him little, if any, attention, he nodded a greeting to Albright.

The man was obviously not a regular, as he too looked out of place, getting unfavorable glances from a number of the patrons. He ordered a coffee for himself and, to Albright's surprise, asked if he could join him.

Albright said, "Sure. Why not?"

Remember the plan, Albright told himself.

The old man spoke with a bear-like growl. Ever word, in fact, came out sounding like an animal noise. When asked what brought him to the north of Scotland, Albright answered, "Ghosts. I'm a writer for a Chicago magazine, working on an article about the legends of Great Britain."

"Are you, indeed?"

"Yes. I plan on heading up to Thurso and Wick before returning to the states," he lied. "When

I was here years ago, as a teenager, I was told a tale about a woman who was able to turn herself into some kind of beast."

"Ah. That would be the Witch O' Glen Tromie."

"You've heard of it then?"

Christmas was just ten days away; and as he sat across from the old man, whose name he didn't catch, the Christmas spirit was beginning to catch on.

"Have another coffee on me, lad, and I'll tell ye the full story."

"Thanks, but this one should last me for a while."

"Suit yourself. Now it's like this, it is. There was once a cat, a great black one, mind ye, and it gave the shepherds a world o' trouble."

As the old man's eyes remained on Albright, and like the gas station attendant, he rolled his R's as he spoke.

"This cat was something to reckon with, they say. Bigger than any other cat 'round these parts, son. Terrorizing 'em, he was. He would steal out into the night, black as the wind and quiet as yer very shadow. He went all over, killing sheep wherever they might be found, getting his fill and leaving the carcasses for the carrion. Horrible, it was."

"One night the farmers from all 'round came together and decided they'd had enough of this cat. Came from all over to a meeting in *Bail Ur An T-Sleibth,* Newtonmore they call it nowadays, and talked up a storm about what to do with this devilish cat."

"Sure you'll not have another coffee? Very well. Now let me see, where was I? Ah, yes. Had a meeting, they did. I hear tell it was one o' the Camerons, who thought up bringing out the dogs on the hellish monster. Aye, laddie, a monster it was. It wasn't a work o' the Lord, ye can be sure. And don't think I'm takin' the piss out o' ye, 'cause it's true. Every word o' it."

Albright took a long sip of his hot coffee, glanced at his watch, and sat back in the upright chair.

"Nothing happened for months. Some had even given up on the beast until one night, middle o' winter it was, on a farm near Glen Tromie, when a shepherd's pack o' dogs began howlin' like they was mad. Aye, laddie, they'd gotten wind o' the cat this time!"

"The men turned the dogs loose on this beast, but it managed to get away with no more than a wee wound on its hind leg. Ah, but wee wounds leave wee pints o' blood, don't they? The night was all over when the hunt ended and lo! Where d'ye think it ended, eh? In a cave? Not on yer life, my boy. The trail ended at the door o' a house. A house!"

"Well, they were surprised. No, they were bloody shocked when they looked inside this house.

It was all dark and quiet in there, not a soul to be seen but a young woman. Ah, but that wern't the half o' it, laddie. Now don't think I'm making this up 'cause I ain't. That poor woman was bleedin'! From the leg, she was! Aye, there was nae doubt about it, laddie; that hellish cat and the young lass was one and the same!"

"Wanted to do her in then and there, they did, but no one would'a believed 'em. 'Right,' they said, 'we'll try her for what she is, a witch.' Tried her they did in Glen Tromie and sentenced her to the stake. But mark my word, laddie. Ye haven't heard the last o' it. Drink up, my boy, and brace yerself."

"Her final words were strong ones. 'Listen fools!' she shouted, 'I fear neither you nor your cursed stake. Once and for all, you shall fell my power from now till kingdom come! On the hill where my house now rests, from this day forth let no tree flourish. Ever! Their roots shall wither and their leaves shall crumble to the earth! I may die, but my dying will endure. Forever!' "

At that point, Albright, who was rather enjoying the old man's company, took note. The tale brought him back to the legend he and Jennifer and all the American students had heard the decade before from the clan chieftain while touring the Scottish Highlands.

Like many of the Americans on the coach that summer, he found the tale amusing but hardly believable. What this man was saying was almost identical to what he'd been told back in 1969.

Nothing, Albright thought, was without possibility during this trip.

"Ask anyone 'round Glen Tromie, and they'll tell ye the same thing as I," he said. "Even

Captain MacPherson himself will back me up. Aye, his great-great grandfather himself was in on the hunt. If it's a lie, it was them who told it, not me."

***

JACKSON, TENNESSEE

AS ALBRIGHT STRUGGLED WITH HIS BELIEF IN GHOSTS IN THE NORTH OF SCOTLAND, THE MID-

AFTERNOON SUNSHINE BROUGHT LITTLE WARMTH TO THE PEOPLE OF JACKSON, TENNESSEE. Mid-December was normally moderate as far as temperatures were concerned, but a stubborn cold front brought gusty winds of up to 25 miles an hour, dropping the wind chill into the low teens.

"Mr. Lowery?"

The man in the tan smock looked up, wiped a smudge of glue off his fingers, and nodded. "I'm Lowery," he said.

"It is my understanding that you are the best around when it comes to picture framing."

"That's a matter of opinion," Lowery replied. If he did not like Yankees coming around all the time, Lowery certainly did not like foreigners in his establishment. The man had some sort of British accent. "I simply do my best."

The elderly man who stood before Polk Lowery removed his glasses and began to clean them with a burgundy silk handkerchief he removed from his breast pocket. The spectacles had left two red marks on the bridge of his long nose. He cleaned the glasses quickly, placed them back on his face, and beamed at once when noticing a picture hanging on the far wall.

"Nathan Bedford Forrest! An excellent rendition, I should say. Are you a student of the American Civil War, Mr. Lowery?"

Lowery nodded as he looked the old man over. "Yea. I suppose we all are around here. What is it I can do for you, Mister...?"

"Dyson will do, young man. I am looking for artwork," he said, getting straight to the point.

"American work. Like that excellent Ralph McDonald print over here."

Dyson pointed to an unframed print of wild geese in flight at sunset.

"I suppose I can do that," Polk replied. Take his money

and send him on his way. "Anything else?"

"Yes, there is. I have a job for you," Dyson said. "I shall pay you for your skills, but I shall pay you even more for your discretion. I have a document. A document that I want to be able to go to sleep, knowing it will be in a secure and quiet place. It's taken me all morning, in fact, to decide just how I wanted it done."

Lowery looked into the old man's eyes. They were brown, narrow and, more than anything else, they were pitiless. Whoever this British gentleman was that had entered his premises was as suspicious and untrustworthy as anyone who had ever entered his shop. At that moment, Lowery became aware of the song coming from the ceiling speakers from radio station WKIR. It was "Season of the Witch," a Donovan tune with that unmistakably slow introduction.

Dyson extended a hand across the counter. Lowery shook it, an unexpectedly powerful handshake coming from a man of Dyson's years. This was his first encounter with a Brit in his shop. The films he'd seen portrayed them either suave and sophisticated or dashing and happy-go-lucky. Lowery's impression of this Dyson was nothing like he expected of the British.

"Show me your very best molding, laddie."

"That's Lowery," he said. At least, he's spending money, Polk thought. Of the framing shops in Jackson, his was hardly the largest and was certainly not the most expensive. Others were doing twice the volume as Polk's Picture Framing and were charging their customers a hefty price. What Lowery was doing was primarily getting by.

His business was located in a small red brick building on Airways Boulevard near State Street. For the past two years, Lowery had supplemented his income by teaching an art class at Lambuth College one night a week. In three months, he and his wife would be expecting their second child. His wife, a dental hygienist, actually made more money than Polk. It hardly mattered. They were happy and living well within their means. Most of Polk's money, in fact, went into his massive record collection. He had hundreds of LP titles. So much so that whenever he went into Sounza Muzik, he would invariably drop anywhere from ten to twenty bucks a pop on rock and roll. Doors. Eagles.

Marshall Tucker. Charlie Daniels Band.

Anything but disco.

Polk looked over his samples. He took down an L-shaped, gold-painted wood piece and laid it on the table.

"How's this?" he asked.

As Dyson picked up the molding, Lowery noticed the splotches on the hands of the old man. His nose was long and bent. His thinning white hair was parted from right to left and curled upward across his ears and at the base of his neck. There was clearly something about this Ambrose Dyson that didn't sit too well with the framer.

Dyson looked the molding over carefully and said, "This will do admirably. How soon can you get to it?"

"Christmas, as you might imagine, means more business for us here. The earliest I could to it would be ten days."

"Tomorrow morning," countered Dyson.

Lowery laughed openly. "That might be a bit difficult. There's a small matter of these work orders that were here before you, sir."

"How much?" Dyson asked.

"How much for what?"

"To get what I need by tomorrow morning."

"I don't think you understand me, sir. I have customers who were here first."

"Five hundred?"

Lowery shook his head.

"Very well. One thousand dollars."

Polk thought about the repair work he'd been putting off on his Ford pickup. About getting his wife that watch she'd seen in the window of Robert's Jewelers. About getting his dad a new workbench from Sears.

"Noon tomorrow. It'll be ready. I will need five hundred as a down payment."

He watched Dyson reach inside his heavy overcoat and pull out a billfold. Without so much as batting an eye, he peeled off five one hundred dollar bills and laid them on the counter. He looked up at Lowery with a look that seemed to say, "Don't waste my time, country boy."

The money remained on the counter. Lowery did not take too well to the man from Scotland or the attitude in his shop. He was used to Jacksonians, people who spoke to you in a friendly manner when they walked in, not like this British snob.

"See you tomorrow, then," said Dyson.

"Right. One more thing," Lowery said. "I need a bit of information for my invoice. At what address can I reach you if there's a problem?"

"Hopefully, there won't be any problems," Dyson said. "In the unlikely event, I can be reached at the Holiday Inn." He gave him the room number and walked out.

Lowery looked at his watch. He picked up the money, deposited it in the cash register, and pulled off his smock. As was his habit, each day at noon Lowery would lock up his framing shop and have lunch at the Little Rebel. Today was the exception—thanks to a surge in holiday customers, as his watch read 2:10. It was a short drive, and Lowery found himself zipping up his black leather jacket in a useless effort to stave off the bitter cold. As a southerner, it was something he simply was not used to.

He drove down Airways to the Little Rebel and pulled his four-wheel drive into the parking lot.

As he walked in, he smelled the unmistakable odor of chili and hamburgers. A Don Williams' tune was playing on the jukebox. The usual lunchtime crowd of construction workers, utility linemen, policemen, and other members of the working class all trying to grab a bite of lunch before returning to the grind was long gone.

Lowery sat down at the counter and ordered a cheeseburger and a large unsweetened tea. To his left (the only other person at the counter) sat a Madison County Deputy. He'd seen him in there a time or two. He nodded a hello. The deputy did likewise. One thing Lowery did not do much of was hang too close to the law. Most of his friends were bikers, others members of the counter-culture who preferred their homegrown to Marlboros.

What had transpired in his shop was troubling him more and more. His instincts were telling him that whatever it was he had been hired to do was trouble, and that was practically unthinkable for a man who framed pictures and needlepoint for a living. Plus, for some unknown reason, his conscience was beginning to gnaw away at him.

The deputy was in uniform, a middle-aged man with a hard face and inquisitive eyes. He was working on a bowl of chili and a small Coca-Cola to wash it down. He looked at the young man next to him. Long hair. Black leather jacket. Beard. Hands of a working man. Something was on his mind, the deputy perceived.

Lowery's meal arrived. He took a swallow of iced tea, still contemplating what to do.

"You look like a man with something on your mind, partner," said the deputy, looking straight ahead.

Lowery turned to the deputy with a surprised expression on his face. "It's known as hunger," he replied, taking his first bite out of the cheeseburger.

"I know who you are. My wife is taking one of your night classes this semester. I usually pick her up and I've seen you a couple of times. Alice Chappel's her name. My name's Elford," he said.

"Well, small world." This deputy may not be too bad after all, thought Lowery. "Pleased to meet you, Deputy Chappel."

"Elford."

"Polk Lowery." Since they were both eating, they did not

shake hands. It seemed odd for Lowery to be having a conversation with a man with a badge. Throughout his young life, he'd had his share of run-ins—nothing major, but enough for him to develop fear and suspicion of policemen.

***

AS LOWERY SAT AT THE COUNTER EATING HIS LUNCH AT THE LITTLE REBEL, AMBROSE DYSON HIMSELF WAS BACK AT HIS MOTEL. He had driven his rented Bonneville back to the Holiday Inn after dropping off the parchment. He returned to his room, where his wife sat reading a copy of *The Jackson Sun*. He closed the motel door, grunted a hello to his wife, picked up the phone, and asked for the overseas operator.

***

EDINBURGH

ACROSS THE ATLANTIC THE LIGHTS FROM THE CHRISTMAS TREE TWINKLED FROM ACROSS THE ROOM. DANGEROUS WATERS LAY ON HIS BACK ON THE COUCH, READING A MAGAZINE, ENJOYING THE SOFT PIANO MUSIC. The widow sat at her piano, wearing nothing but a sheer silky gown, new sheet music before her. She was playing Chopin's "Nocturne Number 19 in E Minor." Suddenly, out of nowhere, she broke into "The Holly and the Ivy." Perhaps it was the sight of the Christmas tree. It may have been Waters' presence. In any case, the sound of the Christmas music brought Waters over to the piano.

"I still don't understand," he said.

"What don't you understand, my darling?" asked the

widow.

"How I ended up with someone as wonderful as you," he said, stroking her hair. "I'm a common ex-criminal, little education, from the sewers of Dundee."

"You're doing all right for yourself, James."

"But I don't have all of those things your posh friends have. I'm no industrialist. I'm not a peer.

I have no titles, no land, and no wealth."

The widow continued playing her Christmas carol and said, "That's precisely the reason we ended up together. You have something they lack. Strength. Courage. You make your living putting your very life on the line protecting others. You are dauntless."

"Besides," she chuckled, "you didn't get your nickname from being soft, did you?"

"If you have no objections," Waters said, "I'll just pop round the shop to get a sporting sheet. For some reason, I'm feeling lucky tonight."

He kissed her forehead, grabbed his leather jacket, and headed out the door. Moments later, the phone rang.

"Hello."

"It's Dyson, ma'am."

"You're late and I can't talk long. I'm expecting James to return any moment. Be quick about it."

"I'm finally in Tennessee. Beastly place, really."

"Is it ready?" she asked.

"Not quite. But it will be. Noon tomorrow, actually."

"What about the name?"

"I plan on visiting the public library this afternoon. The people in this town are without a clue.

We've nothing, whatsoever, to worry about. I've never seen a lot like this. They are far and away the most trusting people you'll find anywhere. If I don't have any luck at the library, I've looked into a couple of local historical groups that might help us."

"Don't be too presumptuous about those Americans, Mr. Dyson. Remember, tell them only what is absolutely necessary," said the widow.

"What about the girl?" he asked.

"Don't you concern yourself with her! Your business is in America, not the castle. She's being well-guarded."

"Are you certain? For some time I've had my doubts about the others," growled Dyson.

"Duncanson, particularly. He's a bit too weak. Perhaps you would have been better off sending him to America and leaving me at the castle."

"Would you be questioning my judgment, Mr. Dyson? I sent you to America for a reason. From this point on, our timing is critical. You have little time to get what I need, so I suggest you get to it straight away. I must go." The line went dead.

***

"THIS IS TOO INCREDIBLE," WAS ALL ALBRIGHT COULD BRING HIMSELF TO SAY.

"Aye. Incredible it is, laddie. You still think I'm taking the piss out o' ye. Can't blame ye, I can't. An old geezer tells ye about the Witch o' Glen Tromie. Laddie, there's tales about this land that'll keep ye from sleeping tonight! Aye, I can't tell 'em like the others.

Like Angus, there." Duncan motioned with his head towards a robust man across the pub which led Albright to believe that the old man did know at least one person in the establishment. "Why, if some o' the old ones were about tonight, you'd be right afraid. So afraid ye wouldn't even return to yer hotel room by yerself."

"Speaking of which, that's where I'm headed, my friend. Thanks for the chat," Albright said, "but I must be moving on."

Since the coffees were already paid for, Albright left a ten pound note on the table as a tip. He returned to his room, made himself comfortable, and lay down on the bed. As he had done the previous night in Scotland, Albright placed the framed photograph of Jennifer given to him by her father, on the bedside table. There was no doubt about how he felt about her. In spite of what had transpired between them ten years ago, his heart still belonged to Tolly Chamberlain.

Jennifer's face stared back at him. The photographer had highlighted the right side of her face. Her cheek bones had just a hint of rouge about them. The trademark dimple in her chin reminded Albright how he used to tease her about it. She never failed to have a comeback line, no matter how much he tried to insult her. Her wisecracks were never coarse; in fact, Albright could not remember ever hearing Jennifer curse.

His old man had asked him. Eulus and Madelyn had asked him. Everyone wanted to know the same thing; why was he doing this? As he drifted off into sleep, Albright thought of the last time he saw Jennifer Tavistock, walking away with her parents at JFK Airport.

There were tears in her eyes.

***

JENNIFER TAVISTOCK REMOVED THE BROADAXE FROM ITS HIDING PLACE. It was the only solution for her escape. The man she feared the most had gone away, leaving the best opportunity for her chance at freedom. Jennifer had no money. No passport. Her best hope was to get out of the castle, find a telephone, and call her family in Boston.

She learned from Seth Duncanson that Dyson and his wife had gone off for a couple of days. That meant that Abigail Overby and Duncanson were the only ones left. That put the odds that much in her favor. Duncanson had agreed to send the birthday card to her contact in America, who hopefully had delivered it to Boston by now.

Was she wasting her time? Would the message in her mother's card go unnoticed?

It was entirely possible.

In all of her 27 years, Jennifer Tavistock had only had two serious physical encounters. The first was in 1973 when she had to fight off a would-be purse snatcher at an outdoor jazz concert in the Boston Common. The other was when she got into a fight with a girl while at college over the use of her hair dryer. Both had minimal consequences and had ended as briefly as they had begun.

She considered neither incident to be a life-or-death matter.

Could she actually do bodily harm to her captors?

Absolutely.

A mere search for her ancestors had led her to this. Captivity. She discovered the intent of the parents of Malcolm Fraser and in doing so uncovered an unknown morsel of history in the process.

The fate of Malcolm's mother left her saddened and angry. Such an unfortunate way to go at such a young age. She died at 24, three years younger than Jennifer's present age. As for Malcolm's father, that was the real shocker. Not so much who he was, but what he had done.

***

AS HE WAS LEAVING THE LITTLE REBEL, DEPUTY CHAPPEL LEFT ONE OF HIS BUSINESS CARDS ON THE TABLE.

Once the cop was gone, Lowery, as he finished off his cheeseburger, thought long and hard about what to do. Never in his life had he turned anyone in for anything. He was not a snitch; in fact, he hated informants. Yet what Lowery and millions of other Americans felt in the last days of 1979 was a feeling of unprecedented patriotic fervor, resulting from the seizure of American hostages in Iran. Had the visit from the foreigner been under different circumstances, his reaction would have been less temperamental, less vehement.

But these were different times. What was it that Jim Morrison sang about? "The future's uncertain and the end is always near..." Lowery picked up the business card and slipped it in the front pocket of his Levi's. He thanked the cook as always and walked out to his truck. He drove past his shop along Airways eastward until it turned into Main. Once reaching the stoplight at Main and Highland, he started looking for a place to park. He circled the block only once, got lucky, and parked his four wheel drive in front of the Madison County Courthouse.

The Madison County Sheriff's Department in 1979 was located in the basement of the Courthouse. In the early 1990's, most of the offices moved to the Old Union University campus on College; but on that cold December afternoon, the man Lowery was searching for was in the Courthouse. He walked in through the south entrance and took the stairs to the basement and turned left. His mind had been made up. He walked through the doorway of the Sheriff's Department and looked around. A uniformed female dispatch sat at her desk talking on the phone. She eyed Lowery with indifference and kept talking. Polk waited patiently until she hung up the phone.

"May I help you sir?" she asked.

"Yes, ma'am, I hope so. I'm here to see Deputy Chappel."

"One moment, please." She picked up the phone once again and dialed a number.

Lowery felt uncomfortable standing there, facing this woman. He slipped his hands into the pocket of his jeans and stared down at his boots as he awaited the arrival of the deputy. He heard the sound of a door closing down the corridor and looked up to see the man who had been seated next to him at the Little Rebel earlier that afternoon.

"Mr. Lowery, how are you?" Chappel asked as he shook Lowery's hand. "Come this way."

Lowery followed Chappel down a narrow hallway into a tiny office.

"Can I get you a cup of coffee or anything?" asked the deputy.

"Sure. One sugar, please." Lowery sat down on a dark green chair across from Chappel's desk.

He noticed the awards on the wall in front of him. Judging from the hunting trophies in the small office, Chappel was obviously a fairly good deer hunter. Chappel reappeared with the coffee and sat down across from Lowery.

***

WHILE POLK LOWERY SAT IN THE OFFICES OF THE MADISON COUNTY SHERIFF'S DEPARTMENT, AMBROSE AND CORRA DYSON TURNED THEIR RENTED PONTIAC BONNIVILLE ONTO NORTHWOOD AVENUE. Located just off Highland Avenue in central Jackson, the wide boulevard was home to some of the more prestigious domiciles and well-to-do families the city of Jackson had to offer. Even Dyson was impressed at the splendor. The house they were in search of was near the end of the dead-end street. Dyson himself was still adjusting to driving in America and found some of the habits of the locals a bit archaic. The mighty oak trees were bare in the winter sunlight; and as he pulled to the side of the avenue, he noticed the house in point still had a yard full of leaves.

Their appointment was for 3:30. Dyson was dressed in a brown suit and wore a gray woolen overcoat and an expensive black Homburg. Dyson wore the hat turned to one side, and his age and size made the Scotsman look not unlike an undertaker. Corra was dressed handsomely in a dark blue suit with a long suede overcoat to keep the Tennessee winds off her back. They walked up the steps; and before Dyson could reach the doorbell, the door opened.

***

ELFORD CHAPPEL SAT BACK IN HIS CHAIR, TOOK A SWALLOW OF COFFEE, AND REMOVED A NOTEPAD FROM THE DRAWER ON THE RIGHT SIDE OF HIS DESK. He extracted a pen from his breast pocket and placed it on the pad.

"What's on your mind, Mr. Lowery?" he asked.

"It's gonna sound stupid to you," Lowery said. "Real stupid. But at least hear me out. I'm sure you'll think nothing of it."

"Don't be so negative," replied the deputy, doing his best to reassure the man sitting across from him. As a law enforcement officer, establishing trust was vital.

"I run a picture-framing shop on Airways. Guy walks into my place this morning. He's a foreigner.

Some kind of Englishman or something. All proper like, if you follow me. Looks around my shop.

He had some kind of document with him. Real old and fragile-like. Keeps it wrapped in plastic inside of this fancy leather portfolio."

Chappel worked furiously as he wrote down what Lowery was telling him.

"He made a few comments about some prints in my shop. I was intrigued that he actually knew who N.B. Forrest was."

"Did he leave his name?" Chappel asked.

"Yea. Said his name was Ambrose Dyson. He wanted this work done by tomorrow, which is next to impossible. This close to Christmas—I'm totally covered up."

"I can imagine." Chappel watched the man across from

him closely. As Lowery talked about what had transpired in his shop, he began to loosen up a bit. His voice was a bit high to begin with, and he had a habit of raising his voice even higher whenever he was making his point. His hands were rough and calloused. Lowery's face, what Chappel could see of it through his beard, was covered with acne burn.

"Anyway, this guy says he needs this document framed by tomorrow. I tell him there ain't no way.

No way! He insists on tomorrow, so we start talking money. He asks me what it will take. Knowing it was out of the question, I tell him ten big ones."

"One thousand dollars?" asked Chappel.

"10-4," he nodded. "One thousand dollars. Reaches down and pulls out a roll as big as anything

I've ever seen and peels off five one-hundred dollar bills as a down payment, with the remainder upon completion. Doesn't bat an eye."

"What's a job like that normally worth?"

"By the time you look at labor, materials, especially molding, which is going through the roof these days, probably two, two-and-a-quarter."

***

IN THE FIREPLACE, THE BLAZING OAK LOGS GAVE OFF NOT ONLY WARMTH BUT AN ESSENSE OF THE HOLIDAY SEASON INSIDE THE NORTHWOOD RESIDENCE. The Dysons had been among the first guests to arrive at the afternoon meeting. The hostess prepared enough food for a professional football team that afternoon: Swedish meatballs, vegetable medley, and fresh strawberries, dipped in chocolate, regular and decaffeinated coffee, wine, and hot cider. Dyson carried on his Scottish theatrics to the hilt, and most of those present drank it all up.

A bald man in his early forties sat with the host, thin and conservatively dressed, a banker known for his extensive knowledge of local history. He answered in detail the Scotsman's questions about the early days of Jackson. Told Dyson about the early days of Jackson, including the story about Davy Crockett.

"So Crockett," said the banker, "told the crowd in front of the Madison County Courthouse "You can all go to hell because I'm going to Texas." True story."

Dyson shook his head in genuine amazement. This American food still took some getting used to.

For the better part of the afternoon, he had experienced what he believed to be heartburn from the spicy southern cooking over the past couple of days.

"King of the wild frontier, wasn't he?" said Dyson with a moderate dose of sarcasm.

At that moment, the doorbell rang. The maid, a slim, uniformed Black woman in her fifties opened the door to two men. One was a bespectacled chap in a crew cut and ill-fitting suit, wearing no overcoat. He spoke his greetings in a manner that was indicative of a Jacksonian with money.

The other man was an inch or so taller, thick dark hair, steely-eyed, more reserved.

The hostess introduced the British couple to the newcomers. The man wearing glasses was the Madison County Executive. He extended a hand at once, shaking hands with Dyson and Corra. The second man nodded a hello. It was Dyson, who had to extend his hand to the stranger, something not lost on those around them. He did at least manage a smile when he was introduced to Corra.

After all, the mayor of Jackson was a gentleman.

Dyson stared at the mayor of Jackson for a brief moment. Temperaments must be controlled, he told himself as he forced a smile and extended his own hand. The mayor stared back at him.

"Mr. Dyson is visiting us all the way from Scotland," said the hostess to the mayor.

"Scotland? You're a long way from home," the mayor said, eyes remaining on Dyson.

"Aye."

"Enjoy your visit to Jackson," said the mayor.

***

WATERS LAY SLEEPING WITH THE WIDOW AT HIS SIDE. He had dozed off less than an hour earlier. She had fallen asleep, as was her habit, in less than ten minutes. When the phone rang, it was he who was the first to wake up. Considering the situation, he never answered her calls. She was, after all, a lady of considerable influence in the city of Edinburgh.

When she realized the phone was ringing, the first thing she did after turning on the lamp was to look at the clock. It was late. She knew it had to be important. This was the first time this had happened with Dangerous Waters present. Three rings. Four. Five. Waters bore something of a puzzled expression. She wasn't answering her telephone. The widow realized something must be done.

"Hello."

"I have news for you. Most urgent. Concerning Alan Albright."

The widow knew her lover's ability at reading situations. She knew her inability at hiding her emotions around him. This was something she had been dreading since his return to Scotland. Yet, what was happening with the Secret could not be taken half-heartedly.

"Indeed. What sort of musical opportunity is it?" she said, hoping to maintain her composure.

"Albright is in Scotland. Arrived sometime this week. I told you he might be trouble."

"Very well. Thank you for your call."

Dangerous Waters was not a jealous person. His relationship with the Widow, at least up to this point, had been one step past the casual level. His new crime-free life kept him away from commitments. North Africa today, who-knows-where tomorrow. Her odd behavior, since his return, was acceptable.

After all, she was a musician.

Wee Ronald's failure to track down the Americans angered him. Being back in Scotland had given him a break from the constant vigilance of guarding against terrorists. He simply did not have his guard on, for there was no reason to do so in a town like Edinburgh. He lay back against the pillow and ran a hand down her back. He understood there was a good possibility there could be others. That was the understanding. He knew perfectly well the conversation had nothing to do with music but accepted the fact that in a little more than a fortnight he'd be out of Scotland. She did, after all, have the right to do as she pleased.

"I have something to tell you," she said looking into his eyes.

Waters braced himself.

"It's possible that someone may be trying to harm me. An American. It's quite a long story, David. I will tell you that his name is Alan Albright, and he's somewhere in Scotland."

"Of course! Those Yanks we saw in the pub!"

The widow had given no more thought to the mild-mannered couple.

"The librarians?" she asked.

"The same," Waters replied. "I have something to tell you. Since we ran into them the other day, I've had a bad feeling about the both of them. Put a man on their trail the other night while you were out. There's been no word."

The widow lied to Waters for the first time since they

met. She regretted it at once. What was happening to her? The Secret of St. Andrews took precedence over everything.

Even love.

Why then was she feeling remorse over what she had done? More importantly, was it possible the soft-spoken book hound sitting in the pub could have been Alan Albright? Her first thought was frightening... Castle Craig and its occupant.

"I have an idea where he might be, darling."

"Where?"

One lie always leads to another, she thought. Of all times for this to be happening! There was no time to come up with an alternative plan. This was it. Tell Waters everything or tell him another lie.

Risk him not going along with what needed to be done to protect the secret.

The Secret of St. Andrews.

This was no time to be indecisive. She loved him and knew his capabilities when it came to something like this. If Alan Albright had been in that pub yesterday, she had little choice. Stuart Cashmore still lived. Ross Burnham still lived. Neal Edwards still lived. They lived because the work had been carried out by sloppy amateurs. The man who lay before her had been trained by the very best in the world. His work would be anything but sloppy.

"Answer my question. Where?" said Waters.

"The Highlands. Inside a castle along the Great Road North."

"You believe that's where this...what did you say his name was?"

"Alan Albright."

"Then what are we waiting for? Let's go find him and have a wee chat."

***

CHAPPELL AGREED TO MEET POLK LOWERY AT HIS SHOP IN TEN MINUTES. He had to let his supervisor know about an unresolved matter about transferring prisoners from the county jail to the Madison County Penal Farm. That took five minutes. Once he left the courthouse, he stepped into his automobile, turned onto Highland Avenue, and headed south. He was tired. It took him less than five minutes to reach the picture framing shop. He entered the business, at once impressed at the quality of work that Chappell had done.

"Hey there," said Chappell, back at work already on a needlepoint of the Nativity Scene.

"Nice place you got here. Good work." Chappell noticed the Nathan Bedford Forrest print Lowery had spoken of earlier.

Lowery entered the back of his shop and returned with a bundle loosely covered in brown wrapping paper.

"This is the thousand dollar work order," he said as he unraveled the paper.

***

THE CONVERSATIONS WERE LESS FORMAL. Many of the Jacksonians, primarily those associated with the Jackson Symphony, were warming up to the Dysons. The hostess told Dyson all about the early families who settled in the area.

"Of course, Jackson wasn't the original name of our community. Prior to its present name, Jackson was known as Port Jackson," said the hostess.

"And before that," said the banker," this place was known as Alexandria."

For the first time that afternoon, Corra Dyson showed a glimpse of her true disposition, dropping the empty china cup, once filled with hot cider, onto the floor. She sat up from the couch and gazed at the banker in disbelief.

"I'm so sorry," Cora said. "What did you say?" she asked.

Dyson remained calm, placing his hand over hers. He did not approve whatsoever of his wife showing any sudden interest in something that might give away their plans.

"Alexandria."

"But what about the other Alexandria, Tennessee?" asked Corra, ignoring her husband's warning.

"That's a small town in East Tennessee. Established for some years."

"Do you know when Jackson was referred to as Alexandria?" said Corra.

The banker nodded.

"For a brief time in 1821."

The Dysons looked at each other and smiled. The maid promptly appeared to clean up the broken cup and saucer. There was no need to waste any more of their valuable time with these people. In spite of the fact the gathering was for their benefit, Dyson's mind raced, looking for a reason to return to the Holiday Inn.

The mayor of Jackson stood quietly nearby. He had listened intently to every word that had come out of the mouths of the foreigners since entering the premises, and by no means did the mayor miss Corra Dyson's reaction to the Alexandria reference. Even though he was engaged in light conversation with one of the guests, his ears were trained on what was coming from the mouths of the foreigners.

***

LOWERY REMOVED THE PAPER. Two thick pieces of cardboard were covered with masking tape.

Whatever was inside the document was no more than eight by ten inches by Chappell's estimation, one-half to three-quarters of an inch thick. Lowery picked up a box cutter and cautiously sliced through the tape.

To their surprise, there was velvet inside. Neatly folded, bright and smooth, red velvet. Lowery looked at Chappell. He guardedly opened it up. What lay underneath took away the breath of both men.

***

A PAGE FROM A LETTER, WRITING ON ONE SIDE ONLY, LAY BEFORE THEM. The age of the document was impossible to determine. The handwriting was not in English.

"So you've not seen this before?" Chappell concluded.

"Have not," Lowery said. "I was in somewhat of a hurry. His attitude did nothing to help matters."

Lowery did not touch the document. He spent a few moments rummaging through his tools until he found a dust-covered, heavily-scratched magnifying glass. He held it over the document, examining the edges of the paper in particular.

"This is fascinating. Here, take a look." Lowery handed the magnifying glass over to the policeman.

Chappell did not observe the letter as a law enforcement officer. The man was in awe, near disbelief.

It read:

'Tha mi sgìth. Ged bu mhath leam fois bho m' eallach, cha téid mi nas fhaide.

Chan eil mi ag iarraidh ach sìth agus mathanas bho Dhia

airson na rinn mi.

Tha m' anam ann an àmhghar. Chaidh mi an toir air rud nach ghabhadh ghlacadh.

Tha mi air na bliadhnaichean mu dheireadh de m' bheatha a chur seachad agus an crùn coirbidh orm.

Thàinig mi dhan tìr ùr, a dh'Alexandria, is mi 'n dòchas dèanamh nach ghabhadh dèanamh.

Tha mi air gabhail ri daoine mì-ionraic, air gèilleadh gu beartas an t-saoghail.

Mura faigh mi mathanas bho Dhia, chan eil m' fhulangas ach air tòiseachadh.

Air sgàth mo shannt, tha an dùthaich air fad a-nis air a sgriosadh.

Bidh Alba, àite mo ghaol 's mo bhreith, fo riaghladh nan Sasannach gu bràth agus tha mi ag iarraidh

mathanas airson a' pheacaidh as motha a rinn mi na mo bheatha airson'

The chirography ended abruptly.

***

DANIEL HARPER AND CHARLOTTE HEALY HAD BEEN BUSY SINCE THEIR ARRIVAL IN SCOTLAND. They had followed closely the people who came and went from the Rothesay Gardens residence. One such person was Rosie Carstairs. They knew she arrived around eight each morning and left between three and four. Daniel and Charlotte casually hopped on the same bus one afternoon and observed the stop where Rosie departed.

Earlier that evening, in one of the city's hot dancing clubs; two young people were dancing the night away, oblivious to anything but the driving dance music, mostly coming from the States. They had indifferently found their way to the table, directly behind the group of young women who were making the most of the evening. A small white handbag was casually removed from under the table by the young woman while the girls were on the floor. Keys were removed, and the bag returned to its original spot. The couple literally danced their way out of the club and into the cold Scottish night.

They returned by taxi to the Rothesay Hotel, changed into clothing they had purchased earlier that day, and departed once again onto the streets of Edinburgh. Their destination: Rothesay Gardens.

Once and for all, Harper was going to accomplish, with no mercy, what he had set out to do.

***

IT TOOK SEVERAL KNOCKS TO AWAKEN ALAN ALBRIGHT. He opened his eyes in the darkness, looking around. The soft knocking persisted. Fully awake, Albright realized just where he was. Who would be knocking at his door at this hour? He sensed trouble. There was no weapon to speak of in the room, save breaking off a leg from the round bedside table. There was a way out of the windows if necessary. Before destroying the furniture or diving out the window, he decided to find out just who was at the door.

"Yea," was all he said.

"Mr. Albright?" said the man's voice on the other side of the door.

"Who wants to know?"

Albright had turned on the light in his hotel room. He was wearing pajamas and stood in his bare feet on the cold hardwood floor.

"It's the chap who bought you the coffee tonight. The storyteller."

A relieved Albright opened the door. He was understandably edgy, judging what he was about to do the next morning. The old man stood there, bent over.

"What do you want, man?" he asked.

"Five minutes of your time."

What the heck, Albright thought.

"Why not?" he said.

Once the door closed, everything changed. The shabbily dressed commoner looked Albright in the eyes, extending a hand.

"Never told you my name. Troy Swithuns," he said, as he shook hands with the American. "Been in touch with your father since you left Urbana."

The accent was still there, but there was something familiar about the way he spoke. Traces of central Illinois were mixed in with the Highland brogue.

"I know what you were expecting at our rendezvous. A firearm. Your dad and I spoke of this, and I convinced him not to give you what you asked for. I am here to help you, however. I know what you came here for, and I sort of know why. I also consulted with Tom about your plan of attack."

"How do you know my father?" asked the clearly dumbfounded Albright.

"Grew up in Gibson City, not five miles from your grandparents' farm. Your dad is about ten years or so younger than I am. I married the woman of my dreams back in '44. Scottish lass. War ended. I stayed. I've been back to Illinois periodically over the years. Got a call from your old man the other day asking for my help. How could I say no?"

***

THE TWO DECIDED A STRIKE IN THE DARKNESS WAS OUT OF THE QUESTION. So was sleep as far as Albright was concerned. They would move at dawn.

This changed everything. He had an ally. Someone he could trust. Someone from his own state, even.

Swithuns briefed Albright on some last-minute modifications on the original strategy on rescuing Jennifer Tavistock. Getting in, finding Jennifer, dealing with whoever was inside Castle Craig, and getting not only away from the castle but out of Scotland was discussed.

Chances are she would be without a passport. Particularly, if it was determined she was being held against her will, and that was, to both of them, a fore-drawn conclusion.

"I realize I dominated our conversation tonight with all of that ghost story mumbo-jumbo," said Swithuns. "But that was for your own good. Whether you realize it or not, you probably didn't get three words in edgewise and that's good. You are so close to ground zero, there's a good chance that who was in that pub tonight could very well be in that castle tomorrow."

Albright failed to take that into consideration. The Colonel had advised him over and over about him not being careless. An American, in spite of his cover story, could draw suspicion.

"What do you do for a living?" asked Albright.

"I'm a minister. Methodist Church. Got the calling in '55, believe it or not. I also do a bit of theater as well in Perth and surrounding areas. Nothing major, just small groups. I'm doing Scrooge at the moment."

He looked at Albright and correctly knew what he was thinking.

"The shabby look, right?"

"Yea...."

"The Scots are a bit different from others. I'm not what you call a dandy, but in this case I wanted to be convincing. As I mentioned, we don't know who was in that place tonight."

"So you've been tailing me since Perth?"

"I have, indeed," answered Swithuns. "I gave Tommy my word I'd look out for you while you were over here. Just look at me as your surrogate Scottish father."

"But you're American."

They talked about God. About life. About Jennifer's escape. Swithuns was an interesting old fellow. His plan was daring, but brilliant. They discussed all possibilities about what would transpire the following morning. Best-case, worst-case. They were former soldiers from two different eras, two different wars. There could be repercussions affecting the old man, since he would be remaining in Scotland. He understood that if he were traced back to Perth there could be trouble. Particularly being a man of the cloth.

It was a chance Swithuns was willing to take.

***

FATE OFTEN INTERVENES WHERE THE BEST OF PLANS DO NOT. Had Charlotte Healy not pleaded with Harper to stay one more night in Edinburgh, they would not have found themselves in Rothesay Gardens, Alan Albright's plan would have blown wide open, and the future of Jennifer Tavistock would have been very much in doubt.

Rosie Carstairs had six keys on her ring. Harper, by simple deduction, concluded that three of the keys would not fit the residence of the widow. Dressed completely in black, he and Charlotte waited until they entered the inside of the building, which happened to be unlocked, before donning their black ski masks.

They would have to determine in a hurry which was the correct key. Harper was operating purely on anger and emotion. They climbed the two flights of stairs—two at a time. The hallway outside of her apartment had ample light being cast from an antique brass fixture, something

Charlotte admired as they approached the widow's front door.

Harper had enough sense not to fumble with the keys. They were separated from the key ring, and he carried all three of them inside of his fist. After examining the single deadbolt lock, he removed the first key, making certain it was going in the right way. He turned the lock. Nothing. He removed the first key, stuck it in his back pocket, and tried the second. Still, no luck. Harper was beginning to think that Rosie Carstairs did not have a key to her boss's residence after all, until he tried the third and final key.

It worked. He opened the door in a rush, and within seconds he and Charlotte were inside the widow's apartment.

***

"WELL, WHAT DO YOU MAKE OF THIS?" ASKED THE MADISON COUNTY DEPUTY.

"Darned strange," Lowery answered. "I'm beginning to understand why he wanted to spend that sort of money."

Chappell shook his head as he looked around the shop. Sawdust covered the floor in Chappel's work area behind the counter. The front of the shop, where customers browsed, surprisingly was pristine. The work orders impaled by the thin metal spike on Lowery's desk indicated to the policeman just how busy this guy was these days. After all, it was Christmas.

"At the present time, there's nothing we can do," Chappel said, noticing the look of frustration clouding over the young man's face. "This man has done nothing, unless some crime is associated with this...."

A smile crossing Chappel's face made Lowery understand what the deputy was thinking.

"You think this... thing might be hot?" Lowery asked.

"It's entirely possible," said Chappel. "Just think. Why come all the way to Jackson, Tennessee, to have this work framed? Not that you aren't capable of doing as good a job as anyone else, I might add."

"I see your point."

"Good. Don't need any hard feelings. This Dyson fellow could just as easily have had this done anywhere. That's what I don't understand."

"I have an idea."

"Which is?"

"There's a guy over at Lambuth who might be able to tell us more about this gem. Classes are out, but I know just where to find him. What d'you think?"

"Let's go."

***

WATERS WAS REACHING FOR HIS SUITCASE WHEN HE HEARD SOMETHING. The bedroom door was open at the moment, and Waters knew at once that something downstairs was wrong.

"Don't move!" he whispered.

The first thing Waters did was to reach over and turn off the lamplight next to their bed. He was familiar enough with the apartment by now to find his way about in the dark. He had no idea how many intruders there might be, how well trained they were, or what sort of weapons they might be carrying. Protecting the widow was crucial. Taking immediate action, he grabbed her arm and led her across the room. He opened the closet door and pushed her inside, closing it behind her. No more than ten seconds had transpired since he first heard the downstairs noise.

For the second time since returning to Scotland, he was frustrated at having no weapon. He remembered seeing a pair of scissors at her vanity. Not particularly effective against guns but something that would take a man down at close range. The darkness was his advantage but would be short-lived. Striking first would give Waters somewhat of an edge on the intruder or intruders. That worried him. How many were there and what were they carrying?

Harper acted quickly in the darkness. He popped on the flashlight and found the outline of a piano.

His target.

Before entering, Harper had managed to loosen the gallon container of adhesion promoter he carried. Once inside, he wasted no time in prying the can open, moving to the piano, and pouring the thick, gooey substance into the Widow's beloved piano. When Harper saw the light flick on at the top of the stairs, he heard Charlotte shout, "This is for Leigh Katalinic! And The Secret of St. Andrews!" They dropped the can and disappeared through the door.

To Waters' complete surprise, the voice was that of a woman. The accent—distinctly American. He dropped the scissors at the landing, took the stairs two at a time, ignored the piano, and ran to the door.

They were gone.

The piano was fully engulfed in the adhesion promoter.

The Widow emerged from the bedroom, ran down the stairs, and screamed in horror at the sight of her adored piano.

"No!" she shouted.

Once he realized there was no catching the intruders, Waters closed the door to the apartment. He picked up the telephone and called the Edinburgh police, gave them the address, and hung up. He walked across the floor and stood at the Widow's side.

Ten minutes later, two policemen stood at the opened door.

Waters hadn't said much through all of this. The acrid odor from the adhesion promoter permeated up from the clearly ruined piano, and Waters realized to his dismay that his hunch had been right after all, as the two Americans had been up to no good from the beginning. What he learned from the Israelis about suspicions actually was paying off. Prepared as he was at all times in Morocco, this situation in Edinburgh was the second example of not being too careful under any conditions and not trusting anyone anytime.

Without that training, without that discipline, he never would have thought twice about those people in the pub again, which could have very well cost him and the Widow their lives.

The cops walked in, saying nothing at first, eyeing what was left of the piano and the people in front of them. A shirtless man wearing only a pair of trousers, noticeable scar running across one shoulder was standing next to an older, beautiful woman, wearing nothing but a white silk robe.

"Thank you for coming," said the Widow. "As you can see, we had unexpected guests tonight. Two Americans broke into my home and destroyed my piano." Her rage, in spite of the thing she cherished the most now destroyed, was well under control. The man whom the Widow believed to be Alan Albright had walked into her home, right into her hands. It was the perfect opportunity to finish him once and for all, and he had managed to get away.

"Very good of you to get here when you did," Waters said.

He was puzzled at the inexplicable rantings of the American girl. These people were on the offensive with a mission that he was certain did not include boosting the sterling silverware. Neighbors from nearby apartments peered out of cracked doors at the commotion. Her name meant nothing to the lead policeman at first. Then, after noticing a photograph of her late husband on a nearby end table, it hit him. He realized this woman was someone well-known, respected, and revered.

She was a luminary—a beautiful one at that.

David Waters did not ring a bell to the policemen either. The only concern Waters had, in fact, was for the Widow. She did not need the heat from being associated with a man of his background. The report took ten minutes to complete. The American burglars were good. The only thing left was the empty metal container of adhesion promoter. The Widow at one point nearly revealed that the male suspect's name was Alan Albright but, at the last moment, decided against it. All kinds of hooliganism was going on in Edinburgh these days, concluded the policemen.

As a precaution, the fire department was summoned and showed up some twenty minutes later to make certain the substance in the piano was not a fire hazard.

Once they were alone, she was relieved. Until she saw the look in her lover's eyes. Gone was the concern and warmth he had shown her since arriving from Morocco. What was left hardly could be defined as adoration.

"Now is a good time to tell me what's really going on," he said.

***

Daniel Harper and Charlotte Healy had done it. Harper concocted a number of things he'd wanted to do to the Widow; but because of the woman he loved, he chose this option.

To destroy her piano. Harper was well aware of the damage the adhesive had done. He had used the product often and knew of its uses.

"Tomorrow we return to West Virginia, sweetheart. Now let's get back to the hotel. We need to pack."

***

THE MAN LOWERY NEEDED TO SEE LIVED IN A BRICK SINGLE-STORY HOUSE ON ROLAND AVENUE, JUST EAST OF LAMBUTH BOULEVARD. He was in his early forties. His name was Warren Price, but everyone on Roland and in Jackson, for that matter, knew him as Sonny. Lowery was determined to catch up with the man that afternoon. His decision to take a separate vehicle from his shop was not out of disrespect to the deputy. Chappel was turning out to be halfway all right as far as cops went. But Lowery had to live in this city, and Jackson was too small. Too many people knew him.

Being pegged for a narc was the last thing he needed.

He had phoned Sonny from the shop and was told it would be fine to drop over. The document was carefully re-wrapped, tucked into the cardboard, and currently lay in the seat of Lowery's four-wheel drive. He pulled into Price's driveway while the deputy, in his personal vehicle, parked on the street. They met on the steps and walked up to the front door. Before they could knock, Price opened the door.

"Must be something important," quipped Price.

Chappell looked him over. Tall, bookish-looking fellow. Dark eyes behind a pair of reading glasses. Brown corduroy trousers. Navy cardigan sweater with suede patches. From out of nowhere, an Irish setter appeared and began to sniff at the cuffs of the deputy.

"He's harmless. Unless he's hungry." Price extended his hand to the policeman. "Sonny Price. Come on in."

Chappell shook hands with Price and followed Lowery into the home. The first thing about Price the deputy noticed was the diamond stud earring in the left ear, something he found distasteful. The smell of fresh coffee permeated the warm house. They walked into the living room. Chappell and Lowery got straight to it. For the second time in the last hour, they opened the cardboard and removed the document.

Price put two cups of coffee out for his guests. The dog that they learned was called Moose sat lazily beside the fire. Chappell and Lowery drank as Price pored over the document. He said nothing for several minutes. Classical music played from the stereo as daylight waned outside. Price looked up at the two men several times, saying nothing. Finally, he shook his head.

"Do you know where this came from?" he asked.

"Sort of," Chappell said.

"I need to talk to the owners of this...chronicle. Are they here—in Jackson?"

Lowery nodded.

"Incredible."

"What can you tell us?" asked the deputy.

"I have no idea whatsoever."

By nightfall, Price was at his desk on the telephone. He returned the mysterious document to the two men, who left his home more curious than when they had arrived. They thanked him improvidently, assuring Price that he had seen neither the last of them nor the document.

***

BY 1:30 THAT MORNING, THE PLAN WAS SET. Albright's adrenaline was on the rise, excitement from what was about to happen finally beginning to settle in. Since leaving the Marines, this sense of going into battle simply did not exist in the young man's psyche any longer. He and Troy Swithuns were seated in the small hotel room; Albright, on the edge of the bed; Swithuns, sitting with ease in the upright wooden chair in the corner. Albright was bringing the older man up to date on Illinois football when, for the second time that evening, there was a soft knock at the door.

"Are you expecting anyone else?" Albright whispered.

The old man simply raised his eyebrows.

"I don't like this at all." Not having a weapon handy was frustrating to Albright. Walking over to the door without even bothering to ask who it might be, he flung the door open. Swithuns, by this time, had moved alongside Albright. When he saw who stood at the door, the old man's eyes closed; and he simply shook his head.

"Hello, Father," said the man in front. There were three in all.

All wearing policemen's uniforms.

"Why don't you come inside?" said an astonished Albright, escorting the visitors inside the small room.

"Alan Albright, say hello to my son, the police lieutenant. Although well out of his jurisdiction."

"Who are these guys?" Albright asked...

"Ah, the Golspie Police!" Troy Swithuns replied, slipping on his spectacles.

"What, pray tell, might this visit be all about?" said Albright.

"We don't want you killed, Mr. Albright. Chief Inspector Angus Swithuns." He extended his hand to Albright. "Say hello to Sergeant Jack Cameron and Constable Paul Fleming."

The younger Swithuns was dressed in full uniform of the Perth Police Department. Albright had had but one question. "Are you armed?"

"We are," answered the chief inspector.

"Great! We'll move at dawn," said Albright.

The Golspie police sergeant spoke up. "We'll move now."

Everyone looked at the American. Seconds passed. Suddenly, a smile broke out across his face.

"Like you told me earlier," Albright said, "we don't know who was in that restaurant tonight. With all you uniformed policemen converging on this place, I would be inclined to agree with us moving now and not in the morning. Let's go!"

Angus Swithuns nodded. "The officer in charge of this operation will be Sgt. Cameron, since we're in his jurisdiction."

The five men were standing in a circle, listening to Chief Inspector Swithuns. Unlike his father, Angus Swithuns stood only about five feet eight. He was stocky with long bushy sideburns and a moustache. He wore his blonde hair parted to the left, with the part half-way down the side of his annular head, trying in vain to conceal the fact that his hair was thinning on top. He was as stout as an ox, with a resolute gaze as sharp as a scalpel.

"You don't realize what's involved in this," said Troy to his son. "There are only five of us."

"Or who," added Albright.

Angus Swithuns acknowledged all of what he had heard without saying a word. He was a quiet fellow, seemingly good-natured. He, like his father, spoke with a sharp Perth accent. "I suppose it doesn't matter, does it? If a crime's been committed, or about to be committed, it's our business to do something about it, isn't it?"

***

BACK IN JACKSON, WARREN PRICE SETTLED DOWN AT HIS DESK. Papers were strewn about. Like most educators, he had plenty of books and magazines and hardly enough space to put them. Normally at this time of day, he would be reading the afternoon edition of *The Jackson Sun*. This document brought to his door would not let him carry out his routine. His wife had arrived home, and his two young daughters were upstairs in their bedroom playing with dolls. From his desk, he made a phone call to a former colleague, who lived in Halifax, Nova Scotia. Being two hours ahead of Jackson, he was relieved when his friend answered the phone.

"Hello, Barry. Sonny Price, here."

"Talk about a voice out of the past!" exclaimed the man on the other end. His name was Barry Parker. He worked in the personnel department at Dalhousie University. Knew something about everyone in the academic world of eastern Canada, active or retired, English-speaking or French, living or dead. In fact, he was but three weeks from retiring himself.

At 68, he was ready to do a little fishing.

"How's the family?" asked Price.

"Wonderful. Pauline can't wait for me to retire. Thinks we're going around the world." He laughed heartedly. "To what do I owe the pleasure of this phone call, Dr. Price?"

Sonny Price wasted little time. He told his old Canadian buddy his dilemma. Spelled out several of the words to him.

"I haven't a clue," Parker said. Price's heart sank. "There is a man, however, who might shed some light on the matter for you. Lives up near Cape Breton. This sort of thing is his specialty. His name's Donald Barbour. With any luck, you'll catch him at home tonight."

"What does he do?"

"Teaches at St. FX. Saint Francis Xavier University. Resides in a small farmhouse on the outskirts of Antigonish in a small community known as Bayfield. Pertaining to things British, the man's a walking historian. Trust me, he'll know. If you just hang on, I'll get his number. By the way, I think what's happening to those American hostages is criminal."

"Thank you," Warren replied.

Moments later, Parker was back on the line with Donald Barbour's telephone number. They chatted an additional ten minutes before ringing off. Price rang the number given to him by his old friend, got a busy signal, and hung the phone up, elated. At least, someone was home!

He waited five minutes and dialed the number once more.

This time it rang. A man's voice came on the other end, soft and cheerful.

Price introduced himself to the Canadian, using Barry Parker's name as a reference. Like the first phone call to Canada, the man from Tennessee wasted little time explaining what was puzzling him.

Price's realization that he had struck what could very well be pay dirt came when Donald Barbour asked him to describe the document itself. He asked the American numerous questions about the parchment— its thickness, its color, its condition. The color of the ink. The description of the letters. How broad the pen strokes were. How far apart the words were from one another.

This went on for nearly twenty minutes. Spelling out each word, letter by letter. What happened next, Warren Price was hardly ready for.

"Where did you say you were calling from?" Barbour asked.

"Jackson, Tennessee. We're located roughly halfway between Memphis and Nashville."

"Nashville, did you say?"

"Yes."

"Always wanted to visit Nashville. I like country music. Waylon and Willie, George and Tammy, Bill Anderson. Are you a fan?"

"Actually, I prefer Peter, Paul and Mary."

"I shall be on the first available flight from Halifax in the morning. Depending on my travel plans, I shall be arriving in either Nashville or Memphis sometime tomorrow."

"What?"

"Tomorrow, I realize this may be something of an imposition, but is it possible that you could meet me once I've finalized my itinerary? My driving's not so good these days."

It did not take Price long to realize what was happening.

For someone to stop what they were doing in far away Bayfield, Nova Scotia, and travel down to Jackson, Tennessee, meant something was very, very important.

"Mr. Barbour, I'll be happy to meet you when and wherever you so choose."

Price gave the Canadian his telephone number before hanging up.

Looking for her reading glasses, his wife strolled into the study. Noticing the perplexed look on her husband's face, she walked behind his chair and began massaging his shoulders. They were tense. She glanced down at the manuscript before him and inquired what was going on.

He simply stared at the parchment and shook his head.

***

THEY ALL LEFT THE HOTEL TOGETHER. Albright and Troy Swithuns in Albright's hired Jaguar while the policemen led the way toward Castle Craig. Whoever was inside would be discovered; and if it happened to be Jennifer Tavistock, and she were alive, she would be a captive no longer. The road leading from the hotel into the A-9 was, not surprisingly, virtually abandoned at that hour. There was no sound, save the wind and the sea and the motors inside the automobiles. Albright followed close behind the police car as they inched their way toward their destination.

Suddenly, there it was. Castle Craig, what little they could see of it through the darkness, came into view. The police car drove through the gates up the narrow black gravel driveway with the two men from Illinois following close behind. The policemen opened the car doors almost in unison. Sgt. Cameron waited until Albright and the elder Swithuns converged.

"Right, lads. This is it," Cameron whispered.

Going into a dangerous circumstance with someone as

confident as the sergeant was reassuring to Albright. Cameron and his men were putting it all on the line on this night. Little did Albright realize that prior to their arrival, the policemen had summoned for backup from Golspie and their counterparts in Brora as well.

Cameron knocked on the ancient doors and waited for a response.

Two people were left in charge of attending to Jennifer Tavistock. Both of them were in bed. Seth Duncanson, alone in the east wing. Abigail Overby, nearest the great hall. After two minutes of knocking, Cameron pulled out his service revolver and was about to shoot the handle off when the door creaked opened.

Abigail Overby wasn't pretty, even when she worked at it for hours. The sight of her after being awakened from her sleep, baggy eyes void of makeup and uncombed hair straddling a long, wretched face made her something, which Albright could best describe as that of an unkempt harridan. The reaction of the men at the door, glancing at each other, was not without a touch of merriment.

The woman's face was ill-favored.

The realization of what was to come was troubling. Kidnapping was not a frivolous offense in Scotland. Abigail, as well as her three conspirators, was being well paid to do what she was doing. The uniformed policemen were bad enough. Troy Swithuns, white hair flowing in the wind, dressed in his black leather greatcoat, looked at her without mercy. The other man, however, younger, wearing a parka and standing quietly in the back, disturbed her the most. It was all over and she knew it.

"What the... "exclaimed Duncanson. Wearing a robe and slippers, he hobbled into the great hall.

"We're looking for someone," said Sgt, Cameron. "Young American lady. Haven't seen her about, have you?"

They all stood inside the great hall underneath all the splendor of the history surrounding them. Before Cameron or both Swithuns could protest, Albright had bolted up the stairs of Castle Craig.

***

SHE HAD NOT BEEN TO SLEEP THAT NIGHT. Her decision to escape or die was unwavering. After a bath, Jennifer Tavisock dressed in a hurry, found her battle axe, and resolved that she would either die fighting or kill the first person to open up the door where she was being confined.

Albright had no idea who was in this castle. He did not care. Having flung himself up the broad stairs, he was having no luck finding his way around. All of the rooms he'd searched so far were dark, cold, and empty. Some doors he opened in a civilized manner; others were kicked open. He made his way along the last darkened corridor, frustration growing in him by the second. He tried one door and found yet another empty room. Still another. At the end of the corridor, he was about to kick the last door in when he noticed it. The key.

An enormous, worn, smooth brass key.

There could have been armed men on the other side of the door. The door itself could have been booby-trapped. He was doing the very thing his father had warned him against— thinking irrationally. He should have waited on Sgt. Cameron and his men to conduct a thorough search of Castle Craig. A logical man would have shown equanimity and self-possession.

Others would have simply been afraid.

Alan Albright took hold of the key with his right hand and turned it sharply to his left and opened the door.

***

WATERS WAS TRYING TO ACCEPT THE FACT THAT THE WOMAN IN FRONT OF HIM HAD MANAGED TO CONCEAL AN ASPECT OF HER LIFE FROM HIM AND WAS ANALYZING EVERYTHING SHE WAS TELLING HIM. He waited for her response, disbelieving what was transpiring in sleepy Edinburgh mere weeks before Christmas.

"Looks as if what you told me about this Albright fellow was on the mark. Except for his location. Rather than being where you thought he might be, he's here, isn't he?"

What the Widow had been through up until that moment paled by comparison when she thought of Castle Craig. Albright was surely heading north from Edinburgh to that destination. There were but two guards looking after the one woman, besides herself, who knew about the Secret of St. Andrews. Dangerous Waters or not, she walked over to the telephone, dialed, and waited for an answer.

***

JENNIFER TAVISTOCK WAS STARTLED. No one had ever come to her chambers at this hour before. All of her fears about her life, being without value any longer, were abruptly returning. The Dysons could have come back. Abigail may have been given the orders to kill her. Or even Duncanson. Perhaps someone had intercepted her mother's birthday card and determined the truth.

It mattered not. The broad axe was poised just past her right shoulder. The light in her room had been turned off the instant she heard movement. As the door swung open, she brought the axe down with everything she had.

***

THANKS TO THE BEAM FROM THE FLASHLIGHT, ALAN ALBRIGHT SAW THE GLEAM OF THE AXE BLADE A SPLIT-

SECOND BEFORE HE DUCKED. He would later discover a lock of hair, where the blade had missed his skull by a fraction of an inch and wedged into the antiquated door, which had kept Jennifer Tavistock in captivity for so long.

***

SHE HAD MISSED! She still held onto the axe handle. The blade had found its way into the door and was not budging. Suddenly, another set of hands gripped the axe handle over hers. A man's hands.

"I would have thought that you learned your lesson back there in University Hall," cracked a relieved Alan Albright. "First, the tennis racket—now this."

Ten years since St. Andrews. Ten years since being rushed away by her impatient father at JFK. Ten years since she first wrestled with the obnoxious pest over her tennis racket. None of it made any sense. He had gone against her wishes and gone off to Viet Nam. She had gotten on with her life. Put Alan Albright behind her once and for all.

She had come within inches of taking his head off.

This was the first time since her captivity that Jennifer Tavistock had actually smiled. The first thing she noticed about the man in front of her was his heavy black parka and gloves. The flashlight lay aimlessly on the floor. The first time, in Scotland as well, their hands had collectively gripped the handle of a Wilson tennis racquet.

He wasn't wearing gloves then.

The smile! The same smile in the photograph given to Albright by the doctor was on the living face of Jennifer Tavistock. The same smile he remembered from a decade ago. Her hair was long, disheveled, and untrimmed. She wore no lipstick. No eyeliner. No earrings. Despite the lack of womanly accents, her face radiated. Her teeth gleamed. She smelled wonderful.

All she could manage to say was, "How?"

"Let go of that ax handle and I just might tell you," he replied.

Suddenly, Lt. Swithuns appeared at the top of the stairs, gun in hand, followed by his father, who had taken longer to make the trek through the castle. Troy Swithuns broke into a hearty laugh; and his son, in spite of the moment, soon followed, both amused at the sight of the lock of Albright's hair, embedded in the door, thanks to the ancient broad axe.

After several moments, Jennifer Tavistock did, indeed, let go of the broad axe. For Albright, in spite of his quips, this was the awkward moment. He always wondered what he might say in this instance. Every hunch he had since getting the phone call from Tavistock that Saturday morning in Urbana was on the mark. He was still wondering what to say next when he found Jennifer's arms around his neck, holding him even tighter than when they said goodbye to each other in the terminal at JFK airport in the waning days of July 1969.

***

"ANSWER IT," SAID SGT. CAMERON TO ABIGAIL OVERBY. The phone began ringing at the same time Angus Swithuns and his father chased Albright up the staircase. Instead of waiting any longer, Cameron jerked the phone from its cradle and practically rammed it into the woman's face. Judging from the look in the policeman's eyes, Abigail obliged.

"Mrs. Overby." While she was indeed an accomplice, she was nobody's fool. She was assessing damage control while awaiting a response from the other end of the phone, her eyes transfixed on the policeman in front of her. It was over.

She was too old to be spending the next ten years,

probably her last, in some remote women's prison. "Mrs. Overby, indeed!" said the Widow. "Someone could be on to us. A couple of Americans may have found out about the girl being there. Listen carefully. Under no circumstances do you let anyone in, do you understand? I had unexpected company at my home tonight. Those same two Americans, in fact. They may be working alone or they may not. In any case, I'm on my way there straightway. Keep an especially close watch on her in the meantime. Again, under no circumstances are you to let anyone in, is that clear?"

"Yes, ma'am," Abigail replied. It was not the easiest thing to maintain her composure while the burly police sergeant held the cradle of the phone between them. Sgt. Cameron heard every word of the conversation; and before he knew it, the woman on the other end of the line had rung off. He hung the telephone up, realizing his other hand was gripping the arm of the old woman with the same intensity that he used when rounding up drunken hooligans on a Saturday night following a football match.

Lt. Swithuns and the remainder of the men finished their methodical sweep of the castle in less than thirty minutes, even though Mrs. Overby and the mature chap, who called himself Seth Duncanson, insisted no one else was on the premises. Sgt. Cameron left one of the policemen to guard the couple while Alan Albright, Jennifer Tavistock, Troy Swithuns, and his son walked into the library, closing the aged doors behind them. Albright hadn't had time to say much to her, nor she him, before being summoned by the policeman. After confirming by radio that backup had arrived and was stationed outside Castle Craig, he recounted the phone conversation between Mrs. Overby and the other party.

All of the men in the room took note of the hatred coming from Jennifer, who suddenly directed it towards the terrified old woman. Jennifer Tavistock walked over to Mrs. Overby. She looked frightened and pathetic. "Tell me who you were talking to before I take your head off."

Her statement wasn't shouted. Even though her face was flushed with anger, there was little sign of antagonism in her voice, which made her seem even more precarious. In fact, she could have easily been a receptionist taking down information from a potential client. The only indication that she meant business, apart from the look on her face, was how she had snatched herself from Albright's arm and held the broad axe to Mrs. Overby's throat.

"Clean off," she calmly added.

No one in the room moved or said a word. This was justice. Even Troy Swithuns, the man of the cloth that he was, said nothing.

Mrs. Overby mumbled the widow's name aloud, "Terryl Kinninmont."

It meant nothing to Jennifer Tavistock. Albright had already informed Troy Swithuns the information passed on to him by his contacts. The policemen, to a man, showed signs of disbelief. That name was familiar in political Scottish circles. Charles Kinninmont was a well known MP, who died tragically of cancer some years before, leaving behind his beautiful widow, herself a renowned pianist in her own right.

"Now give me her phone number!"

Mrs. Overby obliged.

"Does she have the Crucifix and the manuscript?"

"Yes," replied the old woman. Jennifer Tavistock managed to compose herself, glancing around at her rescuers, finally resting her eyes upon Lt. Swithuns. She could not understand his lack of composure. Albright thought fast. Realizing that introductions had not been made, he quickly proceeded to acquaint them all to Jennifer. Beginning with the notable Troy Swithuns, naturally. Jennifer was assured that from this moment on absolutely no more harm would come to her. Albright suggested that she call her parents.

Cameron objected. "The line needs to be free," he said.

He looked for any sign of disappointment on the face of Jennifer Tavistock at his statement. There was none.

All the policemen were nervously fingering their firearms as they left the library. The woman who phoned Mrs. Overby could be anywhere, Lt. Swithuns concluded. Golspie, even Brora for all they knew. When asked by Sgt. Cameron the whereabouts of the caller, however, Mrs. Overby informed them at once that Edinburgh happened to be the caller's location.

"This is what we're going to do, mate," said the lieutenant to Albright. "You, Miss Tavistock, my dad and I are leaving. Now. I'll drive your car. Sgt. Overby and his men are going to stay close and wait on our guests, whoever they are, since we can't get much more out of 'em," he said, pointing his head in the direction of the main hall of Castle Craig.

"Where are we going?" Albright asked.

"Police headquarters in Golspie. From there, we'll be able to notify Miss Tavistock's family and make the necessary arrangements about getting her back to the states. Unless you have your passport handy."

"I do not," said Jennifer. "But I have always wondered just who has been holding me all of this time. There are two others directly involved in all of this," she said. "Ambrose and Corra Dyson. Right now, they're probably in the United States. All four of them have been guarding me since I've been here. Thing is, they have been taking orders. I never realized from whom until now. By the way, I do not wish to press any charges whatsoever in this matter. I just want to go home."

Albright hadn't heard the voice of Jennifer Tavistock in years. In addition to her Boston-inspired accent, he realized she was pronouncing many of her words with a distinct Scottish flair, which he realized was understandable. Based on the information provided him by the hospitalized Stuart Cashmore and the St. Andrews history professor, Albright knew exactly who was behind Jennifer's abduction. What he did not know was why. He decided now was not the time to bring up the subject.

"How long have you been in this place?" Albright asked.

"All but three weeks since coming to Scotland."

"Let's move," interrupted Sgt. Swithuns.

"Wait!" she exclaimed, and headed back down the broad stairs to the rooms where she was being held captive, Albright right behind her. There was but one thing she wanted out of Castle Craig: her Bible.

Albright naturally followed her every step. As she returned to the great hall, she paused to take one final look at the man in the painting. Albright's eyes followed hers. What he beheld was staggering. He could not believe the coincidence. They still hadn't time to say very much to each other; and while they were alone for a brief moment, Jennifer looked at Albright in her direct manner and thanked him.

As they were departing, Jennifer paused in front of the painting that so many visitors to Castle Craig found to be menacing. Albright had scarcely taken his eyes off Jennifer Tavistock since her rescue; but when he did manage to glance up at the man in the painting, his mouth flew open.

"I know," Jennifer responded. "My reaction was the same. There appears to be something of a family resemblance."

"Let's move!" Lt. Swithuns told the American couple. "There's no telling what might happen here next."

Albright was frustrated because he knew the individual responsible for doing this to Jennifer, but it was in the hands of the Scottish police; and there was little to be done to counter that. Jennifer wasn't pressing charges, either. She was the lawyer, not he. Albright wondered about the outcome of that request. He accepted the fact that his responsibility was to stay close to Jennifer Tavistock as he led her out of Castle Craig into his rented Jaguar.

"I'll drive, Mr. Albright," Lt. Swithuns said, drawing his firearm once inside the automobile. His father checked the passengers behind him. Jennifer Tavistock, meanwhile, experienced the inside of a vehicle for the first time in two years as she sat in the back seat with Alan Albright. The car pulled off. Sgt. Cameron spoke to the lieutenant as the car slowly eased through the castle grounds towards the A9. Since there were few items in the line of outerwear for Jennifer to choose from and since she'd been confined to the inside of Castle Craig and hardly used to the cold December Highland air, Albright placed his heavy parka over her shoulders as she shivered in the cold night air.

Jennifer Tavistock was convinced that she would have either gained her freedom or died that night. Why Alan Albright happened along on that very night, the night she told herself enough was enough, could not be explained other than what she had believed all along.

Faith.

It was 2:32 a.m.

"We've got to get you home to Beacon Hill. In time for Christmas, as I'd hoped," said Albright. "Your parents are going to be the happiest people on this planet."

She sat back and took several deep breaths, eyes closed, experiencing freedom for the first time in many months. The hired Jaguar had plenty of rear seat leg room, and Jennifer felt the power of the automobile, even in the back seat, as Lt. Swithuns sped through the night.

"I need to make a stop before saying goodbye to Scotland. Unfinished business, you might say."

Troy Swithuns sat in the front seat next to his son, eyes straight ahead. When he heard Jennifer speak of unfinished business, his head tilted slightly, mindful to respect the privacy of the two passengers seated behind him.

"Sure that's a good idea?" asked Albright. "Considering what's occurred to you lately, Miss Tennis Star, the sooner we get out of this country the better."

"That's Tavistock," she retorted. "I'm not leaving until I've taken care of this," said Jennifer, unable to ignore the reference to St. Andrews and how they first met. It made her smile.

Albright was not altogether surprised with her steadfastness. "So where might we uncover this unfinished business?"

To Jennifer, the smell and feel of the inside of the Jaguar was wonderful. The heater was turned on high, and the experience of being inside a luxury automobile at seventy miles an hour was quite an extraordinary occurrence. There was more than enough room in the back of the automobile, and Albright was making every effort to assure her comfort.

"I'll give you one hint. A university's located there," she said. "Along with a golf course. Might be a bit difficult you to figure out, I know." The Tavistock wit was awakening.

"Let me guess."

"What happens now?" said Troy Swithuns to his son.

"If what that old woman back there said is true, we'll be issuing a number of arrest warrants. No one in this realm is above the law, Dad."

"What about the consequences?" His son merely shrugged.

***

Swithuns was actually enjoying driving the 1980 Jaguar. Liked the way it handled. Appreciated the opportunity, in fact, and told Albright as much as they pulled into the small building that housed the Golspie Police Station. As they traveled from Castle Craig, a plan was being formulated on just how the two Americans would get out of Scotland. Jennifer Tavistock repeatedly thanked the policeman and his father for freeing her from captivity.

Albright, meanwhile, was both ecstatic and hesitant. He had, in a remarkably short period of time, done what some had not done and others felt could not be done. He had reached his goal. There were a number of causalities that had gotten in the way of a woman in Edinburgh determined to keep Jennifer Tavistock from obtaining her freedom. Albright did not want Jennifer or himself for that matter, to be included in that number. Once inside the police station, Jennifer was given a small package by the elder Swithuns.

"Open it up," he said with a broad smile.

Jennifer found Troy Swithuns, this minister, comforting and estimable. Being able to breathe in the fresh night winter air as she strolled from the Jaguar to the police station soothed and refreshed her. The spare, unfriendly, unsmiling company she had been with had been replaced with reassurance. Concern. Understanding. Consideration. She opened the package. To her surprise, she found tubes of lipstick, mascara, eyeliner, chewing gum, candy bars, and something she was completely shocked to discover—

a copy of *Soap Opera Digest*. Albright, remembering the conversations with Jennifer during their summer at St. Andrews, recalled her wondering during their six weeks abroad what was happening on her favorite television program, *The Edge of Night*. He hoped she was still a fan.

She was.

The undoing of their relationship nearly ten years ago over the Vietnam war was forgotten. The abrupt split between the two meaningless.

"You've not seen the *Edge* in how long?" asked Albright.

"Over two years."

"You haven't missed anything whatsoever." The Albright sarcasm. "This should get you caught up in a hurry."

Along with *Soap Opera Digest*, there was a copy of the latest *Time, U.S. News & World Report,*

Newsweek, TV Guide, and a copy of the *Chicago Tribune,* all purchased at O'Hare the day Albright left the states bound for Scotland. He would have preferred to get Jennifer a Boston newspaper but was unable to find one. There had been no assurance, whatsoever, that he would even find her in Scotland, no guarantee Castle Craig was the place, and no absolute certainty of her being alive in spite of the card sent to Claire Tavistock.

Mrs. Swithuns had, to Albright's surprise, picked up the personal items and had sent them up the A-9 via her husband.

The room was filled with anxiety from the officers who had accompanied Sgt. Swithuns to Castle Craig. Unlike Alan and Jennifer, they seemed grave, concerned about what had transpired and what would happen next. Jennifer was still wearing Albright's heavy parka as she sat at the sergeant's desk, examining her care package, smiling at Alan, holding his hand, and poring over her soap summary.

Troy Swithuns motioned with a nod of his head to Albright. Alan had pulled up a three-legged stool opposite Jennifer and had yet taken his eyes off her. He patted Jennifer on her shoulder, stood up, and walked up to the man of the cloth.

"You need to get out of this country," he whispered to Albright. "As soon as possible." Swithuns, like the police officers, was thinking about the consequences of the evening. Once they learned who was involved in the abduction, the policemen quietly agreed there could very well be danger.

"Dr. Tavistock gave me enough money to get us out of this country. That's no problem. We'll drive to Edinburgh, book a flight, and go home. Mr. Swithuns, I want to tell you something, sir. You made," Albright said, pointing his head in Jennifer's direction, "her freedom possible. Granted, my plans were moved up and a bit and altered considerably. The question of the moment will be how to get Jennifer Tavistock on that plane to the states without a passport. More than likely, the American Consulate won't be open for some hours in Edinburgh. Under the circumstances, being who she is and all, there shouldn't be much difficulty in obtaining a temporary passport."

Troy Swithuns gave the young man from Illinois a look Albright did not particularly care for. It was the same feeling Abigail Overby experienced when she opened the door to

Castle Craig and saw the tall figure in black with the white flowing hair. "I don't think you understand, Alan. As soon as possible means now! This woman didn't hesitate to keep your friend in captivity, did she? Who's to say she won't kill her, both of you, in fact? Just listen to me. My son has an idea. It won't be cheap, but he believes it will work."

This man was from Illinois. A friend of the family. Most importantly, Mr. Swithuns had provided needed backup for Jennifer's rescue. Albright continued to return the old man's gaze and eventually said, "Miss Tavistock, got a moment?"

It was all about respect.

Jennifer Tavistock, seated at a desk in the small police station, experimenting with a tube of lipstick in front of a small compact, looked up at Albright.

"Mr. Swithuns would like a brief word with us."

She stood up, drew the chair back under the desk, and headed over to join the two men, nonchalantly slipping her arm into Albright's.

"You say you needed to make a quick stop before we leave this country. Mr. Swithuns says the sooner the better. What do you think?" asked Albright

"I have to go to St. Andrews, Alan," said Jennifer Tavistock very slowly and very distinctly. "Shouldn't take more than thirty minutes, believe it or not. Once I've done that, my business in this country will be finished. For good. It's imperative, however, that I do this. I've been waiting two years, after all."

After brushing her hair, applying the makeup supplied by Mrs. Swithuns, the woman who stood before them was a bit different than the woman they met in Castle Craig. Her fingernails were scarlet, matching her lips. Her dark hair now lay halfway down her back, her high school length and then some. In spite of wearing the same dowdy and uninteresting clothing, the fact that she was now a free woman returned the luster and cockiness Albright had remembered.

Troy Swithuns spoke up once again. "The longer you two ponder over this, the larger your risk factor grows. Now here's my suggestion." He spoke in his best ministerial resonance for five uninterrupted minutes. Like Albright earlier that evening, Jennifer Tavistock found herself captivated not only by Troy Swithuns' presence but his exceptional and sagacious ability to reason. His son strolled over to listen, saying nothing.

Albright and Jennifer looked at each other for a moment. There was no trace of fear or uncertainty in either of them. As if on cue, they both nodded.

"I suppose if Sgt. Swithuns is willing, so are we," said Jennifer.

"How long will it take to arrange this?" Albright asked.

Sgt. Swithuns looked at his father, who raised his eyebrows and shrugged his shoulders.

"Considering the time, with money paid up front naturally, perhaps an hour," said Troy.

"How much?" Albright asked.

"At least a couple of thousand quid." "Each," he added.

"Done," Albright replied.

"Make the call, father," said Sgt. Swithuns.

It was against Jennifer's better judgment. What she had in mind could cost her life, possibly that of her rescuer as well. So what, she thought. Her anger was returning. She sat back down at the desk, where she had been doing her makeup and, without hesitation, dialed the number given to her by Abigail Overby.

"Hello," said the voice.

Even though Dangerous Waters had dressed well for this cold night, he was still having problems adjusting to the Scottish chill. This was, he thought, becoming some Christmas holiday. One he was hardly anticipating, but he felt utterly prepared to deal with anything and everything.

He sat in the living room in front of the ivory piano, crossed his legs, determining how to calm the Widow down somewhat, when he noticed the look on the face of his companion.

"Hello, indeed, Mrs. Kinninmont!" shouted Jennifer Tavistock. At that moment, Albright and every man in the squad room was mortified. With a chilling smile on her face, Jennifer handed the telephone over to Alan Albright, who, dealing with this unforeseen turn of events, grabbed the phone.

"Guess what, sweetheart," he said calmly into the telephone, "your captive has been freed. I guess that's the one thing that your friend failed to share with you."

The vituperative voice, like that of the woman's seconds before, was that of an American. A man's voice.

"Jennifer Tavistock is no longer your prisoner. In fact, the only prisoners around here are your former jailers. By the way, darling, just in case you were wondering who you're talking to, my name is Alan Albright. A-L-B-R-I-G-H-T."

Albright hung up the phone before allowing a response from the Widow." "Well, that should get her attention," he said.

***

Dangerous Waters began to pace the floor inside the Widow's flat. What he had seen earlier in the evening was nothing. But Waters was completely unprepared for the look on this woman's face as the telephone call came in and left her in a completely uncontrollable state of rage. The woman he'd known for so long, the accomplished pianist, the chic lady, the elegant darling of Edinburgh society, had suddenly turned into a predator. When Waters asked questions about this secret of St. Andrews the Yank had been raving about, she simply dismissed it with a wave of her hand. He realized there was trouble but, in spite of any unanswered questions, wasn't about to turn his back on the woman he was falling in love with.

No matter what might be involved, Dangerous Waters would be there for her. He didn't care about his new profession or even his decision to walk away years before from a life of crime. The whiff of danger and adventure was in the air, something simply nonexistent in North Africa in spite of what he was being paid for. Waters had picked up the scent of a wounded animal. If someone in Scotland, besides the two Americans he'd encountered earlier that evening, meant harm to this woman, and judging from her rage at this phone call there was, they would have to get past him first, something not about to happen. Her rage was becoming his rage. In all the times they had been together in the past, Waters' anger had been kept in check. There had been no reason for it to emerge. Until now. She stood there, refusing to hang up the telephone, eyes on Dangerous Waters.

What happened next left Dangerous Waters more astonished than ever.

"I must prepare for a journey, my darling. A long journey, I'm afraid. I'm sure you will choose to remain here in Scotland while I travel to America." The composure was restored along with the coolness and style and grace. The voice was steady once again.

"America?" said Waters. "Whereabouts?"

"A place called Tennessee," she said, putting her arms around him.

"When do we leave?"

***

Alan Albright took note of the disgust in the eyes of Troy Swithuns as he returned from making his own call on the other side of the office. The two Americans were smiling at one another, apart for over a decade, reunited for less than an hour, up to no good already.

"It's done. He'll be here in an hour or so. Downright criminal, what he's asking. Five hundred pounds, each. Firm. Landing in a small airstrip just up the road, in fact. The plane will fly you to Leuchars, where you'll be boarding a private jet." "As if anticipating what Albright was going to say, Troy said," Tom Albright's planning. Courtesy of your United States Air Force. How he did it, I do not know. On the other hand, he knew you would be unreceptive at some point. Like me, he insisted on having the escape module in place from the beginning. I notified the pilots when I heard you'd landed in Edinburgh. Told them to be on standby, awaiting my word." His son was listening to his father with something that could best be described as incredulity. "These ...er....gentlemen work on a cash only basis, Alan. Sterling is the only ticket you'll need, my boy. After the greeting you two just passed along to our friends in Edinburgh," he said, motioning with his head at Jennifer Tavistock," this decision to visit St. Andrews one last time means leaving now would be in everyone's best interest."

The Piper Cherokee was small, loud, and uneasy. To Jennifer, the next step. Freedom. Yes, but an unimaginable opportunity to finish once and for all something she had set out to do.

The plan was to fly into Leuchars Junction, drive into St. Andrews, finish whatever business Jennifer Tavistock had to take care of, return to Leuchars, board the Air Force jet, and fly out of Scotland. All went well on the flight to the East Neuk of Fife. Into a grey and cloudy morning, Alan Albright and Jennifer Tavistock rode into St. Andrews, the very city where it all began. The pilots were doubling as drivers. They had been well paid and asked few questions. Albright quietly asked, and was informed, that both minders were indeed armed.

To Albright's disappointment, he was not.

At Jennifer's request, the two Americans were dropped off in South Street. They would return to the spot where they'd been dropped off in two hours. Sharp. The drivers assured the two Americans they would be. As Jennifer Tavistock and Alan Albright emerged into Market Street, at that moment two unique experiences took place. For one, it meant the first morning of freedom in two years: each step, each sight, and each breath special and cherished beyond description. For the other, a reunion with a young woman in the city where they'd met, grown close, now reunited.

Jennifer Tavistock's first purchase of the morning was an overcoat. Not a slim, black fur-collared overcoat. Hardly. What caught her eye was a heavy, down-filled, hooded woman's parka.

The two, as they browsed through the shop, at last had a moment to themselves. The ice had been broken the moment the axe fell within inches of Albright's head.

"So," asked Jennifer, "how did all of this happen?"

"All of what?" he replied.

"You rescuing me, idiot."

He began with his search for the baseball collection Thanksgiving week and his decision to send the Christmas card to her parents' house.

"What day was that? Specifically. What day was it? Do you remember?"

Albright found himself holding her new overcoat as Jennifer looked over the meager selection of purses in the shop. A far cry from the fashionable stores in Edinburgh and London. The very fact that Jennifer Tavistock was actually able to browse for clothing and accessories surpassed any experience she would have found in those cities.

"Easy. Thanksgiving Day. Thursday, November 22nd."

Jennifer had reached for a simple folding handbag when she stopped, stared straight ahead, then looked into the cobalt blue eyes of Alan Albright, that same look Albright remembered from one memorable summer.

"We remembered the JFK assassination. Sixteen years ago," Albright continued. Jennifer still stared at him. "Why?"

"You'll think I'm making this up. I was listening to Radio One that day. I remember the newscaster talking about it being Thanksgiving Day in America. I took an oath that same day, Alan. Based on something I could not understand at the time. I felt," she paused, "that I had a prayer."

Albright tried to come up with a plausible explanation that moment why he decided Thanksgiving night to send a Christmas card to Jennifer Tavistock that next day. Had the events of the previous weeks not taken place, he would have simply chalked it up to sentimentality.

Before he could respond, Jennifer was strolling up to the front to pay for her purchases.

The lady behind the counter had wished them a Merry Christmas when they walked in the small shop. Now, as she totaled up the order, Jennifer Tavistock became aware of something she had never been aware of in her adult life.

"I'm afraid I have no means to pay for my purchase, Mr. Albright."

Albright felt like an idiot.

"Of course. Here you go." He reached into his hip pocket, removed his black leather wallet, and promptly handed Jennifer Tavistock a wad of ten pound notes. "Courtesy of Doctor Tavistock."

"Thank you, sir," she said with that captivating smile. She returned her attention to the shopkeeper and said, "I was in here a year or so ago. My name is Jennifer Tavistock."

"So you were!" exclaimed the shopkeeper. "We get lots of Americans in here these days, you know. You purchased a sweater and asked us to monogram it for you! That's right. We thought you'd gone back to America without it."

"Do you still have it?" asked Jennifer.

"We should, indeed. I'll just have a look, dear."

Albright glanced at his watch. He wasn't about to take

away the enjoyment Jennifer Tavistock was clearly experiencing by telling her to hurry up. If she bought the sweater and paid for it, it stood to reason she should get it. Nevertheless, his sense of urgency was growing. Neither of them had slept. The triumph of finding Jennifer Tavistock made the lack of sleep worthwhile. The fact that they needed to get out of Scotland as soon as possible pressed on his patience.

The shopkeeper was smiling when she brought in a box neatly wrapped in green paper.

Being Christmas, she'd even topped it off with a white ribbon and bow.

"Here you are, dear. Better late than never. Happy Christmas to you both."

As they walked back into South Street, they spotted the car, engine running, and minders inside. Albright and Jennifer walked over, climbed in the back, closing their doors.

"Where now, ma'am?" asked the driver.

"We have a plane to catch," Jennifer said. "Let's get going."

Surely not, Albright thought to himself. Surely, this "unfinished business" Jennifer referred to was not a sweater! He gazed out the window as St. Andrews whizzed by. There has been hardly any time to truly appreciate this town. He smiled to himself as he thought back to the night the cops apprehended Albright and his buddies in the graveyard while on a ghost hunt.

Jennifer Tavistock, meanwhile, had slipped on her new parka, removing the tags and putting them into one of the parka's many pockets. In spite of the lack of sunshine outside, the quaint seaside town looked good.

The two drivers sped up as they eased out of St. Andrews. They had been polite to the American couple, had been well paid for what they were doing, and asked few questions. Albright knew people, but even he was at a loss when it came to determining exactly which side of the law these two gentlemen were on. The driver was the eldest, seemingly in his forties, while the husky chap in the passenger's seat couldn't have been more than thirty.

"So what's the first thing you're going to do once you get to America?" said Albright.

"You asked me that same question a day or so before we left Paris," she replied. "Don't know why I remembered that all of a sudden. Like I told you ten years ago, I suppose I'll get off the plane."

***

Jackson, Tennessee

As promised, Donald Barbour was on the first available plane from Nova Scotia to Tennessee. Warren Price was waiting for him in Memphis as he emerged from the American Airlines gate. Shorter and younger than Price had imagined, he offered to assist the Canadian historian with his carry-on luggage. Once they had retrieved the additional luggage, they made their way eastward toward Jackson.

By one that afternoon, following a true Tennessee lunch, the two men were in Warren Price's study, poring over the document in question. Barbour removed a legal pad from his briefcase, reached inside his breast pocket for his Mont Blanc, and began to write. Price felt as if he were invisible, as the Canadian professor who was so engrossed in the document, failed to answer questions from his American host.

Professor Barbour, Price observed, jotted down the size and width of the document itself, the color of the ink, and the texture of the paper. At last, he acknowledged his host.

"Where's the rest?"

Warren Price laughed openly. "As I mentioned earlier, Sir, this is all there is."

"Ah, yes," Barbour replied. "You did, indeed."

Professor Barbour spoke out of thin lips. His downturned mouth gave way to a slightly droopy chin. His ears were larger than average. His eyes were dark, and his fixed gaze showed strength behind the disheveled appearance that comes from a lifetime spent in the world of academia. Although completely gray, Barbour still had all of his hair and wore it in the fashion of an English barrister, parted on the left and swept back over the forehead. He wore a blue dress shirt and had flown in from Nova Scotia wearing his favorite navy tie.

Full Windsor, naturally.

Mrs. Price brought coffee into her husband's study and promptly disappeared to get on with her Saturday priorities, leaving her husband and guest to ponder what lay before them on Price's desk. For the next two hours, the professor from Canada and the professor from Tennessee discussed possibilities and, finally, what to do about the owner.

"So, about this British fellow who brought this to Tennessee," said Professor Barbour. "Just who is he?"

Warren Price was blunt and to the point. He conveyed to his guest what was told to him by Polk Lowery. Lowery, Barbour learned, came to the police due to his suspicions about the foreigner who called himself Ambrose Dyson. The police approached Price to try to shed light on what the document was, who might have written it, and what it all meant.

***

As Sonny Price and Professor Barbour sipped coffee, Elford Chappell and his family were attending the birthday of his wife's mother at a local restaurant. Being full at that hour, Chappell saw more than a few people he knew. There were kids in front of him in the buffet line; and as he reached for a glass of iced tea, someone tapped him on his shoulder.

"Hello, Mayor," said Price as he turned around. The mayor was dining with his wife and knew the deputy. Not well, but knew him, nevertheless.

"Mr. Chappell. How's the family?"

"Very good, sir, and yours?"

The mayor had a small dish of peach cobbler in hand. "Everyone's well. Got a minute?"

Chappell had finished his meal, looked over to notice that the birthday party was going along nicely; and since this was the mayor of Jackson, he sensed it might be important enough to give the man a few moments of his time. Chappell stepped out of the buffet line and stood off to one side to hear what the mayor had to say.

"I spoke to Ed late yesterday afternoon. It came to my attention that you are aware of a newcomer to Jackson. A foreigner. England or somewhere." The mayor's blue eyes narrowed for an instant when he mentioned England. "Fellow by the name of Ambrose Dyson."

Chappell was no fool. Mayors in that town normally did not get involved in law enforcement matters. Ambrose Dyson was certainly becoming known in the short time he had been in Jackson. First, the outlaw picture framer; now, the mayor and the Chief of Police.

"Ambrose Dyson. I am aware of him, sir." Chappell briefly summed up his meeting with Polk Lowery, what troubled the young man, and how the mysterious single page of manuscript was being examined by a Lambuth professor.

"A manuscript?" said the mayor, nodding a greeting to a couple who were being seated in the restaurant. At six-two, the mayor stayed fit by playing tennis regularly. His full head of hair was dark brown, and he could break out into a hearty laugh if amused.

If crossed, he could be intimidating.

"Yes, sir," Chappell answered.

"Have you been watching the agony our hostages are

going through in Iran, Mr. Chappell?"

"I have, Mayor."

"Iran's a long way from Jackson. Long way. We don't need anyone in this town breaking any laws, period. We certainly don't need any foreigners here who might have ideas of getting away with something just because we're a small town in West Tennessee. Ambrose Dyson is what you policemen call dirty. I smelled the sonavabitch the minute I laid eyes on him at that Symphony meeting the other day. Ed's got his people doing a background check on him. While he's in this town, he doesn't move without our people watching him."

"Symphony meeting?" asked Chappell.

"Mr. Dyson is in Jackson in preparation for some special Christmas gala. Some world famous piano player has chosen Jackson, Tennessee, for a concert with the Jackson Symphony. Her name's Terryl Kinninmont. Seems this lady has found it in her heart to come all the way here and play for one night only. Next Saturday night. A week from today, in fact. Mr. Dyson claims to be her manager. He's been meeting with the Symphony Board putting this concert together. All very sudden. The Symphony people were notified a short time ago. Here's the strange thing about all of this, Mr. Chappell. She is performing this concert at no charge."

Chappell listened thoughtfully at what the mayor was saying. He was just a county deputy. Not a detective by any stretch of the imagination. He patrolled county roads and carried out the day-to-day duties of the Madison County Sheriff's Department as best he could. At a chance luncheon, he'd noticed a troubled man and offered his help.

Now he stood fact to face with Jackson's mayor. He took a deep breath, looked around at the throng of people at the busy restaurant and, once again, over to the table where his family sat. What the mayor had said about the American hostages in captivity was bringing out the worst in him. Elford Chappell had yet to meet this Ambrose Dyson—had no idea what he even looked like. Chappell had never spent much time around the British and, up until that moment, had given them little thought. Suddenly, a conversation years ago with his father and his uncles at a summer barbecue came to mind. His father, Chappell remembered, had blamed the English for getting America into too many wars. Chappell couldn't have been more than eleven or twelve at the time and thought little about what was being said at the time. He'd always listed to his father's advice and relished his wisdom.

The fact that Ambrose Dyson was, in fact, Scottish and not English mattered little to the deputy sheriff. He did not like him and planned on meeting Mr. Dyson very soon.

***

Jennifer Tavistock looked back at the last several hours. She realized that family was an essential part of the existence of mankind. The portrait of the man in the great hall of Castle Craig was in plain view for everyone. The portrait of the woman she'd discovered inside a remote wing by accident was not in plain view. She was a pretty woman. A soft face.

The face of a Black woman.

***

The widow was also looking back at the past several hours. Her beloved piano was damaged beyond repair. Waters had luckily contained the spill to the piano before things spread throughout her flat, but the damage was done. She paused to reflect on two names out of nowhere that popped up in her very apartment. Alan Albright and Leigh Katalinic. To discover that the perpetrator she believed to be Albright was, in fact, someone else was bad enough. That this strange American shouted Leigh Katalinic's name was too much. That Jennifer Tavistock had been freed by the man the Widow had been warned moments after her piano was destroyed about was incomprehensible.

After breaking down and telling her lover everything, Dangerous Waters did not turn his back. He was consoling. One of the last things the Widow did before leaving her Edinburgh flat was picking up the telephone and placing a call to America. A city called Boston.

A call to Claire Tavistock.

They met as children. The Widow was six, Claire was fifteen. A family reunion in the Widow's home in Halifax, Nova Scotia. Her name was Terryl Fraser, and she and her older cousin became fast friends that summer, in spite of the nine years difference in age, and only grew closer through the years. Castle Craig belonged to Claire Tavistock, and there would be questions surrounding the captivity of Jennifer Tavistock. The conversation was brief. Terryl Kinninmont informed Claire Tavistock that her daughter was no longer under the Widow's watch.

She was a free woman.

After hanging up, the Widow packed through the night. Her passport was in order, and so was her agenda. Dangerous Waters, after being told completely everything, had no misgivings whatsoever about traveling to America. In fact, he was looking forward to the trip. They would be departing Edinburgh on an eleven-thirty flight that morning to New York.

***

Alan Albright and Jennifer Tavistock landed on a snow-cleared airstrip at Loring Air Force Base in Limestone, Maine. They were just over 400 miles from Boston. Just over 400 miles from Jennifer's Beacon Hill residence. The couple disembarked from the plane into the blustery frigid Maine air and freshened up inside a spare hangar, where

Albright used a phone to call Urbana.

To the Colonel.

He broke the good news to his father, excited beyond belief at having successfully fulfilling his mission. At Jennifer's request, as difficult as it was to understand at first, they would not be notifying the Tavistocks.

Jennifer Tavistock, at last, would be able to visit the cities where she was a phone call away from attending college.

Champaign-Urbana.

Albright had given up wondering what his old man would come up with next. Less than an hour after touching down at Loring, he and Jennifer were airborne once again, flying in a southwesterly direction. Destination: Chanute Air Force Base, ten miles north of Champaign-Urbana.

It was on the flight to Illinois when Jennifer opened up to Albright.

"Remember the portrait back in Castle Craig?" she asked.

"Of course. Noticeable resemblance. Particularly about the chin."

"Well," Jennifer said, "there was another portrait you did not see. The wife of the man."

The plane seats were uncomfortable. There were no drinks served, no hot chocolate or hot meals. Albright sat upright, staring out the window at the frozen landscape below.

"The wife," he repeated.

"My reason for leaving Boston to Scotland was to find out who my ancestors were, Alan. Everyone's doing genealogy these days."

"Yes, because of *Roots*. Mrs. Tavistock briefly alluded to the fact."

Jennifer looked at Albright and shook her head. "What my mother did not tell you, and I am certain now that she knows, is that our family tree was unknown to us on the Fraser side of the family beyond Malcolm Fraser."

"Right! Saw his portrait inside your home."

"Malcolm Fraser's father was the man you saw in the portrait in the castle. Angus Fraser. I have his Bible with me. His wife's name was Matilda. Seems Angus met her as a sailor on a sugar plantation in the Barbados, fell in love with her, bought her freedom, and returned to Scotland with her as his wife. She was Black."

Jennifer remained silent for several moments. Albright was unsure to attribute the silence to shame, anger, or just making a point.

Malcolm Fraser was a mulatto. Another uncomfortable moment for Albright.

"Did you ever read about the Triangular Trade in school?" Jennifer said, breaking the silence at last.

"I did not," said Albright.

"American merchants would take goods by ship to Africa. These goods, Alan, were exchanged for slaves. Slaves! These slaves were loaded up and sent on these same ships to the Caribbean. The slaves would then be traded for rum. Rum and molasses. Guess where the rum and molasses ended up? America. The new world."

"I see."

"No, you don't! Our family fortune was built on the Triangular Trade. Every cent my family owns is tainted with this, this filth! The true irony is that Malcolm Fraser, the son of a Black woman, engaged in slave trading and died a very wealthy man in Boston. That's why I went to Scotland, Alan. To find out more about Malcolm Fraser."

Albright was unsure what to say. As if sensing his awkwardness, Jennifer said," I learned about what Malcolm Fraser really did for a living before I left Boston. I shared this information with my mother."

"How did that go over?"

"Not very well," she replied. "My mother told me that history cannot be changed. That's it. That's when I decided to take things a step further and go to Scotland and once and for all find out who Malcolm Fraser was. Who his family was. I discovered Castle Craig through the help of Ross Burnham from the University of St. Andrews."

"Right! He was most helpful to me as well," said Albright.

"I was taken captive at Castle Craig. Two things were taken from me at that time. One extremely valuable to me. The other not so valuable."

"That would be the Crucifix you referred to back there?"

"That's right."

"And the other?"

She looked straight ahead and smiled. She turned to Albright and looked him over. Jennifer, at that point, decided it was time to find out more about the man who had rescued her. There was no wedding ring. How could there be? What married man would go off and find another missing woman other than his wife?

"So tell me, Mr. Albright. What have you been up to these days? What do you do for a living?"

"Currently unemployed. Looking for work."

"Oh. Who is the special woman?"

An uncomfortable question, to be sure. Albright's steadfast refusal to discuss his relationship with Tolly Chamberlain was unknown to Jennifer Tavistock. The hum from the plane engines did little to dampen the uneasiness he felt. Jennifer picked up on it at once.

"I was engaged. We broke it off this past Valentine's Day." Albright gazed past Jennifer out the window at the frozen landscape below.

"Oh. Well, for what it's worth I haven't been doing much dating lately myself," Jennifer replied.

The perfect comeback line.

"I suppose if you'd grown your hair out like Rapunzel, you could have used your hair to escape from that ghastly castle."

"But that would have spoiled me being rescued by you," she replied. "By the way, did you ever get those tennis lessons?"

"I did not. In fact... Come to think of it, I haven't played since I beat you back at University Hall."

***

The non-stop flight from Edinburgh to New York on British Airways was leaving at 11:51 A.M. and was completely booked. The Widow and Dangerous Waters, no sleep whatsoever between them, managed to get last-minute reservations through a well-connected Thomas Cook travel agent.

After hastily packing for America in the early morning hours, they took a taxi from the Widow's flat to Turnhouse Airport. There would be plenty of time to sleep once they reached the United States.

The chances of acquaintances running into each other at an airport the size of Turnhouse was unlikely, but not impossible. Edinburgh is hardly the size of a New York or London, and its airport was not nearly as large as Heathrow or JFK. It was Charlotte, who shivered at the sight of the profile of Dangerous Waters. She was unsure, at first, but the woman walking alongside him confirmed whatever doubt the man might have had. She grabbed the hand of Daniel, who was busy holding on to not only the woman he loved but his carry-on luggage as they headed toward their boarding gate. They were a few feet behind the two people walking in the same direction, whose home they'd invaded the night before, destroying an ebony Wurlitzer piano forever.

"It's them!" Charlotte whispered.

"What are you talking about?" Harper said, keeping in step with the airport flow of people.

"That woman! Look there, just in front of us!"

It took several seconds for Harper to see exactly what Charlotte was talking about. When he did, he has a nightmarish vision of being led off to jail, separated from the love of his life, unable to leave Scotland for the vandalism he had caused. Suddenly his hatred for the Widow returned, and he did not care about the consequences of the night before. To Charlotte's dismay, Harper jostled his way past the people in front of them until he and Charlotte were walking directly behind Dangerous Waters and the Widow.

***

Jennifer Tavistock had never visited the state of Illinois. She'd been accepted to attend the University of Illinois ten years earlier, sight unseen. Of course, Albright had described it to her, and she'd read over the pamphlets during her senior year in high school. When she and the man traveling with her went their separate ways, that visit to Champaign-Urbana never came to pass. Now, on a brutally cold December afternoon with snow clouds overhead and unmerciful prairie winds whipping about, they emerged onto the tarmac at Chanute Air Force Base.

"Dennis Albright." He vaguely resembled his younger brother, with a thick pair of eyeglasses and just an eyelash under six feet. A young woman stood beside him, bundled up for the winter, who introduced herself to Jennifer Tavistock as Bonnie Albright. They both hugged Jennifer.

On receiving the phone call from his son, Tom Albright made the call to Daniel and Bonnie to meet them upon arriving at Chanute. They grabbed Albright's luggage and Jennifer's few possessions and piled into a warm station wagon. Bonnie and Jennifer climbed into the back seat while Alan sat up front with his older brother.

"How was the flight?" asked Bonnie.

"Restful," said Jennifer. "Thanks for asking."

"Well, this isn't Boston or New York. Not even Chicago. But we do have a number of great stores in this town; and with the U of I being here, we're going to do a little shopping. Believe me, it's Christmas time, and there's gotta be something you'll like. And, if you're game, I'll take you to my favorite salon for a little pampering. Hair, nails, the whole bit."

Jennifer found Bonnie to be wonderful. They hit it off at once. In the front seat, meanwhile, the Albright brothers were quiet. The old man brought Dennis up to speed that morning about what Alan had been up to, and obviously the task he'd taken on was successful. In no time at all, they were in Urbana, heading for their parents' house.

***

Dangerous Waters looked over his shoulder into the eyes of the man who had tapped him on his back. He stopped dead in his tracks to the surprise of the Widow, who wondered what exactly he was doing. She was impatient, and he knew they had a plane to catch within twenty minutes. She was about to tell him to come along when she saw who was behind them.

"How's the piano?"

Daniel Harper, being the country boy that he was, looked nothing like the timid bookworm at The Last Drop some days before, when they'd first seen him. He said nothing else to the man in front of him. Charlotte was afraid, unsure of what was about to happen. All she wanted to do was get out of this country and back to West Virginia. She looked at the Widow. Saw the shot of hatred pointed at the man she loved. Daniel and Dangerous Waters were inches from each other, as Waters had turned to face them both. Like Daniel, Charlotte thought she was going to jail.

"Come, my dear," said the Widow, grabbing the arm of Dangerous Waters. "We have a plane to catch."

Waters did not move. No one took notice of the exchange occurring in Turnbridge Airport as the two couples stood facing one another.

The man before her was not Alan Albright, as the Widow found out from the phone call the night before. Whoever this man was had, yes, destroyed her piano, and yes, was acquainted with the most unfortunate Leigh Katalinic.

But he was not Alan Albright.

Waters obliged and walked away from the American couple to the relief and dismay of Daniel and Charlotte.

Harper could not believe it. He looked at Charlotte and said, "Why didn't they do anything? Why didn't they summon the cops?"

"What are they doing here?" Charlotte asked.

"I don't know. And I don't know why they just walked away from two people who broke into their home and destroyed their piano. Even though we were face to face, they just walked away. Explain that, Miss Charlotte."

"I can't. Look, there's our gate!"

"Good. Let's go."

They walked into the waiting area and sat down.

Backs to the wall.

The plane was due to board in 28 minutes.

The Widow and Dangerous Waters, meanwhile, found their respective gate five minutes later. They would be boarding a flight to London, which would in turn take them on a non-stop flight to New York.

Once airborne, she planned on drinking plenty of coffee, as neither she nor David had slept.

Waters was taking this trip for two reasons. First of all, he was falling in love with this woman. Secondly, his sense of adventure was aroused. Morocco paid well, but the boredom had set in. As long as he was back in Morocco by the 3rd of January, there was no problem.

Whit Campbell, he vaguely remembered, was the name the American gave back at the pub. How had they discovered them? How did they know where the Widow lived? How had they gotten in? Had they stayed in Edinburgh for one more day, Rosie Carstairs would have inevitably confessed to losing her key to her boss's flat the night before. That would explain how the Americans got in.

The Widow briefly mentioned this Leigh Katalinic fellow during Waters' enlightenment of the events that led to the night before.

What Waters did not know was that Leigh was born in Croatia some twenty-five years before. His father had left for England, while Leigh was at the age of five, to take on a position teaching biological science at the University of Reading. Young Leigh took a healthy interest to British life while growing up in the Thames Valley. He quickly mastered the English language and spent most of his free time out of doors playing football, swimming in the summertime, fishing on the banks of the River Kennet, and, as he grew older, with girls. By the time he was fifteen, Leigh began dating the older girls. Liked to sneak into pubs because he enjoyed the dancing.

His biggest weakness in life was money. He loved the flash, the finer things. He went against his father's wishes at seventeen and chose not to attend University. He found work in a department store in the Butts Shopping Center and quickly moved up the ranks to management. He found it easy to cook the books and began stealing a few pounds at a time. His trusting demeanor and convincing presence made it too simple.

In the summer of 1978 on a sunny Monday morning, he was called to the manager's office. He found not only the manager there but two policemen ready to place him under arrest, which they promptly did.

He appeared in front of the magistrate with the certainty

that his young life would be altered by the prospect of jail time. He was given an option: pay back the money he had stolen over the years and do service work helping less fortunate children in the local housing estates, or face a sentence.

The choice was easy.

His life, fortunately, changed for the better. He found a second chance by following his father's wishes, enrolled at the University of Reading, and began studying geography.

While in Torquay one weekend with his buddies, he spotted her. He'd always liked older women. She was beautiful. Elegant. They were having dinner in a licensed restaurant, and she was dining alone at a nearby table. Leigh's group of friends from University were all smooth, well-to-do, and, for the most part, well-behaved. They all wore ties and blazers that night.

All women were fair game in Torquay that weekend.

Leigh had his usual glass of gin and, on a dare from the table, asked the waiter to place a glass of wine at the table of the lady. The waiter obliged. She looked around the restaurant in faint surprise until she noticed a young man quietly raise a glass in her direction. He was seated at a table full of young men.

Practically schoolboys.

She did not decline the glass.

What was to be a weekend in Torquay for Leigh turned into a two-week holiday. He was love-struck with an older woman who, it turned out, was still in mourning for her recently departed husband, who had succumbed to a tragic illness in Scotland.

Katalinic's downfall came during an unannounced visit to Edinburgh that fall. He'd written to her often. Followed her career in the newspapers and TV. She did not return the letters, but she did speak to him once by telephone. One Saturday morning, when the Widow answered the door at her flat, there to her surprise, stood the young man she'd met down at Torquay.

Reluctantly, she'd let him come inside. He was a happy-go-lucky young man, full of confidence and full of stamina. The physical attraction they felt did not make up for the fact that she felt unwilling to get involved.

With anyone.

He told her he had to be back at University the following Tuesday and promised her he would be leaving for England that Sunday afternoon. It was while the Widow was fixing coffee that he discovered the book. Being the studious young man that he was, Leigh picked up a book sitting on a shelf on the wall in front of her piano. What was unusual was that the entire shelf was void of any books, save that one. His curiosity overtook him as he opened the book to discover a simple handwritten note inside. By the time he'd read the note, the Widow had returned with the coffee.

For Leigh Katalinic, it was the beginning of a nightmare.

He was told to leave at once.

Fear bubbled inside him as he pondered what he had just read. He left her flat overnight bag in hand and walked two blocks before finding a taxi to take him to the train station. Before he could board the train to London, he was arrested and taken to the police station. He was being charged with theft from one of the most prominent women in the city of Edinburgh. He'd thought nothing of the gesture of the Widow, handing him his jacket when she told him to leave her flat. Failing to thoroughly check his pockets was his biggest mistake. The four British Sovereigns, struck in 1919, were found by the police. The sovereigns, bearing the image of King George V, were brilliant in luster and valuable in price.

That did it.

When the authorities learned of his earlier crimes while in Reading, they threw the book at him. Katalinic did sixteen months in jail and came out with no money, no University, and few friends. He came out of jail with a vow that he would seek something he'd had sixteen months to think about what was in that letter.

What he lacked in resources, he made up for with brains and cunning. First France, then Germany. He fell sick from giving too much blood, following a trip to the Netherlands in search of information at the University of Leiden, only to meet up with a helpful American, whose name was Daniel Harper.

***

Ambrose Dyson had awakened early that morning. He'd risen from bed, bathed and dressed, and took a look at the local newspaper over what he could only describe as a mediocre breakfast at his hotel. Everyone found his accent and British demeanor to be charming. Little did they know of his disdain for all of them, the lot. His journey to Tennessee began in Nashville, where he and his wife promptly hired a luxury vehicle at the airport and driven west. Their first stop was a small hamlet near the Tennessee River. The people in Clifton were helpful, as he found the small hotel in Clifton, which housed a log book from 1937 and contained the name he was indeed looking for.

Erwin Rommel.

Rumor had it that Rommel traveled to America in 1937 to study the military strategy of Confederate leaders and how their Civil War battles were won by these men. Most of that was true.

Rommel, in fact, was in Tennessee for an entirely different reason, and had he not been summoned back to Germany for a family emergency, he may have found what he was in search of, Alexandria.

Where Rommel was unsuccessful, Dyson planned on finding out once and for all what secrets lay hidden in Jackson. As for the high and mighty Miss Terryl Kinninmont, her agenda and his would soon be going different directions. She was harmless, had no means of protection, and would hardly be a threat once she found out that Dyson meant business. He'd signed on to baby-sit that American girl at that remote, desolate castle. He'd been well paid to do her dirty work. His failure to eliminate that posh English estate agent had been unfortunate. How was he to know that Neal Edwards would schedule maintenance the very day the bomb had been planted?

Dyson was certain there was money involved in all of this. A large sum of money. That picture framer, as Dyson knew he would, had jumped at the money and would have the job completed.

Step one.

***

Blakelyn and Bonnie doted on Jennifer. Alan and Dennis, once arriving at their parents' house, hung out with the Colonel as Blakelyn left with the ladies. Alan gave Jennifer the American Express card, plus five hundred dollars in cash before they left to go shopping.

"So how is she?" asked the Colonel. They were standing in the Albright backyard ignoring the Urbana chill, waning afternoon sunlight illuminating golden tones over the neighborhood. The Colonel and his two sons. Hands in pockets. Eyes glancing at nothing in particular.

"I'm not sure. We haven't had time to see a doctor or anything. She appears to have lost weight. There's no way to judge what being holed up in that castle back there for so long did to her well-being."

"Consider that done," the Colonel said. "I'll call Doctor Taylor shortly at his home."

Dennis spoke up. "Why doesn't she want to return to Boston?"

Albright brought his older brother and his father up to

speed as to what Jennifer had told Albright about having "one more step."

"So what's your role in this 'one more step'?" asked the Colonel.

"I'm unemployed at the moment with little else to do. I suppose I'll tag along and see what happens."

"Exactly where does this 'one more step' take place?" said Dennis.

"Tennessee."

***

Jennifer Tavistock, Bonnie Albright, and Blakelyn Albright returned to the Michigan Avenue home at 9:30 that night. Packages and boxes were everywhere. Albright and his brother were in the basement playing ping-pong when the women arrived.

Naturally, they finished their game before coming upstairs. Dennis lost.

Jennifer's back was to them when the two brothers emerged into the living room. She turned and smiled at her rescuer; and when she did, Alan Albright almost did not recognize the woman standing before him. Everything was different about Jennifer Tavistock. She'd spent two hours at a salon getting her hair done. Bonnie Albright, learning of Jennifer's fashion tastes, took her new friend to the very best boutiques in Champaign-Urbana. With school still in and Christmas season in full swing, the shops were not only open late but full of the very best in that season's *haute couture*.

Her hair had been trimmed, styled, and four inches cut to get that perfect look she wanted. For a moment, ironically, Albright was reminded of the night he met Claire Tavistock at the Parker House in Boston. Jennifer was dressed to the hilt with all the poise and self-assurance that went along with her Bostonian aristocratic background. New shoes, slacks, blouse, sweater, the works. The makeup and lipstick left him impressed.

The smile left him speechless.

Jennifer Tavistock was back.

As late as it was, the Albrights had dinner. It was especially out of the ordinary for Tom and Blakelyn Albright. Their son seemed full of life again, no longer brooding from not having Tolly Chamberlain around.

For Jennifer Tavistock, it meant a return to America, surrounded by sincere, caring people, energized by a college town environment she almost called home ten years earlier. They all sat at the dining room table. The Colonel asked the grace. She was amazed at this family. The Colonel wore his usual old sweatshirt and slacks. The food was wonderful. Dennis kept her in stitches with his sense of humor. The Colonel made an appointment for Jennifer, against her wishes, to have their family physician give her a check-up the next morning. Albright, meanwhile, would catch a ride at six the next morning with his older brother to Chicago to pick up the Big Jag. Once back in Urbana, Albright and Jennifer would be taking "one more step."

To a city known as Jackson, Tennessee.

***

At Edinburgh Airport, two flights left out within thirty minutes of each other. The Widow and Dangerous Waters left for a non-stop flight to New York, while a stunned West Virginia couple boarded a plane that flew them to Heathrow without incident. Once in London, they boarded a jet that took them to Washington, D.C. Daniel Harper and Charlotte Healy arrived home in West Virginia some five hours after landing in Washington. Their beloved state was covered in snow, the drive in from D.C. was slow going, but they were home.

Daniel Harper swore he would never return to Europe again.

***

Alan Albright slept deeply and slept well. The last time he slept, in fact, was in the hotel in Scotland the night before the rescue of Jennifer Tavistock. No one disturbed his slumber. When he eventually did awaken, it was well into the noon hour.

He found his way downstairs, looked out the window, saw that his parents were both gone, and remembered that he and Jennifer were supposed to be catching a plane that day. Someone had the wisdom to let him sleep. Suddenly, he thought of Jennifer Tavistock. She, like Albright, retired for the evening following dinner, equally as exhausted as Albright. Mrs. Albright had prepared the guest bedroom for her visitor; and as far as Albright knew, Jennifer was still asleep.

During the flight to America, Jennifer promised to tell Albright everything once they were in Illinois. Albright's job was to find her. He had done so. The thought of getting paid by Martyn Tavistock was the least of his concerns at that moment. Albright simply wanted to be there for this "one more step," whatever it might be.

***

As Alan Albright stood in his parents' house, Dangerous Waters and the Widow enjoyed room service in a smart hotel room in mid-town Manhattan. Their late breakfast was excellent. Waters had showered, shaved, and dressed early. This unexpected trip to America might have its share of risks.

He placed a call from his hotel room to Tel Aviv, spoke

briefly to his employers, told them what he needed, where and when he needed delivery, and rang off.

He casually finished off his breakfast with his companion.

***

In Jackson, Tennessee, Sonny Price paced his living floor, unable to keep still. He'd brought wood in that morning, and the fireplace roared away, the oak logs crackling. The Christmas tree stood in the corner of the living room, a simple pine adorned with bright-colored lights and shiny ornaments. The gentleman from Canada was the opposite of his host. His demeanor was calm; his mood was surprisingly composed, considering what he had in front of him.

Mr. Barbour wrote a number of notes throughout his examination. Once satisfied with his assessment he called Price over. Two sheets of note paper lay in front of him, side by side.

"Here we have the original," he said, pointing to the sheet of paper to his left. "Written in Gaelic."

"Over here," he pointed to the sheet on the right," is the English translation.

He read the original out loud to his host.

'Tha mi sgìth. Ged bu mhath leam fois bho m' eallach, cha téid mi nas fhaide.

Chan eil mi ag iarraidh ach sìth agus mathanas bho Dhia airson na rinn mi.

Tha m' anam ann an àmhghar. Chaidh mi an toir air rud nach ghabhadh ghlacadh.

Tha mi air na bliadhnaichean mu dheireadh de m' bheatha a chur seachad agus an crùn coirbidh orm.

Thàinig mi dhan tìr ùr, a dh'Alexandria, is mi 'n dòchas dèanamh nach ghabhadh dèanamh.

Tha mi air gabhail ri daoine mì-ionraic, air gèilleadh gu beartas an t-saoghail.

Mura faigh mi mathanas bho Dhia, chan eil m' fhulangas ach air tòiseachadh.

Air sgàth mo shannt, tha an dùthaich air fad a-nis air a sgriosadh.

Bidh Alba, àite mo ghaol 's mo bhreith, fo riaghladh nan Sasannach gu bràth agus tha mi ag iarraidh mathanas airson a' pheacaidh as motha a rinn mi na mo bheatha airson'

Price was in awe of this man. His friend had recommended a true professional and, with Price himself being in the world of academia, he was that much more impressed.

"Now", continued Barbour, "this is what it means in English." He began reading aloud once again.

'I am tired. Though I would desire to ease my burdens I can go no further.

I seek only peace and forgiveness from God for what I have done.

My soul is in torment. I went in search of the unobtainable.

I have spent the last years of my life wearing the corruptible crown.

I came to the new land, to Alexandria, with the hope of fulfilling the unfulfillable.

I have embraced the unrighteous, surrendered to the richness of the world.

Unless I be forgiven by God, my suffering is only beginning.

Because of my greed an entire country is at ruin.

Scotland, my beloved birthplace, lies forever under English rule and I ask forgiveness for the greatest sin of my wretched life for'

"Wow." Price could not manage another word.

Price studied Barbour's face. He wouldn't make a good poker player, he thought. There was more to come, to be sure.

"This certainly has a historic ring, doesn't it?" asked Price.

"Yes, it does," answered the Canadian. "The man seems to be British, obviously well-educated, quite possibly a peer of the realm. From the way it reads, he was every bit a traitor."

"I'm not sure I understand what you mean by traitor," said Price.

"This man is speaking with a guilty conscience. Clearly. He is asking for forgiveness. This is a remorseful declaration of guilt. He is asking for forgiveness. 'An entire country is at ruin' and the fact that it's written in the Scottish Gaelic tongue has to be referring to Scotland."

***

"Good morning, Mr. Albright."

Albright looked up to see Jennifer Tavistock fully dressed, looking rested.

"Hey there."

"You slept a bit longer than the rest of us," she said.

"Us?"

"Yes. Someone said we were going to catch a plane for Tennessee first thing this morning.

Of course, you didn't factor in that neither of us has had sufficient sleep. Oh, I woke up in this wonderful bed inside this extraordinary home and had breakfast with two amazing people. Your parents. Who both happen to work for a living. The decision not to wake you was unanimous. By the way, I went to see a doctor this morning. First thing, while you slept. Says I'm okay. Your brother, meanwhile, is awaiting your call to drive us to the airport. He, unlike your parents, took the day off."

Albright could not get over her dry, matter-of-fact delivery. Not unlike Dr. Tavistock.

"Looks like I need to get a shower."

"Smells like it, as well."

***

Dennis was there when Albright came downstairs. His big brother has sacks of fast food on the dining room table. A request from Jennifer Tavistock, naturally. She did not wait on Albright to tear into her cheeseburger and fries. She wasn't worried about calories or fat grams or anything. Just the savory experience of something she'd dreamed about for months.

Albright opened his sandwich and looked at his brother.

"Thanks, man," he said.

As soon as they finished lunch, they packed the luggage of Jennifer and Albright and loaded it up in Dennis's auto. All the purchases Jennifer made the day before were still in their bags.

They headed south for Willard Airport.

They arrived at the airport twenty minutes later, giving Jennifer a brief tour of the southern stretches of the University and were dropped off at the terminal. Dennis helped them with their considerable amount of luggage.

After dinner the night before, the Colonel pulled Albright aside. They spoke about what Albright and Jennifer Tavistock planned to do next. Albright initially wanted to go to Chicago and drive the Big Jag from the Windy City to Tennessee. The Colonel felt that was a bad idea. Rent a car, he suggested, something nondescript. Jaguars, especially a 1960 MK9, would stick out where they were going.

Albright reluctantly went along with the idea. Once again, as he slept, his sister-in-law purchased tickets for him and Jennifer. Their itinerary would be from Champaign to Memphis by way of St. Louis.

Once in Memphis, he would pick up an automobile, which would carry him and Jennifer to their ultimate destination.

Before retiring, Albright did manage a phone call to his best friend. He told Eulus about finding Jennifer Tavistock alive, that they were both in Urbana, and the fact they planned on leaving for Tennessee that next day. He asked Yew one small favor and his best friend told him not to worry; it would be taken care of.

***

Jackson, Tennessee

Ambrose Dyson was furious. He paid a visit to the shopkeeper the next day, as was the agreement, to pick up his work. To his disgust, it was not ready. He found a sign posted on the front window stating that the business would re-open at 9A.M. Monday morning.

Dyson arrived at the shop that Monday morning at 8:30. He sat inside his automobile, motor running, heater on full, waiting for the shopkeeper to arrive.

***

As Ambrose Dyson sat fuming in his automobile, a phone call was made to a New York City hotel room. The caller asked for the room of Terryl Kinninmont.

"Hello," said the Widow.

"Good morning, Terryl; it's me. The police have found out about the document. Whoever this chap you have in place down here brought it to a shop to be framed. The shopkeeper became suspicious and notified the police. They have no idea that I've even seen it prior to coming to Tennessee; much less know where it came from, and from whom. Are we any closer to finding the remainder of the epistle?"

The question drew the Widow into disappointment and anger as she looked back at the escape of Jennifer Tavistock. "No we are not. The fact that I'm due to arrive in Tennessee this afternoon means you need to leave America at once, Donald. Find a reason to return to Canada. Health reasons, family emergency, anything. Just leave!"

The fact that the Widow hailed from Nova Scotia was a stroke of luck. Dr. Donald Barbour had, ironically, been the one who interpreted that very document at the request of the Widow, who happened to be an old family friend. He was widely regarded as the eminent expert on all things Gaelic in North America. Once he learned that people in Tennessee—of all places—were inquiring about that very same document, he'd called the Widow at once. Dr. Barbour was unaware that Jennifer Tavistock had been detained or that the Widow had recently tried to kill a number of people. Her angle was that she was working on a historic breakthrough and needed the doctor's help. Barbour naturally became interested, once he read the document and was eager to discover not only who had written it but what the remaining content might be.

The Widow now realized the true inability of Ambrose Dyson to take care of a simple matter. His carelessness placed something as vital as the document into the hands of the authorities.

Yet another setback.

***

Elford Chappell had been in position since Dyson's arrival. Since his encounter with the Jackson mayor over the weekend, he was aware that this Dyson fellow had been tailed virtually everywhere he went in Jackson. There had been yet another visit to Northwood, at the home of the symphony board member the evening before that lasted an hour. Chappell sat in an unmarked vehicle one half-block up the street from the shop. Directly across the street from the shop, inside a drug store, stood two uniformed Jackson Police officers. Like Chappell, they watched every move Dyson made.

Polk Lowery left for work at the same time he always did. His cooperation with the Madison County Sheriff's Department aside, he took comfort in knowing the bulging .38 Special inside his leather jacket was there. As he drove into the parking lot of his shop, he noticed the late model automobile, engine running, parked in front. Lowery stepped out of his truck, walked straight ahead, eyes on the occupant of the automobile.

He was ready for anything.

Ambrose Dyson was fuming. He'd shown up on Saturday morning, as promised, to pick up his work. He was fed up with the attitudes he'd encountered with many of these southerners. To make matters worse, the Widow had phoned from New York, and Dyson was due to meet with her once she reached Jackson later that day. He slammed his car door behind him, heavy frame in stride, as he approached Polk Lowery.

Lowery slipped a hand into his pocket and found comfort in the pistol grip. His eyes were covered by his old sunglasses. He looked the old man over as he drew near. Steady walk, upright stance, and unblinking eyes in spite of the bright sunlight.

***

As the two men faced each other in a Jackson, Tennessee, parking lot, Dangerous Waters stepped foot onto Tennessee soil for the first time. With the beautiful elegantly dressed woman at his side, he strode through the Memphis Airport with the unexpected anticipation of not knowing what lay around the corner. He wore a set of navy slacks and casual dress shirt underneath a camel-hair double-breasted overcoat, a gift from the Widow, that fateful Saturday morning while shopping in Princes Street in Edinburgh.

The flight from New York arrived on schedule, and once they gathered their luggage from baggage claim, he found the rental car desk. While in New York, Waters made arrangements to rent a Buick Riviera and, as promised, the shiny white coupe was waiting for them.

As Waters hoped, the specific automobile he had hired had what he needed. Once he opened

the trunk, he noticed a black duffel bag. He hauled the Widow's considerable luggage into the Buick, his own spare gear, and casually unzipped the duffel. He breathed deeply in satisfaction as he eyed what lay inside. The Heckler and Koch MP5K was barely three years into production. A year earlier, Waters went through vigorous training with the short-barreled German-made machine pistol, disliked by many of his bosses due to the reduced range of effectiveness, but put into the hands of his security firm, nonetheless. One particular advantage the weapon boasted was its easy conceal ability. In addition to the weapon itself, Waters found eight 30 round magazines inside the duffel bag.

No questions had been asked.

He closed the trunk, and after opening the passenger door for the Widow, walked around the Riviera and climbed into the driver's seat.

Once again, Dangerous was back in America.

It was wonderful.

***

"I believe you have something for me that should have been ready a couple days ago," growled Ambrose Dyson.

"Family emergency, I'm afraid," Lowery replied, eyes locked on the old man. "I have it ready for you now, sir. If you just come inside, you can pick it up."

Lowery reached into his pocket, grabbed his keys, and opened the bolt lock on the wooden door of his shop. He walked in, turned up the thermostat to warm things up inside, and walked behind the counter. He hung his leather jacket on a hook and put on his well-worn smock.

"Here you are, Mr. Dyson. Hope it meets your expectations." Lowery placed the frame gingerly in front of his customer.

Dyson ignored the sarcasm in Lowery's voice. He beamed at once when he noticed the excellent work. Dyson noticed the outside edges of the frame and how squared they were. He examined the document itself, how the double matting neatly covered the historic work.

He nodded in approval. "Well done, young man. I believe I owe you payment." Dyson reached inside his breast pocket and paid the framer in full.

What was unknown to Dyson was that a man who was in the process of leaving Jackson, Tennessee, at that very moment had placed a telephone call to New York City. His conversation was brief and pertained to the now-framed work in his possession. Had Dyson spoken to the Widow, he would have known that Lowery was lying about the family emergency and that a lot of interest was being directed at what lay inside that frame. As it was, Dyson picked up his work, not bothering to thank Polk Lowery, and walked to his car. He left the frame shop and returned to his hotel.

***

Alan Albright sat on the aisle seat, dozing. Jennifer Tavistock, meanwhile, was wide awake, observing the city of Memphis from above as the plane banked and approached its destination below. The sun shone over the city. It was mid-afternoon. Neither Albright nor Jennifer had ever been to Tennessee. With a nudge to her traveling companion, she awoke Alan Albright, who still suffered from jet lag.

"Okay, Rip Van Winkle. Time to wake up. We're about to land."

***

The city of Jackson was simply buzzing about the upcoming concert. The Jackson Symphony itself suddenly became the envy of the respective Memphis and Nashville symphonies at the ability of landing the renowned Terryl Kinnimont. Newspapers and television stations from the two largest cities in Tennessee were devoting considerable coverage on the event. As Saturday approached, the Jackson Symphony found themselves bombarded with phone calls of people as far away as Atlanta looking for tickets.

By Wednesday afternoon, all the seats at the Jackson Civic Center were sold out.

Jennifer Tavistock, who was in a hotel room next to Albright's, watched television as she finished up drying her hair. It was Thursday evening, and she and Albright had spent a third day of frustration in Jackson. Since returning from Scotland, Jennifer felt an urge, for reasons she did not understand, to take a least two showers a day. When she saw the story on the Jackson television station, she ran to the phone, called Albright's room, and screamed into the line that he come next door at once.

Albright was there in ten seconds, not even bothering to close his hotel door. Jennifer opened the door, transfixed to the TV screen, not saying a word. By the time Albright walked in, the maestro for the Jackson Symphony was concluding an interview about the excitement building around Saturday's upcoming concert. Albright, jumping to conclusions as he often did, could not understand Jennifer's hysteria, until the report ended and the news anchor came back on the screen with a tag line stating the Jackson Symphony Orchestra's upcoming performance with Scottish performer Terryl Kinnimont was sold out.

Jennifer continued to stare at the TV screen as she said, "She's here!"

Albright was staring at the television but for a different reason. He kept looking at the anchor who was in the process of having a conversation with the weatherman about the outside chance of snow. There was something familiar about the man. Too familiar. He knew this fellow.

Knew him from Urbana High School. Hargrave Washburn, he was sure of it.

Strangely enough, the weatherman did not refer to the anchor as Hargrave. In fact, during the weather transition he called him Jack. As they went to break, the announcer's voice came up, telling audiences they were watching the news at six with Alison Hopper and Jack Stockdale, weather with Ted McClure and sports with Sam Rowland.

As if the Widow being in the same town wasn't enough, what was his old classmate from Urbana High School doing on TV down here, and why was he calling himself Jack Stockdale?

"She's here," Jennifer said once again. "Obviously, she's after the same thing we are. By the way, that man they interviewed just before you came in here is Ambrose Dyson, her so-called manager. This is too good!"

"Ambrose Dyson? That's the name you gave to the police. The man who was part of the group, holding you captive in Castle Craig. Well, well, well. Looks like you might have the chance to even things up right here in Tennessee after all, Miss Tavistock."

Things had not gone well in Tennessee for Jennifer

Tavistock. As least as far as what she was looking for was concerned. They arrived in Jackson earlier that week, found rooms at the Old English Inn, and went to work at once. They'd been to the public library, spending the day poring over records provided by a local genealogical society. The librarians had been most helpful; but, at the end of the day, she was unable to find the name of the man she was looking for. Jennifer did manage to leave a one thousand dollar donation to the society as a gesture of goodwill, and they, in turn, promised to call her if someone in that city might know of the name. Later that day, they visited the Madison County Courthouse looking through public records. Nothing. She and Albright were looking for a name from the early eighteen hundreds. They were searching for one of the early settlers of Jackson, who had moved, in his waning years, to West Tennessee.

Born in Scotland, the man sailed for America at a very young age and served gallantly in the Revolutionary War. In his later years, unable to care for himself any longer, he traveled to West Tennessee to live out his remaining days with his son, who had secured a land grant in the expanding section of West Tennessee. This man, whose final days were spent in a Tennessee community briefly known as Alexandria, was in the family Bible Jennifer Tavistock carried with her from Castle Craig. The Bible contained the names of her ancestors, the missing link she first set out to find in Scotland. The man in question had written, in addition to his last will, a testament in his native Gaelic tongue.

Jennifer acquired this testament, as least part of it, along with a Crucifix belonging to this man, three weeks into her quest in Scotland. Her first stop had been St. Andrews. While in St. Andrews, she'd made contact with a research consultant. Her decision to go to St. Andrews was purely sentimental, based on the fact that she'd visited it some years before.

Jennifer knew she'd have to start somewhere.

She paid the consultant well and within three weeks was on to something.

She was given the name of a place in the north of Scotland. Additionally, Jennifer was given the name of an elderly woman, in her nineties, who was living at a nursing home in a city she'd never heard of.

The city was called Goldspie, and the woman's name was Henrietta Fraser Sim.

Jennifer spent five days in the company of Mrs. Sim. She fell in love with the charming woman, who in turn felt a bond with her young American, who turned out to be a distant cousin. Mrs. Sim filled Jennifer's head with a history of her sought-after family tree, explaining as best she could remember most of the legacy of the Fraser family.

It was Mrs. Sim, who told Jennifer about Castle Craig. It was Mrs. Sim, who told the tale of the two brothers who moved to America at a very young age when their mother died. The oldest was Malcolm; the youngest, Walter, a man who spent most of his years studying the Gaelic language. One of his last deeds in life was to send by mail a letter back to Scotland to his sister Jane who, unlike her brothers, remained in her native country, having been taken in by a loving family, who eventually moved to St. Andrews.

Jennifer learned that Walter Fraser, in fact, returned to Scotland once as a young man, spending five years in that country before returning to America for good.

Jennifer Tavistock left the company of Mrs. Sim with a sense of excitement and accomplishment. As a gift, Jennifer bought her cousin the care of a private nurse to see to her needs. In return, Mrs. Sim gave something to Jennifer.

A letter, a Crucifix, and one other item. Jennifer found it hard to believe what the elderly woman was saying. Perhaps, confusion had set in with her old age. This item had been handed down through the years, from one generation to the next, beginning with Jane Fraser.

Henrietta Sim, in her frail, soft voice, insisted upon one

thing. Never keep the Crucifix and the letter with the third item. Keep them separate, she insisted. Ironically, Jennifer Tavistock returned to St. Andrews to recover a bag of luggage she'd left in a hotel room prior to traveling to the north of Scotland. She, in turn, would be traveling back up north to introduce herself to the residents of Castle Craig. The words of Henrietta Sim stuck in Jennifer's heart. What she had learned about her missing family tree left her full of anticipation about heading to the birthplace of Malcolm Fraser, Castle Craig.

Henrietta's insistence of the three keepsakes being kept apart was, after much deliberation from Jennifer, obeyed. She had no idea, whatsoever, what to do and how to do it. She was visiting a foreign country and lived out of a suitcase in hotel rooms. She pondered a solution throughout the night in St. Andrews before coming up with what she hoped to be a workable plan. Prior to leaving for the north of Scotland the next morning, Jennifer dropped into a small clothing shop in South Street, made a purchase, and casually slipped the third keepsake into the box, while the shopkeeper walked into the back in search of wrapping paper.

That was her last day of freedom prior to being rescued by Alan Albright. That morning, she placed a call to the University of St. Andrews' professor, thanking him for his invaluable assistance and sharing with him the treasures she'd obtained from her cousin. She'd driven later that day to Castle Craig, introduced herself to the occupants, only to be told by Ambrose Dyson that same day that she would be kept at Castle Craig until further notice "for her own good."

Unknown to Jennifer, Ross Burnham would later come within an inch of losing his life on his way to Golspie that evening while driving up from St. Andrews.

Everything she brought with her that day disappeared. Even her hired automobile. She surmised that her captors had somehow returned the auto to the place she'd rented at the Edinburgh Airport, since all the rental paperwork lay in the glove compartment.

Once being rescued, she realized that to try to recover her money, passport, and luggage was useless. Her deepest fear lifted the day she and Albright, while standing in the shop in South Street in St. Andrews, picked up the gift-wrapped box she'd left what seemed like an age ago.

***

Moments after Ambrose Dyson left for his hotel, Elford Chappel and three other law enforcement officers walked in to see Polk Lowery, standing behind the counter. Lowery was left with the same sense of foreboding as he was the first time Dyson walked through his door.

"Good job," said Deputy Chappel.

"Bastard," replied Lowery. "By the way, what about this money he left?"

"Keep it."

On that note, Lowery rang open the cash register and deposited the money. "I hope you bury the bastard," he said, looking at the deputy.

"Oh, we plan on it. Seems like Mr. Dyson's made some enemies during the short time he's been in this town." Chappel didn't like what he saw in front of him. "You all right, Polk?"

"I'm good. I never want to see that man again. For the record, did you guys ever figure out what that document said?"

Chappel nodded. "Sort of. It's written in the ancient Scottish language of Gaelic. Some sort of confessional. We know what it says, but we're unsure what it means. A Canadian fellow flew in Saturday and translated it."

"So what's Dyson's connection?" asked Lowery.

"We're in the process of finding that out."

***

The dinner party was to begin at 6:30 that evening in Northwood. The hosts had invited key members of the Jackson Symphony Orchestra's board of directors, the Symphony conductor, Ambrose and Corra Dyson, as well as Terryl Kinnimont and David Waters. The hostess was pleasantly surprised to receive a phone call the morning before from none other than the mayor of Jackson. The mayor had, once again, congratulated the Jackson Symphony for their golden opportunity of putting on such an elaborate event and asked if any additional help needed to be provided from city hall. Naturally, the hostess had extended an invitation for the mayor and his wife to attend the upcoming dinner party and have the opportunity to meet Terryl Kinnimont herself.

He gladly accepted.

Two hours earlier, Dyson was shocked when, in the lobby of the Holiday Inn, Terryl Kinnimont strolled in with a strange man. He thought it odd the day before when the Widow informed him it would not be necessary for Dyson to pick her up at the Memphis Airport.

Now he knew why.

He'd looked the chap over. Average size. Smooth dresser. In spite of the man's firm handshake and steadfast gaze, Dyson felt assured that this David Waters was nothing more than a companion who, if necessary, would meet the same fate as the Widow if either tried to get in his way. As it was, he had plenty of dirt on the Widow. The kidnapping of the American girl. The unsuccessful car bombing of that English estate agent in Bristol. Dyson's agenda was simple. Find out the real reason for coming to Tennessee. This mystery of Alexandria had to mean but one thing.

Money.

Dyson had the document translated for himself before leaving Scotland. It is not the most difficult thing to do to get Gaelic translated into English while living in Edinburgh. Even though he had less than 24 hours before leaving for America when the Widow had given the document to Dyson, along with her orders of what to do with the document, he'd managed to find out what it said.

That document ultimately turned the man.

Why should she, this posh woman with plenty of money of her own, get even more money?

Corra went along with the plan as well. Whatever this Alexandria business turned out to be, Terryl Kinnimont would not be the benefactor. In fact, Terryl Kinnimont would probably not be leaving the United States alive.

As dinner was served that evening, the guests from Britain mixed wit and merriment with the residents from Jackson. David Waters, as he introduced himself to the Tennesseans, left quite an impression when he told everyone what he did for a living.

Ambrose Dyson was the exception. There was a momentary sense of apprehension when David Waters explained to the dinner party that he was employed by an Israeli-based protection agency.

The mayor of Jackson happened to have his eyes on Dyson the moment Waters disclosed the news about his employment. The evening had been a difficult one for the mayor. His rheumatic hip had bothered him all day. He could have easily bowed out of the dinner party invitation and stayed home to tend to his sore bones. The mayor was smart enough to understand that whatever business these people had in Jackson would probably be concluded by the time Saturday's concert was over, so that meant he absolutely had to be at this dinner party.

When David Waters told everyone his occupation, the mayor watched the eyes of Ambrose shift from his knife and fork to the man seated two places down and one across from where Dyson sat. He watched Dyson look past the elegantly decorated dinner table, replete with the very best food and wine, to the young black-haired man. It was momentary but discernible, nonetheless. The mayor correctly deduced that these two men were strangers, and the younger man from Britain just made the older British fellow uncomfortable.

***

As the dinner party unfolded in Northwood, Jennifer Tavistock and Alan Albright continued their exploration of the city of Jackson. The people at the Old English Inn earlier that day recommended a popular nightspot to the visiting couple. It was a nightclub that catered to the hip crowd of Jackson, known as TJ's. They decided to give it a try.

Dancing wasn't one of Alan Albright's pastimes. Once inside of TJ's, with the music and the atmosphere of the nightclub all upbeat, he had a sudden change of heart. He and Jennifer danced the night away, drank their share of beer, and hung out with the friendly regulars.

For Jennifer Tavistock, the escape into the nightclub was undoubtedly what she needed to get away from her stumbling blocks in Tennessee. She was, by nature, a socially outgoing person, made friends easily, and had the ability to converse on any level with just about anyone. Being mid-week, TJ's wasn't overly crowded, which meant it was easy for them to find a good table. By the end of the evening, their chairs were full with new-found friends and their table chocked with beer bottles.

***

Terryl Kinnimont, being the woman of charm that she was, did not disappoint those at the dinner party. As she had done in an earlier interview with a Nashville television station, she explained to everyone her reason for putting on her very first American performance in the heart of West Tennessee. So many residents of Tennessee she said, and the southeastern United States at that matter, had their roots in Scotland. Why Jackson? Because, she explained, the setting was conducive to what she wanted to experience in America. The small town charm and the intimacy of performing with a smaller orchestra at Christmas time was something she'd dreamed of doing for years.

Dangerous Waters, always the analyzer and strategist, left no hint of what he was thinking that evening at the dinner party. The women, both young and old at that table, were swept off their feet by his good looks and appeal. He spoke little, listened attentively, and smiled constantly. He was actually enjoying the meal.

Waters did manage to conclude that evening that Corra and Ambrose Dyson were up to something. He'd lived amongst treachery for most of his life. He understood when people had hidden agendas and growing up in Dundee taught him to know when people were hatching a plot. The Widow had spoken little of this man since opening up their last night in Edinburgh. He knew he was her manager of sorts and was a liaison between the Widow and the Americans, putting on this upcoming concert.

He did not know what this man and his wife, for that matter, were really up to. When he'd walked into the Holiday Inn lobby from the Jackson cold, luggage in both hands, he'd picked up on his vibes the moment their eyes met.

All this, coupled with the break-in at Ramsay Gardens and the revelations about this Alan Albright fellow wanting to harm the Widow made this latest development with these two older people even more puzzling.

***

Without a doubt, the funniest part of the evening was watching Alan Albright try to dance. He was hopelessly out of step on the fast numbers; and when he and Jennifer tried slow dancing, she kept dodging her feet to prevent them from being stepped on. Nevertheless, they both had a time that evening at the nightclub and by eleven called it an evening.

***

Friday was a busy day for the Widow. She spent the morning going over her musical selections for the following night's performance. There were two selections of music in particular she insisted upon, which she and the conductor were at odds upon the exact arrangements of how they would be played.

She was extremely fastidious, as was the conductor, and by noon they reached an accord. There would be two rehearsals. The first that afternoon, the second the day of the concert itself.

The Jackson Symphony, she had to admit, was much better than she realized.

***

Alan Albright, after finding the number of the local television station in the white pages, placed a call to Jack Stockdale at ten that morning. He was informed that Mr. Stockdale would not be in until 1:30. At 1:45 he called back and was put through to the newsroom.

"Jack Stockdale."

"Hello, Hargrave, or do you prefer Jack Stockdale? This is a voice from the past. Urbana High School, to be exact. Class of 1970. Go Tigers!"

Ten seconds later, after the shock wore off, Stockdale asked, "Who is this?"

"My name is Alan Albright. I'm not sure if you remember me or not."

"Alan Albright? What a surprise. Yea, I remember you, buddy. Where are you?"

"I'm in Jackson. Been watching you on the television. How are things going?"

Stockdale was seated in the cramped newsroom going over the rundown for the six o'clock newscast. There was precious little so far. The lead story was yet to be determined.

"Not bad. Not bad. What in the world brings you to Tennessee? And call me Hargrave. Jack Stockdale, in case you're wondering, is my air name. Not entirely unusual in my business, by the way, to use a different name. I chose Jack Stockdale because it is a good news name. But enough of me. What brings you to Jackson?"

"Long story, you might say. I was wondering if you might be free for a drink. I have one heck of a story you might be interested in. One heck of a story!"

"I'm tied up here all day, Alan. I'm not free until 10:30 tonight."

"Do you get a dinner break?"

Stockdale thought a moment. "I do get an hour for dinner after the six. I suppose I can take a break and hang out with a homeboy. Where are you staying?"

"The Old English Inn. North Highland Avenue."

"Oh, I know where it is. Tell you what. How about meeting me in the restaurant at 6:45. I won't have more than an hour."

"Deal. See you then. Hargrave, this thing is huge. This could mean big things for you, my friend."

***

Ambrose and Corra Dyson had spent very little time alone

with the Widow in Jackson. Since the Dysons had been in America, the last contact they actually had with Scotland was the phone call with the Widow shortly before her departure to Tennessee. They were unaware of the events that had taken place regarding Jennifer Tavistock. They did not know about her rescue from Castle Craig, and neither knew at that moment that Jennifer Tavistock was not only a free woman but happened to be in none other than Jackson, Tennessee.

***

At 6:30 that evening Alan Albright stood in the foyer of the Old English Inn, alongside Jennifer Tavistock, awaiting the arrival of the television personality. Jack Stockdale walked in ten minutes later, fresh from his six o'clock newscast.

"Urbana Tigers!" Stockdale exclaimed, walking over to Albright. They shook hands, all smiles, seeing each other for the first time since leaving high school.

Being a Friday night, the restaurant was full of people, and most of those nearby recognized the anchor. Stockdale stood an inch or so shorter than Albright. The Afro was much shorter these days, the beard Albright remembered from school long gone, and what remained was neatly cut, with two inch sideburns and a thick moustache remaining. Jack Stockdale, like Albright, spoke in a Midwestern accent, typical to those from Urbana, not quite the Chicago nasal, but a smoother enunciation deemed perfect to those in the broadcasting business.

His complexion was medium brown, with a broad nose and thick eyebrows. His news director had recommended contacts when he was hired on as anchor, but Stockdale insisted on wearing glasses. It gave him a somewhat bookish look, and over the years the signature glasses had grown on the viewing audience.

Albright introduced Jennifer to the anchor. Being the gentleman that he was, Jennifer was taken aback momentarily when Stockdale addressed her as "ma'am." People were walking through, recognizing the news anchor, some speaking, others nudging one another.

"Jennifer, we are in the presence of a celebrity."

Stockdale shook his head. "Hardly." He looked down at his polished Stacey Adams. "This is Tennessee."

They followed the server to their table. Once they were seated, and iced tea was served to all three, with the small talk over, Albright got to the point.

"Hargrave, are you aware of this thing the Jackson Symphony is putting on tomorrow night?"

"Yea. Who isn't? Is that why you came all the way to Tennessee, Albright? To see Terryl Kinnimont?"

Alan Albright proceeded over the next eight minutes, with a few clarifications from Jennifer, to tell the anchor the real reason they had traveled to Jackson, Tennessee. By the time their meals arrived, Stockdale wasn't even interested in the mouth-watering pork chops in front of him.

Hargrave Washburn, a.k.a Jack Stockdale, left Urbana following graduation for Nashville. Following a degree in journalism from Tennessee State University, he interned at a Nashville television station while at TSU and for the past three years held the job as anchor in Jackson. Like most journalists, he had a nose for a good story, and what had been laid out in front of him was a honey. Being hyperactive and full of energy, his excitement was evident.

"Jennifer, are you willing to come forward on camera with all of this?"

Jennifer Tavistock, being the free woman she was in spite of being in the company of Alan Albright, was still dealing with her captivity. To the disbelief of the Scottish police in Goldspie, she insisted on not pressing charges against anyone in Scotland. Now, in America, traces of apprehension were returning, particularly since seeing the face of Ambrose Dyson on the interview days before. She reverted to the Scripture she'd read flying to Illinois from Maine days before, while Albright dozed in the seat at her side. It was a passage from the Book of Deuteronomy. It read:

"Be strong and courageous, do not be afraid or tremble at them, for the LORD your God is the one who goes with you. He will not fail you or forsake you."

Jennifer's reply took the anchor aback. "Are you willing to put this on the air? There could be consequences, which you cannot imagine."

"These are dangerous times, Jennifer. It's part of my job. Kidnapping is serious business. Based on what you tell me, Miss Terryl Kinnimont is a powerful and dangerous person. Does this woman know you are here in Jackson?"

"To my knowledge, she does not. The gentleman your reporter interviewed the other night, Mr. Ambrose Dyson, isn't aware of my presence here, either."

At that moment, Albright spoke up. "This guy is pure scum. I cannot believe the nerve these people have. When Jennifer escaped, the last thing we expected was for them to actually put on a performance. It's as if she's defying everything and everyone. How brazen can you get?"

Washburn had a habit of adjusting his glasses at the bridge of his nose. His news director had convinced him not to do it on the air, but it was a nervous practice, particularly when he was thinking. He raised his right index finger to his nose while looking at his friend from Illinois.

"This could be our lead story at ten." He stood up from the table, excused himself, and went to the front of the restaurant to find a telephone.

***

Rehearsal ended at nine. Everyone was comfortable with what was expected of them. The orchestra seamed flawlessly with the Widow, held together by the maestro and his meticulous attention to detail. As they exited the Civic Center, he opened the door to the automobile for the Widow, planted a kiss on her cheek, and, before Dangerous Waters drove off, told her that tomorrow night will be unforgettable.

***

Jack Stockdale introduced the lead story that night in the A-block on the ten o'clock news. He hoped to control his on-camera demeanor enough to not come across as being angry or displeased. His news director had climbed all over him while on the phone at the Old English Inn and continued the aggravation once returning to the station. The reporter, assigned to cover the concert since the Widow's arrival in Jackson, sided with the news director. In all, it was an unpleasant time span leading up to the ten o'clock newscast for Jack Stockdale.

"Good evening, I'm Alison Hopper."

"I'm Jack Stockdale. Our lead story tonight: Scottish virtuoso Terryl Kinnimont tells us that tomorrow night's concert in Jackson will be her last. Caroline Walker has the details in this exclusive report."

Back at the Old English Inn, watching the news in the lobby, Jennifer Tavistock and Alan Albright watched the local news with renewed interest.

Neither was at all surprised at the sudden announcement.

Once Stockdale returned to their table earlier that evening with the bad news that the story idea was impossible, disappointment set in. Jennifer made it clear that it was all wishful thinking, and they were certainly not naive enough to really think they could get a story like that on the air without proof. After thinking the situation through, all three came to the conclusion that it was probably for the best that the story not be pursued any further.

Stockdale, meanwhile, when returning to work and pressed about his source, claimed it had been an anonymous phone call. That really made his news director angry.

Furious, in fact.

Journalism 101, Stockdale was told, was not to believe nonsense from crank callers. Like most Jacksonians, the news director understood that this was one of the biggest events to take place in Jackson in a decade. Everyone was excited about Saturday's concert.

Everyone, except Jackson's mayor. He, too, watched the Jackson ten o'clock news that evening. He read over a report, given him earlier that evening, detailing the step-by-step activities of Mr. Ambrose Dyson. There was little in the report that told him anything. Whatever this man's business was somehow connected with the lovely Terryl Kinnimont. The mayor was certainly charmed by the Widow. He'd learned of her fame and her late husband.

Impressive.

Her celebrity status, notwithstanding, the mayor failed to buy into the fact that whatever their business in Jackson, Scottish pride and a tribute to the Americans, whose heritage hailed from that nation wasn't the real reason. Now the news that she was retiring following Saturday's concert. The mayor did find Terryl Kinnimont's interesting companion to be different, based on the events he observed at the dinner party.

Ambrose Dyson, the mayor concluded, did not like David Waters.

***

As the mayor listened to the report on Saturday's concert being Terryl Kinnimont's last, the Widow at last got the opportunity to meet with the Dysons. Dangerous Waters remained at the hotel during rehearsal, and she sat in a restaurant over a cup of coffee across from Ambrose and Corra.

"Where is it?" she asked.

"It's safe in the hotel room," said Dyson.

"Do you know what it says?" asked the Widow. She brushed a lock of her long brown hair back and looked at the old man before her. Her brown eyes were anything but friendly. She tapped her fingers against the tablecloth and waited for an answer.

"I do not," he replied.

"Lots of people speak Gaelic these days, don't they? After all, we're all Scottish. This historic artifact means a lot to me. In fact, this is partly why we're all here."

You don't say, Dyson thought.

"I'll be leaving America first thing Sunday morning. Our business will be complete. As promised, you'll be paid in full."

"Going back to Edinburgh, are you?"

"Where I'm going, Mr. Ambrose, is none of your concern. Incidentally, you've done well."

Cora Dyson had sat quietly, looking as graceful as ever, sipping a coffee. She spoke up for the first time. "What about the girl?"

The Widow looked at Corra. She wore a blue suit over a ruffled white lace blouse. Age aside, the Widow trusted her as much as she trusted her husband.

"She's being taken care of."

"Taken care of?" Corra asked. "Abigail and Seth are hardly capable of..."

"Of what?" the Widow snapped.

"Nothing."

"Let's get back to why you're here," the Widow said, returning her attention to Ambrose Dyson."Were you able to confirm the location?"

Dyson nodded.

"Are you absolutely certain?"

"No doubt about it. Once we landed here, I was able to find, with the help of the local historian of this place, the chap you were looking for and where he lived out his final years." Dyson reached into his breast pocket and handed over a sealed envelope.

"Well done. Meet me at eight o'clock sharp tomorrow morning. Have the car ready. David and I will be waiting."

***

At 10:45 the news anchor returned to the Old English Inn. Stockdale introduced his wife to Albright and Jennifer Tavistock. Elise Washburn should have been in Hollywood. Her complexion was a shade darker than her husband's. In spite of her age, streaks of grey were mixed in with her wavy black hair. Like her husband, Elise wore glasses, had a small nose, and her lips were covered in a dark burgundy shade of lipstick. She'd had trouble finding a job in her profession in Jackson and currently worked in a department store selling cosmetics.

Washburn wore an overcoat over his suit, and, as was his habit at the end of his work day, his tie was nowhere to be found. They piled in the Washburn's Datsun, cramped as it was and, at the request of his friend from Urbana, headed to TJ's. Unlike earlier in the week, the club was packed and the atmosphere that night was stimulating. The music was deafening, lights flashed, and beer was everywhere. Albright and Jennifer enjoyed being in the company of the local celebrity, as total strangers were constantly walking over to their table speaking to Jack

Stockdale. They'd been at the club thirty minutes when several people from the station dropped in and quickly filled up their table.

The news director was not one of them.

Jennifer learned that Elise had a degree in interior design. She hailed from Nashville and reluctantly took the job at the department store to be with her husband. Albright and Stockdale talked more about what the Widow had done, with speculation on the real reason this woman would be in Jackson. Stockdale could not believe that Jennifer Tavistock did not press charges against the people who held her captive. Yes, she's famous. Yes, her late husband served in government. Kidnapping is kidnapping, no matter who she was or who she'd been married to, Stockdale insisted.

Jennifer pulled Albright onto the crowded dance floor. It was a Friday night, and those who danced alongside the beautiful young woman had no idea what she had endured for so long or what freedom to let loose on a Friday night really meant to her.

***

The Widow arose at 7 A.M. on the day of the concert. Waters was already up, showered, and dressed. His instincts told him that today would be life-changing. For whom, he wasn't exactly sure. He'd asked few questions since that night at Ramsay Gardens. His convictions to guard the woman he'd suddenly realized he was in love with was unconditional.

Dangerous Waters knew of Alan Albright but had no idea of who Jennifer Tavistock was or how she might be connected with the Widow. Since leaving Scotland, Waters knew that the upcoming performance with the Jackson Symphony Orchestra in Tennessee was the primary reason for the sudden trip to America.

He did question the timing.

The Widow responded that she planned on telling Waters the same night of the break-in. Dangerous Waters was not a nosy man. His station in life this Christmas holiday season was to stand by a woman who dealt with personal matters that did not concern him.

That's the kind of man he was.

He found the old man, who called himself Dyson, to be anything but entertaining. Her so-called manager fancied himself as something of a tough guy. From the moment Waters walked into the lobby of the Holiday Inn to the dinner party, Dyson tried to come off as being hard. As intimidating as he tried to be, Waters was almost amused by Dyson's attempt to stare him down across the dinner table. Waters, too, noticed Dyson's reaction when he told the hosts what he did for a living.

As Waters helped the Widow with her overcoat in the lobby, he noticed that Dyson's temperament had not changed. He looked at the older man and noticed that he had a look of implied malice about him. What bothered Waters the most was that the malice seemed not to be directed just at him.

It seemed to be directed toward the Widow, as well.

Waters felt comfort in knowing that in one pocket of the camel-hair overcoat rested his Heckler & Koch MP5K and in the other an extra 15 round magazine. He wasn't sure where he and the Widow were going this morning, but the Dysons were driving; and Waters wasn't about to go out and about without any defenses.

***

Albright's phone rang and rang. He turned over, answered it, and said good morning to Jennifer Tavistock, who sounded wide awake on the phone.

"What time is it?" he asked.

"10:30."

They shut down TJ's the night before. They retired to their respective rooms and both fell asleep.

"You know what you told me last night over dinner?"

Albright struggled to collect his senses. It had been a number of years since he'd drank so much.

"I told you several things as best I remember, Jennifer."

"About me contacting someone."

"Oh, yea! Your brother and your best friend, what's her name... the Rhode Island Redhead?"

"Franconia despises being called that. It's clear that you and Oliver had a good conversation. Anyway, I can't seem to go any longer. I need to speak to Roger. Let him know I'm okay."

"Do you know where he is?"

"I believe I do."

"Give me thirty minutes to get a shower, and I'll see you in the lobby for breakfast. We'll call whoever you need then, fair enough?"

***

Once the Widow reached their destination, a look of grave disappointment had come over her. What she expected and what stood before her were completely different. They were parked in front of a warehouse, having seen better days, four blocks west of the Madison County Courthouse. All four passengers got out of the car into the frosty morning air. Ambrose Dyson led the way, walked up to the front of the building, and knocked on a rusty metal door.

The door opened and an elderly Black man, dressed in overalls and wearing a weathered hat, stood there. He said nothing, and the look on his face gave no indication whatsoever what he could have been thinking at the time.

The inside of the warehouse had an oily smell. Dust was everywhere. A single bare light bulb provided illumination. Old tires lay scattered about and there were signs that once upon a time a garage of some sort might have called the warehouse home.

"Here it is," Dyson said. "The Silver Post. Final home of Walter Fraser once stood here."

Dangerous Waters observed the disdain Dyson showed towards the Black man. He was still very much in the dark about what was transpiring in this warehouse. It was clear that Corra shared her husband's sentiments about the occupant of the warehouse. The Widow, meanwhile, looked the place over, seeing nothing whatsoever that so much as resembled a home. Being in the 20th century, she understood that what once stood in the 1800's would be completely different than what was standing in December 1979. Ignoring the dust, the rubble, and the smell of oil and gasoline, she began to walk about the warehouse.

"Sir, what is your name?" she asked the stranger.

"My name is Samuel Weatherspoon."

"How do you do, sir?"

Mr. Weatherspoon seemed taken aback by her politeness. "I'm fine, thank you. And yourself?"

"Did Mr. Dyson tell you why we're here?" she asked.

Weatherspoon looked Dyson in the eyes. Dyson tried staring Weatherspoon down, but Weatherspoon was having none of it. His gaze remained on Dyson as he said, "Did not."

"Have you ever heard of the Silver Post?"

"Yes, ma'am, I have. It was a home. Before all this was here." Weatherspoon turned his attention away from Dyson and looked back at the Widow. "Before all this was developed, before the war, houses stood along this street. Years later, the railroad came back behind here, and most of the houses were torn down. Businesses came along. Like this one, or what used to be this one."

"Do you know anything about the owners of the Silver Post?" asked the Widow.

"Little bit. There's a connection that my family had with the Silver Post."

"Connection," chucked Dyson. "I'm sure there was."

"My family worked for the Frasers," Weatherspoon continued, ignoring the sarcasm. "They're all gone from here now. Died off or moved away."

"The man who lived here was an ancestor. His name was Walter Fraser."

A flicker of recognition in Weatherspoon's eyes at the mention of Walter Fraser brought, for the first time, a smile on the old man's face.

"So if anything belonged to him, it would now belong to you," Weatherspoon said.

***

Outside the warehouse sat three unmarked cars, all within several yards of each other, heaters running to stave off the cold morning. Deputy Elford Chappell was one of them. JPD officers sat in the other two vehicles, like Chappell, unsure of what was going on inside the decrepit old warehouse.

"That's Spoon's place," said the officer seated beside Chappel.

"Yea, I know. There's nothing inside that place that should interest our friend Dyson, is there?"

***

There was no heat going inside the warehouse. Samuel Weatherspoon trudged slowly to the far end of the warehouse and walked over to a sliding panel that was secured with a rusty padlock. The panel was made of wavy corrugated metal and extended from the floor nearly to the ceiling. Being an elderly man, he was slow and deliberate with his movements. He took his time reaching into his pocket. He brought out a small key ring and unlocked the padlock.

Before he could open the door, Dyson snorted, "Where is the owner of this warehouse?"

"Standing in front of you." Weatherspoon was a quiet man. He probably had five, perhaps ten years on Ambrose Dyson. When he turned to answer Dyson's question, he looked him straight in the eyes, and continued eye contact following his answer. Crime was getting worse these days, and for the last twenty years, he'd carried the same 45 Colt in his right hip pocket. He wasn't a dangerous man. He did, however, believe in self-protection.

"Mr. Weatherspoon, we are forgetting our manners." The Widow glared not at the elderly owner of the warehouse but at Dyson when she spoke.

Dangerous Waters suddenly noticed how the Widow and Dyson seemed to be more than just musician and manager. He took in the flash of hatred, however momentarily, from Dyson at the scolding he'd just received from the Widow.

All of the tension subsided when Weatherspoon proceeded to roll open the door and revealed the carriage.

***

The first call Jennifer Tavistock made was to Franconia Edge. The Dove was at home, having a lazy lunch with her boyfriend, and was astonished when she heard the voice of her best friend. Twenty minutes later, after swearing her best friend to secrecy, she rang off.

The next call placed by Jennifer was Boston. Roger Tavistock failed to answer the call at his home. Being just before noon in Massachusetts, and a Saturday, he would be hard to track down. Then she had an idea. One of the band members, a keyboard player, still had a crush on his band member's older sister.

Albright was against it. One phone call to an outsider like this fellow might usher in a wave of gossip and rumors that could easily reach her parents. It took several minutes of persuasion for him to convince Jennifer not to make the call.

Reluctantly, she agreed.

"Feel better after speaking with the Dove?" he asked.

"I do. My best friend in this putrid world. I suppose I do feel better." Jennifer looked straight ahead. She turned her gaze to Albright and said, unexpectedly, "You still love your ex-fiancée, don't you?"

Albright stiffened. "What on earth brought that on?"

Since rescuing Jennifer Tavistock from Castle Craig, flying her back to the United States, spending time in Urbana and now, in Tennessee, the only affection they had shown one another was the holding of hands as they drove away from the castle in Albright's rented Jaguar. Since then they had been together—drinking, dancing, sourcing out libraries and courthouses, dining, and talking.

Nothing else.

This was the first time she'd mentioned Tolly Chamberlain since the flight to Illinois.

"Your sister-in-law schooled me a bit. After all, she is part of your family. Bonnie told me about you and Miss Tolly Chamberlain. Nobody in your family seemed to care much for her, from what I understand."

"Bonnie needs to mind her own business. Besides...."

"The only reason I'm bringing it up is that if you two hadn't broken up, I'd still be locked up in that bleak place, facing a certain death. Talking to my best friend was wonderful, but not as wonderful as seeing your face on the other side of that door in Castle Craig. When we were at your parents' house, I noticed those photographs of you and your dad and your brother on the mantelpiece. In your full dress uniforms. It made me understand what serving in the military meant to you back in 1970. 'The Albright tradition,' I believe you called it. Do you have any idea how grateful I am?"

Before Albright could answer, the phone rang.

***

A dusty tarp cover lay over it. Weatherspoon slowly pulled away the tarp to reveal a black four-wheeled Brougham carriage with the gold letters WF on each side. The carriage was like new, following years of restoration from Samuel Weatherspoon. Since the body shop had closed down, it became a hobby for the old man—something to work on.

"This is all that is left of Walter Fraser. His carriage." Weatherspoon looked at the Widow. She, unlike the man who had looked him up days earlier and now glared at him as he stood in front of the carriage, was friendly. He opened up the storage case under the seat of the Brougham. "And this."

Inside the storage sat a weathered strongbox.

***

The caller on the phone identified herself. She was the lady from the library. Her call was brief and simple. She called Jennifer Tavistock to notify her that she, indeed, did have knowledge of the man she inquired about earlier in the week. Before she could explain her reasons for not coming forward, Jennifer said, "Let me guess. Older man. Scottish. Evil. Am I close?" asked Jennifer.

"One and the same. I went to church Wednesday night and prayed. I broke down and told my husband what I had done. Miss Tavistock, I was afraid. I've never met anyone like that man. My husband told me I have nothing to fear. I feel terrible about lying to you."

"I can assure you that I completely understand how you feel."

Two minutes later, after ringing off, Jennifer looked at Albright, told him to grab his coat, and they both bolted out of the hotel, climbed into their rental car, and sped off. Jennifer wisely asked for directions from the librarian and screamed at Albright to speed up, despite the posted limits on North Highland Avenue.

He ignored her and drove on at 35 miles per hour.

***

No one spoke as they stared at the strongbox. For Samuel Weatherspoon, the legend of what lay inside prevented him from removing the contents for himself. He wasn't poor, but he was a far cry from being financially comfortable. He was a widower, drew a meager social security pension, which was his sole source of income. He paid his city and county taxes on the warehouse, lived in a small house on Stonewall Street, and considered himself fortunate. He'd heard the story from his father about the Frasers and their tragic demise following the Civil War.

At the age of twelve, following the end of the Civil War, William Weatherspoon was not only freed but without his mother and father. Young William, an only child and an orphan, was told he was to be apprenticed in Jackson to the family of carriage-makers until his twenty-first birthday. The Frasers took in the frightened child, fed him, housed him, and taught him to read and write. William was seventeen that dreadful summer when tragedy, in the form of yellow fever, struck the Fraser family. Mister Peter, the man who had taken in William, took ill and died along with his wife, two daughters, and one of two sons.

Within the course of eight days, five members of the family of six were dead.

The oldest of the two Fraser brothers, according to William Weatherspoon, left Jackson in the middle of the night with one of two strongboxes belonging to his grandfather, Walter Fraser, off to New Orleans a year earlier. The story was that James Fraser, in a moment of greed, exchanged the contents of the strongbox at a bank in New Orleans for American gold of the day. James Fraser returned to Jackson six months later and, in a moment of fear and indecision, chose to bury the majority of the money in three locations throughout Jackson.

In 1985, a group of construction workers unearthed the smallest cache of the gold, creating a fever of its own at its discovery. The two remaining troves remain undiscovered to this day.

James Fraser fell into disrepair in spite of the theft of his grandfather's gold. He died—childless and broke at the age of twenty-nine. The family carriage-house business folded, and William Weatherspoon, a freedman, continued to scrape away in spite of the difficult period known as Reconstruction. He married, sired three children, the youngest being Samuel, who stood quietly over something his late father insisted to his dying day was cursed money.

They were intoxicatingly beautiful. William and Mary 5 Guineas. Struck in 1692, the gold coins featured the images of King William and Queen Mary. The strongbox was full of the brilliant coins. Weatherspoon took note of each of the four foreigners as they beheld the treasure. The oldest man's eyes gleamed with lust. His wife blinked at what she beheld, unable to control her excitement. The polite lady, descendant of Walter Fraser, showed to Weatherspoon's surprise little reaction to what lay in front of her. The younger man, after taking stock of what lay in the strongbox, focused his attention on the old Scotsman.

Dangerous Waters, at that moment, reached into his camel-hair overcoat and took comfort at what lay inside.

Nevertheless, Waters regretted not taking his own vehicle to this meeting. Traveling with Ambrose Dyson meant anything could happen, which made him grip the Heckler & Koch even tighter. The discovery of this gold meant anything might be happening with these people.

"Ma'am, this carriage," Williamson said quietly," and all that goes with it is, as far as I'm concerned, yours."

"Why are you giving this money to me?" asked the Widow. It was something they were all wondering about.

"Doesn't belong to me," Weatherspoon replied. "Mister Peter gave my father a life. In fact, what I have here came from the Frasers. This building, this property. Left to my father. He had to struggle to keep this. But he kept it. Left it to us. This carriage," Weatherspoon said, "belonged to Mister Peter's father. Not me. What's inside that box there ain't mine. I will say this, Ma'am. All of the people in that family died tragic deaths. My daddy says it's because of that money. That money has been in that carriage inside this shed since Mister Peter died. Since Mister Peter's son died. You're the first to know about this. Being who you are, Ma'am, kin to that family and all, I feel that this is the time to pass it all over to family. That's why I'm giving the money and this carriage to you."

"This money," said the Widow, "belongs to Scotland. That's where it will be returned, I can assure you." At the sight of the gold, the mystery of the missing remaining testament written by Walter Fraser suddenly became irrelevant.

At that moment, there was a knock at the door. Samuel thought he had seen enough strangers for one day.

He was wrong.

***

Weatherspoon left the carriage and slowly made his way to the entrance. He opened the door to see two young people:

a man and a woman, standing there.

***

Elford Chappel watched from across the street as the strange couple approached the warehouse.

What concerned him was the speed in which the vehicle, which drove past the warehouse a half-block before turning around, pulled into the graveled parking lot.

He watched as the man spoke to the woman before they walked to the door. She seemed to be in a hurry while the man appeared to be more reserved, grabbing the woman's arm to keep her from rushing inside the building.

***

London

Neal Edwards had seen better days. He'd been holed up in London, pondering, debating, and afraid for his life. He drank himself into a nightly stupor, holed up in his hotel room in the West End. He'd been away for five full days. He awoke Wednesday morning, poured coffee and, in desperation, turned on the radio. Interestingly enough, the cleaning people the day before left the radio tuned not to a pop music station but one featuring news and classical music.

They were having a discussion about the war. Edwards' hands shook as he poured coffee. He poured cream, added sugar, and opened the curtains to the grey skies of London. Then he heard the voice of the man he truly admired. He'd wept on that late January day in 1965, when young men his age simply did not cry, when he'd learned of his death. The recording was scratchy but the voice unmistakable:

"One ought never to turn ones back on a threatened danger and try to run away from it. If you do that, you will double the danger. But if you meet it promptly and without flinching, you will reduce the danger by half."

It was the voice of Sir Winston Churchill.

This was to have been his last day in England, leaving behind all he had built with his estate business and not even saying farewell to family and loved ones. He thought about everything his father had taught him. As the program continued, Edwards began to think about the courageousness his countrymen displayed during the Second World War. Churchill's brief motivational statement, coming from the radio in the luxury hiding place, suddenly changed the mind of the young man planning to run from England because someone had tried to kill him.

Edwards put the cup down, undressed, and walked into the shower. As he shaved for the first time in three days, he looked at the man who was going to run away from it all. He dressed, ordered a full breakfast from room service, and placed a call to the Bristol Police. He proceeded to tell them the truth. He explained why he took a trip to Scotland. He told the police about the American couple wanting to buy the castle. He shared his visit to Castle Craig, the icy treatment, and told them about the note placed in the pocket of his Macintosh he thought to be a joke at the time.

He was still talking to the police when room service arrived.

Edwards left London with a clean conscience and a renewed sense of courage. There were too many people in his life that he cared for, and if he had to die for standing up for what he believed in, so be it.

It took two days for the Bristol authorities to notify the Goldspie Police. Once that happened, things took off. Whereas Jennifer Tavistock had insisted she wasn't pressing charges about being held in Castle Craig, the bombing in Bristol took on a much bigger priority. After all, the Prime Minister herself had paid a visit to the young bombing victim, and finding out who was responsible was being handled by authorities larger than a small police force in a small

Scottish village.

***

The mayor of Jackson received a phone call at home just as he was about to walk out the door to get his weekly haircut. It was the Chief of Police. As promised, the chief told the mayor the news as soon as he himself found out.

Scotland Yard was interested in the whereabouts of Mr. and Mrs. Ambrose Dyson, regarding a car bombing in Bristol, England. Meanwhile, the chief of police in Jackson, Tennessee "flagged" the name the same day he received a phone call from his boss, and the chief himself was called at home when he received information that Scotland Yard was interested in Mr. Dyson. An arrest warrant wasn't issued as yet, but people were wanting to talk to him nevertheless.

***

As the door slid open, Jennifer Tavistock and Alan Albright stood before an elderly Black gentleman. Jennifer took note of the curious face. His right eye sat slightly lower than his left, gazing steadily under the grey eyebrows. He was a dark-skinned man, tallish, with years of hard effort and toil evident in his gait and on his face.

"Are you Mr. Weatherspoon?" she asked.

"That's right."

"My name is Jennifer Tavistock. I'm looking for information about an ancestor of mine by the name of Walter Fraser."

The face of Mr. Weatherspoon gave away nothing as to what he may have been thinking at the moment. He simply beckoned them with a wrinkled hand for them to come inside. Albright, for the first time since leaving St. Andrews some days before, took the hand of Jennifer Tavistock and walked inside, following Samuel Weatherspoon to the rear of the stuffy garage, where four people stood in front of an old carriage. Albright felt Jennifer's grip tighten in his hand when she saw Ambrose Dyson, and at that moment, Albright experienced the same sensation as the picture framer he'd never met and the mayor of the city of Jackson when seeing the man for the first time.

"Hello, Ambrose. Hello, Corra," said Jennifer, regaining her composure. "Fancy meeting the two of you here."

The expression on Ambrose Dyson's face was one for the ages. The evil within him seemed to converge within his eyes as he looked upon Jennifer Tavistock.

"You must be Terryl Kinnimont," continued Jennifer, looking at the Widow. "We spoke by phone briefly a short time ago."

"I'm Alan Albright, by the way. That's A-L-B-R-I-G-H-T."

No one in the Widow's group said a word. Dangerous Waters' mind was blown for the second time that morning, totally bewildered as to just what in the world was going on. By now he understood that the Widow may very well have told him half-truths and possibly outright lies about who she really was and why she was really in America. In spite of that, he still loved her and was too aware of the danger he sensed from Dyson and felt, in spite of all the surprises, compelled to protect her from Dyson. Like her husband, Corra Dyson was in shock at the sight of the young American woman she'd enjoyed keeping in captivity.

The Widow suddenly felt very cold. She looked upon the face at last of Alan Albright, the man who she'd been warned about, who for a brief time, she believed, destroyed her beloved piano until she heard his voice coming over the telephone in Scotland. He stood next to Jennifer Tavistock, who the Widow decided needed to know the truth once and for all.

"I must say I am sorry, Miss Tavistock." Her voice was crisp and steady, full of truth. "I did what I did to keep you alive. You know me as Terryl Kinnimont. My maiden name in fact was Fraser. Yes, I am your cousin. I placed you under my protection while in Scotland to keep you from being killed. Hate me, as you may, I cannot put a member of my family to death. You came to Scotland and two things happened. First, you discovered things from our dear cousin Henrietta Sim that should have not been disclosed. Secondly, and what would surely have gotten you killed, your genealogical mission revealed the truth of Malcolm Fraser's parentage. Yes. For that reason, Jennifer, the fact that the wife of Angus Fraser happened to be a Negro, and you might disclose it to the world, Claire Tavistock, whom I have known since we were children, wanted you dead. I kept you in Castle Craig for your own protection."

"Mister Dyson?" said Elford Chappell. There were six officers of the Jackson Police Department and two Madison County Sheriff's Deputies standing there, one being Elford Chappell.

Ambrose Dyson was a dangerous man, but he wasn't foolish. He took one look at the policemen, glanced down at the gold; back at the policemen and decided what sat in the carriage wasn't worth going to hell for.

"I'm he."

"We'd like to ask you and your wife to come with us, please," Chappell said, experiencing for himself what so many others had felt when looking into Dyson's eyes for the first time. Somewhere in the back of his mind he was hoping that Dyson would make a move so he could put a bullet in his brain.

That moment passed.

Although he would never know the man in Scotland, known as Wee Ronald Mackey, who made the remark after shooting over the heads of the would-be robbers in the Keithleigh docks, the thought in his head was similar.

It was too close to Christmas for any killing.

***

Terryl Kinnimont and the Jackson Symphony did not let the audience down that night. The cabaret tables were full, with the lower level of the Civic Center turned into the recreational area of the wealthy and powerful, while an empty seat was not to be found in the upper level. A concert of unparalleled excellence, the daily newspaper would later call it. Terryl Kinnimont and David Waters returned to Memphis the next day, dropping off the rental car in a pre-determined parking garage area at the Memphis airport and boarding a jetliner that would take them back to Scotland. The Heckler and Koch remained in the boot of the automobile, to be removed by the same contact from the Israeli security firm who placed it there.

Ambrose Dyson was arrested for attempted murder in the Bristol, England, car bombing. Following expedition to Great Britain, he was tried and convicted and given a fifteen-year sentence. Corra Dyson was not charged with the crime. During the trial, there was no disclosure whatsoever of anyone else's involvement in the car bombing other than Ambrose Dyson.

Evil as he was, Dyson was not a snitch.

Prior to leaving the garage in Jackson, Tennessee, the Widow told the kind Mr. Williamson that the carriage was his to keep. What Mr. Williamson did not know was that the gold that Walter Fraser absconded to America with, more than two hundred years earlier, and the Widow was taking back to Scotland to be returned to its rightful owners, was to be used to help in Scotland's fight against the English. The two strongboxes, containing the William and Mary 5 guineas gold pieces, were to be used in the struggle for the House of Stuart.

The Jacobite Uprising of 1745.

***

Alan Albright and Jennifer Tavistock did not attend the concert that night. Following the arrest of the Dysons and the revelation from Terryl Kinnimont, they walked out of the garage, returned to the hotel, and checked out. They were in Urbana by the time the first note was being played by the Jackson Symphony Orchestra.

Albright was unsure during their flight home of what he should do. He looked over at Jennifer as they flew back to Illinois and saw her quietly weeping. Following her rescue from Castle Craig, things had been decidedly different, since Jennifer was jubilant just knowing she was at last free from captivity. He had tried to talk to her about her mother, and she was having none of it. She wasn't cold or anything; she was just Jennifer. She finally opened up and asked Alan how she was going to tell her father that the woman he married actually wanted their daughter dead.

"Why did she do such a thing?" asked Albright.

"Because of the world we live in, Alan. Sadly, fame and privilege come at a cost. Proper Bostonians, Alan, come from English stock, not African. Social no-no. Even though this is almost 1980, the way I see it anyway, few people would even care. It wasn't like I was going to come back from Scotland and broadcast to the world that the mother of our family patriarch, the founder of our family fortune, had a mother who happened to be Black."

"I suppose it's a good thing that I didn't spend that half million dollars your father promised for your safe return."

"Not funny!" she snapped.

"Believe me, it wasn't meant to be funny, Jennifer." It was all Albright could do to keep from smiling.

The following Tuesday morning, Albright dropped Jennifer Tavistock off at Willard Airport. While in Urbana the day before, she'd re-established contact with her bank, obtained credit cards, and booked reservations through Bonnie Albright, naturally, to Key West. She and Franconia Edge planned on hanging out through the New Year. Alan and Jennifer hung out in Campustown for the rest of the day, with one request by Jennifer to go to the Urbana Post Office.

Prior to leaving, she walked over to the Albright's Christmas tree and did two things. First, she placed a large present under the tree with Alan's name on it. Secondly, Jennifer removed the smaller box she'd picked up at the South Street shop in St. Andrews. They went to the Albright dining room table, found scissors, and opened the box. Inside were the white cashmere sweater and a simple wooden box.

"Remember how you felt when you learned that Reverend Swithuns left you a Bible rather than a gun?"

"Of course I do, Jennifer. You don't just forget things like that."

"Right. Remember what Reverend Swithuns told us as we were leaving Scotland? To trust God, because He has a plan for all of us?"

Albright remembered.

"One of the first things we all learned back in 1969 when we arrived in St. Andrews," said Jennifer, "was the history of the town itself, how it came to be and why."

"Okay."

"Andrew was a disciple of Christ. He was crucified in Greece, in the town of Patras, and became the Patron Saint of Scotland."

"Indeed. And the legend was that a small part of his remains was brought to Scotland by St. Regulus. Oddly enough, I read up on all of that when I was trying to find you."

Jennifer tapped the small box with her index finger. Albright looked at the box, then up at Jennifer. He said nothing. He could not say anything.

She opened the box. Inside the velvet-lined container, no more than one inch in length, lay the distal and middle phalanges of a human finger. The bones were brown.

"During my visit to Scotland, while visiting my cousin Henrietta Sim, she gave this to me along with a cross and a manuscript. Cousin Henrietta gave me implicit instructions to always keep them separate, and I know why. I stashed this at the woolen shop in St. Andrews the day before I arrived at Castle Craig. The rest, as we say..."

Albright still could not bring himself to speak.

"That's why I left this under your tree. Had anything happened to me in Tennessee, at least this would have been safe. This, Alan, is what my cousin, Terryl Fraser, was talking about when we were in that garage down there. This is The Secret of St. Andrews. Our family secret. This is what I feel prompted Terryl Fraser to behave the way that she did. I'm sending this back to Scotland. To Troy Swithuns."

"Could this be the..." he could not finish his sentence.

"I honestly don't know. If it is or if it's not, it will be returned to Scotland. All of what happened to us, as Reverend Swithuns said, is God's will. And Reverend Swithuns doesn't even know about this."

Jennifer went upstairs to her room and returned with the Bible she brought out of Castle Craig. She'd carried it to Tennessee, and now, at the dining room table, she opened the Bible to the faded writing on the first page. Here was the family history, introduced by Angus Fraser. She ran a finger down to the passage that simply stated: "protecting that which belongs to God."

Five days later, Troy Swithuns received a box from America. There was a blue sweatshirt with the face of Chief Illini, emblazoned in orange on the front. There were several other items of memorabilia as well, each covered in orange and blue with the University of Illinois or Fighting Illini on them. A small box, in its own gold wrapping, contained a note from Jennifer Tavistock. When Swithuns read it, he sat down, opened the box, and found himself unable to keep from choking back a tear.

A tear of joy.

He would keep the promise.

***

Jennifer Tavistock was helped with her substantial luggage, accumulated in a relatively short period of time while in Illinois, at Willard Airport by Alan Albright. Since she was traveling to warm weather and since she had nothing to wear in Key West, she would have to do additional shopping. She was going to meet up with not only Franconia, but her younger brother Roger Tavistock. He would advise her how to tell Martyn Tavistock that their mother, his wife, was a would-be murderer.

She invited Albright to come along, but they both knew she needed time. Time with her best friend, who she was terribly close to and time with her baby brother.

She did promise to call.

Albright arrived home in his brother's car to find that his best friend had kept his promise. There, sitting in the driveway of his parents' house, was the Big Jag, driven down from Chicago by Eulus. Albright spent the remainder of the days to Christmas in Urbana, hanging out mostly with Eulus and Madelyn White. All of the Christmas presents he bought for his family while in Boston were placed under the tree. On Christmas Eve, Dennis and Bonnie came over, keeping with the Albright tradition. They drank eggnog, sang Christmas carols, and listened to the Colonel, as he always did at Christmas; tell them how much he loved his family.

Albright and the Colonel spoke at length over the events that transpired since Thanksgiving. The Colonel offered his assessment. Blunt and to the point. Even on the night before Christmas, there was a discussion between father and son. Albright felt the fact that the family patriarch had chosen a Black woman as his bride meant little. The Colonel disagreed. Some people would still have problems with mixed blood, however distant it might be. They agreed on the fact that Walter Fraser and his theft of gold, meant for the Jacobite Uprising, could have spawned something of, for lack of a better term, a family curse.

As for the contents of the box and who the contents once belonged to, the Colonel was skeptical. He wasn't discounting the theory altogether. He did feel that unless comprehensive scientific analysis was conducted on the remains, the truth would never be fully known. Jennifer had explained to Albright while in Tennessee about the testament of Walter Fraser and how the discovery of the missing gold, in her mind anyway, accounted for what was in the lost page or pages that brought them to Tennessee in the first place.

Albright agreed.

They retired for the evening with something from the Colonel that Albright still sought from his father, even at his age.

Praise. For a job well done.

On Christmas morning, the traditions continued. Breakfast was served, Albright was the last up as always, and Christmas music was played on the new stereo system Albright bought his parents. In addition, the Colonel hooked up his brand-new video tape recorder, assuring the fact, his younger son told him, that he wouldn't miss another Steelers' game.

The phone rang just after ten. To his surprise, Blakelyn Albright told Alan the call was for him.

Well, Albright thought to himself, Jennifer Tavistock did keep her promise.

"Merry Christmas," said Albright.

"Hello, Alan. It's Tolly."

John Scofield

Main Street Publishing, Inc.

206 E. Main Street Suite 207
P.O. Box 696
Jackson, Tn 38301

Toll Free #: 866-457-7379
or
Local #: 731-427-7379

Visit us on the web:
www.mainstreetpublishing.com
www.mspbooks.com

E-Mail: mspsupport@charterinternet.com